# Spontaneous Combustion

Luba Burtyk

🐾 BURROW BOOKS

Spontaneous Combustion
Luba Burtyk

COPYRIGHT 2021 by Luba Burtyk

ISBN: 978-1-7365285-0-1

Cover illustration: Kiki Smith. Congregation, 2014

For the ones I love
"bigger than my whole heart."

# BILLY
He Should Have Known

I blame Robert. Me and Darcy, we were just kids. What did we know? We'd never been more than fifty miles out of Glen Eddy. But Robert was a grown-up.

Sure, now he boo-hoos twenty-four seven about how much he loved Darcy. The question is – what did he do to stop her?

She was hard to resist. I know all about that. Letting her have her own way was easier. Way easier.

For a minute there, everyone wanted to claim her. Wanted to be part of her thing. Including me. Especially me. And Robert too.

Darcy's army. That's what Robert called us. As if. More like a bunch of wannabe hipster dudes trying to get in on a media moment and some old hippie types like Robert on a trip down memory lane.

The day it all went down, Robert no-showed; came running out of the Ramble hand in hand with some babe after everything was over, acting like he'd only been out of sight for a minute or two. By then, it was old news that people were hurt and missing. He probably really did expect to find Darcy sitting on a rock next to Belvedere Castle waiting for him. And when he saw that she wasn't there, he started spazzing, grabbing onto anyone and everyone, "Where's Darcy? Did you see Darcy?"

Well, duh. Thanks to that cyborg freak, M3, her face was all over TV and the net. But no one had actually seen her, just like I told him.

"They got Darcy. She's gone."

When that bit of 411 finally sank in, what did Robert do but sit down on a rock, a sobbing, useless wreck.

The tears didn't cut any ice with me. "Dude, get a grip," I told him.

The biker-looking babe with Robert, she figured things out right away.

"I know people who can help," she said and hugged Robert. Held the big baby's hand.

Turned out she did have some connections, though with her

wild licorice-black hair, and funky leather get-up you wouldn't think so.

Good thing, too, that she could call on her friends because by then Darcy's so-called army had taken a look at what was happening and was gone. Gone and not coming back. Yeah, in a heartbeat everyone moved on.

Everyone, except me. And probably Robert. I have to give him that.

"Whoa," Darcy said the day the cops got her. "Whoa." barely loud enough for anyone but me and the spooked horse to hear her. I mean, I was that close. Running with her.

Me on foot. Her on the horse. Even on foot, I was that close.

"Whoa," she repeated as the horse reared way the hell up.

It wasn't a big horse, or a beautiful horse. And it definitely wasn't made for speed or charging up slippery hills. It wasn't a horse made for heroics.

"Whoa," Darcy said, but it was too late.

"Whoa."

# ROBERT
Like a Daughter to Me


Robert wanted to forget that day in Central Park and everything that came after. Especially everything that came after. He worked at it the way he once worked on sun salutations and the full body prostrations of Buddhist practice. The peace of satori eluded him.

Each morning he awoke to memories that assembled themselves in the form of a Medieval triptych. Dominating the central panel — a single iconic image of a barrel-chested horse, body reared up, front legs pawing empty air, mouth splayed wide, pink tongue thrust out, exposed. And Darcy — small, determined — clinging to the horse's neck, her whole body strained, straining, her lips at the creature's ear whispering consolation. The sun appeared as a silver disc burning high above a landscape of scorched darks gashed through with vermilion. No way could Robert stop imagining the piercing neigh of the horse's distress.

Much as the central image terrified Robert, the hinged side panels with miniatures from every part of his life with Darcy broke his heart – infant Darcy riding high on his shoulders, toddler Darcy "planting" Tinker toy flowers in his garden, young Darcy astride his pasture fence declaiming poetry, or at his side, trailing him from barn to apiary, hanging on his every word, eager to learn, eager to be taught.

From day to day, the vignettes arranged themselves in shifting configurations without respect to real-life chronology – ever different but ever the same.

According to Professor Sovern, who'd taught the freshman survey art course that Robert had taken at Columbia, the order of the scenes on the hinged panels didn't dictate the ultimate narrative of the Medieval triptych. A heartening notion that Robert clung to, given that his memories of Darcy never seemed to add up to a sequence that felt final or satisfactory. On the rare occasion that he was able to invest the images with a story that felt like it offered insight and understanding, another memory would intrude, forcing him to realize that his knowledge of Darcy remained incomplete.

One day he hoped to make sense of the memories. Until then, much as he wanted to forget, Robert went on remembering.

***

From the middle of the apiary, Robert watched Darcy climb over the split-rail fence of the back pasture, her hair a halo of light.

To see Darcy was to glimpse her mother, Isabelle, age eighteen, gliding across the campus green in front of the Columbia library... Bella, he used to call her, before she decided to marry Jack. Bella. Bella Donna. Belissima Bella...

Darcy moved with a simple animal grace despite the *djellabah* she insisted on wearing.

"My poor girl," Robert sighed. For two, going on three days Darcy had stopped wearing jeans and t-shirts. The billowing blue Moroccan robe that had started out as a Halloween costume had become a daily uniform.

How much longer would Darcy go on shrouding herself like that?

Shrouding. What else could he call it? Clearly the whole *djellabah* thing was about Darcy concealing her developing body. Had to be.

A tough age, thirteen. Uncomfortable. Boys starting to notice girls and to ogle their budding breast, and to make dirty jokes, dumb comments. Darcy — too smart, too serious to do the girly girly, flirty flirty giggle thing to make their dumbass bullshit seem OK.

"Over here," Robert called and waved.

Darcy waved back, the sleeve of her robe sliding down to reveal her strong, tanned arm.

Without a doubt, she was going to have a beautiful body. A sexy body. Inside his jacket pocket, Robert made a fist. Just let some little snot-faced teenage boy mess with his Darcy.

Yeah, his Darcy. She was like a daughter to him.

The bee yard – a mini Stonehenge of twenty hives — hummed around him. A few slow moving bees emerged to probe the chill air. Though the sun still shone bright between the gathering clouds, the sky promised rain. Like people, the bees preferred not to venture outside in bad weather.

"Hurry," he called out to Darcy. Smoking out the hives needed to be finished before the foraging bees returned from their daily rounds. Prepping the apiary for winter should have been done weeks ago and it was too late to put it off any longer.

Beekeeping had not always been a part of Robert's life, but he could hardly remember that time. Even though caring for the bees had turned out to be more about sweat, and worry, and stings than about honey, he had no regrets.

He wasn't going to get rich off the bees. The income from the honey was a supplement to what he earned from the organic produce he sold. Even with the honey, his income barely added up to enough. Especially in a bad year like the last one when each hive delivered about thirty pounds of honey instead of the usual hundred. He kept at it because he liked the idea of making a buck by messing around with bugs — bugs that flew wherever they damn well pleased, did their own thing and just happened to be useful and good for the earth. How cool was that?

Beekeeping had taught Robert a whole new way of seeing his patch of the world, gave him a new take on the weather, the changing of the seasons. Tulip trees behind the barn becoming sag heavy with deeply cupped flowers meant spring. The black locusts at the edge of the pasture acquiring a drapery of lacey, sweet, sweet blossoms that the bees loved would come later. It was summer for sure when clusters of bell-shaped flowers, dripping nectar, hung in the green canopy of the sourwood trees.

To hear the bees deep, slow autumnal drone coming from the hives saddened Robert. Like the bees, he mourned the passing of summer.

SAD – seasonal affective disorder. Both he and Isabelle suffered from it. Luckily, Darcy seemed to have escaped any tendency towards the blues.

"Hurry."

"Okay. Okay. Okay," Darcy shouted and, gathering the *djellabah* into her fist, began to run.

Or rather, from Robert's vantage, to levitate across the field. It was the long robe combined with a trick of perspective that

5

made it seem so, and yet Robert could not shake the feeling that Darcy was a creature of air, soaring out of the dark wood at the back of the pasture, flying towards him.

The blazing colors of the trees that had nourished the bees were all well past their peak. Only a few furled husks hung from the branches of the sourwoods, a sad remnant of the foliage that just a week ago had burned crimson and scarlet. Soon all the trees would be bare.

Robert eyed the thunderheads beginning to roll in over the brown line of trees.

"Hurry-up girl, come on," he whispered, stamping his feet against the cold. Against impatience.

*These are the desolate, dark weeks when nature in its barrenness equals the stupidity of man*, Robert muttered. William Carlos Williams got that right. And as if to confirm it, a gust of wind knifed through the pasture.

\*\*\*

"Hey," Darcy said, her hand raised in a half-hearted high-five.

Robert flicked his leathery palm against her small, soft one.

They geared up in silence. Not their customary, easy silence. A disagreement over her admiration for Doefen and her crazy plan to support his fight against Burgundy Enterprise, abandoned rather than resolved the day before, had come between them.

Quickly, deftly, Darcy slipped the protective, white bee suit over her *djellabah*. Not her *djellabah* exactly. Her mother's. Robert knew for a fact that it was a memento from Isabelle's happier days – a college summer spent backpacking across Morocco.

He remembered Isabelle dancing around in that *djellabah* on the grassy rectangle in front of Lowe Library the fall of sophomore year. Remembered slipping his arm around her tiny waist to spin her, to spin with her... Remembered her letting him spin, wanting him to spin with her. Wanting him...

The smoothness of the fabric – his first taste, probably Isabelle's too, of sumptuousness in a lifetime of wearing cheap synthetics – stunned him. He'd wanted to let the blue silk flow through his hands like water, but it caught and snagged on tiny rough spots and calluses on his fingers that he'd never noticed before. Dismayed, he'd buried his hands deep inside the pockets of his jeans and contented himself with watching Isabelle sway to a tune only she could hear. The breeze draped the silk ever so subtly over her bra-less breasts, the firm buds of her nipples, which showed, oh yes — just barely, but they did show — beneath the delicate fabric.

No doubt Isabelle had imagined that she was dressed for a life as amazing as the garment. How could she have known that she'd end up working the red-eye shift in a crappy little hospital in Glen Eddy ventilating dead people? Or that her big crush, Jack — Mr. Jumpin' Jack Flash, 'call me Jack Dharma the Street Fighting Man' — would morph into a husband who spent his days stringing phone wire, and his nights shouting encouragement at perps on rerun TV cop shows he knew by heart?

Fucking sad – the whole lot of them, himself included. In their heyday, he, Isabelle, and Jack could never have envisioned the life that they were living now. But neither could they have imagined having a child like Darcy in their lives. She was their greatest gift. Their greatest pleasure.

As Darcy zipped the front of the bee suit coverall, Robert could not help but notice the faint contours of her still-developing breasts, which he admired in much the same spirit that he appreciated a well-proportioned hive. Another couple of years and she'd be a knock out. Some guy would snatch her up. She'd leave Glen Eddy. Leave him.

He swiped at a tear that threatened to roll out of the corner of his eye, overcome by a heart-palpitating kind of sadness mixed with a thrilling tenderness.

Darcy held up a hand. "What?"

"What do you mean, what?" he stammered, face flushing.

"You're staring."

"Not staring, dear girl, just thinking that we need to get a move on." Turning away, he busied himself with preparing the smoker.

He loved the special bond he shared with Darcy. Intense, but innocent. Definitely innocent. Nothing even remotely wanton or genital.

At his age he knew what he liked. When he first came to Glen

Eddy, Robert had tried to make it with the local women. Or more to the point, make do. Problem was that all of the women in town were either of the soft, plump variety — pale and indeterminate as bee larvae. Or they were the thin sort with sharp noses and laughs to match. In the end, he couldn't get past their too big hoop earrings, and too tight jeans and the smell of menthol cigarettes on their breath.

And then there was Isabelle... Tender Isabelle, his best friend. Belissima Bella. The crush of his life back in college. But he'd gotten over that. Had to, once she married Jack. Chosen Jack over him. Carrying a torch was not Robert's style.

Robert couldn't remember exactly when he discovered the men's magazines that he favored now. Or when they became a habit. A girl a month. Each month a new one. A magazine girl for every mood, every fantasy. And no morning after. No cigarette breath. Just glorious Mistress Jade. Or Madame Silk. Or Vikktoria...

"Let me help you tuck-in," he offered gently, overcome with sentiment as he watched Darcy fumble with the protective bee gear.

Oh how he loved that girl! Loved her like a daughter. Always had. In his heart of hearts, he believed that she was his daughter.

"I got it," Darcy said, bending to stuff the pants legs of the jump suit into her worn, black combat boots. Against the delicate lines of the *djellabah*, the boots looked particularly disproportionate.

Robert could have asked for a paternity test. The thought had crossed his mind. But Isabelle never for a moment suggested or acted like he was or could be the father. And who would know better than her, the mother?

Anyway, it was just that one time with Isabelle. In all the years he'd known her, yearned for her... Belissima Bella — the brightening in the sky that announces that winter is over, that the rain is done...

"O.K. How about I help you with the duct tape?"
Isabelle married Jack. Chose Jack over him. It would have been uncool to insist on paternity testing. Totally un-groovy. And it would have so complicated things that were already complicated enough. Now it was too late.

"Thanks. I'm good," Darcy insisted, pushing past Robert.

"Be myself?" he said, quoting the governing refrain of Darcy's babyhood with which she'd refused all offers of help with anything from knotted shoelaces to brushing her teeth. Without a doubt, she'd inherited Isabelle's stubborn resolve.

Just that one time, long after Isabelle had married Jack ... her legs locked around Robert's hips, the heels of her delicate feet pressed into the hollow of his back, the assuring mantra of her quickened breath moist in his ear ... just that one time... Robert at the mercy of their desire, helpless... What did he know about the timing? Just that one time... What were the chances?

Anyway, what did it matter how Darcy came to be? The important thing was that she — glorious creature — did come into the world. His world. A blessing to them all.

"Yes, be myself," Darcy said with a sarcasm that instantly made him feel like he was just another grown-up she had to make nice with.

"The hell with you then," he muttered, and slammed a veiled helmet onto his head.

He could hardly have loved Darcy more. Or been more of a father to her. She came to him with her problems, confided her secret worries. Without a doubt, she shared more of her life with him than she ever did with Jack. Or even Isabelle. "The hell with you."

"I heard that."

It pained Robert to be on the outs with Darcy. Their argument about Doefen and Darcy going to the protest rally he was planning in the city was stupid. They needed to put it to rest, clear the air.

Robert lit the smoker, inhaling deeply to let the familiar, narcotizing smell of smoldering sage and sumac soothe him. Once he was certain that Darcy had actually duct taped the legs and sleeves of her coveralls and tied the veiled helmet securely around her neck, he handed her the smoker.

He could do the hives perfectly well without her help. But it was so much more of a pleasure to do them with her.

"Now remember," he said, "no wild motions. Just take it slow and easy and you won't get stung."

"I have done this before."

"Yeah, you have." And done it well. She was his daughter, alright. If not in the flesh, then in most of the ways that really counted.

To her credit, Darcy began to smoke the hive entrance at the leisurely pace that allowed the bees time to respond. Just like he'd taught her.

When Darcy was little, the bees buzzing in the pasture – each fat and thick as a finger – used to send her screeching to cling to Isabelle's leg. And Isabelle, bless her, after patting Darcy's head would encourage her to be brave. Unlike their other Glen Eddy neighbors, Isabelle never once dismissed beekeeping as weird, or urged Robert to switch to keeping dairy cows. In the end, Darcy would end up peering out from behind her mother's skirts to watch the bees balance like acrobats on balls of purple clover.

Darcy turned seven before Robert finally succeeded in introducing her to his girls, as he called the bees to make them seem less scary. Putting a drop of honey or his arm, he waited for a foraging bee to find him. Darcy, her face a mask of fierce concentration, watched as a stubby worker bee landed to suck up the sweet lure with its long, grooved tongue. She didn't turn and run, just squeaked, "My turn. My turn now," capturing his heart completely

With Isabelle standing alongside Robert, and Jack watching from behind the trunk of a large oak and calling out unnecessary cautions, Darcy let a bee crawl up her arm. The insect raised goose bumps on her flesh with its tiny steps, but she stood silent and unflinching. When the bee flew off, she laughed, and jumping up and down, clapped her hands, "Again! Again!"

In the years since, Darcy had learned to overcome any show of nervous excitement around the bees, except when the smoke riled them into bolting from a hive. Robert loved to glimpse this tiny *pentimento* of the skittish child Darcy once was. Much as he enjoyed every phase of her growing up, even the 'tweens that most adults seem to hate, the years of her childhood stirred him most.

"Heads up," Robert said and pulled her to stand behind him. "I'm going in."

Gently, he pried the lid off the hive. A cluster of bees stared up from the top bars of the frames. After a moment's hesitation, Darcy expertly dispersed them with a few puffs of smoke.

"Good job. Excellent work."

The veil prevented Robert from being able to tell if the compliment had any mellowing effect on Darcy. She continued to squeeze out plumes of smoke, forcing the bees to forget all about folding themselves into stinging position to defend the combs. Instead they began provisioning themselves with honey, and hurried to flee. Their panicked frenzy brought to Robert's mind unpleasant images of anti-war demonstrators being dispersed with tear gas, and of protesters on the run.

"Easy, man. Easy," he exhorted the bees and Darcy both even as he remembered his younger, militant self — choking on tear gas, running blind for fear of being trampled by cops, or by the other routed demonstrators. "Easy does it."

He inspected the hive from bottom to top, just like all the apiculture pamphlets and bee geeks recommended. At first glance, the bottom chamber seemed to have plenty of honey, but there were no eggs, no developing brood. The few remaining caretaker and worker bees were clustered in a single group of cells.

"Not good," he said.

Darcy came alongside to peer over the edge.

The honeycomb on the first frame he pulled out of the hive body was patchy. Broken. Luckily, there were none of the red dots that would indicate the presence of verroa mites, the dread parasitic infestation that every beekeeper feared. But it didn't take long to see that the scattering of intact cells of the honeycomb were infested with grubby, maggoty, dirty white, blind wormy things.

"Wax moth larvae!" He shook the frame hard. All but a few of the squirming bastards that were chewing up the walls of the honeycomb held tight.

"Don't stomp on them," Darcy warned even before he had lifted his boot.

"Yeah, I know. I know. Respect all life," he said, wishing now that he hadn't asked Darcy to come. "You do realize that any normal kid would be screaming yuck and running for the hills."

"And we know I'm not a normal kid." Darcy said. All sarcasm. No laughter.

"Out of the mouth of babes," Robert muttered, steeling himself for Darcy's usual lecture on the sanctity of all life, including insect life. In her presence, he wasn't allowed to so much as swat a mosquito.

Darcy remained silent, no doubt still sulking over his refusal to OK her plan to go to Doefen's protest rally in the city.

"I'm going to take the bees that are left and put them into another healthier hive," he told her managing to make it sound like something routine, rather than the one beekeeping task that never failed to freak him out.

He took the smoker from Darcy, waved it at the open hive.

The elegant and elongated queen with three black rings was easy to spot in the depopulated frame. He glanced at Darcy — a small monolith sheathed in white, barely discernible behind a scrim of smoke. Really, how much could she possibly see?

Quickly, he seized the queen and sacrificed her under the heel of his work boot, poked the dry grass to cover her.

A few agitated bees flew out of the now queenless hive.

Pooft... Pooft... Pooft... With a practiced hand, he streamed a wash of smoke that would sweep the bees towards a new home.

Pooft... Pooft...

Not a word out of Darcy. Robert could not see her eyes, but felt her watching him from behind the bee veil. Could she have seen him kill the queen?

Pooft... Pooft.

The sound failed to have its usual wonderfully calming effect, for which he blamed being forced to kill the queen of the hive, and Darcy's infatuation with Doefen.

Dofen, Doefen, Dofen. From the minute Darcy first read about him in the newspaper, it was Doefen 24/7. From a big picture point of view, he was basically a big to-do over a lot of nothing; a small town guy that local papers played up to sell copy. But to hear Darcy talk about him, you'd think that Doefen walked on water. He should be the next mayor, or governor, she said. Or even president. Especially president.

Robert had to admit that there were a few things about Doefen that did look pretty good on paper. Researching him on the library computer, he came up with plenty of hits, a lot of them positive. And Doefen's critics were exactly the ones he should have pissed off. Big business hated him. So did the cops. As far as Robert was concerned, it was important to have the right enemies.

And yet, strip away all the media to-do, and Doefen was just a guy out to protect a piece of his own turf. Not that Robert blamed him. But the scope of his so-called action that Darcy swooned over didn't even come close to the feats Chuck Lorraine pulled off as head of the Farmers Coop.

Just last year, Chuck had single-handedly mobilized the whole county to keep pastureland from being seized through eminent domain to add another lane to an already too large highway. He'd also rallied the entire Farmers Coop to do battle with Burgundy Enterprise over their scheme to plant test plots of genetically-engineered crops in the fallow fields around Glen Eddy. None of that got Chuck national coverage.

Without a doubt, Doefen sitting down in front of a bulldozer to keep a fast-food franchise from being built was sexier than a farmer in dirt-stained overalls addressing town councils about Burgundy Enterprise's dangerous pesticides. And it didn't hurt that Doefen had movie star eyes, and a messy ponytail that was a good kind of messy, and a little exclamation mark beard on his chin that made you notice his smile. Unlike most of the Glen Eddy farmers, Doefen also had all his teeth, and they were white, not brown like rotted out corn cob rows. His body was straight and thin. No belly on him.

Meanwhile, Chuck was pock-scarred by teenage acne, and wouldn't have passed for attractive even before cancer started eating his body down to bone.

Even Isabelle, who adored Chuck, had a little thing for Doefen. "If anybody could get me to march for anything again, it would be Doefen." There was no mistaking that the smile she smiled didn't have a whole lot to do with Doefen's politics.

Sure, Doefen's story struck a nerve. David going up against Goliath. But he wasn't any kind of visionary. Let alone a real hero.

At least not the way Darcy thought.

In the barn, Darcy hurried to get out of the bee gear. And still she didn't have much to say. Sullen and silent was not her usual style. She knew about the queen, Robert decided.

"You OK?" he asked crouching down a little so that they were eye to eye. He loved her eyes. So like her mother's. A deep

deep greenish-blue, spangled with amber. Like sea water after rain with glints of sunlight

She nodded.

"You know I had to do that thing with the queen bee, right?" he murmured.

"You mean kill her?" her eyes flashed with a hard brilliance that scared him.

"It was for the good of the hive," he muttered and quickly busied himself with sorting and stacking the empty bee frames. "I had to do it."

"Right." Darcy watched without offering to help. "Which is why you of all people, should understand about Doefen," she said. "And why I have to do what I have to do.

"You mean grind him under your boot," Robert said looking to get a laugh. No one could make Darcy laugh like he could.

"Don't be a jerk," she said.

If memory serves, he went off on her then. Told her that tangling with Doefen and the whole rotten world of politics and low-life corporations like Burgundy Enterprise with who knows what kind of agenda was much, much worse than dealing with the sickest of sick hives. It meant going up against cops, real live cops, not a bunch of fat guys with shiny badges like the ones who spent their time playing cards at the Glen Eddy sheriff's office. Cops with riot gear and guns. Guns loaded with real live bullets. Cops twitching like a finger on the trigger of a gun.

None of which scared Darcy in the least. Robert should have known better than to think that it would. The girl was nothing if not fearless. Not the reckless, naive-kid kind of fearless. Her sureness felt like a solid thing, unbreachable as a wall.

"You're just jealous because I care about something and you don't," she said when he paused to take a breath.

Jealous? Jealous! "As if!"

But as usual, Darcy had nailed him. In his heart of hearts Robert had to admit that even as he cranked out objections to Doefen's planned rally, and spelled out the risks of so-called peaceful protests, he missed the thrill of putting himself on the line, of being a part of something big, bigger than raising bees in Glen Eddy. He might have been warning her about the dangers of Molotov cocktails hurled by demonstrators, but he was remembering that, like skunk, they smelled good from a long way off.

"I'm only concerned about your safety," he insisted.

"So then come with me to Doefen's rally. Help me get there. You know that I'm going to go with or without you."

Robert could have, probably should have outed her to Isabelle and Jack right then and there. But she trusted him like no one else. And he loved that. And she knew that he loved it. In fact, she counted on it. So yeah, his decision to go along with Darcy's plan was kind of a done deal long before he said yes. And mostly he was OK with that. The only part that still bugged him was that it was all about Darcy putting herself out on behalf of Doefen.

Why Doefen?

Because there was a voice that told her she had to, she said. Robert struggles to remember Darcy's exact explanation. There was something about a cloud. A white shiny cloud hanging low over the Fairy Tree where she used to play. And a voice coming out of that cloud telling her that she was would have to leave Glen Eddy and take up Doefen's cause. The voice said it would guide her and tell her how to act. She never saw the cloud again, but heard the voice quite often. The voice of truth she called it, and said it looked and sounded like the poet Allen Ginsberg.

It did strike Robert as a little weird at the time, but only a little. Darcy's descriptions of the world were often vividly poetic. Charmingly over-the-top. Memorable. The sound of leaves rustling before a storm was orangey-brown, and pale yellow right after the rain stopped. In the summer, the grass was loud with the silver blue of insects' breathing. The wind that came up before sunset had the voice of an old, old woman. The moon was a button on the dark dress of the sky. He figured the imagery she chose came from her love of all the poetry that he and Isabelle had read to her over the years.

Voice of truth, Allen Ginsberg in shiny cloud? How different was that from Darcy's insistence that the ribbit, ribbit of frogs floated out of their mouths like purple stars.

Still Robert does recall that he lost patience with her, shouted, "Get real!" and pointed out that Doefen's run-in with a fast-food chain was nothing more than an attempt to secure his own little plot of land, to fulfill an ambition that went no further than raising a few goats.

Darcy just shrugged and smiled. "It's not like Doefen has to be the best person, to be the right person, the necessary person for me to help."

And there it was in a nutshell. Doefen was the one. That's all Darcy knew, and all she needed to know.

# BILLY
Doefen, Doefen, Doefen

I didn't get what Darcy saw in Doefen. At least not right away. I mean there was his whole look for starters.

In all the pictures she dragged me off to the library to see, he was dressed in denim top and bottom. I was the geekiest geek alive and even I knew that was a fashion no-go. Ditto the hair – thin, scraped back into a tiny grey ponytail. Add to that a soul patch on his chin, and you're talking sad. Really, really sad. "The dude needs a decent haircut, at least," I told her

"You sound like a sixth grade mean girl," Darcy said. "Forget about the clothes and focus on Doefen's actions."

I had to admit that she had a point there. What Doefen did was cool. Way, way cool.

I mean what a story!

There he was just some farmer dude out in a nowhere town called Swan Lake minding his own business, grazing goats, making cheese.

Me personally, I could live in a world without any goat cheese whatsoever. Once when my Mom was feeling fancy she bought some in Center City, and nagged me to try it. Problem was that I couldn't get past the smell – like old socks at the bottom of my gym locker. But that's me. I know there are all kinds of people out there who swear by the stuff.

Anyway, Doefen was busy doing his thing to provide all-natural, wholesome goat cheese to all the people who love it, when along came a developer with a plan for putting up a fast-food place right there in the middle of goat grazing country. Not in Doefen's field exactly, but right next to it.

Crazy, Doefen called it. Except that it wasn't, really, now that I think about it. Route 27 was right there at Doefen's property line, and the Interstate was just a mile further up with Glen Eddy, and most of the towns all up and down the valley strung along it.

Anyway, where there are roads, there are drivers who want to be fed. That's how the developer saw it. And the mayor backed him up.

Swan Lake really needed an economic boost, Mr. Mayor Man

said at the town meeting. Nobody gave him an argument on that part. But then he said that one little crummy diner just wasn't enough to generate the kind of money the town could really use.

Of course, everybody knew he meant the White Swan Diner and it kinda, sorta pissed people off. Just like it would if anybody around Glen Eddy dissed our Hawk's Crest Diner. So, the good citizens of Swan Lake were willing to give Doefen a listen when he got up to say his bit at the meeting.

Not that I was there to hear him. I was like eleven at the time. It was just that everybody in my life at that point – meaning Darcy, and my Mom and Dad were all going on and on about how Doefen stuck it to the mayor of Swan Lake. Which only goes to show how hard up a small town like Glen Eddy was for something to talk about.

Swan Lake didn't have any Golden Arches, or Taco Bells, or Burger Kings, and it didn't need any, thank you very much Doefen told Mr. Mayor Man and the good people of Swan Lake. Fast-food chains would destroy local businesses, and the kind of life people loved and wanted to live, he said. Not to mention, that all those big buck operations got meat on the table by mistreating animals from birth to slaughter. Cruel. Inhumane. Totally cruel, he called them. Of course, Darcy and her Mom were all over that considering that both of them were against eating animals in any shape or form. But they were the exception. Pretty much everybody else in Swan Lake had no problem with a nice, juicy burger, as long as they could keep on ordering it at the White Swan Diner. Me personally, I was with them.

Truth is that no amount of Darcy going on about how cows have beautiful eyes, or how chickens are really pretty birds like robins and sparrows, only bigger, ever made a dent in my taste for meat. But the cool thing about Darcy was that she knew that, and was still willing to be my friend. My best friend.

Anyway, most people were like my Dad on the subject of fast-food places. I mean, he was totally okay with them getting built. Live and let live, he said. And my Mom was for it too, as long as they prettied up the property by planting some petunias or something.

Me, I didn't give a shit about what they were going to do or not do in Swan Lake, except that it mattered to Darcy. I mean, my taste buds were shaped by the burgers, and fries, and fried chicken at the Hawk's Crest. All of which, in my humble opinion, were totally awesome. No Burger King or KFC or whatever was going to beat them. But they could go ahead and try.

Anyway, the story of Doefen's showdown with the mayor and the developer made all the papers up and down the valley. Got a big buzz at the Farmers Coop. Which was where Mr. Farmerman Robert came into the picture. Not that keeping a bunch of bees and picking some half rotten apples from trees he didn't even plant, and then selling them at the side of the road to city people made Robert any kind of farmer in my book. But he thought he was. Or made like he was. The point is, the first time Darcy ever heard about Doefen was from Robert talking with her Mom about how the whole Farmers Coop, and Chuck Lorrain especially, were psyched for Doefen. And if Robert was interested in something, then Darcy was going to be interested in it too.

Because that was how it was with her. Robert was *The One*. The go to guy. *The Answer Man*. Darcy was forever going on about Robert this, Robert that. What she saw in the dude, I'll never know. I mean he was old, as old as her Mom and Dad, way old for Darcy to be calling him her good friend. But that is a whole other story.

Right away, the Farmers Coop got behind Doefen.

Protest, protest, protest. That made the valley papers too, along with a photo spread of Doefen and his goats, but in the end Mr. Mayor Man did not give a shit about what a few farmers wanted. The developer got the go-ahead to build his junk food place, just like Burgundy Enterprise got the okay to plant monster corn in the field behind the high school in Glen Eddy, which Chuck Lorrain and the Farmers Coop had protested against for like a whole year.

In the beginning, the protest against the junk food place was all about marching, marching, marching. Then came the petitions and filing legal stuff at the State legislature and the Governor's office. The number of protesters went up and up, but the result was the same.

Bulldozers and diggers came anyway.

Which was when Doefen and his protester friends lay down at the entrance to the construction site.

Dozers went around them. Dug a hole.

Came night, Doefen and his friends filled in the hole.

Darcy loved that part. Farmers "armed" with shovels undoing the damage done by huge machines.

Next day, more of the same thing. Only this time, a local paper covered it and ran some pictures.

The developer hired guards.

Maybe those dudes slept on the job, or maybe they had a soft spot for the farmers, but overnight the hole got filled again.

Problem was that the farmers just couldn't fill the hole that the developer dug fast enough. Three days later, the developer pulled way ahead. Foundation got poured, the shell of the building started to go up.

Doefen and his friends came in the night, took it down. Easy work. It was all prefab crap.

At which point the developer went ape shit, accused Doefen and "his gang" of a zillion dollars worth of damage, and had Doefen's ass hauled off to jail.

And that's when the story went big and bigger. Civil rights people got involved. There was talk and more talk about the right to protest and free speech. Next thing, all kinds of local groups buddied up in support of the farmers and started to call themselves a coalition. Named themselves WE, as in Whole Earth, not wheeeeee, which is what I thought at first. TV cameras rolled.

But while Doefen sat in jail, and his legal aid lawyer from Center City tried to get him out, and his farmer friends marched outside the jail with Free Doefen signs, the fast-food place went right on being built. The whole protest thing got pretty tired, pretty fast once there was no more man-against-the-machine drama to spice it up. So, by the time Doefen got out of jail a month, or maybe it was two months later, people were already okay with eating at the fast-food place, and couldn't imagine how they ever got along without it.

For a while, my Dad would think of the fast-food place in Swan Lake on a Friday night and tell my Mom that we should go over there and check it out. In his mouth, "over there" sounded like it was as far away as the moon. Or at least that's how my Mom reacted to it. Maybe next week, she'd say.

Truth is I was tempted. I mean, it wasn't like I was thinking of bailing on our usual once-a-weekend fest at the Hawk Crest or anything. I just wanted to check out the competition. But knowing how Darcy felt about my eating shit food, especially shit food made from animals kept me from taking my Dad's side to push my Mom into driving out to Swan Lake.

More than anything, Darcy was always looking to make the world a better place and to keep people from acting like the bunch of dumb fucks they are. Not that she called them that. Or even thought of them that way. That's on me. Darcy was a way better person. All heart and dream. I mean, she was a dreamer, capital D, big time.

So, I tried my best to not let her down.

Too bad she believed that her dream for Doefen was his dream too. Which it wasn't. No way, no how. Not that you could tell her that. Or that she would listen if you tried. Anyway, somewhere along the way she decided that she was supposed to work with Doefen to make the dream become real.

"When the mode of music changes, the walls of the city shake," she said like that explained everything.

It was some quote from Plato that she got from reading Ginsberg, her all-time favorite poet. Idol, actually.

I didn't get the quote then, and I'm still not sure I really know what Darcy meant by it. It had something to do with a theory she had that Doefen's ideas would act sort of like a sound, a vibration, a music that would set people's bodies moving in a new way, and the new rhythm of their bodies would make them think and behave in new ways, send the old ways, the old walls tumbling down. Instead of people settling for the same old same old, they would try for something better, she said.

"It's just poetry," I said. "You can't live by poetry."

"I can. And I do."

End of discussion.

That's how it was with Darcy. Once her heart was made up, there was no reasoning with her.

Doefen, Doefen, Doefen.

"He should be President," she said. "The world would be in such a better place."

"The goat guy?"

I couldn't picture it myself. Presidents were dudes they taught you about in school, not somebody you could run into on the street if you happened to be in Swan Lake. President Lincoln.

And Washington. Those were the two names that stuck with me. I pictured Presidents kinda, sorta like superheroes, but more boring. Except for that *I have a dream guy*, Martin Luther. He was way cool. But then, they shot him

"When the mode of music changes, the walls of the city shake." Darcy treated it like it was a personal marching order.

Doefen , Doefen , Doefen.

Darcy dragged me off to the library so that I, we could read all about him. And I went, even though I hated the place. All those aisles to get lost in. No landmarks.

But the library was where the computers were. Never mind that there were only six of them and that half the time they were crashed. If by some miracle all of them were up and running, the sign-up sheet was filled up for like hours ahead of time.

I didn't see the point of the library's so-called resource room. But Darcy, she had patience. She'd be in there five days a week, if she was researching something.

We waited for like two hours for some lady with haystack hair to finish looking at Thanksgiving Day recipes, but once we got on line Darcy showed me article after article on Doefen. And yeah, her anti-junk food hero did look pretty good. I mean who wouldn't be against messing with nature and doing stuff like putting fish brain genes into tomatoes. If I had to eat a tomato, I sure as hell didn't want it to have anything in it that was even a tiny bit related to fish brains. And just like Chuck Lorrain, he was against spraying food crops with the Burgundy Enterprise stuff that for sure could make people's hair fall out and cause babies to wind up being born with extra eyeballs and fingers just the way the frogs all around Glen Eddy were hatching with extra legs and tails and shit.

Monster frogs. Nobody could fault Doefen for wanting to stop that.

For sure the whole frog thing really hit home with Darcy. I mean if you knew Darcy, you had to know that she was haunted by suffering.

Most of the kids in Glen Eddy just wanted the monster frogs gone. When they caught sight of them, they shot them dead with BB guns, threw rocks at them until they drowned. But Darcy made a hospital for them behind Robert's barn.

"Don't you worry, no one is going to hurt you here," she'd coo at some ugly-ass specimen and slide it into the old porcelain tub that Robert donated to the cause.

Mostly she found the frogs along the short cut that we took to school.        It was a route that only Darcy loved. No question that it eliminated a quarter mile of terror that came from dodging the truck traffic that tore down Route 27 toward the Interstate. And it bypassed Mrs. Mustache, the lady crossing guard with bleached blonde whiskers who stood on the quiet corner by the school where like two cars an hour went by. She made you wait ten minutes before she got around to stubbing out her cigarette and holding up the round red stop sign at the empty street and let your cross. Ten minutes that made you late enough to get detention.

The problem for me was that the short cut meant going into the woods between where Darcy and I lived and the back entrance to the school. And those woods were dark. Not to mention, totally spooky and creepy silent. Snap a twig and it was like a rifle going off. A rock tumbling sounded like a pack of ax murders crashing after you.

Even with miles of string to mark the trees, I would have gotten lost if I wasn't with Darcy. Beats me how she knew every log, every mossy rock as if it was a point on a map, but she did.

For long stretches, the shortcut followed a stream with mud-slick banks. Darcy made a game of jumping from one side to the other.

"Cross like you're a leopard," she'd say. "Use only three jumps." Or, "Make like you're a flamingo."

She'd launch herself off the muddy bank, teeter on a wobbly stone with one leg tucked up, arms flapping until she was perfectly balanced, and then cross like it was nothing.

Me, no matter what animal I was supposed to be, I'd inch out onto the nearest, widest rock and half the time land ass first in the water.

Darcy could have called me out and treated me like a clumsy rhino, or hippo, or water buffalo, but she didn't. She just got right in the water with me, and splashed around until her jeans were as soaked as mine.

So, there we were one morning running, laughing at the squelchy, farty sounds our wet sneakers were making, when Darcy suddenly came to a dead stop.

"Look at that," she whispered pointing at the ground. "Look." And I did. I looked hard as I could, but all I saw was leaf litter.

"Wow, wow, wow," she said and scooped up something green and shiny, held it in her cupped hands for me to see.

"What a beauty you are," she whispered to the frog with bulging eyes that were a picture of total terror. She ran her thumb down the pebbly ramp of the frog's back, stroked its snout. "You are a real beauty," she said, and I could tell she really meant it. "Yeah, you are."

My brain screamed — gross. Way gross. And that was before Darcy found the frog's hind leg, which looked like a shrunken question mark with a fan of stick-like toes.

"You poor little thing." Tears were coming out of her eyes, for real. "No wonder I was able to catch you so easily."

She kissed her finger, pressed it against the rim of the frog's mouth. I mean, if it wasn't for everything her Mom drummed into her about germs, I bet she would have kissed the thing on the lips.

Gross my brain screamed again, but my heart knew that, really, Darcy was totally awesome — a sort of good fairy, kind princess, and best friend all rolled into one.

"Here you hold it," she said.

I was willing. It wasn't so much to ask. I really did want to show Darcy how much I loved her. But my hands refused to obey, and I shook my head so hard I could practically feel my brain smacking the walls of my skull.

"It's OK," she said, which started me boo hooing like a total baby, and blubbering.

So why did I repay Darcy kindness later that day by grabbing her slimy little darling out of the tub hospital and shoving it down the front of her t-shirt?

Maybe it was because something I saw on TV gave me the idea that boys were supposed to do that to girls, or maybe I just wanted to get Darcy away from the frog so she would come skateboarding with me. I don't know.

What I remember is the buzz of the frog's heart against the palm of my hand, and the pukey feeling in gave me in my stomach.

And I remember Darcy gently pulling the frog out from under her shirt.

No screaming. No flipping out. She just gave me a look, a look of such sadness that it ran straight through my heart like one of those long barbecue skewer things my Mom used for vegetables when my Dad fired up the grill.

"I know you won't ever do anything like that again," she said, her hand on my shoulder.

It was like she was forgiving me and giving me a command, both at the same time.

"I promise," I said. It was all I could do to keep from falling down on my knees at her feet. "I promise."

I owed Darcy big time and I knew it. Not that she made me feel that way. But still, when she told me to read about Doefen, I read and waited for her to tell me how I fit into her plans. I knew Darcy well enough to know that if she was interested in something, there was going to be a plan. And it would involve taking action.

My usual contribution to her projects was to make posters. Which I loved to do. To me they were kinda, sorta like street signs. Maybe because I was always getting lost, I had some definite ideas about what made a sign work. I mean when I was little, I used to tie string all over the place to help me find my way. Three loops of green around the pine at the end of my street marked the starting point of the shortcut to school. Two windings of brown twine on a lamp post let me know which of the five look-alike driveways was the one to my house. A thin red rubber band on the stem of the front doorknob was for making sure I really was in the right place.

The Boy Scout handbook said to mark a trail by piling up stones, making gashes in trees. But doing that wasn't going to tell me if I was headed for the supermarket or school. Darcy knew about my strings, and never made fun of them. She totally got that most of the world, and me especially, didn't have her sense of direction.

Direction. That is basically what a poster is all about. Darcy had no problem with that part. It was just that she couldn't make direction into a picture. Lucky for me, of all the things that she was really good at, drawing wasn't one of them. Which meant that there was at least one little thing I could do for her. Give her.

At the start of that school year, I made the great, big red signs that she used in her fight to get the fish-stick things that smelled like old bait off the cafeteria menu. And then a month later, I made the yellow and black posters she wanted for the protest against the Frankenstein corn that the school let Burgundy Enterprise plant next to the football field.

Those corn signs were some of my best. They had the same look as the yellow and black nuclear Fallout Shelter signs that were still bolted to the walls all over the school from who knows when. I used yellow for the background — the color of warning, and put pictures of the toxic corn plants inside the three triangles. The lettering was all in black – because there was destruction and death hidden in the screwed up Burgundy Enterprise seeds. Principal Toul sure as hell hated my signs. Tore them down as fast as I could make them and Darcy could put them up.

My favorites, though, were the ones I did the year before for Darcy's campaign to save Wood Park, the schoolyard playground that she, and I, and all the kids loved so much. Toul and the PTA called it a splintery, vermin-infested hazard, but for us the wooden platforms and nooks underneath were sometimes a pirate ship, sometimes a mountain top, or a cave, or a castle. I used a spring green for the background of the poster – as in, natural, calm — and timber browns for the lettering. I drew the ramps and platforms in rainbow colors. For a minute there, I think the grown-ups looked at the lines and squiggles on the poster and saw Wood Park as the magical place that it was for us kids. Even Toul swore that he was sorry that the playground had to come down.

But it did come down. The school put up an all plastic, modular swing and slide set – rust-proof, bug and rat proof, and pretty much imagination proof too. I can't say I was surprised. That was just the way things worked in the world. Bigger, stronger always beat out the little guy.

All the kids were sad at first, but it didn't last. Darcy was the only who never really got over losing Wood Park. She acted like its destruction was somehow her fault. Which made me worry about my part in the whole thing. Maybe if I had made different signs, better signs, the battle to save the park would have turned out different.

So, when Darcy told me that her plans for Doefen included

making a really, really good, unforgettable poster for him and the Whole Earth movement, I totally flashed on Wood Park and got really nervous.

It didn't help that Darcy wanted it to be something that would speak to anyone and everyone, regardless of their language.

"It will have to be read with the heart," she said.

I sketched a blue and green globe with a stretched out W on one side, E on the other. Simple. To the point.

Darcy called it alright, but said it didn't tell the whole story.

Usually, the signs she asked me to draw just came to me. But this time, I sketched for a week. At home. At school. None of the drawings that filled my notebooks and the margins of my textbooks looked right. I was just about ready to bag it, and tell Darcy that I was a complete and total failure, when this picture of her dressed like a knight and carrying a banner came into my head.

The banner was bright white and it was flying high above her head. And anyone who saw it, magically became a knight too, and lined up to march behind Darcy. All around the banner there was a clear, clear light without any dark or shadows in it.

I started a design with two boxes on a white background – one labeled Truth, the other Lies. Truth in a white box on the left. Lies in black box on the right.

Truth because Truth was what Darcy was all about. No one fought harder for it, or was willing to sacrifice more for it. The lettering was made up of tiny human and animal footprints. You had to get up close to see them.

Lies was spelled out in tiny dollar and cent signs.

A black and white choice in black and white. That was so Darcy.

Below the boxes, right in the middle was the earth – watery blue, the way it looks from space. All around it, I drew cupped hands in a rainbow of colors. From a distance it looked like a giant flower.

At the top in bold black I put the letters WE.

The cool thing was that anyone could copy the design. From day one, every kid knows how to draw one of those loopy flowers. And with or without the tiny symbols in the lettering, the words were the same. A totally readable sign.

Excellent, Darcy said and made one change. In place of

Truth and Lies, she put Right and Wrong. Which was perfect. The design pulled the eye first to the word WE at the top, then to the white box on the left, and finally the black box on the right. WE RIGHT WRONG. Typography at work – I didn't know the word or concept back then, but somehow I'd stumbled onto the combination of sizes and shapes that made the words come together as a sentence – WE Right Wrong.

Three little words. They became a slogan for WE. For Darcy, they were already the only words to live by.

## ROBERT
No Talking to Them


Robert did his best to convince Isabelle and Jack to let Darcy go to the WE rally. Whatever his misgivings about Doefen, he couldn't bear to disappoint Darcy.

"No way," Isabelle said, hunched over the kitchen table, a thick ceramic cup clutched in her hands.

He remembers her hands, so pale against the yellowed cup. Not an old woman's hands, but no longer young either. Veins showing a little, the skin starting to bunch up over her slender fingers like a stretched out glove. He wishes he could have kissed those hands. Kissed them smooth.

"No way," Jack echoed from his side of the table, creaking back and forth on his chair until he managed to balance it on the two back legs.

Robert imagined the chair sliding out from under Jack, his head going splat against the red wall. He noticed that the red was no longer as red as the red that he remembered helping Isabelle to choose. When had that red faded from poppy to the color of bleached brick?

"Hell, I'd rather see my kid take up with the yahoos around here, or even the summer yuppies sooner than let her get involved with all that WE shit," Jack continued, allowing the chair to thump down onto all four legs for punctuation.

"Oh yeah, right on Mr. Helter Skelter, Street Fighting Man," Robert said.

A dim image of Jack back in the day came to Robert – wavy chestnut hair so thick and shiny it was the envy of women and men both, long legs looking miles longer in striped bell-bottom pants, paisley shirt open down to there, smoky-dark eyes peering out at the world over the top of blue-tinted glasses perched half-way down his enviably straight nose, half-stoned smile on his pretty boy lips. How and when did Jack become the paunchy slob with a frizz of grey hair floating around his head like electrified iron filings?

Helter Skelter, Street Fighting Man — snippets of the twin anthems of their freshman year buzzed in Robert's head.

*Everywhere I hear the sound of marching, charging feet,*
*Cause summer's here and the time is right for fighting in*
*the street*

*Look out*
*Helter skelter*
*Helter skelter*
*Helter skelter*
*When I get to the bottom*
*I go back to the top of the slide*
*Where I stop and turn*
*and I go for a ride*

"Come on, man," he said looking from Jack to Isabelle to Jack to Isabelle again. "You remember what it was like being young — doing your own thing."

"I do," Isabelle said, her tired eyes locked on the day's worth of leavings and crusted dishes littering the table.

"So," Robert said, a tiny trill of hope pitching his voice up and higher. "So!"

"I also remember that we were in college, not thirteen years old. Times were different. Way different."

Jack smiled. "Yeah, me too. I remember." His voice sounded gummy.

Robert shifted in his seat to get Jack out of his line of sight.

"Bella," Robert sighed, daring for the first time in a long time to address Isabelle by the nickname she'd banned him from using years ago for being too infantilizing. Or was it patronizing? Maybe patriarchal?

"Bella." He remembers wanting to awaken the dreamy girl in her, the girl who once planned to weave tapestries with yarn that she would spin from the wool of her own sheep.

"Listen to me, Bella." The name felt round and ripe as a plum in his mouth. He saw Isabelle stiffen, but couldn't resist indulging in the forbidden name one more time.

"Bella," he whispered, voice hoarse with pleasure, "Darcy really wants to do this."

Isabelle — determined, sensible, mother of girl-child Darcy — slammed down her mug on the table. Spoons, bowls pinged and clattered. "Is it really too much to ask people to put their dirty plates in the sink?"

"Not my stuff," Jack offered, neither defensive nor aggrieved, and began drumming on the edge of the table with a knife and spoon.

It was hellish, Jack's habit of drumming on every surface of the house, and pummeling his own chest when nothing else was available, yet Isabelle acted like she didn't hear it. Without another word, she downed the dregs from her cup like it was a shot of tequila and began to clean up.

Robert jumped up to help. The clatter of the dishes as he and Isabelle stacked them in the sink set up a satisfying counterpoint to Jack's persistent drumming. Robert happily removed the last empty bowl from the table, depriving Jack of his improvised tom drum. Unfazed, Jack banged the top of a honey jar like it was a cymbal, and pounded the table leg like the pedal of a bass drum.

Isabelle washed. Robert dried. The thick dishware was just like the stuff in his own cabinets, Salvation Army salvage, each cup banded with coffee residue like the growth rings of trees. A record of slapdash housekeeping. How was it that he'd never noticed how crude, how ugly it all was?

Before long, the hot water from the sink steamed up the kitchen window and Robert was glad. The sky outside was the color of faded mums which he didn't like to see. Mums made him think of funerals. He was happy to be indoors, standing alongside, close to Isabelle.

"OK. So think about this," he said between trips from sink to cupboards. "Darcy really believes in Doefen. And who knows? Maybe she's right. Maybe this guy can make a difference."

"Man, that is such shit," Jack said. "Doefen is part of the System." He scratched the stubble on his chin with a spoon without interrupting the complicated rhythm he had going with a knife on the table edge. "He's bullshit and so is WE. All part of the System"

First Isabelle, then Robert rolled their eyes. Only Isabelle smiled. Everything for Jack was about the System.

"BU·LL·SH·I·T," Jack chanted to the rhythm of spoon and knife. "BU·LL·SH·I·T."

Robert's head seethed with images of fiery, vaporizing rays shooting out of his eyes at the cutlery in Jack's hands, but, adopting, a neutral, soothing tone, he said, "Well, Chuck thinks WE is on the up and up."

Both Isabelle and Jack adored Chuck. Everybody, all the right people, adored him. The guy didn't have a buck in his pocket, cancer was chewing up his insides, but he was busy sheltering a barn full of cows too old to milk, and race horses past their prime, not to mention greyhounds who could no longer run fast enough to escape being put down. And sick as he was, Chuck never failed to show up at the Farmers Coop and to make himself heard loud and clear at town meetings.

Robert waited for Chuck's name to work its magic, but Jack kept on drumming and Isabelle continued slamming dishes into the drainer.

"Don't forget, Chuck likes Doefen's politics," he nudged. Fact was fact, whatever Robert's feelings on the subject. "He thinks Doefen has gotten kids excited about WE. And you know that for things that need to happen to start happening, you've got to have kids involved, you need some young blood."

Too late, Robert realized his mistake.

"Well WE will just have to do without the blood of my kid," Isabelle said with a tone of terrible finality.

"Come on, she believes in Doefen ," Robert said, eyes on Isabelle, willing her to remember her own passions of years ago. "And maybe Chuck is right. Maybe this guy can make a difference."

"So let her sign a petition." Isabelle's voice was thick, threatened by stormy emotions. "Or she can raise money for WE. I don't want her getting busted. Or worse."

"Damn straight," Jack said beating out a complicated rhythm of twos against threes that Robert recognized as a prelude to what could only become an ever louder and more unbearable riff. Almost without thinking, Robert held his hand out for the cutlery.

Jack gave it up without a word of protest, and proceeded to make a drum of his chest.

"Fucking hell," Robert remembers shouting at Jack, "Give it a rest."

To which Jack whimpered, "Sorry, Man. Sorry."

Isabelle was at Jack's side in a heartbeat, patting his shoulder. The way she touched him revealed much about how they'd

32

managed to stay together for eighteen years. More than Robert wanted to know.

"Babe," Jack whimpered, kissing Isabelle's fingers. "Babe. Remember that drum kit I used to have, the one that came in a little suitcase?"

"Yeah," Babe answered, kissing the top of his frizzled head, apparently not the least bit put off by Jack's failure to use her proper name. "It was totally sweet."

"Wasn't it, though? Best snare ever. Sound of it went right through you."

Very touching, Babe's little dreamy stroll down memory lane with Jack. And shameless, considering that she knew, Jack knew, they all knew that back in the day Jack had hocked that oh-so-wonderful drum kit for drugs.

As far as he was concerned, the fucking pair of them deserved each other. Could have each other. His only concern was for Darcy.

"It's not like Darcy would be going to the whole WE thing by herself," he pointed out. "She'd have me." Subtle emphasis on me. "I'll watch out for her." As if to highlight his responsible nature, Robert turned to the sink to finish washing the dishes.

"Shit, now there's something that will let me sleep at night," Jack laughed, wheezing like a stuck accordion. In short order, Isabelle laughed too, softly at first, then louder succumbing to a fit that seemed as much like sobbing as amusement. And finally Robert couldn't help but add his own staccato yelps.

Admittedly, adult style responsibility was not exactly a strong suit for any one of them.

"Come on, you guys" he said once he could speak. "Don't be like that."

Like it or not, the three of them – him, Isabelle, Jack — were lifers. They belonged together. Whatever kind of life they'd made, it was the only life they knew. The only life they could live. They'd been together too many years to ever break up. The three of them were all the friends, and lovers, and family each of them had in the world.

Headstrong, passionate, fiery Darcy had arrived late in their lives. But they each loved her more and better than they had ever loved, or could love anyone else. Even if none of them agreed on what was best for her.

33

"Enough," Isabelle said, turning suddenly sober. "I need some air."

At which point Jack decided to mellow out with a favorite cop show – Double Doink he called it for the sound in the opening credits. Robert joined Isabelle outside, found her lighting a joint.

Robert loved that she still smoked. It was so retro. So Sixties. And he loved that she sneaked it from Jack whose idea of a wild time these days ran to drinking two diet colas back to back. After squandering the equivalent of a small country's gross national budget on drugs, Jack had managed to twelve-step his way out of all of his addictions. Ten years sober and counting. He'd become as unforgiving as an Old Testament prophet on the subject of drugs and alcohol. More than once, Robert found himself wishing that he'd fall off the wagon.

Standing alongside Isabelle watching the sun sink behind what was left of the woods at the border of the development, Robert couldn't help but think of the bungalow colony that used to be there.

"Don't you wish that old man Glasdale hadn't sold the cabins?" he said, gently resting his hands on Isabelle's shoulders.

To his surprise and delight, she didn't shrug him off. She even leaned back against his chest as she took a long toke of weed, held it, offered the joint to him.

Robert savored the sweet, sweet smell of cannabis that perfumed the air, but his memory of the paranoia that had prompted him to quit smoking remained vivid enough to keep him from being tempted.

Isabelle exhaled a long plume of smoke. "We couldn't go on squatting in a bungalow colony forever," she sighed.

"Yeah, but the price was right."

They'd lived rent-free, at first, in the boarded-up cabins, then paid a few bucks to Glasdale once he discovered them squatting on his property.

"Free is about what it should have cost considering it came with no electricity or running water."

Isabelle and Jack had chosen cabin 11 — the largest. Robert decided on cabin 9 — close, but not too close to Isabelle and Jack. "Liberating the property" they'd called it.

The Beach Tree Garden Complex that Isabelle and Jack and

Darcy now called home had been built over the bones of the bungalows. The development of forty more or less identical townhouse threaded along spirals of arbitrarily placed cul-de-sacs was a "Disney does cute village" abomination if ever there was one. How Isabelle could stand living there was beyond Robert.

"Remember Cabin 7?"

Isabelle took another long toke. "Sure. Mouse turds all over the place. Not to mention mosquitoes, the size of B52s."

Insect life didn't figure much in Robert's memories of the Wreck Room as they used to call that cabin. He recalled long nights of smoking dope, drinking cheap beer, playing cards, passing out huddled together on a mattress pulled up to the blazing heat of a cast iron stove they'd stoked with wood collected from around the cabins.

"We were happy there," he said. He blamed Isabelle's job as an ICU respiratory therapist for having darkened her perspective on things. "Really, happy."

Isabelle neither confirmed nor denied it.

"I mean if Glasdale hadn't sold the place, you could have raised your sheep."

Isabelle toked up again, held the smoke long and longer, finally exhaled. "You think?"

"Definitely."

He still half-believed that they could have pulled it off. The clearing at the center of the circle of cabins was perfect for a sheep pasture. An underground spring fed right into an abandoned swimming pool that could have become a pond to water the animals. The utility shed would have made a perfect shearing room and there was no shortage of places to build a loom. And Jack had actually hit on a "redistribution of wealth" scheme, as he liked to call his dealings outside The System, that could have generated some start-up money.

*What a time it was, it was a time of innocence...*

With the economy tanked and gold prices going through the roof, Jack was buying up Glen Eddy's broken jewelry, unloved trinkets and taking them to the diamond district in the city where he earned double what he paid the locals for them. Part of the profit went into dope — mostly weed, a little mesc, peyote — which he scored in the city, and then sold in Glen Eddy.

Isabelle worried about the money having bad karma, but Jack gave her an earful about how all the sad shit with bad vibes that the people of Glen Eddy kept hanging onto weighed them down. By buying the unloved mementos that they'd stashed in attics, and the keepsakes they'd inherited from relatives they despised, Jack unburdened them. Cleared their psychic space, gave them all a little room to breathe. Not to mention, paid them a fair price for the shit, better than they could ever hustle for themselves, even if they'd been able to get it together to travel to the city. And last but not least, he brought back a little brain candy for them, some sweet drugs to color their world happy.

Robert had to hand to Jack, in his heyday, he really could charm a bird out of a tree. Not only did he convince Isabelle that the scheme was righteous, but he got Robert to come along for the buying and selling, and, in no time at all, had him tucking an unregistered gun into the waistband of his jeans "in case there was a problem."

"The Man never sleeps, you know what I'm saying?" increasingly paranoid Jack insisted to explain the need for a gun.

Except, that The Man wasn't the problem. It turned out that from day one, Jack lied about their earnings, short-changed Robert on the split, and put a whole lot of money up his nose in the form of white powders that fried his brain.

By the time the developer's bulldozers came to take down old man Glasdale's bungalow colony, Robert was glad to bail on the whole scene. He took the wad of bills from his cut of the deals, which he'd stashed behind a wall panel in cabin 9, walked down the road and rented a room at a defunct dairy farm.

Totally broke thanks to Jack's drug habit, Jack and Isabelle refused to budge from their cabin. One town house after another went up around them. In the end, somehow Jack sweet talked the developer into offering them a deal on a town house of their own.

"That's crazy. Don't do it," Robert said. By then the dairy farm where he was living had been put up on the block for taxes, and he had enough cash for a down payment. "We can all move to the farm and start over."

Except that there was no going back. Jack was too strung out to think about anything but drugs. Isabelle declared that even though the whole back-to-the-land thing was totally groovy, she wasn't into it anymore. Having read the library's entire holdings on massage, and nursing, and respiratory therapy, she'd decided to forego raising sheep and to embrace the healing arts.

Robert bought the dairy farm anyway. Because he could. Because he had no other plan. Because he wanted to stay near Isabelle. It took him years to accept that she was not going to change her mind, wasn't going to leave Jack.

"You can't say we didn't have some good times in those cabins," Robert murmured into Isabelle's hair.

She sucked down the last bit of the joint. "Listen, I don't really have anything against Doefen. It's just that Darcy needs to focus on her schoolwork, and to start thinking about getting into a decent college."

She didn't say make a better life for herself, avoid ending up like us. But Robert knew that was what she meant.

In the almost dark, he kneaded her shoulders gently. "Darcy is a good kid. You don't have to worry. She'll do fine."

A breeze lifted Isabelle's long hair. Robert inhaled deeply. *Trailing clouds of glory do we come.* Something, something. *Youth by vision splendid is on her way attended.* Wordsworth's exact words escaped Robert, lost as he was in the scent of Isabelle's hair.

He remembers that it smelled inexplicably of wood smoke, and ever so faintly of apples.

***

On his way home, Robert stopped off at Chuck's house. Chuck could be counted on to listen and keep a tight lip. Over the years, he and Chuck had become friendly without being friends, Robert having kept a careful distance because Chuck's activism attracted the kind of attention that scared the hell out of him. The last thing he needed was for some Pig to link his name with Chuck's. He didn't have the stomach for jail that Chuck did.

The guy was likable. Admirable, really, without ever morphing into enviable. Chuck's recent cancer diagnosis was a clincher as far as envy was concerned. Given all the stats, Chuck shouldn't have been dying of prostate cancer. Not at his age, anyway. And yet, against all odds, he was. Nothing to envy there.

Cancer had definitely left its mark on Chuck's body, but his eyes had not lost their vigor. He smiled and nodded knowingly at Robert's complaints about his unsatisfactory discussion with Isabelle and Jack.

"They're good people, you know that," Chuck said, voice brimming with kindness, even love. "But they're rabbits. Scared little rabbits. You can't expect them to suddenly act like lions," Robert was quick to agree, lest Chuck deem him a rabbit-like creature as well.

"Now Darcy... Darcy is a whole other story," Chuck continued. "That little girl is a true spitfire... I'd go to hell and back for her. Do whatever she asked me to do."

"Even if it was for a guy like Doefen?" Robert snapped, ready to recite the litany of reasons why Doefen was unworthy of Darcy's admiration.

Wagging a finger, Chuck directed Robert to sit in an ancient overstuffed chair with wadding spilling out at the seams.

"You miss the point," he said. "Let me share a little story with you."

Robert did his best to settle into the chair knowing that with Chuck there'd be no avoiding the story, and that it wouldn't be brief. Chuck, who always seemed to know everyone — important and not — or at least to know someone who knew the person in question, launched into a story about Duke Burgundy.

A friend of Chuck's, or a friend of a friend of his attended prep school with Duke. Or maybe it was college. Robert can no longer remember which.

Apparently, Duke was a popular, rangy, rich kid with a long dark pony tail down his back, who was known for wearing Hawaiian shirts in all weather and a suede hat with an eagle feather, which he claimed to have found hiking the Appalachian Trail.

"Everyone pretty much suspected that the feather came from a fancy sporting goods store," Chuck said. "You wouldn't think that mattered, except that it ties in with Duke's dumpling thing."

"Dumplings? What about dumplings," Robert remembers having asked more than once that evening in an unsuccessful attempt to steer Chuck towards the point of the story and away from one of his many digressions. Instead, he had to hear all about how in college Duke became a stoned-out drug hound who never met a mind-altering powder or pill he wouldn't try, but never once experienced a moment of true awareness. Another tale that stayed with Robert had to do with Duke's inability to hear the whisperings of his heart over all the ideas that buzzed around his head. Such as whenever a girl fell in love with Duke – he was, according to Chuck's source, irresistibly charming, charismatic – Duke's response was to ponder the mystery of why he should reciprocate; why he should choose to love that girl over another with similar intellect, interest, and intelligence. Apparently, he longed not for love, but for a science to elucidate love and attraction.

The actual explanation of the dumpling phenomenon when it finally came concerned Duke's often stated ambition to make the world a better place. "Better" turned out to be founding Burgundy Enterprise, which was meant to change farming into a science of economy, and to separate the whole idea of agriculture from emotional issues like feeding nations.

"Burgundy Enterprise is the damn dumpling story all over again," Chuck said, "writ large."

That story, as Chuck told it at last, concerned Duke's claim that he was able to taste MSG, and that he liked the taste very much. One of Chuck's sources apparently recalled with fondness and bemusement that he and his friends spent many a Saturday afternoon in Duke's kitchen rolling dough, chopping ingredients to make dumplings from scratch in a city where there was Chinese take-out on almost every corner. Duke insisted on heaping the dumplings full of MSG, even though he knew that many of his friends got a headache from it. He claimed that MSG was key to getting the taste right. Amazingly enough, he had no trouble convincing his friends to eat the dumplings anyway. And, headache or not, they wound up pronouncing the dumplings the best they'd ever had.

"That's it?" Robert practically shouted, his voice bristling with irritation. The fairly obvious point of the MSG dumpling story hardly required an hour's worth of parables. "That's it?"

"Absolutely," Chuck said, smiling like a goddamn Buddha waiting for Robert to attain *bodhi*. "A lifetime history of inexhaustible enthusiasm, and persuasive, seductive charm masquerading as sincerity. That's why Duke has no problem selling genetically altered seeds laced with killer chemicals while maintaining his image as an ecologically concerned businessman."

"Darcy is right," he continued. "Duke's whole more-Eco-than-thou snow job has to come to an end before he poisons the entire world. He deserves to be shamed, needs to be brought down. Exposed."

"*Satyam muktaye,*" Chuck said by way of closing, with the serious look of a judge passing sentence. "Truth liberates."

"Ah," Robert sighed, feelings of *bodhi*, and *satya,* and *prajna* all rolled into one awakening in him. "I grok, brother."

He left Chuck's place, floated out into the night. Chuck was right. Who better that Darcy to shame Duke out of his lies? He had to believe that she would do fine, just like Chuck said. Never mind that according to the Farmer's Almanac, which Robert read every morning, Mercury had just gone retrograde. Until it returned to its normal path, chaos, misinformation, miscommunication in more than usual amounts were predicted to prevail on Earth. Not really an auspicious time for the journey, the quest that Darcy had in mind, but Chuck's voice kept playing in his head, "Take her. The time is ripe. Do it. No time like the now."

Chuck had also suggested, no urged Robert to bring, *Black Lightening*, his one and only good horse, to the protest. "Can't you just see it," he'd said sweeping the horizon with his hand. "Cops, corporate goons all around and then there's Darcy, above it all, up on a horse."

Robert dismissed the idea as the cancer talking. But crazy as it was, he couldn't get the picture of Darcy riding into the fray on Chuck's spirited stallion out of his head.

On his way home, Robert stopped in his orchard to study the sky. Jupiter, Venus, and Saturn were a silver zipper holding closed the black vast of the night. And Mercury? It was a mote, a scintillation at the horizon that the eye could barely make out.

Chuck was right. Darcy would do fine.

# BILLY
Maize Fire

Maybe things would have turned out different for Darcy if the field of Burgundy Enterprise's monster corn didn't catch fire. Maize, Toul kept calling it. An ancient, very important food crop that Glen Eddy was helping Burgundy Enterprise to test and improve so that people all over the world could grow more, eat better, he said. As if.

The Farmers Coop spread the real 411 on why the Glen Eddy high school said yes to Burgundy Enterprise planting the stuff next to the football field. It was all about cash. Cold hard cash so that Toul's pets — the football and ice hockey thugs — could get new uniforms. We're talking the same guys who beat the shit out of me every other week just to work their muscles. Fuck if I cared about them having uniforms.

But that was just me.

The Farmers Coop was pissed off because of the way BE screwed around with seeds and made them a one-shot deal. The plants that grew from BE seeds couldn't make any new seeds of their own. I didn't see why that was any kind of biggie. I mean, I guess I should have known that messing with nature like that was not cool. But maybe I missed the science class about plant reproduction, or maybe I was used to seeing my dad buying grass seeds at Home Depot all the time and figured it was just what you had to do if you wanted to grow stuff.

It took Darcy to set me straight. Turned out that the reason anybody wanted to buy the BE seeds at all — even though they cost a lot more than regular seeds — was because they produced a kind of super plant that no bugs could eat and no weeds could get near. Which sounded good to me, until she explained about Whack, the special bug and weed killer made by, you guessed it – BE. It was better, stronger than any other bug and weed killer out there, and it worked when all the others didn't. The BE plants that grew from BE seeds could suck up Whack like it was water. Meanwhile, regular plants would keel over dead. Ditto bugs.

Nobody wanted weedy fields and buggy plants, but the catch was that Whack also killed bees, birds, and small animals. Dead bees were where Robert came into the picture. And of course, wherever you had Robert, you had Darcy.

And that was before she found out about what *Whack* did to frogs. Turned out that once rain washed the stuff off the plants, it soaked into the ground, and worked its way into rivers and lakes where frog eggs that were exposed to *Whack* chemicals wound up hatching into monsters.

BE said it was trying to work out the kinks, but a lot of farmers didn't want anything to do with test driving their so-called new, improved seeds. Only a place as small, and stupid, and broke as Glen Eddy was willing to do that.

No question that Toul had it in for Darcy after the whole Wood Park thing, but he was definitely looking daggers at her as soon as the anti-maize posters went up. So, of course, he was more than ready to blame her for the fire.

Or me. Not just because I hung out with Darcy but because of my whole Pyroman rep. I mean kids were calling me that since I was like seven.

Okay, there was that time in the playground when I lit a couple of matches and threw them at a bunch of kids who had been beating up on me since I was in kindergarten. Not a single match even came close to one of those brats, never mind catching them on fire. Truth is I would have been okay with seeing flames eat up their jeans and jackets and spit them out as ash. I was that mad. Maybe if Darcy had not shown up, I really would have put fire to them. Who knows?

I mean, I even wave a lit match at Darcy when she tried to stop me from lighting any more.

She didn't blink. "I know you don't want to hurt anyone," she said. "And I don't want any hurt to come to you."

Next thing I knew, my cold and shaky hand was in her warm one, my box of matches was in the pocket of her jacket. Just before the recess monitor hauled the two of us off to Toul's office, Darcy kind of stared up into the sky, and whispered, like she was taking directions, "Look in your heart. Be bold and careful at the same time."

A poetry-speak moment. That's what I called the times when she spaced out like that. The recess monitor didn't even notice, or didn't make anything of it. I mean, nobody ever did until after the maize fire. For one thing, everybody was used to Darcy quoting poets at them. She did it all the time.

I put that right on Robert. He was the one who got her reading the stuff and memorizing it. I admit that there was a point where I thought it would be way cool if I could share in the whole poetry thing with her. So, I tried reading a few of her favorites. But I didn't get them. Ginsberg, especially.

Toul went ape-shit over the matches. Darcy said they were hers and stuck to the story, even though the recess monitor said different. And because Darcy wouldn't give them up, Toul put us both into detention for like a month.

"Dude, you didn't have to do that," I told Darcy, feeling super, super bad for getting her in trouble.

She just smiled. "Resist much, obey little."

I was so impressed, so grateful that when I got home that night, I took my Mom's red laundry marker and drew a flame on my chest, right over my heart. For Darcy. And as soon as it started to fade, I drew it again. And again. And again. I never stopped.

"Get it inked, dude," a friend recently told me. "Make it permanent."

I mean, I could. I'm old enough now. But a tattoo wasn't and isn't the kind or permanent I want. Permanent like a mole you're born with is permanent – always there and forgettable. Forgotten. Drawing the flame keeps it always new, fresh in my mind.

Anyway, no matter what Toul thought, or what the kids at school called me, I wasn't any kind of Pyroman. Really, I was just an average kid with an average kind of interest in fire.

I mean, I loved toasting marshmallows. Find me a kid who doesn't. And I loved when my dad burned leaves in a barrel, back when you could still do that without getting a ticket. I'd get close and closer to the flames so I could really suck down the sweet smell of the moldy leaves and damp twigs going dry, blazing up in smoke, and the tang of rust burning off the metal, glowing orange on the lip of the barrel.

The amazing thing was that my dad let me do it — no pulling me back or telling me it wasn't safe. "Go for it, tough guy, warm up those hands," he'd say, his voice all melty. It's as close as I can remember him being kinda, sorta thrilled with me as a son. I mean, how sad is that?

Anyway, it is true that when Darcy and I went skateboarding

by the empty houses in the neighborhood, we did try to get dried grass to catch fire by holding a magnifying glass over the buried lights in the driveways. But that was only because I was working my way through my Boy Scout handbook and trying out everything in it – different kinds of knots, measuring trees using a stick and shadows, and starting a fire without matches.

It never worked. Starting the fire over the driveway lights, I mean. Somehow, I missed the part about how it had to be sunlight, not just any kind of light.

It was sunlight that burned up our Christmas tree when I was ten. That's what the insurance guys said. They checked the whole house about ninety-nine times and couldn't find any other explanation. No bad wires. No electrical shorts. Furnace all nice and clean, doing what it was supposed to do. Nothing to point to arson. The way they had figured it, sunlight came in through the picture window and got concentrated on some straw ornaments my Mom bought at a crafts fair.

Spontaneous combustion, they called it.

Of course, my mom and dad freaked. My dad especially. Bad wiring, he could understand. But spontaneous combustion was another story. Home Depot didn't sell any kind of gadget to protect against that. It was like he suddenly found out there was black magic running around loose in the world.

Spontaneous combustion.

Nothing to do with me. But still, that year my mom and dad decided I was too old to dress-up in my firefighter coat and hat. And they disappeared the collection of toy fire trucks from the shelf above my bed. Lighting the stove had always been off-limits. Ditto the barbecue grill, or plugging in anything electric, even my toothbrush. But suddenly, making microwave popcorn became a no-no too. The paper bag might burst into flames they said.

Spontaneous combustion.

The day that the maize field went up in flames the sun was fierce bright. And hot. Like summer.

I was sitting in detention, sweating, staring out the window, dying to get the hell out of there. I should have been out skateboarding with Darcy. And I would have been, except for stupid Mr. Sullivan in 5th period asking me why my homework was all dirty and crumpled. I wasn't about to explain about the shortcut to school and landing in the water. But telling him a dog tried to eat it really pissed him off. Especially, since I didn't have a dog, and he knew it, and everybody cracked up because they knew it too.

Anyway, when I saw the bright orange light on the cornfield, I figured that the sun was going down and it was finally time for the detention monitor to let us go home. But then I noticed smoke.

"Fire," I shouted. "Fire."

By the time the hose and ladder truck came, there was hardly a row of corn left. It burned that fast.

Toul was way pissed. But no matter what, he couldn't blame me for the fire. Pyroman or no Pyroman, I was right there in the detention room. And he knew it. Never mind that he eyeballed me like I could somehow be in two places at once. Or acted like just because I saw the fire first meant I had to have something to do with it.

"Dude," I wanted to tell him. "Fire isn't like farts. The 'he who smelled it, dealt it rule' does not apply."

But I kept my mouth shut. I didn't need any more detention.

Darcy, on the other hand, got up and cheered when I told her about it. And when she got to school the next morning and saw the burned field with her own two eyes, she did a little dance of celebration in the playground. Her *djellabah* rose and fell around her like she was a mast and it was a sail.

"Oh yeah, oh yeah, the Frankenstein corn is dead," she sang because nature had taken care of the problem that her petitions and picketing had not.

Toul saw her and was not amused.

"My office, at three o'clock sharp," he told her, his jaw clenching and unclenching like a fist.

# PRINCIPAL TOUL
Voice of Truth

Evidence suggested that the field had been torched. The Sheriff's short list of suspects included first and foremost the Farmers' Cooperative. Their opposition to the genetically engineered Burgundy crop was well-known. The Sheriff had already decided that Chuck Lorraine, the coop's most vocal spokesman, was a person of interest.

Toul didn't think so. His money was on the Pucelle girl, Darcy. Ordinarily, he would have suspected Billy Dalon, well known for his unhealthy interest in fire. But the attendance record showed that the boy hadn't cut any classes that day, and wound up in detention for failing to turn in homework and going to sleep in seventh period.

Darcy was the one to look at. She had made no secret of how much she hated the maize field. Miss Activist. Miss More-Committed-than-Thou. Always running around with a petition in her hand for something. Save the whales. Save the spotted owls. Ban aerosols, and Alar, and God knows what else. Not to mention her endless lobbying for the impractical and undoable – vegetarian meals for the cafeteria including organic milk, and sprouted grain bread, unsulfered raisins. And then there was the unpleasantness she created over the playground renovation. Eight years it took him to squeeze the money out of the district for good, clean plastic equipment and she managed to stir up a school-wide sit-in to protect the splintery, vermin-infested Wood Park playground from the contractor's demolition squad. She had to have been all of what, a fifth grader at the time.

Most recently, there were the papers she wrote for science class. From his littered desk, Toul picked up a copy of the latest one.

> Millions of Dead Sea snails have piled up along the Bay of Bengal. The stench is unbearable.
> In the US, including our own town, an alarming number of frogs, toads and other amphibians are being born with horrible deformities, including extra legs

and missing digits.

Both problems can be traced to changes in the animals' habitat that are caused by humans. Industrial and municipal waste pollutes the Bay of Bengal. Run-off from nitrogen-based fertilizers used in monoculture agriculture allow the parasites suspected of causing the amphibian deformities to flourish.

A screed, Mr. Speck called it and gave it a C. A little harsh, to be sure. Toul really couldn't blame the girl's mother for protesting the grade. Not that he would ever in a thousand years give her the satisfaction of saying so.

Especially after she made light of his concern about the girl running around in a Lawrence of Arabia get-up since Halloween. The nerve of the woman, laughing right in his face, giving his blazer a long hard look and telling him that at least her daughter's outfit was made of one hundred percent organic fabric – as if that explained anything. After preaching to him about freedom of self-expression, she had proceeded to quote chapter and verse from the school dress code to demonstrate that it didn't prohibit her daughter's choice of outfit.

Darcy presented herself, as directed, at 3:15 sharp. Punctual. He had to give her that. And maddeningly silent. He looked up from the paperwork that he loathed doing to find her standing at the door of his office, like a soldier at attention waiting for him to notice her. God only knows how long she'd been there.

"Enter," he commanded and the girl moved toward his desk without a sound, despite the heavy, black combat boots that he glimpsed under the hem of her robe.

"You must be cold wearing that get-up in this weather," he said trying his best not to sound judgmental

The girl shook her head no.

"Speak up."

"I'm comfortable," she declared.

"Are you wearing something under that thing?" He scrawled the air with his meaty fist to indicate the *djellabah*. It wasn't exactly the way he'd intended to start out.

The girl nodded and stared at a point somewhere over his right shoulder.

"Shirt? Pants?" He resented that the girl was forcing him to sound like a bully.

"Layers," she acknowledged.

"In that case, the caftan is a coat."

"*Djellabah*, not caftan," she corrected him. The little snot.

"*Djellabah*, *bhurka*, *caftan*, whatever it is, it functions as a coat. And it's against school regulations to wear a coat and hat indoors."

The girl glared at him.

"I must insist that you remove the coat and hat."

"These are my clothes."

"No. The layers *underneath* are your clothes. The robe and headdress you've been wearing since Halloween constitute your outer wear. Take them off."

"I don't choose to wear a coat and hat, and nothing in the dress code says that I have to."

"You will remove your coat and hat, or you will spend the rest of the month in detention."

He came out from behind his desk and positioned himself between Darcy and the door in the event she was planning to bolt.

She turned to face him.

Scared. She had to be. Should be. Toul searched her face. Not a trace of uncertainty.

"Off, now." He smiled, but stood with legs planted wide, arms crossed against his chest to show her that he meant business.

"Mr. Toul... I..." Her voice quivered ever so slightly and her eyes glistened like she was about to cry.

"Take the coat and hat off, and the whole thing is over." He fought the urge to say please. To beg. "Done. Forgotten."

"I don't wear these clothes to annoy you or anyone else. It's just that they feel right for me."

In theory, Toul admired the girl's perseverance. But he had to consider the chaos that letting her get away with this could unleash in the school. "I'm sure they do," he murmured and chucked her under her chin. With his other hand he untied the closure at her neck, and slipped the loosened garment off her shoulders. It fell right off and lay in a pool around her feet.

"Don't," the girl snapped, but he'd already given the turban thing on her head a yank, and off it came too.

Her hair cascaded down onto her neck in soft waves. A strand

48

fell across her face. His hand ached to tuck it behind her ear.

The girl stood trembling and struggling not to. In her gym shorts and t-shirt she was actually less naked than the average rock stars in an average music video. But she somehow managed to look stripped. Small. Stricken.

Toul burned with a shame he could not name.

"There," he consoled her. "Now you look like a perfectly nice young lady." He could not help but eye her appreciatively. Next to her, he felt, at age forty-two, worn and old. "A lovely, young lady."

The girl responded with a roll of her eyes. A teeny, tiny roll of her eyes. No doubt she thought that he wouldn't catch it. The much loathed gesture of teen insolence steeled Toul against her.

He retrieved the robe, balled it up and threw it onto his desk.

"Sit," he said pointing to the chair alongside his desk. To his surprise, she obeyed without a word of protest.

"So then, let's talk about the fire in the maize field, shall we?" he said, all business. "And I expect an answer to every one of my questions. An honest answer. Is that understood?"

Darcy measured him with a long and level look. "It depends," she said at last. "You could question me about things that I certainly would not tell you."

"Don't get smart with me young lady," Mr. Toul warned, though in truth Darcy hadn't sounded in the least bit sassy. "I mean all questions related to the maize field."

"It's better that the crop is gone," she said without a moment's hesitation or uncertainty.

"Better?" he fairly shouted. "That was school property."

"The earth's genetic legacy belongs to everyone and all the generations to come."

If that wasn't straight out of the Farmers Coop party line, Toul didn't know what was.

"As you well know, the monies that the school was going to receive from the Burgundy Enterprise for completing the research project was going to pay for much needed sports equipment."

"The present can't be bought at the expense of the future."

More sloganeering. No doubt something she picked up from her hippie-dippy parents.

"You approve of the fire, then," he said, not bothering to conceal his disgust.

"I approve of not tampering with genetic structure."

"And what about progress?"

"Putting fish genes into plants like tomatoes and strawberries violates nature. It isn't progress."

"Who appointed you judge of that?"

Derailed. How the hell did the girl manage to so totally derail him from his intended line of questioning?

"I listen to the voice of truth."

The principal laughed out loud. "And where does this voice of truth come from?" No more Mr. Nice Guy. The gloves were off. "The radio? TV? The fillings in your teeth, perhaps?"

"It speaks to me directly, as clearly as you and I are speaking in this room."

"You're telling me that you hear voices," Toul said, amused and alarmed in equal measure.

"I hear truth."

"How does it sound, this voice of truth."

"Clear and beautiful, like a poem, a song."

"And what does this voice say to you?"

"To live in truth and speak truth and serve it."

"And serving it means burning down the maize field?"

"It means acknowledging the truth about genetically altered crops."

"And that truth is that they should be set on fire?"

"If that's what it takes to stop dangerous and damaging crops from spreading and destroying the balance of nature."

"So you're telling me that you burned down the maize."

"That's not what I said."

"You have said it. Not in so many words, but you have said it."

"I answered your question."

"I demand that you tell me everything."

The girl smiled. "I already told you. You might ask me about things that I certainly won't tell you."

"Then be prepared to face the consequences, young lady."

"I am more afraid of saying things that would displease the voice of my conscience."

For an hour Principal Toul and Darcy repeated the round. He did not succeed in making her say that she'd burned down the maize, nor did Darcy retreat from the position that it was a good thing that the crop was gone. Twilight had lapsed into darkness as the principal marched Darcy down the dim and empty corridors of the school to the front door.

"It's almost winter," he said by way of parting. "See to it that you come to school tomorrow dressed like the young lady you are, and that your clothes are appropriate for school and the weather."

The girl said nothing, just stood there like a deaf mute waiting for him to unlock the door.

Fine, let her be like that.

He ushered her out in just the t-shirt and shorts, and locked the door.

Luckily, the girl hadn't claimed that her get-up was religious dress. One word about being a practicing Muslim, and the whole robe thing would have been untouchable. Protected under the Constitution.

But all the talk about voices was troubling. He didn't want to find himself in a position where he could be accused of having missed a red flag. With all the horror stories about kids shooting up their schools, there was no being too careful.

In the morning, he'd call the guidance counselor and tell him to check out the girl.

# BILLY
Apokatastasis

So there I was in the car with Mom and Dad coming back from our 999th trip of the week to Home Depot — *Home Despot* is what I called it. And I was looking out the window at the dark, seeing nothing, just my own reflection when Mom slammed her arm on the dashboard like it was a brake, and said through her teeth, "Watch out. Watch out. You'll hit the kid," and my Dad yelled back, "I see, OK. I see," and slowed the car to a crawl.

I looked to where my Mom was pointing, and there at the side of Route 27, in the almost dark, all alone on the shoulder, I saw a girl. It was like 2 degrees outside and she was wearing a t-shirt and gym shorts. Her socks, all baggy, were down around her ankles.

You would think that she'd be shivering and trying to hug herself warm, but no. She was dancing. Or at least I thought she was. She had her arms up over her head and she was spinning, and when my Mom rolled down the window I could hear that she was chanting.

The voice was Darcy's. For sure.

One word over and over again. I didn't get it then, but later she told me it was *apokatastasis*, which means transformation or renewal or something like that in Greek.

"I picked it up from Allen Ginsberg." That's how she explained it. Not – something I read in Ginsberg. Or – a thing that Ginsberg writes about like most people would say. No, the way it came out of her mouth made it sound like Ginsberg was some dude she sat down with for a regular face to face chat. Which to my mind is another good example of where all the confusion about Darcy and voices came from.

But all the concern and to do about the voice stuff came later. At that moment, the only thing that happened was that Mom stuck her head out the window and pulled it back in.

"Oh my goodness," she said pulling on Dad's sleeve. "I think it's the Pucelle girl."

They both spent like three minutes staring out the windshield to make sure.

By then I had my seat belt unbuckled and my head out of Mom's window since Dad still used the child safety buttons to keep the back ones locked.

"Darcy, Darcy," I yelled, but she didn't hear me, just kept spinning slowly down the road.

Dad inched the car to catch up, and Mom called out, "You OK, hon?"

Darcy stopped long enough to shout back, "Fine."

Like what was she supposed to say? "No, I'm crazy, completely out of my head, out on the road in the dark with hardly any clothes on."

"We can give you a lift."

"No thanks, I'm good." Darcy waved, and broke into a run. I mean, took off at like Olympic speed.

"You ought to wear something warmer," Mom called after her, never one to pass up an opportunity to say the obvious.

"Nice girl, but a little strange," Mom said to Dad, like suddenly it had slipped her mind that I was in the car and that she was talking about my best friend. My only true friend.

"Haven't I been telling you that all along?" Dad said.

"I blame the parents. They really do let her run wild."

There was a lot I wanted to say. But none of it would have done Darcy any good and it would have gotten me grounded. So I sank down into my seat and made like I was invisible.

"What do you expect from a bunch of burnt out hippies," Dad said like Darcy's Mom and Dad had some kind of disgusting disease.

"Actually, the mother is nice. Works really hard. She's just not around enough."

Go Mom. Her tone gave me hope that they would drop the subject. But no, Dad kept right on trashing Darcy. "What? She can't see that her kid is going around dressed like some kind of Arab terrorist since Halloween?"

"Earth First Commando," I said under my breath. That was what Darcy said she was supposed to be. An activist who went around saving redwood trees from being cut down and other cool stuff like that. It's not like she didn't explain all that to Dad when she rang our bell to take me trick or treating.

Earth First Command.

Really to me she looked like a Jedi knight, or Obi Wan Kenobi from *Star Wars* or something. And her mission the night of Halloween was to save me from being beat up by the kids who were prowling the neighborhood dressed up to look like the serial killers from all those horror movies that I was too scared to watch.

"Bottom line," Dad said as we pulled up to our house, "Billy shouldn't spend so much time with that girl. A boy should hang out with boys. He needs to make some guy friends. Play some ball."

"Hear me son?" He looked for me in the rear view mirror, then twisted to look over the top of the front seat. "You hear me?"

"Yessir."

"Tomorrow we'll go out in the yard and play some catch. You and me."

"Okay." But it wasn't okay, because the only thing I hated almost as much as looking at stuff at *Home Despot* and watching horror movies was playing ball. Baseball especially.

The wet cement at *Home Despot* – pukey looking like oatmeal — was bad, and movies about killers jumping out of dark doorways were worse, but fucking baseball was way up there with things that I could live without. Stupid and boring as all hell — standing around trying to whack a knob of leather that looked like a shrunken head covered with stitches. I mean, it almost made hanging around *Home Despot* look good.

"I don't know," Mom butted in. "Won't running all over the yard after the ball wreck the grass?"

"Good point." Dad turned to face front again, and inside I was like cheering, "Yeah, Mom. Go Mom. You rule," but then Dad said, "I guess we'll just have to go to the playground. Alright?"

"Sure thing," I croaked. Cleared my throat. "No problem." I was down so low in the back seat, I was practically on the floor.

"I had a mean fast ball in my day," Dad said into the rear view mirror. "And a decent curve ball."

I'm pretty sure he couldn't see me, and wasn't really looking for me anymore. But from where I was sitting, I had a clear view of his reflection. His mouth was going a mile-a-minute. Same old blah blah blah about his varsity letter in high school, his winning homer in the last game of senior year, his MVP award. Sad thing was, he was telling all of it like it was brand new news, like it wasn't a story he'd told a godzillion times before, and the whole time he had a smile on him like a carved Halloween pumpkin.

## PRINCIPAL TOUL
Cause for Concern

The counselor's preliminary report was not exactly enlightening. He refused to disclose the specifics of his session with Darcy, insisting that they were privileged. But Toul managed to pry out a few details.

Yes, the Pucelle girl described emotional experiences which she associated with a "voice of truth." No, it wasn't a hallucination. It was unclear whether this voice gave Darcy directives. Quite likely, it was a metaphor, a personification of her ideas and ideals. Or possibly it represented inspiration manifesting itself with commanding urgency. In any case, the voice was not frightening to her, but rather correlated with a sense of great pleasure, great comfort and sometimes a bright yellow light.

As far as the clothing went, the counselor alluded to a sublimation of sexual yearning and maybe some gender confusion. A case could also be made for a mild underlying depression precipitated by the underlying sexism of teen peer relationships he said, but it was a stretch. He advised continued observation and referral for counseling as necessary.

The counselor's conclusions struck Toul as unduly sanguine and partisan on Darcy's behalf. A page of the counselors' transcript of the session which Toul found on the floor next to the shared printer confirmed his suspicions.

> "When did you last hear the voice?"
> "Yesterday. Today."
> "Where do you hear the voice?"
> "Anywhere. Everywhere."

If that wasn't a hallucination, Toul didn't know what was.

> "What does the voice sound like?"
> "Poetry."
> "Is it a male voice, or a woman's voice?"
> "It depends on the poet."
> "Does it tell you to do things?"
> "Only in the way that poetry does."

So much for not getting directives from the voice.

"Give me an example."

"'Resist much, obey little.'"

"The voice said that?"

"Walt Whitman said it."

Nice evasion.

"Is that why you are wearing the *djellabah* again, even though Mr. Toul asked you not to? To resist?"

"Mr. Toul took the *djellabah*. Today I'm wearing a caftan. But my Mom is going to get the *djellabah* back."

Clever. Crafty. The girl was too clever for her own good. Whatever the damn get-up was called, it was over-sized, inappropriate, and deliberately provocative.

"Would you like to wear your other clothes again?"

"I'm happy with what I've got on."

Armed with what he'd read, Toul took another go at the counselor.

"In your professional opinion, there is absolutely nothing to worry about in the case of the Purcell girl. Is that correct?"

"Well... Let me say..."

The little weasel did his best to hedge, qualify, and avoid stating the obvious.

"Yes or no?" Toul pressed.

"She is at a vulnerable age," the counselor had to concede at last. "Without intervention, she could start forming troubling relationships, get caught up in fringe groups, dubious causes. Act out."

As if it wasn't already too late to prevent that. Toul reminded him of her attachment to the Dalon boy. Billy. Two years younger. Unhealthy interest in fire.

And her involvement with the radical element her parents cultivated, like the Farmers Coop people – Robert Baudry, Chuck Lorraine and the like.

And then there was the incident of the white lab rats being set free from the biology lab. Toul, for one, had never been persuaded that it was due to the custodian's failure to lock the cages. The man was an alcoholic, but otherwise totally reliable.

And there was also the matter of her general insubordination, disrupting science class to lecture on frog spawn hatched with deformed limbs instead of doing the required dissection, handing in some scribblings that she called an epic song-poem instead of the personal essay that her English teacher assigned.

And her chronic tardiness. As though, she was the only child in the school who fell outside the cut-off for the bus and had a long walk. A tenth of a mile or ten miles. A cut-off was a cut-off. A start time was a start time.

And last but not least there was the issue of her academics. Shaky, at best. Despite years of working with the learning specialist, she still struggled with the rote math and reading skills that came automatically to other students her own age. She was not cutting it on standardized tests. The idiosyncrasy of her writing, which may have been charming when she was younger, and the invented spelling which was acceptable in the lower grades would not serve her well in high school. And no amount of her creative thinking ability, innate empathy and complex emotional reasoning that the learning specialist made so much of was going to change that.

"There is cause for concern," the counselor was forced to admit in the end.

How could he not? For Toul, the evidence was overwhelming. It was just a matter of seeing through the girl's clever evasions and double-talk. Seeing her for who she really was. A troubled girl. A trouble-maker.

"Thank you for this very interesting consult," Toul said by way of good bye. Smiling, he left the counselor's office, quietly closing the door behind him.

# BILLY
## Hearing and Seeing

Toul had nothing on Darcy, and he knew it. So, no wonder that he took one thing, one little thing that she said and twisted it all around. By the time he was done with the whole voice of truth comment, he had her looking like a total psycho.

But no matter what he said, Darcy was not some crazy person walking around hearing and seeing things that were not there. At least not the way he meant. For most people hearing and seeing are two completely different and separate things. They hear a doorbell and it's just a sound. That's it. Period. End of story.

That wasn't the way the world worked for Darcy. When she heard a doorbell, it was a sound *and* it was pink triangles flying through the air. A Chihuahua's bark was jagged and pointy and silver. A Labrador's was the color of copper and it curled like wood shavings. I mean, it took me forever to wrap my brain around it, but for Darcy every kind of sound — rain, a truck horn, a door slamming, a poem being read out loud — was also something she could see. Who know why or how, but Darcy could see sound, really, truly see it with her physical eyes.

She was like ten, which means I had to be eight, before either one of us had a clue that her way and my way of being in the world were way different. And both of us were too young to know if either one of us matched up with how everybody else experienced things.

We were playing at the far end of the neighborhood under this huge beech tree. The Fairy Tree Darcy called it because of some story Robert told her about how, once upon a time, tiny Tinkerbells would come there to dance and drink from a spring that would keep them young forever.

The story sounded totally bogus to me. For one thing, there was no spring. Robert said that was because it had gotten covered up over time, but I wasn't buying it. Probably deep down inside Darcy didn't really believe it either. I mean we were both old enough to know that fairies were about as real as Santa Claus. But it was the whole Robert thing. Whatever the dude said, whether it made sense or not, Darcy at least acted like she was down with it.

So one really hot summer day when we were like drop-dead thirsty, she decided we should dig for that spring. After an hour and a hole that came up to like our waist, all we had to show for it were worms and beetley things with long antennas. No water.

"I don't care," Darcy said, and started dancing around me. "It's still the Fairy Tree, the Fairy Tree, Fairy Tree."

I begged her to stop, to shut up, but there was no stopping her once she got going on something. So I covered my ears and did my best to ignore her.

She pried away my fingers. "Fairy Tree," she whispered, her breath making a tiny breeze on my sticky skin and sending shivers – cold, electric – from my neck to my feet. The feeling was insanely intense, good in an embarrassing kind of way. I did and didn't want her to stop.

"Fairy Tree," she said, "don't you love the way that the blue of the F and the white of the T melt together into a smooth and shiny bubble?" She was twirling and sweeping her arms like there was a huge cloud of bubbles flying around her head. "Soooo beautiful."

Probably because I was hot, and thirsty, and tired, I didn't feel like playing along the way I usually did.

"What Blue T? What white F? What bubble?" I said and pushed her away.

"OK, be like that," she said after staring at me for awhile like I was some kind of alien or something.

"Be like what? I don't see any letters with any colors. No bubble shape," I told her. I knew that much for sure.

"For real?" she said, not right away, but after thinking about it for a while. Her voice sounded kind of like she was shivering or something.

I nodded, and her face went all surprised like I'd told her that the Fairy Tree didn't exist even though the branches were right there over our heads.

We sat there for a minute, all quiet, just hugging knees to chest. I saw a look come onto Darcy's face that I'd never seen before, and more than anything I wanted it gone.

"Let's play Rabbit Scientist," I offered, because it was her favorite game. I got down on all fours, ready to be Thumper the

Rabbit and to let Darcy the Rabbit Scientist feed me pretend carrots, and save me from the pretend wolf who wanted to eat me.

"So if the F isn't blue and the T isn't white, what color are they?" Darcy said.

"No color," I forced myself to tell her. As the words came out, my throat all of a sudden felt hot and scratchy like I was coming down with the strep that I got a million times every winter. "I have no idea what you're talking about."

"D is always red, B orange, R blue," Darcy explained real slow, her voice getting loud and louder, like slow was going to clear things up, and loud would make me understand.

I couldn't picture it. Closest I got was R, as in R is for Red, and B is for Blue.

"No," Darcy said. "No. Not like that."

Every letter had a color and that color stayed the same no matter what word it was in. And some words had their own color too. Monday was green. Tuesday yellow. It wasn't a mood thing, she said. Wednesday was always brown, "soft and warm like chipmunk's fur," she said, "not a sad, crunchy brown like dried leaves."

The longer she talked, the more confused I got. One minute I was feeling sick to my stomach just picturing what a page in a book would look like with every letter a different color. The next minute I was feeling like I was missing out on something.

I was used to Darcy knowing more than me, so at first I just figured she was right about the whole letters and colors thing. But then she started talking about the shape of sounds, and I freaked. I mean, maybe I didn't know a whole lot about a lot of things, but I was pretty sure that the sound of a doorbell ringing or a dog barking was not something you could see. And no way were the words of some poet guy a beam of rainbow light.

"You're weird." That's what I told her. "Really, really, capital W weird."

She looked at me like I'd hit her. Her lips got all white. She started to run.

I ran after her, blubbering, snot dripping out of my nose, "I'm sorry, I'm sorry, I'm sorry. I'm sorry."

I grabbed her t-shirt.

She pulled free

Finally, she stopped and grabbed both my arms. "Promise you'll never tell anyone, I mean anyone, about the things we talked about today? Not ever. Not anyone."

Of course, I promised. I swore a cross-my-heart-and-hope-to-die pinky swear. Gave my word. And I kept it, just like she asked, no matter what.

And I'm OK with that, because a promise is a promise. The part that still keeps me up at night and makes me feel like a total shit is my calling her weird. What kind of friend does that?

Who knows, maybe calling her weird was the reason that Darcy didn't really push to defend herself from Toul. I mean, if her best friend was going to call her weird when she explained about the colors and shapes of sounds, what could she expect from a prick like Toul. For sure, the way I reacted must have made her feel all alone in the world.

Other times, I think it had nothing to do with me. I don't know what it means that Darcy saw things the way she did. And really, so what if Darcy heard poetry and saw a man-shape of some dude with glasses and beard, or pink triangles when a dog barked? For sure, it was different. But it's not like Darcy was crazy or dangerous.

Maybe, a little fierce. But only when she was defending anything and anyone who was hurt or hurting – like a geek kid, for instance. Or fucked up frogs.

The point is, nobody I ever knew had a kinder, bigger heart than Darcy.

So, OK. She saw things that other people could only hear. What can I say? It had to be really scary and totally, totally awesome to be her.

# BILLY
Darcy's Oath


Catherine's black eye. If you ask me, that was the thing that made Darcy decide to keep on wearing the *djellabah*. She probably would have switched back to regular clothes otherwise.

At school we all had a sib from one of the upper grades assigned to us. They were supposed to buddy up with us little kids and do stuff like help us with homework, look out for us. Of course, none of that ever happened – too uncool. But Darcy and her sib, Catherine, at least said hello to each other in the hall. I think they even kinda, sorta liked each other. Maybe because there was a little bit of rebel in each of them and they knew it.

Story was that the morning after Halloween, Catherine showed up at school with a huge shiner. She didn't have much to say on the subject except, "Leave me alone. Nothing *really bad* happened."

Which meant that whatever did go down was probably pretty skeevy. I mean it was pretty much a no-brainer to figure out what kind of stuff probably did happen to her considering that all the guys I saw on Halloween were out there in hooded sweat shirts and Freddie Krueger masks, waving plastic axes and knives, hollering at all the girl witches, and princesses, and Catherine. Especially Catherine, because she was the one and only girl dressed up as a punk band rock star in a short, short skirt and a teeny top that showed off the glittery jewel stuck to her belly button.

I heard the boys call out to her, "Baby, baby come 'ere. I'll let you hold my knife."

All those Freddie Kruger wannabes cracking up like nobody got their dumb shit joke except them. Bunch of assholes being their usual asshole selves.

The only thing that was really different about them that night was that they didn't go after Darcy. Usually, she was their first target because she never laughed at their sicko dirty jokes, and she really, really hated it when they tried to touch her butt, or accidentally-on-purpose bump into her chest. I mean, she hated it for real. Not like some of the other girls, who just pretended.

Anyway, no one bothered her. It was like the *djellabah* was some kind of magic cloak of invisibility or something. And maybe because I was with her, they didn't bother me either. No one tried to beat me up, and not one single person called me Pyroman, even though I was wearing my fireman costume.

Darcy's mom seemed to know all about Catherine's black eye and then some. The only way to explain that was that whatever happened was bad enough for Catherine to end up at the hospital where nothing stayed secret for too long. Not that Darcy's mom said a whole lot about what she knew, but she hugged Darcy a lot, and told her to be careful. And Darcy's Dad just ranted more than usual about watching out for the yuppy out-of-towners. No surprise there. He pretty much blamed them for everything and anything that was wrong in the world, or Glen Eddy.

But it was hard to imagine that the yuppies could have had anything to do with the how and why of Catherine's black eye. I mean, they were mostly summer people. It wasn't like any of them were still hanging around Glen Eddy after Labor Day.

For sure, nobody in Glen Eddy had a whole lot of good things to say about the city people. They came up on Friday nights and invaded the Hawk's Crest Diner, took over the place so there wasn't an inch of space for us regulars. And then they mocked the diner – called it the Culinary Institute of Fried.

Saturday mornings they crashed through the supermarket and stripped it. But not before they bitched out Catherine, or whoever worked the checkout register, about how the carrots were wilted, the fruit wasn't organic. Like it was the cashiers' fault. Or like the store owed them a discount or something.

All weekend, the city people tore up and down 27 in their supersized SUVs with tinted windows like it was a NASCAR speedway, and left a trail of road kill — rabbits, squirrels, raccoons, skunks, sometimes deer. One summer, they got Crayons, the librarian's calico cat, and Dave's dog, Lucky. Dave closed his hardware store for like a week and went around crying like a little kid over that dog. I mean it was way sad. Dude had the dog for like twenty years or something.

The town more or less put up with the city people like they would with a thunderstorm or an invasion of grasshoppers.

The only one who had any use for them was Robert because

the city people were the ones who cooed and aahed over the honey and buggy organic apples he sold from his stand on 27, and had the big bucks to buy them. Plus, the city women with their fancy shades and Dracula nail polish drooled all over Robert when he started in about his thing for bees. I mean, nobody in town gave a shit that Robert designed and built his own frames because he thought the regular ones were too unnatural or confining or something. Like what — the bees could really tell the difference?

For a minute I wondered if maybe Darcy's dad did have a point in blaming whatever happened to Catherine on the yuppie dudes who hung around Glen Eddy doing their version of country casual in brand new jeans and soft leather jackets. They did sometimes kinda, sorta flirt with the girls around town in a snarky way – like the girls were squirrels and they were throwing pebbles at them to see if they'd pick them up for acorns. But I really couldn't see them dirtying their hands to rough up a young girl.

More likely Catherine had her run-in with some of the Freddy Krugers out on the street that night, or maybe with one of their older brothers who were tearing around in their pickup trucks — drunk, yelling out the windows, shooting guns off into the sky, or at the signs along the highway. They were the assholes you saw during hunting season with a dead doe, strapped to the roof of their truck, windshield wipers spattering blood all over the road.

Them — you could picture messing with a girl like Catherine.

Of course Robert was in the know about what went down because he spent his whole life glommed onto Darcy's Mom and Dad. But Darcy was only able to squeeze out a few details out of Robert, her oh so precious, tell-it-like-it-is, straight-up, no-bullshit source for answers to all questions. Catherine was dumped at the supermarket parking lot by her shit boyfriend Dominic after some kind of stupid fight. And then he went off to a party with some slut from Senior year. Catherine wound up walking home alone, in the dark. A bunch of guys in a truck offered her a ride. They were not Catherine's friends, but not strangers either.

Darcy and I had both seen the way the dudes at school looked at Catherine. And we'd both sat through Mr. Houghey's health class — the 3P curriculum of pee, poop, and private parts Darcy called it. So we could pretty much figure out the rest of the story on our own

The hardest part for Darcy was to see Catherine go from being bright as a Fourth of July sparkler to walking down the hallways at school hunched down into herself like she was cold and needed another sweater.

It was a couple of days past Halloween, and Darcy was still wearing the *djellabah*. We were huddled under the Fairy Tree, soaked to the skin waiting out a thunderstorm that caught us on our way home from school, and she was telling me how she'd heard Catherine crying in the girls' bathroom at school.

"The sound of it was like needles all over my body," she said.

"Dude…" I wanted to say something comforting, but no words came. I kept seeing Darcy, stuck full of long sewing needles like a human porcupine or something, and suddenly I felt pin-prickly all over. "Oh, dude…" My voice was trembly like it gets before I cry, so I shut up before I made things any worse for Darcy.

Suddenly, she stood up, a fierce look on her face. She raised her arm, waved it like she was holding a sword.

"On a moonless night, I creep up to the top of the mountain that is home to a dragon that hunts young girls from the village, carries them off, and devours them. Everyone lives in fear of the dragon. Its roar is louder than thunder, and poisonous flames shoot from its huge mouth. I see the dragon lying at the mouth of its cave. All except one of its dozen eyes is shut, but the one that is open is bigger than the biggest dinner plate you've ever seen, and it's watching…"

Sure, I knew that there wasn't any such thing as a dragon. But as I listened to Darcy's story, my stomach gripped up like there was. "Stop," I said, probably too quietly for her to hear me.

"As soon as the dragon smells me, it rushes out of the cave and rears onto its back legs. It is ginormous. Its head is bigger than my whole body. It opens and clangs its jaws full or saw teeth at me like a steel trap. Its breath reeks worse than a swamp after a week of rain. The tail is fifty feet long and the dragon whips it at me like a scimitar. But neither its fiery breath, or blood red eyes, or clawed limbs can save the dragon from my hand. I lunge…"

"Ohhhh nooo…" I couldn't help it. I covered my eyes.

"The dragon is covered with scales but I plunge my sword

into the soft, unarmored place under its wing and it falls to the ground at my feet. The earth shakes and trembles."

Darcy laughed a kind of laugh I'd never heard her laugh before. I laughed with her, but her laugh scared me.

And maybe she scared herself because the very next minute she stared up through the tree branches and quietly said, "I take it back. I take it all back. Or at least, the part about killing. The poet says, 'Remember the mind. Include both sides of an argument. Balance body, feeling, reason and imagination. Help everyone.'"

She made me stand up, and she put one hand in mine and raised the other one the way people do in court in the cop shows that Darcy's Dad watches all the time. Then and there, she swore never to harm or hurt any living creature. "You are my witness," she told me. "Remind me, if I forget."

I knew I wouldn't have to. Darcy being Darcy would find a way to keep that promise no matter what. Which she had to do like the very next day.

There she was minding her own self, standing at the edge of the playground waiting for the school doors to open. And up came Mark, the class bully, and grabbed the sleeve of her *djellabah*.

"I like your outfit, but I think it shows too much skin," he said, laughing like he'd just told the funniest joke in the word.

The pack of idiots, who always hung out with him, laughed right along.

"Yeah, way too much," one of them shouted. "Aren't you missing a veil or something?"

"What do you have under that thing, anyway?"

Mark went for the hem of the *djellabah* like he was going to pull it up, but Darcy caught his wrist and locked it in her hand.

"I have a little question for you," she said without ever taking her eyes off his. Totally cool, totally calm. "What's the difference between pink and purple?"

Mark squirmed. And pulled. Darcy didn't give an inch. And Mark's gang just stood there staring like they were watching a movie and were waiting to see how it turned out.

Mark tried hard not to show it, but he totally knew that he was at Darcy's mercy. And anybody could see that he was hurting. I mean, Darcy had a grip on him like she was up on a cliff and his wrist was the only thing between her and a really long, long fall. No way was he going to get loose.

"What the fuck is it with you?" he yelled at her. Spit came out through his teeth. "You cunt."

Big mistake using the F and C word!

Darcy hated swear words the way I hated smelly cheese and green stuff like spinach and peas. Her eyes became steel even though she kept her voice soft, almost kind.

"You have my whole attention. Tell me in clearer words exactly what it is that you want me to know."

Lips quivering, Mark just kept trying to yank his arm away from Darcy.

More than anything, I wanted to cheer Darcy and to call Mark a crybaby right to his face. But I settled for saying, "You should have had your Wheaties, dude," not quite loud enough for him to hear.

Darcy pulled Mark closer. "So, nothing more to say? What about answering my riddle? No guesses? Oh ok, I'll tell you. The difference between pink and purple is in the grip," she said calmly, and dropped his arm, but with a look on her face that said she could have broken it.

Could have, but didn't. She let him go basically unharmed. Maybe a little sore. But unharmed, that was the main thing.

Anyway, now it was Darcy's and my turn to laugh as we watched Mark and his gang disappear down the hill.

"I love this *djellabah*," she said and spun around and around.

She swore to wear the *djellabah* forever.

I could see how brave and powerful it made her feel. The loose fit let her move freely, and kept jerks like Mark from looking at the girl parts of her. Weirdly, for the first time, I saw – really saw — that she was a girl with girl parts, and that she and the girl parts were very, very beautiful.

It was like having a vision or something. And like a vision, it was there one minute, then gone. I mean, it wasn't as if I didn't know that Darcy was a girl and beautiful, but I'd never *felt* her beauty that way before. Up until that moment, she'd always been my friend, my skateboarding partner, my detention buddy, the one person in the world I loved — no ifs, ands, or buts. The one person in the world I would do anything for. But now she was also the girl I loved.

When we stopped at the Fairy Tree on the way home from school that day, she pulled out a pair of scissors from somewhere deep down in the bottom of her backpack, and gave me one of those little mirror things that girls always carry around. She told me to hold it in front of her face, and I did. When she started to cut her hair short, above her ears, I didn't try to stop her. I just watched the long, strands sift through her fingers, and fall onto the muddy ground.

"There, much better," she said when her hair was all short like a boy's.

Maybe there was a part of me that was kinda, sorta in shock. But my heart kept saying, "You rule. Yeah Darcy, you rule."

# ROBERT
Aiding and Abetting

He was aiding and abetting a minor. Two minors. Taking Darcy to the WE protests was one thing. At least he'd tried to discuss it with her parents. But Billy Dalon had never been part of the picture. It wasn't until they stopped for gas that Robert discovered him hidden in the back of the truck with a skateboard hugged to his chest.

"I snuck out after everyone was asleep," Billy admitted. "Same as Darcy. Please don't take me back home. I promise I won't be any trouble."

"Wrong. You already are trouble."

Darcy looked daggers at him.

The boy sniveled.

Robert sent them off to the bathroom to give himself five minutes to think. Not many choices. Middle of the night, middle of nowhere. More than half way to the city. Too late to turn back. This time tomorrow, he'd have both kids back and they'd be tucked in their beds, safe and sound, with a little life experience under their belts. Where was the harm in that?

Robert paid for the gas in cash, hoping with all his heart that the bleary-eyed, turbaned attendant had not and would not notice the kids.

He pulled up the truck to the bathroom door where Darcy stood in a small pool of light cast by a bare overhead bulb waiting for Billy to come out.

"Hurry up. Get in."

"Don't be mad, and don't take it out on Billy, ok?" she whispered, leaning into the open passenger window. "I had to tell him I was leaving. I'm like his best friend. I couldn't just cut out on him."

The heart has its reasons. Robert got that. Who was he to argue?

He waited until the kids settled into the cab of the truck to say, in his best approximation of stern, "We'll have to phone your mothers in the morning."

Neither of the kids were taken in by it.

"Thank you, thank you, Mr. Baudry." Billy lapped at him like a puppy.

Of course, he wound up telling the boy to call him Robert.

"You're the best," Darcy yelped and hugged him. "And don't worry about Mom. I left her a note."

Which Isabelle didn't show Robert until later. Much later.

> *It's important to drop everything and devote myself to Doefen. I*
> *would really like to just stay at home and be a good daughter, spend my time listening to music, and dancing around, and having boyfriends, but I have to do this. Please understand. I love you very much. Darcy.*

Neither he nor Isabelle ever succeeded in wringing much consolation from the note.

Aiding and abetting. The boy certainly complicated the situation. If his parents decided to make a case of it, Robert could find himself being locked up for kidnapping. Isabelle and Jack would probably just be pissed, even though his intention in taking Darcy to the city was to protect her. Without a doubt, Darcy would have gone to the city with or without him.

"I'll hitchhike," she said the first time he refused to take her. Robert knew her well enough to worry that it wasn't an idle threat.

The girl had no experience. Except for one vacation on Cape Cod, she'd never traveled much beyond Glen Eddy. Hitchhiking definitely wasn't as safe as it was when Robert had done it. And even back in the Sixties it wasn't exactly safe for girls.

Darcy had laughed off his concern. "No worries" she said pointing to her *djellabah*. "No one can even tell I'm a girl."

She was unfazed by his argument that boys got raped too.

"The person who wants a boy, won't want me," she assured Robert with the impervious illogic of youth.

Robert couldn't actually recall anyone of his acquaintance having been raped back in the Sixties. But more than a few had been seduced. By sex. Drugs. Rock and roll, by the euphoria of making revolution, taking political action.

Oh, how well he remembered the sweet abandon of succumbing to the wordplay of skillful, artful foot-soldiers of the counter culture! Robert doubted that the current recruits to

WE's eco-environmentalist cause and Doefen were all that different from his own long-ago self. Hormonal teenagers were hormonal teenagers.

He didn't blame Darcy for wanting to be at the scheduled press conference bout between Duke Burgundy – Suave Eco – Pretender, CEO of Burgundy Enterprise, big-time WTO mover and shaker in one corner, Charles Doefen — goatherd in faded denim, default rep of the teeny tiny, alternative Whole Earth coalition in the other. Considering Chuck's Chinese dumpling story, Robert doubted that Duke could actually be shamed. Certainly not by the likes of Doefen. But it would be good theater, if nothing else.

He glanced over at Darcy — she sat facing the car door window. Reflected in the glass he saw her squared shoulders and the firm thrust of her jaw. At the very least, during the Q and A she'd give Duke an earful on the subject of crop modification, the evil of inserting fish genes into tomatoes and producing patented crops. The prospect of a Darcy and Duke showdown made Robert feel deliciously young again. Passionate. Excited. Rock and roll anthems from the Sixties played in his head. He pictured the upcoming anti-WTO demonstration and saw himself running down a street with Darcy, hand in hand, flowers in their hair, tear-gas canisters nipping at their heels. Running, like he used to run with Isabelle – all pumped-up with adrenalin, high on the righteousness of the cause, the excitement of taking action.

He laughed aloud.

"What's so funny," Darcy whispered without taking her chin out of her hand, or turning her head away from the nightscape outside the window lest she jostle Billy, who who had fallen asleep and snuffled softly against her shoulder.

"I was imagining the look on Duke's face when he gets a load of you going at him, all fired up."

"You know me. I always do what I say I'm going to do," she said, sounding more annoyed, than amused.

"I don't doubt it for a moment," he assured her, imagining her on Chuck's black stallion. Robert had to hand it to Chuck — the guy had a real feel for the power of symbolic action. And wasn't that what successful protest was all about? Darcy and *Black Lightening* would have publicized WE's cause a hell of a lot better than Doefen ever could. Why hadn't he listened and brought the horse?

Why? Obviously, because he was a loser, a joke, a scared little rabbit. Robert's mood slipped precipitously from exhilarated to sober, sad. All those years of hiding out in Glen Eddy. For what? He wasn't any kind of rebel or threat to the status quo. What a waste of taxpayer dollars for the Washington spooks to have ever kept a file on him.

Robert gripped the steering wheel, leaned against it to steady himself. Taking the horse or not taking the horse wasn't just a question of balls, he reminded himself. His concern had been for Darcy's safety. That had been the deciding factor. Because sad truth – much as he wished otherwise — Darcy wouldn't have been a good enough rider to handle a stallion like *Black Lightening*. She wasn't a trained rider. Her approach to horses was fearless and intuitive, her attempts to ride more headlong and enthusiastic than skilled.

A shame, really, a girl like that — living in the country all of her life — never having gotten the chance to learn how to ride. And all because her mother had decreed riding bourgeois. Isabelle made it very clear to all concerned that she was against riding, unless it was for a purpose, like ranching or something. And maybe not even then. As a vegan she was against ranching too.

In his gut he knew that Isabelle — country girl by way of steel town Pittsburgh — was probably afraid of horses, afraid of any animal bigger than a house cat. Either that or she was afraid of being shown up by her kid. Not consciously or anything like that – but then half the trouble with the world came from people not knowing their own bias.

In the darkness of the truck cab, Robert shook his head. Too bad about Isabelle. And about Chuck's horse. And about sorry-ass Doefen, and smarmy Duke. All one big joke. The whole lot of them — himself included.

Crazy... sneaking away in the middle of the night, hauling two underage runaways to the city — the boy a totally guaranteed go-to-jail-for-good-mother-fucker liability — all for some protest that in the grand scheme of things probably wouldn't make a shit bit of difference.

Crazy to give in to Darcy's constant barrage of cocky, half-formed, maddeningly pure, but unwise plans to save the planet, and rather than stay on the farm to secure the hives in case of an early frost. The bees would be sure to take note. The quality and quantity of honey would go down. Once again, he'd be short for the mortgage.

Save the planet. Lose the farm. How crazy was that?

Even crazier – to sit there wishing he'd taken along Chuck's horse.

And craziest of all – when he got out of his head and actually looked into his heart — to discover that he was happy. Truth. In his heart of hearts, he felt happy. Totally happy. Happier than he'd felt for longer than he could remember.

It was all a trip — a mystical, magical, mystery tour —starting with the truck quietly slipping away, gliding through the empty streets of Glen Eddy, then making its way down the wooded mountain on a ribbon of road that unspooled through dark and silent stands of trees. A gleaming paten moon lit their way towards the beckoning fairy lights of the city. Seven times the truck crossed seven black rivers that snaked under seven spans of spun steel before it spiraled round and round a whorled highway exit ramp that sent him, and Darcy, and Billy sailing into the dawn.

# ROBERT
Demonstration

The demonstration was as big as any Robert could remember. Farmers headed the crowd. Behind them came labor unions walking shoulder to shoulder with ecologists, scientists, students, civil rights activists and concerned citizens. A troupe of dancers at the margins encouraged everyone to move to the beat of a Caribbean steel pan band that was playing protest songs. Some groups sang, others chanted about health, and food, and free trade, and individual rights.

The vibe was unlike anything Robert remembered from his days of college protests. There was no central authority and none seemed necessary. No pre-set agenda. No single ideology. Communists, Christians, Anarchists, Gays, Feminists walked, not marched, alongside one another — a global assembly deriving strength by accommodating differences. No one claimed to have all the answers.

Banners in dozens of languages denounced corporate greed – GLOBALIZATION KILLS – and corporate dictatorship – NO GLOBALIZATION WITHOUT REPRESENTATION – and questioned suspect corporate practices – FREE TRADE OR CORPORATE SLAVERY? Robert's favorite placard featured Dracula — VAMPIRES CAN'T BEAR THE LIGHT AND NEITHER CAN THE WTO.

It was not an angry crowd, but that didn't keep an excess of armed and armored police, FBI agents, and National Guard troops from lining the route. Same as they did in the Sixties.

Slowly, peacefully, the crowd made its way down Fifth to the Waldorf Astoria, where the WTO was meeting. By the time Robert and the kids reached the hotel it was surrounded by a ring of young, and not-so-young men and women who clasped hands to keep delegates from entering or leaving the building. Officials already inside the hotel buzzed from window to window like trapped flies. Long convoys of limos sat stalled in the side streets, powerless to rescue them or to deliver newly arriving delegates. Robert hadn't seen anything like it since the anti-Vietnam War protest in Chicago shut down the Democratic convention.

The stand-off lasted one hour. Two. A third. The protesters made no move to advance on the hotel. Or to leave. Their chanting lapsed into a soft buzz. "Say No to WTO."

Robert watched the double line of police in front of the hotel thickened to three-ranks, then four, then more, always pressing against the protesters. Without a doubt, a similar phalanx was probably forming at the outer reaches of the crowd. Pigs at the front. Pigs at their backs. That's the way it went down in the Sixties.

A cold sweat prickled the back of his neck. None of the demonstrators were going to get out until the Pigs decided to let them out. He should have known better than to think that the protest would end without tear gas and mayhem.

He looked around. No one seemed anxious or alarmed. Billy was peacefully rocking on his skateboard to the rhythm of the crowd's murmur of "Say No to WTO," and even Darcy had stopped jumping up and down and shouting out slogans. The whole vibe was peaceful, more like walk in the park, not a march.

Maybe he was crazy to worry. Protests in the US since the Sixties had all been non-violent. No need to have drilled Darcy and Billy on the absolute necessity of never revealing their identities to anyone. Maybe the bandannas he held at the ready for each of them when the first tear gas canisters exploded were an indulgence of an old and outdated paranoia.

The cops did seem more bored than ready to pounce. And yet... Robert could not help but sense a purse-seine gradually tightening around the crowd.

He remembers taking hold of Billy's sleeve, pulling him off the skateboard and gripping Darcy by the hand, telling them it was time to go. Darcy resisted, of course, and did her best to make it impossible for him to push through to an escape. Within moments, he felt her hand slip away, saw her turn back in the direction of the hotel.

"Stay with me," he shouted at Billy, gripping him tighter, and struggled after her.

She was just a bit ahead, always out of reach, dodging under linked arms, around, through the thicket of bodies, and didn't stop until she'd succeeded in climbing up onto a sawhorse barricade near the hotel door.

"Come out. Come out of there and speak truth," she shouted up at the windows. Emboldened, re-energized by the slight girl on the barricade, the crowd took up the chant.

"Truth... Truth.... Truth...."

A Whole Earth placard materialized in Darcy's hand, and she hoisted it high, waving it a like a semaphore. As if prearranged, a muscular arm reached out of the crowd to hand her a bull-horn.

"Come out now and speak to the people."

The police line answered Darcy's ultimatum by advancing towards her and the demonstrators, unleashing an explosion of pepper spray and rubber bullets.

WHUMP.

Darcy teetered on the wooden barricade. The crowd reached up to brace her, drawing into a tight cluster around her the way a bee swarm surrounds its queen.

WHUMP. WHUMP.

People were sputtering, coughing. As if in a dream, Robert tied a bandanna around Billy's face, then covered his own nose and mouth.

WHUMP.

Blinded and bruised, the crowd turned to flee.

"Stay," Darcy shouted at them. "Stay. WE must stay."

The air grew more poisoned. Shock, then fear overtook the crowd.

WHUMP.

A huge weariness took hold of Robert's limbs. Seen it, done it before, he thought.

Billy yanked at Robert's sleeve, rousing him from his trance. "Do something," the boy blubbered, pointing at Darcy still tottering on the barricade and the line of cops advancing on her.

Robert's mouth filled with the metallic, puke-up-your-guts taste of adrenaline, rage, and fear that he remembered from the Columbia takeover.

As the crowd fled, he pushed in the direction opposite, towards Darcy. A shift in the wind dispersed the pepper spray and created a momentary opening in the crowd large enough for him to reach her. He grabbed Darcy down off the wooden sawhorse just as the demonstrators who were fleeing gathered enough momentum to break through the police perimeter at the end of the street.

"Let go. Let me go." Darcy screamed, kicking like a four year old.

Robert half pulled, half carried her away from the barricade.

The agitated crowd was disorientated, a riled colony without a place to light. Protesters flying down the streets away from the hotel swept Robert and Darcy and Billy into their retreat.

Robert's only thought was to get Darcy and Billy the hell out of there before there was bloodshed. Arrests. Billy allowed himself to be led, but Darcy struggled, making every step a battle. "Don't," she sobbed, trying to yank herself free. "Stop. Stop."

Robert only gripped her harder.

"You're hurting me," she screamed. "Let go."

"Not until it's safe."

Most of the protesters just ran. A few stopped to tear down banners welcoming the WTO as they retreated. Some gouged the sides of parked cars with keys as they raced past. Adrenalized by the melee, a scrawny guy found the strength to hurl a trash can at the plate glass windows of a multinational bank like he was Superman or the Hulk. It bounced off harmlessly. A large McDonald's ad featuring the slogan "Think global – Eat local" was torn down, trampled, and set on fire. The smoke blew straight toward the advancing lines of police.

"Smoke 'em, burn 'em," the crowd jeered.

By the time that the police started swinging clubs and cracking heads, and the crowd was hurling water bottles and soda cans, Robert had succeeded in hauling Darcy and Billy into an empty side street away from the fray.

"What is with you?" Darcy screamed when he let go her arm.

Panting, aware for the first time that he was short of breath, Robert glowered at her. He was in no shape to be outrunning cops half his age.

She rubbed the red indentations his fingers left on her skin.

"What the hell did you think you were you doing out there?" he croaked.

"Protesting."

"You could have gotten yourself, me, all of us arrested. Killed. Those were real cops out there, with real guns…"

"So."

"So I told you to stay out of the line of fire, to stay below the radar. You can't let the cops notice you, or know who you are, or let them put a name to your face. Once they have you, they'll always run you. Your life will be ruined."

"Yeah, right, like it isn't already? Poison in the air, bacteria in the food, toxic chemicals in the water."

Robert attempted a full, deep breath. "I said, no name. No ID. No pictures. Got it?"

"Just chill," Darcy sulked. "And stop yelling at me."

"Then do as I say."

"Stop bossing me around. You are not my father."

*Not my father.* Each word shaped with pitiless precision. Emphasis on *not*. Even though Robert had always been like a father to her, a better father than Jack ever was. And she knew it.

"While we're here, what I say goes. It's called in *loco parentis.*"

"I didn't come here to parade around in the background where no one is looking or listening," Darcy insisted with serene righteousness.

Robert had been privy to that tone before. Usually Darcy reserved it for the likes of Toul.

"Fine," he said through gritted teeth, "you've been seen and heard, and now we're going back to the truck and driving home."

Grabbing each of the kids by the scruff, he started toward the nearest subway station. It hardly mattered which one. He used to know the system. Maybe the names of the lines had changed since he was at Columbia, but the tracks and tunnels were still the same. Any and all lines would eventually lead back to the street in Harlem where he'd parked the truck.

"Loco," he heard Billy whisper to Darcy, "loco."

"Yeah, totally," she giggled back.

"Loco, and koo koo for coco puffs."

The two of them reeled with laughter. He saw, then, that it was all a big mistake, bringing them to the city. For all her smarts, Darcy really was just a kid. Too young.

# BILLY AND ROBERT
123SNR456

Darcy sat squeezed between me and Robert. We didn't talk, just stared straight ahead. Subway stations appeared and disappeared. 50th Street. 59th. Every time the train slid back into the tunnel, the darkness turned the windows across from us into mirrors. I kept checking the reflection of Robert's face, and each time I saw that he was biting his lower lip against his top front teeth. Which kinda made him look like a giant rabbit. It would have been funny, except I knew him enough to know that biting his lip meant that he was totally pissed.

The stations kept coming faster and faster.

66th

I didn't need a map to know that each stop was bringing us closer to going back to Glen Eddy. Me, I could stand it. But Darcy was going to be heartbroken. I mean, she didn't get anywhere near seeing Doefen.

The next stop we came to was 72nd and for some reason a whole lot of people – way more than at the other stops — jumped up, jammed the aisles, and made for the door. Most of them ran to a train that pulled up right across from ours.

I was just sitting there trying to figure out what the fuck, when Darcy gave my hand I squeeze. I squeezed back, saw her roll her eyes in the direction of the door. Next thing I knew, we were moving with the crowd, out of the train. Good thing Darcy and I were small. We just about managed to squeeze out of our train into the other one as the doors stuttered shut. It happened so fast, Robert probably didn't even have a chance to ask himself what the hell was up.

"We made it," Darcy sighed at the back of my head as the train flew back into a tunnel.

I wrenched myself to face her. "Where are we going?"

"Away from Robert. Give him a chance to cool off."

That didn't exactly sound like a plan to me, but it wasn't like I could discuss it. I mean, the train we were on was like some wild ride at the county fair, swinging from side to side, and throwing us around. Except nobody was screaming. Or even talking.

Maybe it was because we were all busy trying to keep our balance. Lucky for me, I had my skate board in front of me to hold on to, and to keep my face from ending up against some dude's butt. I mean, we were packed in that close and tight. Closer and tighter than you ever wanted to be with anyone, never mind a bunch of strangers.

It took, like nine hundred ninety-nine years for the train to get to the next station, and when it stopped there was this screech of metal scraping and grinding against metal – like a dentist drill, only louder. I don't even want to think about what that sound was like for Darcy, but I wished I could reach around and cover her ears. And her eyes.

As soon as the train stopped moving, everybody started pushing toward the doors, and once the doors opened it was like Darcy and I were caught in some huge wave. All we could do was hang on to each other as we were heaved out of the train. When the platform cleared, and we could actually take a look around, Darcy freaked.

"We're at 96th Street,"she yelled over the screech of another train pulling into the station. Like I was supposed to know why that was a bad thing. But before I could ask, she was pulling me down a flight of stairs, and up to another platform.

"That's better," Darcy said.

I looked around. The sign still said 96th Street. The difference was that Darcy looked happier.

Why? Because, as she explained, it meant that now when we did get on a train we'd be going in the opposite direction.

I smiled to please her, but I didn't get it. What I needed was a map. A few decent signs. A roll of string in my pocket.

"We'll find a map and I'll show you," she promised. "Don't worry."

"Ooooh kay. Oooh kay."

Except I was nowhere near OK. In fact, I was sniveling. Sobbing would be next. Anyone other than Darcy would have told me to get it together and shut up. But she put her arm around me like she was my Mom, like it was all going to be alright.

\*\*\*

Robert squinted at the subway map just inside the train car.

The light was poor. His eyes weren't what they used to be. No getting around that. The swaying of the train didn't make it any easier to decipher the spaghetti of colored lines and minuscule dots that represented the transit system of the city.

Think. That was the important thing. What did Darcy mean by bolting like that? Where should he look for her?

Nearly as he could figure out, Darcy and Billy must have jumped on one of the two uptown express lines that stopped at 72nd Street. Both of those trains would wind up taking them to 110th and Central Park North, close to where the truck was parked.

Assuming they stayed on the train. Robert could only hope that Darcy would realize that she'd made her point – scared him, and that the safe thing to do was to get off at the next express stop and wait for him. With any luck that's where he'd find her and Billy.

If he ever got there. The local train was moving at a crawl, sitting for eons at a time at each station and sometimes in the tunnel in between.

Threatening to take Darcy home had been a dumb move. Dumber than dumb. Dishonest. A bullshit *I'm-the-adult-around-here* power-trip thing. Well, he regretted it. And he intended to tell her as much. Admit he was sorry.

79th Street. Minutes stretched into a taffy string of eternity. 86th Street. Robert vaguely, incompletely, remembered something he'd read about Einstein, and the theory of relativity, and trains. The minutes continued to crawl.

96th Street. The express stop at last!

He sprang out onto the platform.

No Darcy there.

Or at the next stop.

He took the subway exit stairs two at a time and ran to Lenox and 112th where he had parked the truck. Darcy and Billy were not there.

Slowly, Robert retraced the route they'd taken from the truck to get to the demonstration. No sign of her at playground near the Harlem Meer, though when they'd walked by it, she and Billy had gone on and on about how much it looked like Wood Park. Nor were they on the paved paths near the ice skating rink which Billy had pronounced excellent for skateboarding.

Robert considered climbing the hill at the edge of the Park to check the Blockhouse that he'd pointed out to Darcy. It was hidden, forbidden. A perfect hideout for a kid.

Except that Darcy wasn't a kid anymore. Not like that. And even Billy was old enough to show hair on his upper lip. This was not some kid game of hide and go seek. It was stupid to even think of looking for them in a kid place like that.

Darcy had come to see Doefen. More than likely, she'd be wherever the hell Doefen might be.

Robert got back on the train to go downtown.

***

"So where are we?" I asked Darcy after we switched trains.

She knelt on the seat to take a look at the map next to the train door. I looked too. All I could see was a scramble of colored lines.

"I think somewhere near here," she said tapping a spot near the top of the map, but the look on her face said she was as lost as I was. "And we need to get back somewhere around here." She pointed to the lower edge of a green rectangle labeled Central Park that took up a big chunk in the middle of the map.

"Yeah, I'm pretty sure the demonstration was right here."

No way, no how did I want to go back to where all those pissed-off cops were running around. But Darcy wasn't worried about cops. Her only fear was that Robert would also turn up there before she had a chance to meet Doefen.

"We'll have to keep our eyes open," she said.

Me, I secretly had my fingers crossed that she was right and that Robert would be there and spot us right away.

I started to give that map some serious attention. Which was when I started to see that the lines were like strings, and that they worked kinda, sorta like the ones I tied all over Glen Eddy. The red one on the map went from some place called Van Cortland Park to Brooklyn College. Back home, my red string was for getting me from my front door to school. And then I noticed that next to the red subway string there was a red circle with either a 1, 2 or 3. The green string had the numbers 4, 5, 6. The yellow one came with letters — N, R. There were dots along each string and they had street numbers next to them. Which meant that if we could figure what street we were at and what street we wanted to go to, I could get us there.

I got all excited explaining this to Darcy. And she got all excited back, and hi-fived me, called me brilliant.

The doors opened. Darcy poked out her head. "14th Street," she shouted, and we searched the map. By the time we found the right dot all the way down near the bottom of the red string, the doors opened again. Canal Street. There it was, the next dot on the red string, but the nearby blue string, and yellow one, and brown one also had a dot labeled Canal Street.

Suddenly, I wasn't feeling all that smart. Who knew if we were on the 1,2,3, or A,C,E, or N,Q,R,W, or 4,5,6. I stared at the map some more. The one thing I could say for sure was that we were headed in the wrong direction. The place where Robert had left his truck was definitely somewhere near the top of the green rectangle labeled Central Park, and Canal Street was way far from that.

So at Chambers Street, we got out and did a flight of stairs up, then a flight down to switch trains. Somewhere along the way, I noticed that the signs in the station had a big red circle with a 2. And so did the window of the train we got on. Which meant to me that we had to be on the red subway string.

A happy moment.

The way Darcy figured it, we could be back at the demonstration street looking for Doefen in like twenty minutes.

"Cool," I said sounding way less than enthusiastic.

Darcy didn't seem to notice.

I spun the wheels on my skateboard and started to count to 60 in my        head. One and, two and, three and... Twenty rounds of counting to 60 and we'd be out of the train. I could ride around a little, do a couple of ollies and slides and kick-flips to stretch my legs, and look for Robert.

Seventeen and... eighteen and, nineteen and... Yeah, look for Robert. I mean I was pretty much done with the whole riding the train thing and wandering around lost in a huge city. Thirty and... or was it thirty-one ... Thinking about ollies and Robert scrambled my counting.

I was about to start over when I happened to zone in on the dude sitting across from me and Darcy. He was working his jaw like there was something he wanted to say but it was stuck somewhere way back in his throat. Which was enough to make him look way scary, never mind that he was also carrying some kind of pole with a big and pointy curved wire at the top. It looked like something you'd use to hook a really big fish. Except we weren't on any kind of boat. And he kept staring at me, at us, like he was just getting some kind of idea about what to do with his pole thing.

I grabbed Darcy's arm, even pinched her kind of hard. "Hey," I whispered. "Let's move, OK?" but Darcy was too blissed out to hear me.

"Just listen to the music," she said.

And I was like what music?

So she sang the notes of the subway doors closing, *beenhhh bonhhh.*

*Beeenhhh bonhh.* Sure enough it did kinda, sorta sound like chimes, or maybe that tuning-up harmonica thing that Mrs. Aves, the music teacher, used to get us started in chorus. Except that my mind and eyes were on the dude with the hook.

Lucky thing, at the very next stop he got up and was out of the door before the *beeenhhh bonhh* sounded.

So I started to relax a little, and as Darcy sang the sound of the doors closing at each stop, I even started to hear the music too. *Beeenhhh bonhhh. Beeenhhh bonhhh. Pleas·don·ho·da·does. Beeenhhh bonhhh. Stan·clear. Beeenhhh bonhhh. Lego·da·closin·does.*

It was music. And it was beautiful. I forgot all about the scary dude. With Darcy next to me, everything was beautiful.

And then we got to 42th Street. Everybody who got on the train was totally soaked and shivering, and talking about a freak storm. Lightening. Thunder.

I didn't need to hear a lot more. No way was I going to get out and get drenched. Especially if there was thunder or lightening. Both of which scared the hell out of me.

Darcy agreed to stay on the train until the rain stopped.

We rode up to 96th again. Came back down to 14th. And then turned around. At 42nd, the people getting on were no longer wet. The storm was over.

The way I read the map, the next stop should have been 50th right near the green square that was Central Park. Our stop. But somehow, when the doors opened, there we were looking at a sign that said 72nd. We switched trains. One stop later, we were at 42nd again. Darcy checked the map, and got us right back on a train going in the direction we'd just come from. Mysteriously, the doors opened at 72nd, not 50th.

Which was when I had the bright idea of getting off at 42nd, and walking the rest of the way. What could Darcy say? I mean, it was that, or yo-yo between the two stations forever.

***

A hard rain was falling when Robert got out of the subway at 51st. Knots of police stood huddled at the corners of the street and in the doorways of the various corporate offices. Some still had on their helmets. Others had pulled their turtlenecks over their heads. All of them had their hands on their sticks, or close to their holsters.

Robert turned up the collar of his jacket, tugged his hat low over his brow. Head down. Eyes on the ground. Face hidden.

It all came back. Take measured steps. Remain quiet. Nondescript. Act like a guy trying to get out of the rain.

He had his name, his alias ready. Tom. Nice, all American guy name. Tom Miller.

Simple. Common. Forgettable. Totally unlike his real name, his real initials. From what he remembered of his 60's SDS training, that was important. Not using your own initials.

They – the cops, the Pigs — had to be watching. He could feel their eyes on him. Watching. But they didn't stop him.

Hah! He got past them.

The cross streets near the Waldorf were still closed to traffic, even though there wasn't a single demonstrator in sight. Garbage trucks with snow plows attached stood hood to trunk blocking access. An enormous canvas tent now sat smack in the middle of Lexington Avenue at 50th street. All along Park and Madison, metal gates and wooden barricades still lined the sidewalk. At the curb, an unbroken perimeter of concrete barricades had been added. The ones in front of large corporate buildings were disguised as enormous planters — nothing in them but spindly evergreens.

The cops near the Waldorf prowled the streets restless as a pack of dogs.

"You can't go this way," they snarled at pedestrians. Robert ducked into the doorway of a bank to scope things out. From under the brim of his cap, he watched the cops tear into a UPS guy, and a pizza delivery guy before turning them away. A woman with a baby stroller pleaded to be let through. Two helmeted cops yanked off the stroller's plastic rain cover, inspected the baby, and all around and under the baby before allowing her to pass.

Traffic, though sparse, crawled along the avenues because the cops kept checking licenses and rerouting most of the cars and trucks away from the hotel.

Pigs.

Undercover cops were everywhere. And they were as obvious now as they used to be when Robert was a college activist. One of them was dressed to look like a street maintenance guy, except that the walkie talkie in his inside pocket was broadcasting loud and clear, and his gloves spelled P O L I C E across the knuckles.

A few others were meant to pass as protesters. They had scraggly hair, wore baggy black pants, and had canvas bags strung across their chests. The look almost worked, except that hanging out, smoking with the uniformed cops was a definite giveaway.

The unmarked police cars were equally conspicuous. More than a few had police hats or other police paraphernalia lying on the dashboard. Minivans with doors ajar revealed multiple surveillance cameras inside.

Getting near the Waldorf looked like it just wasn't going to be in the cards. Not without a photo ID and security clearance. Midtown was in lockdown. The rich — the haves — were inside the perimeter; the undesirables — the have nots — were outside.

The *Police State* in action. It didn't take any great leap of imagination to see how the Nazis were able to do what they had done.

There was no chance of finding Darcy here. While he considered what to do next, Robert watched a lone bicyclist make his way against traffic. Not until the cyclist was quite near did Robert realize that the man was shouting, "Stop Corporate Terrorism Now." Traces of the same slogan were still legible on the hand-lettered, rain-soaked cardboard sign that was strapped to his chest.

"Right on, man," Robert called out, not loud enough for anyone except the guy on the bike to hear.

At that moment, a man on the opposite corner — probably a cop, his raincoat too obviously meant to suggest "tourist" — shot off his telephoto. The motorized shutter whined. Two uniformed cops materialized alongside the cyclist, and dragged him off the bike. Another cop whisked the bike away.

Robert slipped out of the doorway, turned, and walked immediately and quickly — but not, he hoped, conspicuously — away from the scene.

He forced himself not to run. The skin on the back of his neck prickled with an adrenalin surge. At any moment, he expected to feel an unseen hand drop onto his shoulder.

Inside his jacket, Robert made a tight fist. He wouldn't let the fuckers take him without a fight. Moving only his eyes, he scanned the street — left, right, down, up. He wished he could see further, look behind. Left, right, down. On an upward sweep he glimpsed movement on the low roof of a building across from him. A figure, slick and hunched and black – a crow he thought at first — appeared at the rim of the roof and disappeared.

A sniper! Had to be. There were probably nests of them everywhere. Walking fast and faster Robert went back the way he'd come, and slid — panting, sweating and grateful — back into the underground tunnel system of the subway.

# BILLY
Turning Point


Lost. Lost. Lost.

I must have been whining. I do that when I'm tired or scared.

No matter which way we turned in the 42nd street station, we hit another hallway packed full of people in a big hurry. There wasn't even room for me to put down my skateboard and ride. Darcy offered to carry it and I was glad to let her. Big mistake.

Lost.

There were all kinds of signs all over the place, all of them confusing.

"I have to say, it looked a lot simpler on the map," Darcy admitted.

Everybody hurrying past us looked like they knew exactly where they were going, so we tried following them for a while, but kept ending up near exits for the street, or some place called Port Authority.

Lost.

At some point, I started crying.

Darcy stopped, put her free hand on my shoulder. In the other one, she was holding onto my board. "Remember. Be bold and careful at the same time."

We were like face to face, but I didn't feel that she was really seeing me. Her eyes had that weird blissed out look I'd seen her get whenever she quoted some poet dude. Ginsberg especially.

I shrugged myself loose. Maybe I didn't know a whole lot about anything, but I knew that poetry speak was definitely not going to get us out of that tunnel.

"Just cut the shit," I told her. Actually, I probably yelled it because next thing her hand was over my mouth.

For some reason, her hand smelled like pretzels — the soft ones with diamonds of salt that they sell at the county fair. Right then and there, my stomach let me know that it hadn't been fed for like hours and hours. It was all I could do not to lick Darcy's palm the way I used to when we still played cats.

Darcy had put an end to that game when she was around ten. Last time we played it, she'd wiped her hand hard on the back of her jeans. "Real cats have rough tongues like files," she said, as thought that explained why I wasn't allowed to lick her anymore.

"OK. How about dogs," I said. Can we play dogs?"

A dog that belonged to the hardware store in town where my father went for small stuff when he didn't feel like driving to *Home Despot*, never missed a chance to lick my leg and I knew his tongue was soft, probably softer than mine or Darcy's.

But there was no changing Darcy's mind. She said that she was done with animal games. And that was that. No more snuffling her hair until she rolled away paws up, kicking and meowing for me to stop. No more licking the salt off her sweaty neck. No more sucking her sticky-sweet thumb after she'd snuck *Lucky Charms* out of the box at my house — which Darcy liked to do, since in her kitchen it was whole wheat and bran twenty-four, seven. No more tongue-tip touches to her fingers.

Who knew I'd ever miss the old-leaves taste of her fingers on the days when she went on frog rescue missions? Or the vague tang of rust and blood on her skin when she'd been digging in Robert's garden. For sure that taste was kind of yucky and gross, but also satisfying like picking an old scab off with your teeth.

For a while after the animal games became a no-no Darcy would still let me pat-pat the warmy spot on the inside of her arm with my fingers. But it didn't take too long for that to become off limits too. Which is how I got into petting my own earlobe instead – always the left one with my left thumb and pointer finger.

My Dad called it a nasty habit and slapped me.

Cat, I called the left ear. The right one was just an ear, which is why all my piercings now are on that side. I mean, I could not see sticking a needle into Cat.

Darcy never let me taste her ear. But I did get my nose close enough to know that her ear smelled like crayons.

I bit into a brown crayon once thinking it would taste dark like melted chocolate. It didn't.

All of this stuff went flashing through my head as I got a whiff of the pretzel smell on Darcy's hand. I guess I was so caught up in the whole memory thing that I stopped yelling. Darcy took her hand away from my mouth.

"We are so lost," I sniveled very quietly. "What do we do now?"

"Whenever I don't know what to do, I listen to Ginsberg or Whitman, and they help me."

It wasn't like Darcy had never said stuff about the poet voices before, but that time it creeped me out. I mean, she made the voices sound like they were a real thing, like she could hear those dudes the same way she could hear me.

"They're dead guys," I told her.

"Not to me."

Which was about the time that I suddenly got that she probably saw those poet dudes, the same way that she said she "saw" door bells ringing, and dogs barking.

It's a pretty freaky thing to wrap your mind around, so I guess I shouldn't get too down on myself for taking as long as I did to figure it out — she didn't just hear poets, she saw them.

Anyway, there we were, deep under the ground of a city where we'd never been before, totally lost, and we were talking about poets and voices. I went from crying to laughing so hard I thought I'd piss my pants.

Lost. Totally, fucking lost. And what did Darcy say?

"When the mode of music changes, the walls of the city shake."

I'd heard that one more than once before. And to this day, I still don't know what the hell it's supposed to mean, but there I was laughing.

Next thing, Darcy was laughing too, and dancing me around, hugging me like I'd done, or said something brilliant. Of course, my heart just went white hot with love for her.

"Follow me," she said sounding like she knew exactly what to do.

We took off down another hallway, her hand a snug, warm glove around mine, to look for the place we'd seen on the map where all the subway lines came together. That hallway reeked worse than all the others – think portable johns at the end of a ninety degree day at the County Fair. Slimy fingers of wet oozed down the walls. The lights buzzed like flies trapped between a window and screen. And the floor was covered with wads of already chewed gum that kept sticking to our feet.

Somewhere up ahead I hear a kid's voice wailing,

"Nooooooo... Noooooo."

Darcy gripped my hand hard, and pulled me to walk faster. The sound got louder and louder, "Nooooooooo."

At the point where the passageway suddenly widened and sloped down, there was a little boy on his knees.

Some woman – probably his Mom, was standing over him screaming, "Getupgetupgetup. Getup NOW."

"Noooooooo." The boy's face was smeared with tears, and he had his arms stretched to her. "Carry me."

Both he and the woman looked completely exhausted.

Darcy and I kind of stood there frozen, like we were caught up in some bad dream. Meanwhile, everybody else went streaming past the kid the way rain water in a street gutter goes around a stone.

Out of nowhere, the woman hauled off and smacked the boy, her palm making a THWACK when it connected with the side of his face. The boy's head flopped against his shoulder and back up again, like there was a spring in his neck. But his mouth hung open in a dark and silent O.

No one stopped.

I didn't exactly feel Darcy's hand leave mine, only saw her suddenly standing between the woman and the boy, feet planted, hands resting on the nose of my skateboard like she was some kind of knight and it was her shield.

"Tell him you're sorry and that you know he's tired, and you're tired too," she commanded. "Tell him you'll carry him a little, if he walks a little."

The woman stared at her in a way that made me want to scream, Noooooo.

"Tell him," Darcy insisted. "You're the grown-up. Tell him."

"Who the fuck are you?" You could tell from the way the woman's eyes went all squinty that she wasn't used to taking shit from a kid.

"Tell him." Darcy's voice went dangerously quiet.

The woman hauled off at Darcy's face with her big, thick fist. Darcy raised the skateboard. The punch landed just under the front wheels.

"You fucking little bitch!" the woman howled as her fist connected with the board. She raised her other arm

This time Darcy swung the skateboard, and it caught the

woman hard on the chest. By then I'd come close enough to hear the woosh of air that came out of the women's mouth, and to feel the draft of it pass over my skin, and to smell the sour stink of cigarettes and alcohol on her breath.

The woman's body folded at the knees. Silently, slowly she slumped to the ground. A pink wad of gum slipped out of her slack mouth.

And still no one walking by bothered to stop. But I figured sooner or later someone might, and it would be better for Darcy and me to be gone.

I begged her to run. "Dude, I know from bullies. And if you're lucky enough to knock one down, you've got to get away before they get up."

But no, Darcy was all over the woman, feeling for a pulse, checking to see if she was breathing. The look on her face as she held her finger under the woman's nose made me nervous. And it didn't help that the boy stood at the woman's feet screaming, "Momeeeee, Momeeeee."

Somehow I managed to yank Darcy away, and get her up one stairway and down another. I didn't know where I was taking us, only that I wanted it to be as far away as possible from that woman lying on the floor.

"You killed her," I sobbed once we were huddled together on some dimly lit platform. "I think you killed her."

Darcy got forehead to forehead with me.

"She'll be alright," she said, but I wasn't so sure I believed her. The fact that Darcy was crying made me think that maybe she wasn't totally sure it was true either. Unlike me, Darcy almost never cried.

"Yeah, she'll be alright," Darcy repeated, still crying, but already not so much as before. "In fact, she'll be better than alright, because the ache in her chest will remind her to be kinder, nicer to her baby."

Kinder and nicer. That was so totally Darcy. No matter what, she always believed that if your heart was in the right place and you took action, you'd end up with good results

Me? I'd been beat up enough times to know that probably wasn't the way things would go down. I felt afraid for that boy.

"I am sorry I hit the woman," Darcy whispered, kind of as an afterthought. She was already dry-eyed. "I really, truly am. But

93

I had to. I mean, that kid was so tiny and she was huge. Way bigger than me."

Suddenly, it was all very clear. Of course, Darcy had to smack the woman. She was protecting the boy.

I grasped her hands. "Don't feel too bad," I said. "She deserved it. Just like those bullies I threw matches at before you stopped me deserved it. You know, I really did want to put fires to them. I kept thinking how happy I'd feel to see flames eating up their jeans, then their jackets, until they were ashes."

It was Darcy's turn to freak. "You can say stuff like that to me about fires, but not to anybody else because they'll lock you up. Understand?"

I nodded, but I was glad that at least Darcy knew what I meant.

"I really shouldn't have done what I just did back there," she said quietly, more to herself than me.

I couldn't think of anything to say. So, I just stood there alongside her looking down the tracks, wishing a train would come. A train to take us away.

Maybe it was my silence that got to Darcy. I don't know. But the weird thing was that one minute she was cool with everything that went down, and the next she wasn't.

"Okay, I admit it," she said. "I acted like a dumb and stupid girl back there. I mean, I know that violence can't be overcome by violence. Do no harm— that's the whole point of Doefen's actions, right? He sits down in the road and lets the bulldozers roll up to him. He doesn't blow up the development. He plants a tree."

She was back to crying. Big time crying. She made a fist, knocked it against her forehead. "Stupid. So stupid. I have no business going to Doefen. I should just go back to Glen Eddy, and help Robert sell honey and apples at the side of the road. That's all I'm good for."

"Dude, don't do that." I'd never seen Darcy go to such a dark place before, and I was totally freaked. I took her hand, stroked the soft, warm place on the inside of her wrist with my thumb. "Please, don't."

When she finally calmed down, Darcy locked her eyes on mine.

"You are a good friend. I'm sorry if I scared you back there, but I want you to know that I will never again raise my hand against anyone. Never. I swear it. No matter what. Cross my heart and hope to die."

"Don't say die."

"Hey, you know what I mean." She smiled. I smiled. We locked pinkies for a pinky swear. Everything was right with the world again.

The way things turned out, I wish that she'd never made that promise.

# ROBERT
## The Same but Different

Robert took the subway back uptown to check the truck again, just in case. No sign of Darcy and Billy, no sign that they'd been back at all.

"Fuck me," he muttered, hitting the cap of the flatbed with his fist, a growing certainty gnawing at his gut – the kids were never going to show up at the truck on their own because he'd never made sure that they knew where the truck was parked. He'd never for one moment expected the three of them to be separated. Splitting up was definitely not part of the scenario, not what he'd promised Isabelle.

On the off chance that the kids somehow remembered the general area where the truck was parked and might be looking for it, he decided to check for them in the neighborhood. He walked down the nearly empty street past two old ladies chatting near a stoop. He nodded. They looked right through him like he was trouble waiting to happen. No point in asking them anything. Whatever they might know about two out-of-town kids, they wouldn't be sharing with him.

At the corner where 112th Street met Morningside, a bunch of guys with huge, obviously fake diamond studs in their ears, and caps turned brim back watched his approach from under hooded lids.

"Pussy," Robert heard one of them say, and concluded that they meant him. He crossed the street to avoid them.

Hunched down into his jacket, he quickly searched another three blocks, all the while feeling like dozens of eyes hidden behind curtains and window shades were tracking his movements. No doubt, somebody in the neighborhood had already noticed his truck, and would keep on noticing it if he didn't move it soon.

He returned to the truck without speaking to anyone, collar of his jacket pulled up to hide his face.

What to do next? Hang around in the hopes that the little runaway brats might show up?

He dismissed the thought. Back in the day, the neighborhood

was known for taking a see nothing, say nothing attitude towards the cops. Which was why he'd parked there in the first place. But times had changed. He couldn't be sure that one of those ladies still yacking out on the stoop wouldn't take it into her head to call the cops on a stranger sitting for hours on end in a parked truck.

The sun was dipping towards the horizon. Only a few more hours until dark. He'd intended to be on the road heading back home while it was still light. The kids had no money, no food – he'd planned a pit stop at McDonald's on the way back to Glen Eddy to treat Darcy to the fries that Isabelle deemed taboo.

Isabelle! Panic rose to his throat like pain. What was he going to tell her?

Damn it all to hell. He had to find Darcy and find her quick. Swallowing hard, he crawled into the flatbed, grabbed a couple of peanut butter and jelly sandwiches, some trail mix, a bottle of water and stuffed them into his pockets.

Clearly, the right place, the only place to look for Darcy was wherever Doefen was holed up. Had to be. Hands shaking, Robert pulled out the three daily newspapers he'd bought at the subway stand in the hopes that they'd have something about Doefen's whereabouts. But there wasn't a word about him, just lots of bullshit about the benefits of WTO's proposed trade policies, the very policies that WE was protesting.

At the newsstand, he'd searched for the alternative papers he remembered from his student days, which were always in the know, but only found *The Voice*. Hope faded as he glanced through its pages. The one-time adventurous political soapbox had become a give-away advertising rag. Useless for finding news of Doefen whereabouts.

He couldn't resist a quick glance at the personal ads in the back pages that used to be his favorite section — a place to look for willing girls. Surprisingly, the personals had morphed into an amazingly encyclopedic and explicit resource for all sorts of things rated triple X – escort services, phone lines, real and virtual playmates, web sites and chat rooms servicing every sexual persuasion. The ads for she-male bodyworks were intriguing in their unfamiliarity, offers for breath deprivation sessions were equally mysterious and titillating. By comparison, the opportunities available in Glen Eddy for sexual adventure were painfully tame.

Carefully folding the ad pages, Robert hid them deep down into the wheel well for future perusal.

It occurred to him that whatever *The Voice* and other newspapers didn't cover about Doefen, college students would surely know. Despite the rep that the current generation of college kids had for being apathetic and complacent, he'd noticed a lot of young protesters at the demonstration.

Students. That was the way to go if he was going to get anywhere. Never trust anyone over thirty. Words to live by back in his college days.

Smiling, Robert decided to risk leaving the truck unlocked in case Darcy and Billy did show, stuck a scribbled note on the dashboard, and set off for his alma mater, his old stomping ground.

The walk to the campus across 110th wasn't a long one, but the stretch bordering the north end of the Park had a reputation for being unsafe. Robert adopted a look of unhurried purpose — solid strides, arms at his sides, eyes straight ahead – while keeping ears perked for the sound of ambush.

At the Farmers Gate, he stopped to scan the Park for the kids. It was mostly empty. No joggers. No one fishing at the pond. A few mallards, their gaudy green heads iridescent in the sun, sat along the grassy banks preening their feathers.

On the far side of the pond, he knew there was a knoll with a sunny field at the top. Secluded, screened from view by trees. He and Isabelle had once cut class, escaped another dusty freshman lecture on Hume, or Locke, or some other long-dead philosopher, to lie out there under the open sky.

Shirtless. He still remembers the prick of the newly sprung grass on his bare back.

And Isabelle shirtless too. Because girls did that back then — laid claim to the caresses of sun and soft breezes on their naked skin without shyness or shame.

Isabelle. Bella. Her nipples a tender pink, pale as the magnolia buds above their heads. He should have kissed her. Even though it would have been uncool. Even though she was already Jack's.

Even then, they – he and Bella and Jack – were already a troika. Unholy. Inseparable. Unwise.

As he neared the 110th Street playground, Robert noticed a solitary child, her small body swallowed up in fat coils of snowsuit, lurching from sandbox to slide, and back again. Back and forth. Paper cup filled with sand. Cup emptied at the foot of the slide. Cup filled up again at the sandbox. Dogged. Absorbed. Entirely pleased with herself.

He'd seen that same expression – charming, comical – countless times on Darcy's face when she was a baby. In particular, he recalled a warm spring afternoon in her toddlerhood, which she spent "planting" his garden with wooden Tinkertoy flowers. And a day when she "painted" his kitchen cabinets by dipping a brush onto the colored keys of a pull-toy xylophone.

These moments, and other like them, remained vivid in Robert's mind and he pored over them tirelessly. There was a time when Darcy used to delight in the stories he told her of her childhood exploits. Lately, she tolerated his reminiscences with a glazed and bored expression.

Adolescence. Exciting to watch, but not nearly as charming as what came before.

This child's mother, splayed under the weight of her own massive flesh, dozed on a bench. Oblivious. No eyes for her tiny girl. No heed for the comings and goings of the world around the child — anyone could have walked up and snatched her. Not a thought in her head that the child was way overdressed — the bulky snowsuit was much too heavy for the weather.

Robert resisted the urge to shout into the woman's ear, wake her up. The stupid cow would probably just call the cops on him.

Best to mind his own business.

As Robert continued west across 110th Street, fallen fruit from the ginkgoes that lined the edge of the Park rolled under his boots. Beautiful to look at, like tiny silver apricots, the fruit was foul smelling when crushed. Unbearably foul, really. His every step released more and more of a fetid stink. He held his breath. The trees seemed to flutter their leaves as he passed, as though embarrassed by the rank smell of their own seed.

Smell or no smell, the ginkgo was an admirable tree — stately, majestic, a living fossil from the Dravidian era. Slow-growing, long-lived. Resistant to disease, insects, and the ravages of extreme weather. He'd read once that four ginkgoes were among the sole living survivors of the atomic bomb blast in Hiroshima. You had to love a tree like that.

He picked up a delicate, gold, fan-shaped leaf, and an un-crushed fruit from the cobblestone walk, tucking them both into his pocket to show Darcy later.

He'd never had occasion to discuss ginkgoes with her before. None grew in Glen Eddy. All of his little botanical disquisitions over the years had centered only on local trees, trees that were important to the bees. He could hardly wait to tell her all about the smelly white seed in his pocket – esteemed by the Chinese for its health and aphrodisiac qualities, yet poisonous if eaten in large amounts.

Who ever got the idea to eat such a thing in the first place Darcy would wonder, adding it to her ever-growing list of mysti-fying comestibles like mushrooms and shrimp.

Trust Darcy to ask the best questions.

What makes a sunburn? Are the cells in string beans alive before you cook them? Why don't dogs have belly buttons? Do dolphins or monkeys have them? Why do men lose the hair on their heads, but not their beards? Why do women spend a life-time carrying around breasts – round sacks of fat, she called them – just so that they can nurse a baby for a few months?

Simple questions without obvious answers, welcome as gnats as far as most people were concerned. Rather than muse with Darcy about her wonderings, they told her that she was a clever girl and advised her to study hard so she'd get into a good college.

s Robert loved and encouraged her question, especially the "what ifs" that most exasperated others.

What if two people with a cut on their finger were able to hold their fingers together the whole time they were healing? Would the fingers heal joined one to the other?

By way of an answer, he'd offered everything he knew about the immune system and the way it recognized the self, and re-jected all that was other.

A scientific fact. But the metaphoric truth was not lost on Dar-cy. "The cuts would get bigger, wouldn't they?" she said sadly.

What if you ate a sweet strawberry and a sour one at the same time? What would you taste? Sweet or sour?

All of life, Robert told her. All of life.

What if every time you heard a sound, like say a pick-up speeding down the street, or a dog howling, or nails being hammered you saw a shape or a color?

He'd laughed. "With or without drugs?"

"Without," she'd answered looking unduly serious.

He'd explained about hallucinations, talked about the "color" of an orchestra, the "brightness" of an instrument, and the notion of a "loud" shirt, a "sharp"cheese, and still she'd looked puzzled.

So many questions. A whole lifetime of very, very good questions. But not a single one that Robert could remember was about Doefen. Somehow, Darcy had exempted him. Hard to know why. Did she need a saint, a hero, and having chosen Doefen, could not bear to take a closer look?

The sun dipped behind a cloud, momentarily erasing the elongated shadows of the ginkgo that stretched across the cobbled walk. Soon it would be dark.

Robert quickened his pace.

On his right he passed buildings he recognized from his student day — one with yellowed awning was where he'd gone for his first off-campus party, next to it the derelict brownstone where he used to score drugs. In his memory, all the buildings stood taller, appeared grander — no soot outlined their cornices, and the flourishes of acanthus leaves at the top of their doorway columns were not eroded.

The longer he walked, the more the whole city, not just those buildings, seemed oddly diminished. Like revisiting your kindergarten classroom when you're a grown up.

To his left, the wall that separated the Park from the rest of the city was lower than he remembered, more a conceit than an actual boundary. The Warriors gate was just ahead, not really a gate now that he thought about it. No turnstiles or sentries. No charge to enter. What kind of gate was that?

Farmer's Gate. Pioneer's Gate. Explorer's Gate, Woodsmen's Gate, Hunter's Gate... He used to know the locations and names of all twenty of the Central Park gates. Nonsensical names, really. No hunters or pioneers frequented the Park. Not now. Not ever.

Ridiculous or not, his affection for the gates remained undiminished. He rubbed his brow, straining to remember the names of all of them. By the time he'd climbed Morningside hill to the rear entrance of the university campus, he'd gotten them all.

The quad of the university, an oasis of privilege at the point where an exhausted Broadway makes its break out of the city, was more or less the same. He noticed a few new, non-descript buildings. Designed to blend in. The original ones looked spiffed up. Nothing remained to suggest that they'd been subject to a seven day student take over in '68, or that mounted cops had violently forced a thousand student demonstrators off the campus. Nothing, not even a small, discrete brass plaque marked that landmark event.

He shook his head. The '68 protest seemed an ephemeral gesture that hadn't changed much of anything. The university was probably still taking money from the Institute for Defense, still conducting research for the military, and the ROTC was probably recruiting on campus again. Female students had abandoned tie-dyed t-shirts and gone back to wearing tidy little ponytails and sporting outfits that made them look like drum majorettes. Not a single revolutionary sister was anywhere in sight. The male students all looked like business majors. They probably were business majors – hair buzz cut and groomed like privet hedges. The occasional stud earring didn't fool Robert. These guys were the spitting image of the preppie yahoos who used to beat up longhairs like him and Jack.

Hanging out, which he remembered as an essential campus activity, seemed to have gone out of style too. No one was playing Frisbee on the greens. Not a whiff of weed anywhere. No students sprawled on the library steps.

Everyone hurried down the main walkway with urgency and purpose. No one made eye contact. He smiled, no one smiled back, not even a plain, too plump girl. Bitch, he called her under his breath. Didn't she realize that the black fishnet stockings she was wearing were her only asset?

The colonnade of linden trees leading to the main gate – a real gate — was turning gold in the evening light. He walked slowly, enjoying the rustling of the leaves above his head and under his feet. The lindens could sustain a colony of bees, even without the flowering trees that grew a block away in Riverside Park. A waste that the university didn't keep bees. Probably, there were rules against it. University rules, city ordinances, state and federal statutes.

Damn them. Damn them all.

And damn Darcy too. Taking off like that. If it weren't for her, he would have been heading back to the comfort of his farm, the quiet of Glen Eddy instead of haunting the sites of his old life.

He ought to leave her and her little sniveling side-kick to fend for themselves. Give Darcy a chance to see exactly how smart, how clever she really was. He wasn't obliged to go searching all over the city for her. After all, as she had so heartlessly pointed out, he was not her father.

# BILLY
Farmers' Gate

Even before the cop with the walkie talkie showed up on the platform, I was all for hitting the street right then and there, wherever there was, and going back to the truck. But no. Darcy insisted on studying the signs above the platform.

NRQWF. NRQWF. Like that was supposed to tell us something.

The cop was closing in on us, saying "Roger" over and over again into his squawk box. His eyes were on us. Definitely, on us.

I squeezed Darcy's hand. "We've gotta get out of here. Now." My tongue felt thick the way it does just before you puke.

We walked down the platform as fast as we could without looking like we were running. Not a single EXIT anywhere.

The cop was like inches behind us when a train came screaming into the station.

We jumped on.

Maybe the cop was after us and maybe he wasn't. There was no way to tell if he or anybody else knew about Darcy knocking out that woman. The one thing I was sure of was that Darcy and I had no idea of where we were going, or how to find the truck. I mean, we'd never planned on ending up wandering around without Robert.

Both of us remembered that the truck was parked somewhere near the Park. Which was right there on the subway map – marked by that big green rectangle. And running right along the edges of that rectangle were all those colored lines labeled ACBD23Q456.

Q! The sign in the window of our subway car had a big Q in a yellow circle.

Darcy and I got all excited. All we had to do was look at the map, figure out where the train was heading and which end of the Park to get out.

I remembered Robert pointing out a hill with a fort at the edge of the Park that you could just about see through the trees — a secret, hidden place that even most locals didn't know about, he said. A place that wasn't safe to go to alone. Figures that would be the kind of place Robert would know about. But, of course, the fort wasn't marked on the subway map.

Neither was the pond with ducks that Darcy remembered, or the street she said was named after someone important in civil rights. Not Martin Luther King. Not Rosa Parks. Some other name Darcy couldn't think of. We both agreed that the name Cathedral Parkway sounded familiar.

And then I remembered a sign I'd seen carved into a wall that went around the park. *"Farmers' Gate,"* I told her. "We passed it right after we parked the truck."

Of course, there weren't any gates marked on the map.
Darcy insisted that the park didn't have any gates.
But I knew what I knew.

"There was so a gate."

"Was not."

"Was so."

We spent a couple of minutes arguing like five year olds.

We must have been pretty loud and frantic about it because next thing there was another cop with a squawker on his belt giving us the hairy eyeball.

When the train doors slid open, we ran like hell, up the stairs and out to the street.

## ROBERT
Getting Connected


Robert found a copy of the Columbia school newspaper on the same ledge where he used to get it when he was a student. Same dull rag he remembered. The football team still sucked, leaving Jack Kerouac unchallenged as the best thing to ever happen to Columbia on the gridiron, just like he always said.

Near the main gate, Robert spotted a lone leafleteer.

"WE rally tomorrow," the buzz cut kid was calling out. "Don't forget."

Robert took a flier. "Where, and when?"

"It'll be posted on the net late tonight."

Net? Which site? What if you didn't have a lap top?

Clearly, the questions made the kid nervous. No doubt his life had always included all things electronic, leaving him with no concept of a time before cell phones, PCs, laptops, and internet. How could he possibly understand that Robert's knowledge of these things was limited, mostly secondhand, that he didn't own a computer and only logged on at the library, had never gone to a chat room, wasn't sure how it was done?

Much as Robert longed for a computer, he couldn't afford one, and thanks to Darcy his cash flow wasn't about to get any better. In order to humor her Doefen whim, he'd left the bees unprotected, and, therefore, unhappy. Pissing them off was going to cost him in the yield of honey.

"I could text you," the kid offered, but Robert waved him off, preferring to avoid having to explain that the mountains around Glen Eddy blocked reception and made owning a cell phone pointless.

Robert didn't blame the kid for looking at him like he was some kind of narc — or whatever it was that activists now called police infiltrators — and he told him as much, assuring him that back in the Sixties he would have been equally suspicious. That did the trick. One high-five later, the kid was giving him an earful about the Doefen rally.

Rumor had it that the Doefen - Burgundy debate was going to be canceled, or at least shoved off into some conference room in the hotel that would be too small to hold any supporters. The city had refused WE's request for a permit to march, and assigned them to a demonstration site so far removed from the main WTO events that there was no hope of getting press coverage. In response, WE was organizing its people at the last minute by net and cell. Small groups were going to meet all over the city and converge in waves on the hotel. By the time the cops knew what was happening, it would be too late to stop them.

As to Doefen's current whereabouts, the kid's best guess was that he was somewhere in the Park.

Robert carefully repeated the name and address of the cybercafe the kid recommend as the go-to place to check for updates. Lately, he noticed that his memory was not what it used to be. Was it the drugs he used to take, or was the mind like a muscle that went flabby if you didn't use it? For sure, life in Glen Eddy didn't require much exercise of his higher faculties.

"So cool that you're for Doefen," the kid exclaimed by way of goodbye with a slight, probably unintended, patronizing heartiness in his voice that made Robert want to hurt him. The kid took Robert for an old dog, and it wasn't the dog's fine pirouettes that he admired. No doubt, he was amazed that the dog could dance at all.

Feeling anything but cool, Robert decided that the cybercafe would just have to wait until he'd fortified himself with a couple of beers.

He was glad to see that the *West End* was still in business, even if it was now windowed from ceiling to floor. Yuppified. Gone was the dark dive where Robert remembered groping Susan in the back room, and the basement space where drug deals used to go down. But the beer was still cold and cheap, and students still filled the place with the kind of whooping hilarity that came from not knowing just how badly life could fuck them over.

Hard to believe that he and Isabelle and Jack had ever laughed like that.

Robert parked himself at the bar and surveyed the room. Where there used to be an oddball hunkered down over a textbook, now there were students all over the place bathed in the blue light of their open laptops. A few appeared to be doing homework, but most were playing computer games, or chatting simultaneously with their on-line and present-in-the-room friends.

At the table closest to the bar, a student in a plaid flannel shirt tapped avidly at the keys of his laptop. Because of the long, loose hair that spilled down the kid's back that was so like his own used to be, Robert felt an instant kinship with him. He knew it was stupid.

Robert couldn't quite see the kid's screen, but he noticed that it seemed to attract a nearly continuous stream of students who buzzed around the table, settled in loose clusters, then drifted off.

After a second beer, Robert slipped in among them.

A film clip of a demonstration was playing on the screen. The quality was poor. Jumpy. Out of focus. It didn't matter. The images were familiar. Beefy cops with masks and shields and sticks and guns. Bare-headed, unarmed protesters. A skirmish. Heads bleeding. Limp bodies being dragged off into a police van.

The demonstration could have been one taking place anywhere in the world, at any time in modern history. But when Robert glimpsed the figure in a blue *djellabah* astride a barricade, he knew it could only be an instant replay of the demonstration he'd been at that afternoon.

# BILLY
Surfacing


We came up out of the subway to light, and air, and a familiar smell — a Glen Eddy kind of smell.

Horses. Had to be. There is nothing else like the grass and piss smell of horses. And there was neighing, a dead giveaway.

A yellow swirl, Darcy called the sound of neighing, like butter cream icing. Which had to be a good thing since Darcy was such a freak for frosting. Me, I thought the stuff was slimy, like the spackling paste my father bought at Home Depot by the bucket. At the birthday parties we went to, I gave Darcy the icing from my slice of cake and she gave me the cake part.

I was so excited to be above ground that I jumped right onto my skateboard. A long stone wall right near the subway exit looked perfect for jumps. I rode over to take a look. On the other side, there was a huge drop down a rocky hill all covered with shrubs and trees. At the bottom was a small lake. And past that, trees and more trees and more trees.

I shouted for Darcy to come and have a look. It was the Park. Had to be. But she was all busy bonding with a horse. Cooing. Nuzzling.

Which was just about when I really took in the weirdness of the whole scene. Huge buildings, way taller than anything in Glen Eddy, even the fire tower. A zillion cars zipping by. And horses with carriages. Ten, maybe twenty horses, all tied to lamp posts. And Darcy, right there smack in the middle of them, nuzzling the biggest, most muscular one.

I probably could have gotten her away from the horse and out of there, if this geezer dude who was like a walking, talking picture of the *Cat in the Hat* hadn't showed up.

"Careful, lass," he boomed at Darcy sounding like he was channeling the leprechaun in the *Lucky Charms* commercial.

"Best not to get too friendly with Sam."

Of course, she went right on combing her fingers through the horse's long mane. "Officer Warwick doesn't take kindly to anyone getting too close with his horse."

Officer, as in cop. That was all I need to hear. "We have to get the hell out of here," I whispered to Darcy. In my heart of hearts, I believed that cops were on the lookout to arrest Darcy for what she did to that woman down in the subway. And to arrest me too as her accomplice or something. I mean, even if Darcy didn't kill the woman, she sure as shit broke a couple of her ribs.

But Darcy was just getting started on the whole horse thing. In like a heartbeat, she and the *Cat in the Hat*-leprechaun dude got all friendly. They went from discussing Officer Warwick's likes and dislikes in a horse to talking about the other horses tethered along the street.

"Carriage horses, they are," the dude said.

They looked like a sad and sorry bunch to me. Heads down. Hardly moving except to crook a leg up off the sidewalk, and to drop it down again.

"Hard workers, all of them. But my own Flo is the sweetest," the carriage horse guy said, pulling out a piece of apple out from his pocket and giving it to Darcy.

"Go on. Feed it to Flo," he said. "You'll break her heart sure if you leave without so much as a kind word for her. She'll think you have eyes only for Sam."

Maybe it's a girl and horses thing, I don't know. But Darcy couldn't tear herself away from Flo.

She whispered into the horse's freckled ear. Stroked the curve of her back and flank. Which I have to admit was a nice, shiny brown like melted chocolate. The *Cat in the Hat* geezer must have brushed the hell out of that horse.

"I would love to take you for a little run in the Park," Darcy crooned. "Just you and me. No carriage."

"She'd like that, she would," the geezer said. "The old lass still has a lot of spirit left in her."

A discussion of Darcy's riding skills came next. I zoned in and out. There was something about how Darcy had wanted to learn to ride even though her Mom was against it, which had something to do with her Mom being a vegetarian or something.

Whatever. I was with Darcy's Mom on the whole riding thing. No way, no how did I think it was OK to climb up on an animal that much bigger than me.

There must have been some other stuff that I missed while I skateboarded around, but the next thing I knew Darcy and the geezer had moved on to more personal stuff. And because Darcy was not in the habit of telling lies, not even little white ones, she started to explain all about the *djellabah*, and Glen Eddy, and Doefen and the demonstration.

I did a few jumps on my board, banged around, made a bunch of noise to get Darcy's attention, and to stop her before she got to the part about running out on Robert.

She ignored me.

I was scared and couldn't think of what else to do, so I just rode away.

"Bye," I said. "I'm leaving now." My whole body was shaking, but I kept on going. Which I should have done from the start. Because in like a minute, Darcy followed.

"Where do you think you're going and why are you being so rude?"

"Why are you talking to strangers?"

"He's a good man."

"And you know that how?"

"You just have to listen to him, hear his voice, to know that he's got a big and feeling heart." She claimed that the air around the *Cat in the Hat* dude got all shiny like sparklers when he spoke. "Doefen needs people like him. And people like him need Doefen."

Me – I didn't see the connection.

And sparklers? I didn't care if the dude was surrounded by exploding Roman candles. He could still report us.

I was hungry. All I wanted to do was to find Robert and go home. Probably I was crying by the time I admitted that to Darcy. I did a lot of crying back then.

Darcy hugged me, ignored the part about going home and told me she was hungry too. Even said she wished that we had the PB and jelly sandwiches that we left in the truck. Which made me cry more. Because for Darcy to be thinking about a PB sandwich, she had to be pretty hungry, starving even.

I mean, she hated PB and jelly. You'd think that her good friend and buddy Robert would have known that. True, Darcy was a vegetarian, but she was a vegetarian who hated most of the stuff vegetarians eat. Apples were OK and maybe grapes, but forget the small stuff like strawberries or blueberries. No cantaloupes either – smelled like old socks, she said. I was with her on that. And she hated fuzzy stuff like kiwis and peaches, which reminded both of us of a gerbil or some other furry, little animal. She also agreed with me on the yuckiness of eggplants, squash, beans, and broccoli.

I never cared about eating healthy. My taste buds were imprinted on Burger King and KFC. I was all about eating meat. And no amount of Darcy going on about what beautiful eyes cows have, and how chickens are really birds just like robins and sparrows, only bigger ever made a dent in my taste for it.

But if it had been up to Darcy, she would have lived on soy and white stuff – mashed potatoes, macaroni, milk, ice cream.

Still crying, I told her that I wished that Robert had thought to bring some carrots. Darcy and I were both OK with eating them as long as they were raw. Not cooked. Never cooked.

Carrots. Hungry. Home. Find Robert. Go home. Now. Hungry. Hungry. Hungry. That's was all I could talk about, like my mouth was set on instant replay or something.

Darcy and I were standing next to some kind of huge statue of a girl all in gold, leading a horse, also gold, with a gold rider, and I was shouting. Hungry. Home. People were staring.

"Soon," Darcy kept saying, using her quiet, I'm-all-chill, pretend grown-up voice. Soon. Soon. But first Doefen. Doefen first. Doefen.

I covered my ears and started to ride off again.

Darcy ran alongside, still blabbety blabbing about finding Doefen.

"I want to go home. I want to go home, now." The words came out like hiccups because of the way my board bounced over the cobblestones.

Which made Darcy laugh.

And her laugh made it hard for me to stay mad at her.

So I stopped and waited for her to tell me what we were going to do next. I mean, there we were — no plan, no money, starving. And worst of all, freezing our asses off. The rainstorm had scrubbed every cloud out of the sky and left sunlight that didn't have a shred of warmth or color to it. Even the pigeons sitting all over the gold statue had their feathers puffed out trying to get warm.

As we stood there, one of the pigeons suddenly dive bombed onto the sidewalk. Scared the hell out of me. I swung my skateboard at it, and in a flash Darcy grabbed my hand, and gave me a look like I was clubbing a baby seal or something.

Next thing I knew, Darcy let go of me and started staring at that statue with pigeon poop all over it like it was something she'd never seen before. Something amazing. Sure enough, she got that glazed look she always got when she was about to drop into poet speak.

"Nothing is completely black and white. The mind that insists on either black or white is only a small part of the mind."

A second later, she was head to head, eye to eye with me.

"Gold rider and pigeons. They totally go together, you know?"

I didn't, not really, but I nodded.

"Yeah, it's definitely a thing to remember," she said. "There's no such thing as a hero who isn't also a perch for birds to shit on."

She laughed the kind of laugh that always made me laugh too. Only this time my teeth were chattering so hard I couldn't manage so much as a chuckle.

"Dude, I am so, so cold," I said. Without question, I sounded like someone begging for mercy.

I don't know what changed Darcy's mind – my desperation, the bird poop and gold statue thing, or the goosebumps all over her own arms, but suddenly her plan was to forget about Doefen and just find Robert.

I jumped on my board and did a couple of spins for joy. And to warm up. Find Robert. Go home!

We headed in the direction of the Park. Not too far past the statue, we came to an opening in the low wall that ran alongside the Park. And there, carved in really big letters were the words, *Scholars' Gate*.

I pointed them out to Darcy, did not say, "I told you so," just grinned because it felt so great to be right about something for once.

She high-fived me.

From that point on, the plan became — Find *Farmers' Gate*.

After walking for like a million years, we came to *Inventors' Gate*. We looked around and all we saw up ahead of us was wall, and more wall. It didn't seem possible that a little green rectangle on a map could wind up translating into something so big in real life. I was freaked, but Darcy just walked up to the next person we saw to get directions, never mind the rule about not talking to strangers,

*"Farmers' Gate?"* The scary looking dude in green coveralls who was plucking litter off the ground with a giant tong squinted at Darcy. "Never heard of it," he said. "Park don't have no gates. It's free for everybody."

For whatever reason, the dude sounded pissed. Which, to me, meant it was time to get the hell out of there. But once Darcy had her teeth into a fact, there was no shaking her loose. So, she stood there explaining about the two gates we had already passed, and how we just need to know how far it was to *Farmers' Gate* until the guy told her to get out of his face and snapped his tongs at her.

We kept walking. In like two minutes, we were at the *Children's Gate.* Both of us got all excited thinking that maybe the gates were getting close together and maybe the *Farmers' Gate* would be the next one, until I noticed the street sign. 76th Street. All of a sudden, I could picture the green rectangle on the subway map. I was sure that 110th Street was at the top end of it. Even if we were walking on the right side of the Park, and didn't have to walk around to the other side, we still had a long way to go.

Darcy immediately started to do the math. At a block a minute, it would take thirty-four minutes to get to the end of the Park. The sun was dipping down below the crowns of the trees to our left.

"We can make it before dark, but we're going to have to run," she said like it was no big deal.

The whole idea of being out in the dark scared the hell out of me even before I heard a voice say, "Run? You got that right."

Standing right there next to us was some dude with string mop hair around a circle of baldness.

I grabbed Darcy's arm.

"The name is Matt," the man said and stuck out his hand. Neither of us took it.

"Most people call me M3, short for Mobile Media Man." He tapped his dark sunglasses. "These little babies record everything I see."

I stood there like we were in one of those nightmares where you want to run, know you need to run, but your legs won't do it. Meanwhile M3 explained about some kind of tiny digital video camera hidden in the frame of his sunglasses, and how his headphones were really connectors to a mini computer in his backpack.

"I can move around, walk, and film everything without being detected." To demonstrate, he moved his whole body slowly from side to side like it was a video camera, and ended by leaning toward us.

"Speechless, I see," he said. "I often have that effect on people."

"We've got to go," Darcy said.

M3 tilted his head sideways the way birds do when they look at you. "I recognize you," he said. "You're the kid who climbed the barricade."

He made a slow and clumsy half-circle with his head, almost like the camera glasses made it hard for him to see. "Yeah, you're the one."

You could tell from his voice that he was way happy to be looking at Darcy up close.

"It's the robe. Makes you instantly recognizable." He walked around her in a slow circle. "Very cool what you did. But also useless. You do know that, right?"

Without waiting for Darcy to answer, he pulled a newspaper page out of one of the zillions of pockets on his khaki jacket. "Read it and weep."

He came around behind her, positioned his camera glasses to read over her shoulder.

"Notice that the article about the demonstration is buried on page 10 of the city section, and mentions a few hundred activists. Not the actual thousands of flesh and blood human beings who packed the streets. No mention of the barricades, or the banners, or your climb."

M3 reached to take the page from Darcy.

"Come on kid. Who do you think saw what you did?"

"Everyone."

At which point, I poked Darcy hard. I mean, she was, totally and completely ignoring Robert's warning not to tell anyone anything.

M3 laughed. "You mean all those people blinded by pepper spray?"

"There were others."

I poked Darcy again, but this time she swatted me away.

"Damn straight," M3 said. "All the police cameras definitely saw you. There were plenty of them."

He launched into a lecture about something he called TT, the totalitarianism of technology. Told us that we were all on tape 24-7, watched by hidden cameras while we walked around in malls, or stood on line at the bank, or rode in elevators. Said we were watched without our knowledge or consent, and for no reason.

The guy creeped me out, but I couldn't help listening. Until he talked about the cameras, I'd never given a thought to all the purple bug-eyed ones I'd seen hanging over the registers at Home Depot and the supermarket back home. I figured that as long as you weren't some kind of criminal or shoplifter, they didn't matter. But after what M3 said, I never stopped thinking about cameras and surveillance again.

To hear M3 tell it, the police already considered Darcy and everyone associated with her persons of interest. Security risks. The sad thing was that no one except the cops was ever going to know about Darcy's climb onto the barricades because TV and all the media were in the pocket of big money and politicians who made sure that the public only saw what they wanted the public to see.

"You do understand that unless people see it on TV, it's like it never happened, right?" M3 said.

"But it did happen," Darcy insisted. "And the word will get around."

"Not if the cops can help it. Their job is all about squelching protest and discrediting political activists. Your climb has put you on the short list for pre-emptive arrest. And if and when – most likely just when — you are arrested you will be made to look like a crazed, destructive, unpatriotic fanatic."

Every word out of M3's mouth made me want to run. His effect of Darcy was exactly opposite.

"I'll fight for the truth."

"Doesn't matter. If the media calls you a terrorist, you're a terrorist. People believe whatever they see or hear on TV. Which is where I come in."

He thumped his fist in the general vicinity of his heart. "People like you and WE and Doefen need truthful media coverage."

He tapped his eyeglasses. "I saw everything. The camera recorded it. Unfortunately my equipment is still not as good as my eye, but it's adequate for broadcast. I post the footage on the web. Next thing you know, you've gone world-wide. In fact, you are already playing all over the Internet even as we speak."

M3 paced back and forth, twisting his head this way and that, making fine adjustments in the wires connecting the glasses and backpack. "It's up to you. Leave now and go wander around in the dark – a nobody, a no one whose life doesn't add up to shit in the big picture. Or let me lead you to the place where you can make a difference."

"What about Robert?" I said. "Remember Robert?"

M3 zoomed in on me. "Who the hell is Robert and what does he matter?"

I left the explanation to Darcy.

M3 wasn't impressed. "It's too late to search for this Robert guy, and besides he should be backing you guys 1000% instead of hiding out in some truck uptown – if that's where he is. Trust me, there's nothing happening above Eighty-Sixth Street. All the action is up at Belvedere Castle. Doefen is there, and the WE people are there making plans for a showdown tomorrow that will make the action today look like a wine and cheese party."

Doefen. M3 didn't have to say anything else. Darcy was sold.

M3 smiled. "We need to get going if we're going to make it through the Ramble before dark. It's pretty wild in there."

He turned and started down the path into the park. The monitor light on his headset swept the almost-dark like a tiny beacon.

"Let's not." I held onto Darcy's arm tight as I could.

"We've got to. I came for this."

She scrambled after M3's and the quickly vanishing dot of light on his camera.

All I could think was that this was the way that kids wound up with their faces on Missing posters and milk cartons. But what choice did I have except to follow?

# ROBERT
In the Mirror

Robert swallowed hard. The image on the laptop was a middle distance shot – blurry enough so that Darcy's face was not clearly identifiable. Or at least he hoped it wasn't, though with the kind of enhancement equipment available to cops, the quality of the image probably would not matter. And then there was the *djellabah*. Not many of those on the screen.

Thankfully, he and Billy were not in the frame. The WHUMP of pepper spray that had sent the crowd fleeing must have rattled whoever shot the video. For a while, the main image was lost and the camera caught random glimpses of legs, feet, the sidewalk, the sky. The sound track consisted of hacking, sputtering coughs.

Robert moved back to the barstool, ordered another beer. Things were not looking good. But what to do?

Six, maybe seven beers later he stumbled out of the *West End* hoping that a bit of cool air, a little quiet would help him sort the snippets of information he'd heard into a basis for a plan of action.

- Doefen was holed up in the Park at Belvedere Castle. The cops were keeping him under siege.

- Doefen had taken the Castle and the cops didn't stand a chance of getting it back.

- Doefen was somewhere in the Park, maybe the Ramble. The cops, glad to have him out of the way, didn't give a shit.

- Doefen had skipped town, and just as well. He was acting too much like a pop star to serve as a credible voice for WE.

- The debate between Doefen and Burgundy was off. Doefen said he would only speak with Burgundy if he came out into the street with everyone else.

- Doefen said he would participate in the press conference at the Waldorf, but only if a WE delegation was allowed in too.

Crazy. Crazy shit. Robert didn't know what to believe. All the chatter he'd heard inside was enough to make a sober man's head swim, and he was nowhere near sober, not by a long shot. The only consensus he could glean was that the Park seemed to be the place to look for Doefen.

He wished with all his heart that the cops really were looking the other way while Doefen holed up at Belvedere Castle, and that Darcy was there with him.

Not likely. But possible. The older he got, the more Robert was convinced that life was like that ... crazier than any fucking shit he could make up.

He leaned up against a street lamp to steady himself, considered his next move. Call Isabelle?

"Hi. I lost Darcy. And the Dalon boy too." That would really work well.

Robert checked his watch. The hands and numbers swam in and out of focus — one a.m., possibly two — mercifully too late and too early to call Isabelle.

Call the cops?

"Hi, I'm a Sixties activist with an outstanding arrest warrant for draft evasion, and for slugging a Pig during the Columbia takeover and I'd like to report two minors as missing."

Or he could wait until morning and go looking for Darcy and Billy himself.

The sane and sensible thing to do was to wait till morning.

The chances of finding his way around the Park in the dark were slim. He'd never actually been to Belvedere Castle, only heard about the treachery of its location high on a rocky ledge overlooking Turtle Pond, and the dangers of the Ramble, the thicket surrounding it, which was said to be rife with gruesome occurrence and a kind of prostitution that didn't interest him.

Robert took a deep breath. Morning would come soon enough. Best thing to do was to get a few hours of shut-eye back in the truck.

He lurched out from under the arc of lamplight, weaved along Broadway for a block, two before stumbling up against the plate glass of some storefront.

"You are one sorry asshole," he muttered, resting his reeling head against the cool glass. Gravity threatened to pull him down, lay him flat on the sidewalk, but he forced himself to move, take a step back from the glass. His own ghostly reflection, both recognizable and not entirely familiar, stared back at him – not quite as tall as he imagined himself to be. Lanky without being too thin. A dancer's body, Isabelle used to say. He flexed his bicep, reached inside his jacket to feel the sinewy contour of his arm that came from work, not the overblown cartoon muscle from working out in a gym.

Overall, a decent body, he decided. A good body. Not a body to be ashamed of.

Robert was not in the habit of studying his body. In the daily course of things, he saw his hands, forearms, sometimes his feet. And his dick. A couple of times a week, he looked into the pocked glass of the medicine cabinet door in the bathroom, the one and only mirror in his house, and saw his face. Not his whole face exactly but the parts he had to shave. The annoying ritual of scraping away his beard required seeking out the hollow in his left cheek that the razor somehow always missed, avoiding the white thread of scarred skin on his chin – a souvenir of a childhood look-ma-no-hands bike plunge down a steep hill. Shaving the coarse beard that sprouted from his absurdly soft and sensitive skin entailed facial contortions that in the stark lighting from the single bare bulb hanging overhead, made him look like a grimacing mad man. Whenever possible, he avoided shaving.

In the storefront window, Robert saw a face with scraggly stubble that he preferred to think looked devil-may-care, not merely grizzled and derelict. The whiteness of the beard confounded him, as did the old-geezer furrows running from the sides of his nose to his chin. His hairline seemed higher than he remembered, and came to something like a thinned out widow's peak. And the hair... He'd always thought of it as looking artlessly wind-blown, but saw that it was merely disheveled.

He wagged a finger at his reflection, noticing that in the unmerciful fluorescence of the street light his skin looked an unhealthy blue. The ghostly reflection wagged back.

The minute he returned to Glen Eddy, he'd go to a barber. Get a decent haircut. No more grooming himself with old nail scissors. And he'd shave regularly. Daily. Twice a day, if necessary. Better to patch the nicks on his face a million times, paste them over with tiny bits of toilet paper that would fall off like scabs when the blood dried than to look like this.

A sudden gust of wind blowing up from the Hudson slapped

him hard on the cheek, and filled the street with a familiar smell – the alluvial stink of river mud, and the rot of life forming and unforming. Vaguely pleasant and not, it made Robert's eyes sting.

With fingers stiff and unwieldy as a claw from the cold, he managed to zip his inadequate jacket, and wrapped his arms tight around his chest. In the plate glass he saw a shivering creature huddled in his own embrace.

How long had it been since anyone touched him?

Ages and ages and ages. He exchanged the occasional hug with Darcy. Other than that, nothing. Nothing and no one. No one in a really, really, really long time.

How long? How long? How long?

Months. Years. Too long. Too, too long.

To keep from crying, Robert shifted his attention to the bright wheels of glossy magazines arrayed in the storefront window, magazines with names he'd never heard of, devoted to subject matter he couldn't quite divine.

One minute he was staring at the magazine covers trying to remember what kind of business occupied that store when he was a student — a pizza place, maybe a deli — the next he found himself sitting on an outcropping of rock somewhere in Central Park with tears leaking out of his eyes.

"I am so completely fucked. So, so fucked. Such a total, fucking Fuck Up," he shouted at the sky, overcome by the enormity of having lost Darcy.

Huddling against a boulder, he tried to hearten himself with consoling thoughts. Darcy wasn't afraid of the dark, or of woods, or animals — not even the two-legged homo sapiens kind, which were the only kind likely to give her trouble in the city. She was innocent, but savvy. Savvy enough to find her way to a safe place, to take care of herself. He'd taught her some basic self-defense moves. Tai Kwan Do. She'd mastered the basic ju-jitsu throw. She was a survivor...

Just like him.

No matter what Isabelle said or wanted him to believe, in his heart Robert knew that Darcy was his daughter. Had to be.

How else explain slight and winsome overbite that she shared with his own mother? And weren't her baby pictures doubles of the fading black and white documents of Robert's own babyhood? He too was once a fair-haired, round-faced cherub. And didn't the tiny mole at the corner of her right eye match his own?

Flesh of his own flesh. Surely no harm could come to her without something in him knowing, without something in him being torn, ravaged, extinguished. His body would have trembled as a tree does at the first touch of an ax.

Drunk, and tired, and worried as he was, Robert noted that his heart kept pulsing without faltering. At worst, he felt a hangover coming on. Nothing more.

He took it all to mean that Darcy was alright. He'd find her. In the morning he'd find her...

A cold wind blew through the trees. Robert curled himself tight between two rocks, tucking his hands between his thighs, high up, near his crotch. His favorite sleep position...

Once as he lay dozing on his couch in that very same position, Isabelle had walked into his house without knocking as was her habit and announced, "I found a place in Middlecity that gets fresh tofu, so I brought you some."

She had it in his fridge before he could sit up.

"I just need to use your john and then I'm out of here to take Darcy to the doctor for her shots or Toul won't let her register for kindergarten."

Before he could think of a reason to stop her, Isabelle was half-way through his bedroom and on the way to the bathroom. By the time he caught up with her, she was standing at the foot of his bed with a look on her face that suggested that she'd just learned that the laws of gravity did not apply.

"What the hell... ?

"I'm so sorry," he bleated, sweeping the glossy magazines featuring women in leather that lay spread out on his bed into a pile.

"Really? You buy this shit?"

Thankfully, Isabelle appeared not to notice the thick electric cord that snaked along the baseboard of his bedroom into the dark of his closet where he kept his TV and stash of videos.

"I'm so very sorry," he stammered again. "And so embarrassed. I mean, yeah, they're mine."

"Well of course, they are," Isabelle snapped, the stupefaction lifting from her eyes. "It's your house. Who else's would they be?"

He didn't want to discuss it and he didn't have to. Isabelle spewed a whole bunch of paragraphs about porn's objectification of women while he studied the tongue and groove joinery of the floor boards. Mercifully, most of her harangue had faded from his memory, except the part when she got quiet and sad.

"You, of all people, always talking like you sit at the right hand of Betty Friedan and Gloria Steinem. You get off on this bondage shit?"

He muttered something about fantasy, residual habits from his pre-enlightenment teens. The privacy of his own home.

For a long time afterward, before coming over to his house Isabelle would call to admonish him to clean up. She would no longer let Darcy wander around his house without keeping her in sight. Worst of all, for a while she stopped asking him to babysit.

As if his habits had anything to do with Darcy. Or Isabelle, for that matter. He'd wished he could find the courage to assure her that the magazines she'd found were gone.

And they were. For a little while, they were. But he soon resumed buying the stuff, being careful to hide it better.

When he'd first moved into the farmhouse, he discovered a panel in the bedroom that was actually a door leading into a storage space that probably dated back to Prohibition when Glen Eddy was a pit stop for bootleggers of Canadian whiskey. He'd never told anyone about it. Not even Isabelle. It wasn't exactly a convenient hiding place, but it was where he kept his TV and videos.

Having long proclaimed his disdain for TV, and vowed that would never own one, he took care to watch the videos only late at night with the shades down, and the face of the monitor turned toward a windowless wall. In the unlit night of Glen Eddy, the blue light of a TV screen would have shone as bright as a beacon.

After a while Isabelle seemed to forget about the porn magazines. Or at least she acted like she did. Which didn't keep Robert from living in fear that one day she'd discover that his habits hadn't changed.

But no matter how real his dread, it never became so great that a little session with a magazine image or a video featuring the sultry suppleness of leather, the sweet surrender of bondage could not quell it.

As he lay shivering on the cold, hard ground in the Park, Robert imagined how happy he would feel with a studded black collar around his neck, and the voice of a mistress filling his ear, telling him what to do.

Oh to be securely pinioned by the spike of her heel, to inhale the warm funk of her leather boot, to feel the sting of her whip warming his skin.

Oh Mistress Silk, forgive me my trespasses, lead me into temptation, and deliver me unto the restraint of your rein.

Burrowing his face into the collar of his jacket, Robert slept.

# BILLY
Belvedere Castle


Darcy, M3 and I walked for a long time along a twisting path. Nobody said a word. Birds overhead and in the bushes were settling down for the night. Their twittering got loud and louder, then stopped.

M3 marched on like it was the middle of the day and we were on some kind of field trip. I kept telling myself that if he was a guy who was into doing evil, terrible things to kids, he would have done them already. I mean, there wasn't a single person on that path to see or hear him. And he'd had plenty of time alone with me and Darcy.

I took a deep breath. The soft, sweet smell of dirt and dry leaves – same as in my backyard — calmed me down. I let go of the idea that Darcy and I were going to end up dead, and the minute I did, I realized how totally wiped out I felt. I mean, I was ready to drop and sleep, right there on the path, in the dirt.

"Don't punk out on me now," M3 announced like somehow he had a window into the inside of my head, and succeeded in creeping me out all over again. "We're almost there."

"I can't keep going," I told him as the path began to climb. I felt like any minute I was going to start crying noooooo like the little kid in the subway tunnel.

"Yes you can," Darcy said, crouching down onto all fours like we were playing a game of Earth First Commandos against Redwood Loggers, "Just follow me."

It was kind of dumb, and made me mad that she was treating me like I was just a big baby, but it did get me up the hill. In fact, the climb ended up feeling shorter and nowhere near as bad as the one on the short cut to school.

"Careful, there's a step here," M3 warned right at the moment that the toe of my sneaker caught on it, and almost landed me flat on my face. What he forgot to say was that there were like a hundred dirt and logs steps cut into the side of that hill. By the time we reached the top, I was panting like Mrs. Dipple's old collie. And so was Darcy for that matter. Which tells you something, because usually, she could go all day and not get winded.

But at least I wasn't cold anymore.

At the top of the hill, we stepped out of the woods into some kind of wide open space, all lit up and crammed with people.

"Never mind the little party scene," M3 said. "First let me give you the lay of the land. Follow me."

He swung to the right, avoiding the crowd.

"Castle," he said, drawing our attention to it with a sweep of his arm. As if there was any way to miss the thing. I mean it was huge, with thick walls, slit windows that glowed like orange eyes, and turrets — four of them. Just like you see in cartoons and fairy tale books. A WE flag flew from each turret.

"Castle entrance." M3 pointed to a huge wooden door with a sculpture of a fire breathing dragon crouched over the arch.

I just stood there and stared. Even Darcy was quiet for awhile, hands on her hips, head thrown back, taking it all in.

M3 snapped his fingers in her face.

"Listen up," he said, "The castle is way cool, but what you really need to know about is over there."

We followed him onto a gravel path that went around the back of the castle. After just a few feet, it became narrower, darker, closed in by pines.

Dark. Darker than dark, and very spooky. I was just about to beg to go back, when M3 focused the monitor light on his headset, and said, "Remember this tree."

Who could forget it? The trunk was all warty and shaped like a crooked finger as if a giant witch was buried there and trying to claw her way out of the ground.

I must have shrieked or something because next thing I knew Darcy's hand was over my mouth.

"Follow your breath, in and out," she said. "Open your eyes. Let thoughts form, rise and let them go."

I had the biggest urge to bite her.

M3 stepped behind the tree, and pointed his light at the ground, at a dark hole in the ground, a wide-open, black mouth.

Quick as a lizard, he slipped inside it, and Darcy followed, dragging me behind her.

It was a stairway. An escape route M3 called it.

"Remember it," he said. "You never know when it might come in handy."

Why we needed an escape route he didn't say, and I didn't

want to know, and I was way too scared to ask.

"It will take you east," he said like that was supposed to mean something. "And it connects to the 79th Street Transverse."

Transverse. As in diagonal. The name anchored me. In my head I started making a map. My map of the Park. Transverse – a thick line running from the lower left side of the map, which I thought of as Glen Eddy, over to the upper right corner filled by a big orange sun labeled East. The trick, as always, was to make the map match up with things in the real world.

From where we stood inside the stairwell, I could not see cars, but I could hear the comforting rumble of traffic.

Transverse, as in road. A road east. And probably west too. A road home.

M3 led us back up the stairs, onto the hill, past the castle. The red ivy on the rear turrets and walls made the castle look like it was on fire.

We squeezed our way along the edge of the crowd in the courtyard, out toward the far end of the castle grounds where we came to a platform fenced off by a rusty rail.

"Lookout point," M3 said and waved at the empty air straight ahead.          "Due north this way."

In the fading light it was hard to see much. Far below and to the west, the land curved like a tail. To the right, a steep cliff ended in a bluff with a dark hollow in it like a giant eye. Directly below, there was water. Turtle Pond, M3 called it. It was all straight out of fairy tale book 101 – stone castle set high up on a pile or rock.

I marked it all on the map in my head.

Poking and shoving, M3 led us back into the crowd and inched us around to the western edge of the plaza.

"Notice the dense ground cover," he said pointing into the gathering dark outside the plaza.

It was impossible to see anything but trees, and the gloom between them.

"A good place to know about – just in case."

In case of what? Once again, M3 didn't say and I didn't want to ask. I was tired and hungry, and so done with listening to him.

"Shakespeare Garden is down that way," he said, pointing at

nothing I could see. "And the Delacorte Theater too."

I didn't even try to figure out where they fit on the map in my head.

All I could think was that I wanted to be in the truck with Robert, heading home. Somewhere out there in the almost-dark where I couldn't seem him, Robert had to be looking for Darcy and me, cracking his knuckles the way he does when he's nervous. Or at least I hoped he was looking for us.

"So what about Doefen ?" I heard Darcy ask M3. "Where do I find him?"

"Ah,"said M3 and gave Darcy a smile full of crooked teeth. "That is the million dollar question."

*"I am he as you are he and you are me and WE are all together,"* he sang as if that was that answer.

The words sounded vaguely familiar, but I couldn't place them.

"Right," Darcy said and smiled *"You and me and WE are all together."*

Once she sang the line, I recognized the tune. The Beatles! How could I have missed it? I mean, fucking Robert was always singing some Beatles thing or another. Darcy's mom too. And Darcy had picked up the habit from them.

And now there was M3 doing the same thing. What the hell was up with that? I mean was I the only one who didn't have a Beatles line ready for every life situation?

Anyway, right after quoting the Beatles, the M3 dude up and vanished. Abandoned us. Left us there, in the middle of a zillion people we didn't know. A zillion people who didn't know us and didn't give a shit who we were or what happened to us. And Darcy acted like she was OK with all of it.

It was all one big party out there in the castle courtyard. People spooled and unspooled from one group to another. White-haired geezers were hanging out with dudes who had spiked, dyed hair, and dreads. Little kids were running all over the courtyard even though it was probably way past their bedtime. All kinds of dogs – big, scary ones, little yappy ones chased after each other, barking. There were even a bunch of kids skateboarding along the edges of the crowd.

Here and there, the light from cell phone screens flickered like they were candles, and people gathered around laptop screens like they were campfires.

"Where you from, dude?" everybody was asking everybody else.

Darcy jumped right in, blabbety blabbing about Glen Eddy just long enough to sound friendly before she moved on to the only subject she really cared about.

Where was Doefen?

Nobody in the courtyard could tell her. And it wasn't like they were bothered about it. Everybody looked happy, like it was enough to just be there. Enough to know that they were part of Doefen's thing. Part of WE.

"How long have you been with WE?" was the question that came right after the where you from? And "What are you working on for WE?" came right after that.

I have to say, the answers sounded totally unsnarky to me. Everybody honestly believed every word that came out of his or her own mouth. Everybody was excited. There was all kinds of talk about slow food and organic farming, and about how big farming was poisoning the land, polluting the oceans, making everyone fucking fat, and pushing the country into all kinds of wars. Opt out. Just say no to irradiated, adulterated, genetically fucked, super-processed fake food.

That was the general gist of things, and it was kinda, sorta like listening to Darcy when she got going on the subject. Only multiplied by like a couple hundred people.

And then there was the stuff that was way over my head. Economics. Something about Doefen's health care plan for farmers. Or not just farmers, but anybody who was self-employed. Or actually, everybody.

Bottom line — everybody at the castle was really psyched to be thinking about what WE could do. WE's network grid model, whatever that was, combined with technology would change and restructure the power dynamic, change things for the better.

"You got that right," said a some random guy in a wheelchair who suddenly rode up to Darcy and started chanting,

*I've had enough of reading things*
*by neurotic-psychotic*
*pigheaded politicians*
*all I want is some truth*

The crowd on the plaza joined right in, *"Just give us some truth."*

There it was, the Beatles thing again. Beatles. Beatles. Beatles. Except coming out of the wheel chair dude's mouth, the song sounded dirty – like any minute he was going to crack up the way sixth grade guys do when they tell sex jokes at the back of the playground. Shaking his shoulders like he was dancing, he started swinging his chair this way and that, scaring people into jumping out of the way, and then laughing at them. "Aw baby, did you think the Crip was going to hurt you?"

I have to admit, I just didn't take to the dude. Part of it was the whole Beatles thing. But there was something else too, something I didn't have a name for. Maybe it was the combination of stringy old man hair, and the cigarette hanging off his lip, and the yellow skin around his even yellower fingernails. Or maybe it the way he cracked his knuckles like he wanted you to think that he was some tough, bad guy – like the ones on the TV cop shows that Darcy's dad always watched. And, for sure, it had something to do with his chair – all souped up like the cars that some of the Seniors at school roared around in. And I hated the way he kept calling himself a Crip, as if that made him special, or gave him a free pass to act like an asshole.

Truth is, right from the start I had this feeling that the wheelchair dude wasn't a cripple at all. I mean, his legs looked OK – thick, muscley – like he could go cruising around on them, no problem. I couldn't stop thinking that maybe he did, secretly, when everybody was asleep and there was no one to see him.

As far as I could tell, the only thing keeping his from walking was that he was way fat. I mean whale-sized fat. And obnoxious about it. There were people all over Glen Eddy just as fat as him, maybe fatter, and you didn't see them zooming around in around in wheelchairs like they were race cars and expecting people to get out of the way or get killed.

Bottom line, I felt creeped out by the dude, *and* felt bad for feeling creeped out.

I was about to beg Darcy to leave the Beatles sing-along, when a pale and skinny dude with long, curly hair roller-bladed up to her.

"M3 sent me," he said, high-fiving her. "Told me I needed to give you something to eat." He shoved an apple at Darcy.

She took it and smiled up at him like she'd waited her whole life for him and that apple to arrive, which sent the dude wobbling on his rollerblades like the ground had suddenly shifted.

"Hey," he high-fived her again when he regained his balance. "Good to see you up here. What you did today for WE was awesome."

"I came for Doefen," she corrected him, and passed the apple to me without even taking a bite, passed it like she wasn't every bit as starving hungry as I was. I mean, what she did was enough to steal my heart ten times over.

The apple was highlighter-green. In an anime cartoon, it would have been a poison fruit for sure. But I bit into that apple and it turned out to be the apple-iest apple I'd ever tasted— crisp, and cold, and sour-sweet like those fizz candies. I practically had to force myself to give it back to Darcy.

We chomped down that apple in like four bites, while the dude on the rollerblades gave us an earful about how WE was not about leaders and followers, not about Doefen and an army of supporters.

You could tell from the way Darcy's face went tight that she wasn't liking what he had to say. The dude either didn't notice, or didn't care, but he definitely got that we were still hungry.

"Sorry that you guys missed the pizza and juice," he said, and offered us a plastic bag full of something yellow and crumbly that he pulled out of his jacket pocket.

"Raw ziti," he said. "Tastes like potato chips."

It didn't, but we ate it anyway.

The dude nodded and smiled.

"There's some Chinese take-out floating around too," he pointed into the dark behind the tower. "Course, it's full of salt and all kinds of shit chemicals."

I was all for going in search of it, but Darcy wasn't one to let a little something like starvation sidetrack her from the obsession with finding Doefen.

Where was he?

The dude shrugged, and went on again about how WE wasn't really about Doefen. It was a spontaneous community, a network that gathered, in a flash, by way of cell phones, and pagers, and the web to work on a cooperative project. And when that project was done, then poof, WE would disperse.

Disappear.

Which the dude did after being summoned by a sudden, high *whoooo* from the phone clipped to the waistband of his falling down jeans.

"Later," he called out over his shoulder, gave a toothy smile, and melted away into the crowd.

I expected Darcy to get all bent out of shape by the whole no leaders thing, but instead she got totally psyched about the spontaneous community part.

"It's a great way to help Doefen do what needs to be done. WE – and that includes me and you – have work to do."

Somehow, Darcy managed to overlook the fact that, unlike everyone else in the courtyard, we didn't have a single electronic gadget to call anyone into action.

The way she figured it, our first step was to locate Doefen.

"Nobody will say it, but I just know that he's got to be in the castle. I can feel it," she said pointing at her heart. "And he needs to hear what I have to say."

She circled around to the back of the castle to see what she could see. Of course I followed.

Leaning back onto her heels, she took in the height, the mass of the tower. I did the same. Dark. Just one tiny window way up — too high to reach. The tower looked pretty rock solid to me.

Darcy sank down onto the low stone wall that encircled the castle and separated it from the rest of the hill and the city below. I perched next to her, inched close and closer to warm myself against her.

The lights of far-away buildings flickered through the trees like fireflies. The air smelled Pine Sol clean. The urge to curl up and sleep took hold, bent me to its will. I nodded against Darcy's shoulder. I was already half-dreaming when she suddenly sank her fingers into my thigh.

"Look," she whispered.

A yellow blade of light had appeared at the base of the tower. As we watched, it got wide and wider. A door squeaked open. Out came a dude the size of a football linebacker. After propping an orange traffic cone against the door, he struck a match, lit a cigarette. A bit of smoke drifted our way.

Darcy pointed her nose like a hound, took a little sniff, then another, and then a deep, deep breath. "I so hate cigarettes, but I love that smell," she said, and sucked the smoke way, way down.

## GUARD
Entry


"I love the smell of a burning cigarette."

A pipsqueaky voice came out of the almost dark. The voice of a kid. A girl.

But it was so out of nowhere sudden that it scared the shit out of me. I mean the girl was practically on top of me before I saw her. Either my eyes took that long to adjust to the dark, or she moved that silently.

I recognized her right away. Not from her face, just the robe thing. Same as in that video that everybody was watching on the net.

There was already talk in the tower about whether the girl would be good for the cause or not. I should have scoped her out more, but just then all I wanted to do was have a cigarette in peace. Lighting up inside the tower was not allowed. I was surrounded by health fanatics. When I tried taking out a pack of smokes, everybody reacted like I was mass murderer with an Uzi or something.

I figured the girl was looking to bum a smoke so I offered her one, even though I hate the way people who don't buy have no shame about hitting up those of us who do.

"No, thank you," she said like some little Miss Manners, and started in on how smoking was a vile habit and bad for your health.

"Fuck off," I told her, but she just went right on talking. Told me that when she was little she would go around the diner in her town telling all the smokers that cigarettes were beh, and that they had to put them out.

I blew a nice big lung full of smoke into her face.

She sucked it down. "That smells soooo good."

"Damn, girl," I said and shook a cigarette up out of the pack. "Take one, or scram."

She shook her head no like it killed her to do it, and went right on talking. Told me that smell of burning tobacco was one of her favorite smells, right up there with smell of gas being pumped, and the smell of skunk if it was far off.

I agreed with her on the gas part, but not the stink of skunk.

Weird, I called her right to her face. Not that it mattered. She didn't shut up.

On my next exhale, I blew a great big ring of smoke that hung in the still air like a lasso.

That impressed her. "Cool," she said, inhaled again like it was her last breath on earth, and finally just stood very quiet and still.

I probably managed three more hits off that cigarette with her watching me, and then I was done. I flicked the stub and it flew over her shoulder in orange arc.

"Catch you later," I told her.

"For sure," she said. "For sure."

As if. I headed back inside.

# BILLY
Inside the Tower

It was a no-brainer that Darcy pissed off the smoker dude. Maybe that's why he didn't hang around to make sure that the door really shut once he pulled away the cone. Creaking on its hinges, the door drifted closed behind him, narrowing the rectangle of light inch by slow inch. When only a crack of brightness remained, Darcy wedged the toe of her boot between the door and jamb. I was right behind her.

Very quietly she counted to sixty twice, before grabbing my hand and pushing into the stairwell.

Bare stone walls. Steep steps spiraling up. No place to hide.

We crouched against the wall, holding our breath. A minute. Two. Voices, laughter drifted down from the top of the stairs.

Darcy got down on all fours, and motioned for me to follow. Crumpled coffee cups lay scattered all over the place. I sort of liked and hated to see that the WE people were litterers like the rest of the world. A pyramid of empty beer cans teetered at the edge of the steps like a marker to point the way, or more likely it was a booby trap set for trespassers like us. Super, extra carefully, my knees shaking I crept past it and followed Darcy to the uppermost landing.

Pressed flat against the flagstones, we peered into a room at the top of the stairs, which was dimly lit and crammed full of people – all of them grey-haired, fleshy, big-boned. Even the women. They looked more like the relatives at one of my Mom's family reunions than a meeting of political activists. One thing for sure, no one in that room looked like he or she had ever been anywhere near dirt or live animals.

The room was a total mess. Bunches of WE posters were piled high on a table, and stood stacked against the walls. Leaflets lay scattered all over the sad, shit-colored couch. Empty coffee cups, pizza boxes, soda cans were everywhere.

Slobs. I decided that I liked that. The way I saw it, the last thing the world needed was neatness fanatics setting out to change things.

Everyone boomed at everyone else about WE in what might

as well have been a foreign language. I recognized a phrase here and there.          Something, something "to benefit the rich," which was bad; very, very bad to judge by the tone of voice. Ditto the stuff about the poor paying disproportionately more. But a "uniform charge" – that was some sort of good thing. It took me a minute to figure out that they meant uniform as in "the same," not as in team outfit, which I was used to hearing Principal Toul go on about.

The word – tax — echoed around the room more or less constantly – tax vote, tax cut, tax equity. Somehow, no one sounded as pissed off as my Dad did whenever he talked about taxes.

A boom box set on the only chair in the room blared out reports from a 24/7 news channel. More political speak. Unintelligible.

Every once in a while a single voice would suddenly rise above the babble and deliver a pronouncement about something — conservation easements, end of entitlements.

I don't know if Darcy understood any more of it than I did. Or wanted to. All I know is that she suddenly stood up, and shouted, "Stop."

And everyone in the room shut up.

With an expression of surprise and satisfaction, she stared back at the pack who stared at her. "I'm looking for Doefen."

"Lots of people are," a beefy guy sneered. With his curly sidechops and hunter plaid shirt, he looked like the one of the regulars at the dive-bar in Glen Eddy.

"I need to speak with Doefen."

"How'd you get in here?"

"Through the door."

"Anything you need to say to Doefen, you can say to me." The dude who walked up to us was the hugest human I'd ever seen – way the hell bigger than the smoker and all the other men in the room. He didn't thump his chest, but he might as well have. "The name's Tre Moyle."

"I've got to tell him myself."

"Oh, well then…" Smirking and looking way stupid – kind of like the hunter in the cartoon movie of *Beauty and the Beast*, Tre pointed to a guy with a zit scarred face and droopy mustache. "There he is and be quick about it."

From across the room, in the dim light, maybe, maybe the guy could have passed for Doefen. But as soon as he opened his mouth, even I could tell that his voice was all wrong.

"Come on over," he said, his voice sounding all thin and scratchy – more like steel wool than the wild roses that Darcy went on about every time she played a clip of Doefen on the library computer. Which she did at least a zillion times, or at least that's how many times she made me listen with her.

So Darcy ignored the faker and after scanning the room marched over to a small ropey dude with sun-bleached pony tail and baggy denims. He didn't exactly match the pictures of Doefen that we'd seen on the net either, but without a moment's hesitation, Darcy introduced herself to him.

"What do you want with Doefen ?" he said, sounding surprisingly gentle and kind.

In the clips on the net, he sounded like just another guy trying to make a point, but there was something about him in person that made you want to pay attention. For one thing, he didn't get all loud, or get an attitude like *don't bug me I'm too important*, or *when I whisper, people listen.* Somehow, he made you feel like he really wanted to hear what was on your mind.

Darcy shook his hand, and smiled like it was the first day of spring after a long, hard winter. "I've come with a message."

Doefen started to shift from foot to foot, and look at a point somewhere way past Darcy's head.

"I swore I'd find you even if I had to wear my legs down to my knees," Darcy continued. "I would have preferred to stay home, but I had to do this."

At which point Doefen started to look anything but happy. His eyes never left Darcy's face, but you could see that he was backing away from her an inch at a time.

Darcy kept at him. "You were born to lead WE. Born to lead, period. You, WE will fight and truth will prevail. I'll help you."

"Some guys have all the luck," Tre Moyle shouted. Everyone except Doefen laughed. "Let me know when you're ready for me to escort her out."

Darcy gave Tre a look that suggested that she could see him, see him right down to his boxer shorts, and that they were not exactly clean. But what she said to him was, "Don't fight me. WE needs supporters, worthy people. It needs you. Remember that."

For like a second, Tre actually sucked in his gut and stood taller. Or maybe I only remember it that way because of all the crap movies I've seen where stuff like that happens. It would have been a whole other story if Tre had actually transformed into a one hundred percent hero. Truth is he never really stopped being a stupid hulk with an appetite for throwing his weight around.

Doefen basically ignored Tre, and steered Darcy to a quieter place in the far corner of the room.

"Don't do it," Tre roared. "This one is going to be nothing but trouble. "Don't listen to her, and whatever you do don't encourage her."

I tried to follow Darcy. Tre blocked the way. Words were exchanged. Next thing I knew, two big guys had me under the elbows, and I was out the door lying nose to nose with the orange traffic cone.

A few scrapes. No bones broken. I brushed some dead leaves and cigarette stubs off my clothes. I sat hunched up in the dark — probably it was only for a few minutes, but it felt like hours — shivering, watching the door, waiting for Darcy to finish telling Doefen all about her plans for him and to come back out to me.

## BILLY
Secret Things


Darcy came out of the tower looking like she'd just taken one of her super long, long, long baths — her look of maximum happiness.

For a girl who could hardly sit still — always running, jumping, climbing, boarding or biking — she loved getting into a tub. She'd even take a bath at random times, like the middle of the day when no one was making her get cleaned up. Her favorite place to soak was at Robert's house. He had one of those old, deep tubs with claw feet, and would let her stay in it for like the whole day. Which left me sitting on the grass, or his porch with nothing to do but wait for her to come out and play.

And what did she do the whole time that the water was getting cold and colder and every inch of her skin was turning to prune?

She'd sing.

I could hear her all the way out on the porch. Her singing was way amazing – a huge voice coming out of a small girl body. In the school chorus she was able to hit the high notes like they were nothing. Mrs. Allison probably would have given Darcy solos and big parts in the music concerts, if wasn't for Toul. All the teachers knew that he had it in for Darcy and were scared of getting on his bad side, especially the new teachers like Mrs. Allison. So Darcy spent her time in music class stuck in back row of the chorus with the rest of us who sounded like sick cats.

Until middle school, Darcy used to sing made up songs all the time, and everyone was cool with it. She sang the song of *Windy the bird, bird in the Fairy Tree*, and songs about the pictures in our readers instead of the words that were written there. But all of a sudden, in sixth grade, the teachers started getting down on her for it, and calling her singing disruptive. Sometimes they even gave her detention. All the grownups except her parents and Robert shushed her. I have to give Robert that. He just went right on smiling at all her songs like he was hearing them for the first time.

Trouble was, Robert sang along with her like they were his

songs too — which was annoying as all hell. I mean, his voice sucks, and I hated the blissed out faces he made – like oooh, oooh, oooh is everyone getting what a special thing Darcy and I have going on? I think it bugged Darcy too. But I'm guessing she loved Robert too much to ever let him know.

Point is, Darcy left that tower singing — *"The more WE work together, together, together, the happier we'll be,"* which was straight out of one the kid tapes we used to listen to together.

I wanted to grab her and spin with her like we were little again, but it probably would have just embarrassed both of us.

"So what did Doefen say?"

She shrugged and settled herself with her back against the wall where I'd been sitting. "Not that much."

I begged, nagged for details.

"At first he said I should get an MBA and come back when I'm older."

"He dissed you."

"No. No. He just needed to be convinced that I can be of use to him now."

"Like how?"

"You know. All the stuff I told you before."

"So he was OK with taking on Burgundy and everything?"

"Sort of. I told him that people need to hear the truth."

"Meaning he doesn't really want to do it?"

"Well, he'd rather be back home raising goats. But then we talked and he understood that wasn't an option right now."

I tried to get her to tell me exactly what she said and he said, how she sold Doefen on her plans for him, and her own part in them, but Darcy just smiled.

"We said secret things that no one knows or can know except us."

I sulked at being excluded.

"If I told you they wouldn't be secret anymore," Darcy said and pulled me close, tucked my head under her chin, and wrapped her arm around shoulder. "Anyway, you know all the important stuff."

I was too exhausted to dispute it. Wrapped around each other like kittens, we nodded off.

Next thing I knew, we were sprawled out on the damp ground blinking the morning sun out of our eyes.

141

And M3 was standing over us, camera running.

"Kiddo, kiddo, kiddo," he said like Darcy was the only one there. "Rise and shine. I have orders from Big D himself to bring you inside."

Darcy was on her feet and brushing pine needles off the *djella-bah*, while I was still trying to sit up. She went from dead-sleep to fully revved in like a millisecond. It was totally awesome.

She grabbed my hand, and I stumbled after her and M3 towards the castle. We didn't get very far before the creepy dude in the wheelchair whizzed up at motorcycle speed, laid down some rubber, and stopped dead in front of us.

"I never properly introduced myself last night. The name is Frank Arras," he said, sticking out a Pillsbury doughboy hand at Darcy, and she shook it.

"Pleased to meet you."

Pleased? What the hell was there to be pleased about? For starters, the guy was smoking, and he reeked of that sad, burned-out cigarette stench that my dad carried home on his clothes when he came back from his once a month poker night. And then there was the stink that came from the bulging, greasy bags of food that were hanging off his chair.

"I've been wanting to have a little moment with you," Frank said as he busied himself with lighting another cigarette off the one that was hanging off his lip, burning down to a stub. The way he sucked and sucked on the thing totally grossed me out. His too tight black t-shirt with the body's insides – ribs, and spine and heart and stuff sequined all over it — blinged and heaved over his blubbery chest and gut every time he took a breath.

It must have grossed out Darcy too because she just stood there looking straight past him.

"I know what you're thinking," he told her after blowing out a grey cloud of smoke. "What does this crip want?"

Darcy shook her head. "I..."

He cut her off. "The answer is, I don't want nothing. Nothing at all from you."

Nothing. Except that he was eyeballing her the whole time like he was a cat and she was some dumb cartoon canary he was getting set to swallow whole.

"Yeah. I'm just here to help" he went on. "And to let you know, and to help you understand that you want me, and need me because I'm a really good weapon to have in your arsenal."

Coming out of his mouth, the word weapon sounded like something you definitely wouldn't want your Mom to know about.

"Truth is the only weapon I need," Darcy told him.

Frank slapped the fender covering the fat rubber wheel of the chair. A ring crammed onto his pinky banged against the metal. "Oh, that is rich," he howled throwing back his head, flashing yellow teeth. "I do love that."

Darcy started to walk away, but quick as a blink Frank zipped the chair around to block her. "You getting this?" he called to M3 whose camera was blinking away like crazy, definitely in record mode.

Stretching his neck and whole body toward Darcy the way snakes in nature movies do before they strike, Frank went from laughing to snarling,

"Wrong babydoll, you need *me.*"

"Don't call me that."

"What? Oh you mean babydoll..." He laughed another mouth wide open laugh. "You think I can't see what you're hiding under that baggy rag thing, *babydoll?*"

"I told you. Don't speak to me like that."

"Babydoll and babyface you're going to have to cut the prissy shit if you want to play with the big boys."

Darcy took a step to the side and around the chair. This time Frank let her push past. "OK. OK, Missy, I'm sorry. But listen up. I really can help you. I was doing protest marches back when you were still an unfertilized egg. Hear me out."

Which she did, later that day after her private, little meeting with Doefen.

By then, thanks to Doefen, we'd been moved into a tiny room at the base of the corkscrew staircase in the tower. Darcy was way excited to be a short climb away from Doefen. Me, I was just glad that we weren't going to be sleeping outside again.

In a matter of hours, we went from being treated like crashers, who Tre Moyle was itching to boot out, to being greeted like special guests. Actually, me — not so much. Just Darcy.

All of a sudden, she was the *It Girl* of Belvedere Castle. All morning long, everyone who was anyone in WE came to talk to her. They all wanted to know her, wanted to be her friend. To hear them talk, you'd think they'd all been hanging around, just waiting for her to come along.

Me? I was just the silent little sidekick no one paid attention to. Propped up against the wall, I listened to everything that went down, and tried to understand enough so I wouldn't come off as a totally useless jerk when Darcy wanted to kick stuff around with me.

Frank's spiel, when it was his turn, went something like this:

"I'm supersized and so are my wheels. I'm an ugly, foul-mouthed motherfucker, pain in the ass. People hate me. But like it or not, they got to act right when I'm around because I'm a crip."

To which Darcy said, "Those who demand respect seldom deserve it."

Huddled there against the wall, smiling into my knees, I was thinking, "Take that motherfucker."

Frank didn't even blink.

"No matter what, it don't look good for a cop in a protest situation to get photographed beating up on a guy in a wheelchair. You understand what I'm saying? Stand next to me, and you're safe."

Darcy responded by giving him an earful about faith in the cause, and the power of truth to keep her from harm.

"Blah, blah, blah," Frank said, "very poetic. You can go on dreaming about the ability of truth to open people's hearts and make them do the right thing, but let me tell you, put together a couple of rows of crips like me in a march, and you've got yourself a good, solid first line of defense. Give us some decent weapons and you've got pre-emptive strike capability."

"Words and banners are the only weapons WE will use."

Which amused Frank no end. When he stopped laughing he said, "That's what you say now. But just wait till the mayor and police chief sic *Archangel* on you.

"WE acts through non-violence."

"Oh that's good. Really, really good Missy." Frank poked a sausage finger in the general direction of Darcy's navel. "Let me explain to you about *Archangel*.

I didn't exactly follow the whole thing, but the gist of it was that *Archangel* was like a gang of cops, who were kind of free-range cops who did whatever shit the regular cops couldn't or wouldn't do because it was quasi-illegal. The city's elite security unit Frank called them. He ended by quoting shit he said was from the *Archangel* manual.

"*Archangel Security Officers* use force only as a last resort, when defending themselves or those in need."

"Except that force is not their last resort," he added as if Darcy was too dumb to get that he was being sarcastic.

Darcy didn't give an inch. "WE acts only through non-violence."

Frank flicked a long ash from his cigarette and smiled. "Have it your way, but let me tell you something. There are some people who need a little hurting. Helps them understand things better... know what I mean?"

The way he said some people sounded to me like Frank meant that it could included Darcy and Doefen and WE if she crossed him.

"No!" Darcy turned the kind of red I'd only seen on my Dad when he wanted to punch somebody's lights out. "None of that. I would rather die than do anything that would make blood flow."

Of course, I figured she had to be thinking of the woman she'd hit in the subway tunnel and her promise never to raise her hand against anyone again.

Frank practically choked himself laughing. "Okay, then. But keep my number on speed dial just in case."

He went right into another laughing fit when Darcy told him she didn't have a cell phone.

"What planet are you from, babydoll?" he said as he fished through the plastic bags hanging off the handles of his chair. "Take this one." He handed Darcy something that was the size of one of his cigarette boxes. "It's prepaid. And disposable — like a toothbrush. Use it till it's used up."

Darcy clicked a few buttons. A screen lit up.

I inched over to get a closer look. "We can call our moms," I whispered, but Darcy shook her head. "I didn't come all this way, just to be told to come home."

"Have fun, kiddles," Frank roared as he zoomed off singing "*WE loves you, yeah, yeah, yeah,*" to the tune of the Beatles song. *WE loves you and you know that can't be bad.*

"You have your ways. I have mine," Darcy called after him.

# ROBERT
Waking Up


A long thong of braided leather bound Robert's manacled wrists to the center post of the barn. Down on all fours, he was licking the sharp toe of a red stiletto. Veronique towered over him wearing a black beekeeper's veil and a few bands of studded leather with strategically placed buckles.

She snapped a whip across his bare ass. "Down, slave!"

He pressed his chest and nipples harder into the straw, raised his ass still higher, savored the coolness of the barn's damp air on his stinging flesh.

"Clean it!" The whip burned the command into his skin. His cock, already sprung and hard, swelled still more between his thighs as he licked Veronique's shoe.

She shoved the handle of her crop hard against his forehead, forced him up onto his knees. "Cover that puny prick of yours."

"Yes, mistress." Robert arched, thrust his pelvis up towards his bound hands, But the leather thong held tight. His hard-on stood even more exposed.

Veronique strode over to one of the hives, unlatched it, dipped the handle of her crop inside.

"Please mistress..."

"Silence!"

Robert moaned and looked across the barn... A familiar figure stood silhouetted in the sunlit doorway.

Darcy!

Robert yelped, snatched a handful of straw to cover himself. Woke up.

He drew one shaky breath. Another. Waited for the quaking in his chest to subside. He was alone. Thankfully, all alone. Nothing but cold bare earth below him. Above him only sky. Alone... Alone in the Park. No barn. No Veronique.

Vaguely, the events of the night came back to him. The stumbling attempt to walk back to the truck after leaving the bar. The conviction that took hold as soon as he took a few steps that anything less than an immediate search for Darcy and Billy was cowardly, unworthy. The entry into the Park through the

Stranger's Gate, which he confused for the Warriors' Gate. How ironic. How apt. What was he if not a stranger? Lost in the dark, no idea which unlit path to take. Lost. All alone in a small wood, tripping over unseen tree roots, falling once, and again, and again. Entering a wide and seemingly open field that was mined throughout with boulders that were invisible in the black night. Falling again. Getting up. Turning this way and that.

A hopeless undertaking.

Unable to get his bearings, he sat down. And stayed down. Better to sit than to walk in aimless circles.

He had not intended to sleep, only to rest.

And here it was, morning.

His dick pressed uncomfortably against the metal teeth of his fly. He nudged it through his pants pocket. A big, fat boner. Lately, his morning hard-ons had dropped off in quantity and quality, but this was a really good one. A shame to waste it. If only he could find a nice, private place before it went away.

Robert forced one leg, then the other out of the fetal curl he'd slept in. His joints felt as though they'd rusted. What goes on four legs at dawn, two at noon and three at dusk?

Man! He'd learned the answer to the Sphinx's riddle in his classics class at Columbia. Now he knew it in his bones.

His clothes felt unpleasantly damp, as though he'd wet himself. *I grow old, I grow old,* he thought. Soon I will wake up with pee stains on my pants. Just a matter of time.

What he wouldn't give for a warm place to piss and shit. He longed for his warm bathroom. The half hour he spent on the toilet each morning drinking coffee, reading the paper, picking his nose was the best time of the day — especially if it happened to be a clear day with the sun pouring in through the window behind his head. So pleasurable. So innocent.

A hangover headache declared itself as soon as he stood up. He cursed it along with the misery of his aching joints and full bladder. Several minutes spent rubbing all the acupressure points that Isabelle said were supposed to relieve headaches brought distraction, but not much relief. He wished he'd thought to bring pain medicine.

He looked around. Overnight, the cold snap had ignited the colors in the trees. The maples burned like tongues of flame – yellow, orange, bright red. Pigeons flew amongst them grey as ash.

A pale sun without any warmth hovered at the horizon in a sky the color of tarnished metal. A nearby tree, bent as though reeling in shock or horror, creaked in the wind. Another, gnarled and arthritic, reached toward it as if to console it.

Robert shivered.

He couldn't remember the last time he'd slept outdoors. Probably not since college, when contemplating the blue void of sea and sky at Jones Beach drew him away from a stuffy dorm room or an early morning discussion of Plato in a dusty classroom. Never in all his years on the farm had he felt the slightest urge to forsake the comfort of quilt and bed for raw earth and a bare sky. As soon as darkness fell, he liked to settle into the soft shadowed rooms of his house. From his chair, he relished the ecstatic clamor of night creatures waking from their daytime torpor. The fur-winged moths, steely owls, skittering bats, needle-nosed mosquitoes and all their stinging brethren were welcome to the world beyond his windowed walls. He could do without dodging, and swatting, and being bitten by them.

Sometimes, at night, Robert heard loud crashes coming from the woods around his house probably made by smallish creatures prowling through the brush. He never felt compelled to investigate. It had been years since he so much as stepped out onto his porch at night. Not even the splendor of a starry sky could lure him out.

One night he dreamed that the crashing sound came from trees uprooting themselves and walking around like men. When he awoke and peered out the window, he was vaguely surprised to find the woods standing where they were the day before. The feeling of unease engendered by the dream never entirely left him.

Robert hunkered down into his jacket. His hand closed on a flattened peanut butter sandwich buried in the depths of his pocket. When had he last eaten? Hours and hours ago, his body answered, his whole being suddenly becoming an empty maw. He couldn't unwrap the sandwich fast enough.

Poor Darcy and Billy had to be equally famished. Anxiously, Robert checked his pockets for the rest of the sandwiches. Thankfully, they had survived his night wanderings.

Orienting himself so that the spire of the Empire State was in front of him and the Dakota towers to his right, Robert began to hurry south in the general direction of Belvedere Castle. With each step, his bladder screamed out for attention. He searched urgently for a clump of tall grass, a bush, any secluded place where he could take a piss without his cock being out there for everyone to see.

But eyes were everywhere. Joggers, mostly. Dog walkers. Strangers, but still witnesses.

Robert stopped, did a 360 – in each direction he saw empty stretches of grass punctuated by trees. Incredible trees. Even in his desperate state, he could not help but notice that in the Park's open, sparse style of planting, each tree was unique, unforgettable, a sculpture. Some, molded by wind, bark burnished to a bronze patina by weather, stood posed in mad arabesques. Others stooped between earth and sky, or stretched lanky limbs to improbable heights.

Natural woods, the woods in Glen Eddy, looked nothing like this. They were dense, too dense, to invite study. Rampant underbrush obscured detail.

Despairing of any camouflage, Robert walked over to the biggest, widest tree — an oak — and leaned up against it as though to rest, unzipping only as much as necessary. A slack stream splashed out of his swollen dick, wetting the toe of his boot, the ground, the swirling-skirt drapery of the tree's roots. He tightened his grip on his dick, but failed to create the bright tight arc of piss that used to shoot out of him effortlessly. Widening his stance, he lifted his pelvis fixing his eyes on the delicate pattern of pinching and pleating in the tree bark to avoid thinking about who might be watching.

A moment later, the aching pleasure of relieving his bladder overtook him, driving away shame, making him feel like he was stoned, or tripping.

Emptied, but not quite empty, still wet, dribbling a little, he tucked in.

Stepping away from the oak, he squinted up into the crown.

How was it that in all his life he'd never really seen a tree?

*I think that I shall never see a poem as lovely as a tree. I think that I shall....* Robert hated Kilmer's unfortunate doggerel, but as it looped in his head, he understood for the first time the im-

149

pulse that drove Darcy to dance around the ancient beeches in Glen Eddy when she was little while singing in her high, impish voice, "Yippee, I kissed the tree."

Until he began to keep bees, Robert had never paid attention to trees. Even then, his only interest was in the nourishment they provided for his broods. As for woods, he liked them best when they were a smudge on a distant horizon.

Never in all his years in Glen Eddy had he gone hiking or rambling around in the forests surrounding the farm. Or wanted to. Not once had he set foot in any woods except when Darcy persuaded him to walk with her through the thicket she called a shortcut between her home and his. Usually he insisted on taking the paved road, the long way around.

While she liked nothing better than to dawdle in the shadows of the trees, he hurried to get out into the open. The dense growth oppressed him.

She relished the coolness of the woods in summer. He found them dank.

She exclaimed over the perfumed air. He smelled the decay under foot.

She kept a pricked ear and keen eye on the underbrush for camouflaged wildlife. He watched for hunters.

Robert knew that Darcy sensed his unease. Tirelessly, she extolled the beauty of the woods, unable to accept that he did not love what she loved so well. It was a rare area of disagreement between them, and it irked them both.

He wondered what she would think of the Park.

Probably dismiss it as unworthy. "It's so fake," he heard her adamant voice exclaiming inside his head. "So totally unnatural."

Yes, the trees in the Park were planted in improbable combinations that would never arise in the wild. Spiky evergreens nestled alongside lanky leaf shedders. Ranks of ginkgoes towered over evolutionary newcomers. That was the point. The pairing showed each tree to its greatest advantage.

This would mean nothing to Darcy. The girl was nothing if not uncompromising. Unyielding. Exasperating. Cruel in her honesty, punishing in her inflexibility. She would have been unbearable, if not for the fact that she took the side of the small, the halt, the lame, the injured, the defenseless, the pure.

With his brain feeling like a swollen sponge, Robert was half-glad that Darcy was not yet anywhere in sight. He was in no shape to deal with her. Desperately, he squeezed the acupressure point in the web space between thumb and index finger again. His head throbbed on.

The smart thing to do would be to go back to the truck, abandon the search for Darcy until he felt better. Every minute of his life did not have to be about her. The very thought gave him a momentary sense of relief.

On his best day, let alone a morning like this, he could not live up to her standards. No one could. She was born to be disappointed.

Except... Except... He struggled not to weep. Except — to be in Darcy's presence was to be alive and living at full attention. When he was with her his whole being became a taut string attuned to the smallest breeze, his body a too small vessel that could not contain his heart's circulation. Away from her, his spirit shrank and shriveled. His hands became dull implements, his heart a mere pump.

For what seemed like a long time, Robert stood on the path that ran alongside the oak, unable to move forward, struggling not to turn back. A runner, head turned to her partner, moved past him like he was a stone and she was flowing water. A mother with children in tow gave him wide berth, as though avoiding a hole in the road. All around him, he saw people talking, laughing, people in twos, in groups, people with eyes for each other. He knew no on and no one knew him. He was no one. Nothing. Alone. Invisible.

Darcy, dear, dear daughter, heart of his heart reduced all that was trivial in his life to ash.

He had no choice but to find her. Squeezing the acupressure spot again, he plodded deeper into the Park.

# BILLY
## Robert Shows Up

By mid-morning, Darcy had gotten an earful from at least a dozen WE activists. I could tell by the way she fidgeted that she'd had enough. True, Darcy was probably as smart or smarter, braver, and more determined than most of the adults who'd come to talk with her in the tower, but she was still a kid. She needed some down time to hang out, joke and kick back every bit as much as I needed time to ride my skateboard. Which was pretty much when Doefen's cousin, Allen, showed up.

Third cousin, twice removed or some shit like that. I didn't exactly follow what the relationship was, but it made sense to Doefen and Allen, and produced a lot of back slapping and man hugs.

Turned out that Allen was a freshmen at City College where he'd heard talk about WE and Doefen's involvement, seen the video of Darcy up on the barricades. He couldn't resist coming to check things out for himself. "Beats the hell out of studying for midterms," he said, looking at Darcy.

"The more hands, the better," she said, smiling a girl sort of smile I'd never seen on her face before.

Who could blame her? That Allen dude was born to inspire crushes. Good-looking in a non-movie star kind of way. His part of the Doefen family definitely got the handsome gene. And he was funny, too. A minute after he got there, he had Doefen, and Darcy, and even me laughing. No surprise that he and Darcy became friends on the spot.

Maybe it was because Allen showed up, or maybe Doefen just got tired of discussing whatever plans Darcy had for WE, but the next thing I knew, we were all racing down to the field below the Castle, and tossing a Frisbee at one another.

And right there in the middle of the game, Darcy spotted Robert.

Robert, if it was Robert, was still a long way off, a black dot moving across a field of dry and yellowed grass.

"How do you know it's him?"

Darcy pointed out the hunter's plaid shirt, his distinctive walk that she said looked like he would fly if it wasn't for gravity."

Fly? More like the dude was always half-expecting to step in shit, if you asked me.

"Over here. Over here," Darcy yelled waving her arms as if nothing in the least bit unfriendly had gone down between her and Robert.

"Robert! Robert!" She must have been calling his name for the sheer pleasure of it because it wasn't like the dude could hear her from where he was.

When Robert did finally make it to our side of the field — winded, red in the face — Darcy ran to him, hugged him hard around the middle. "You smell so good," she told him. "Like honey, and beeswax, and clover."

And who knows? Maybe he did. Personally, I kept my distance from the dude.

Robert just held on to Darcy, not saying anything, struggling for breath like he'd run a marathon. You could see that he was working himself up to get all pissy with her. But before he could say anything, Darcy had her arm through his, and was introducing him to everyone on the field.

"I'm so glad that you're here now," she told Robert as we started back to the Castle. "It's all been good, but just not really one hundred percent right without you."

Not one word from her about how he went off on her after the protest, or how he was all set to totally mess with her plans. No, it was all buddy, buddy, best friends forever friendly.

A part of me wanted to shake Darcy and yell, "Are you for real," but another part wanted to hug her and tell her, "You rule! You are so awesome." I mean, Darcy was never one to hold a grudge, always forgave everyone no matter how much they pissed her off or disappointed her. And I don't mean that she just let people off the hook. It was more like she gave them the opportunity to do better, to be a better version of themselves.

Hell, a couple of hours after we got to the Castle, she had everyone, even the people who had made fun of her, looking to be her friend, to please her. Frank Arras couldn't stop offering her snacks out of his food bags.

You just had to look at the size of the dude to know that he didn't usually make a habit of sharing his goodies. Tre trailed after her like an oversized puppy. Doefen didn't seem to mind that she'd crashed his whole party. The way he ended glomming on to her, you'd think that he and Darcy were twins separated at birth. They were constantly consulting in whispers, sitting shoulder to shoulder, making plans for the next day, and the next one after that.

And then Robert shows up and what does Darcy say?

"Thank you, thank you, thank you. I couldn't have done any of this without you."

As if.

# ROBERT
Reunion


Relieved to find Darcy safe, Robert held her, patted her hair. He could almost forget that she had hurt him.

How could she, why would she run off on him of all people, betray their long, unbroken bond?

"You scared the shit out of me," he said, resting his arms on her shoulders, touching his forehead to hers, "You know that, right?" He willed his third eye, the *ajna chakra,* the eye of enlightenment between his brows to open and help him understand Darcy's actions.

"I love you," she replied softly, hugging his waist.

"I love you too," he murmured, voice hoarse with feeling.

"But you know that I have to do this."

Blackness reigned in Robert's third eye. No vision appeared to help him see the unseen, or know the unknown part of Darcy.

He opened his physical eyes to find her smiling up at him.

Have to do this... something about the way she said it, shook him, made him flash on the one image from the Vietnam War that had never stopped haunting him. Not Mi Lai. Not the young girl – napalmed, running naked down a dirt road, her face a scream. But the monk lighting himself up in flames in protest against the war...

"Hungry?" he croaked. Blinking back tears, he reached into his pocket.

Darcy didn't want the peanut butter sandwich, or to wear his flannel shirt and her polite little thank yous uttered with each refusal were a knife in his heart.

Less than twenty-four hours after cutting out on him, she was already creating an independent life. A life that didn't include him, didn't have to include him.

So, what choice did he have but to let her lead him across the field to the Castle?

Her home away from home she called the hovel under the stairs where Doefen had installed her, and pronounced it wonderful.

The tiny circular room was musty and dark with green slime

growing on the hewn stone walls, but it was just a spiral staircase away from her hero's own quarters. For her, that was all that mattered. Robert got that. He swallowed hard, thankful that Isabelle wasn't there to see the filthy foam mattress on which Darcy slept.

Dank quarters or not, Darcy herself looked remarkably fresh and well-rested. Even Billy looked none the worse for wear. Maybe it was an illusion caused by the low ceiling of the cramped room, but the boy looked inches taller.

"How old are you, anyway?" Robert asked.

"Almost twelve," Billy answered making it sound like it was about one minute from being a grown-up.

And maybe it was. There was no mistaking that Darcy had started treating Billy like he was more or less her own age.

A faint fuzz that Robert hadn't noticed before darkened Billy's upper lip, a sure indication that he was old enough to be hormonal. He and Darcy both were. No wonder they had energy to burn.

The resilience of youth. Robert remembered it, vaguely. *I grow old ... I grow old ... I shall wear the bottoms of my trousers rolled.* Scraps and snatches of *The Love Song of J. Alfred Prufrock* blew through his desert mind, a tumbleweed of doggerel. *How should I presume... Do I dare ... Part my hair... Disturb the universe?*

He hadn't showered in two days. Never in his life had Robert felt more stale and rank. *Oh, do not ask,"What is it?" Let us go and make our visit...*

***

Despite Darcy's claim that she and Doefen were in constant communication, Robert noticed that he was a no-show for a meeting with her that she was clearing counting on.

"I'm sure he's got a million things he needs to do," Darcy told him by way of explanation. "Otherwise he'd be here for sure."

Robert couldn't exactly blame Doefen for making himself scarce. It must have taken the guy all of a millisecond to figure out that Darcy was going to be a huge pain in his ass. There she was — a fiery girl dressed like Lawrence of Arabia intent on saving the world – determined to convince him — a reluctant-hero, goatherd — to do all kinds of things he probably had no desire to do, but which she fervently believed he was secretly dying to do if only someone – someone like her — would show up to inspire him, raise support for him. How whack was that?

Robert could so picture Darcy's arrival on the scene at the Castle – Doefen in a room packed with a crowd of self-professed, more-brilliant-than-thou radical thinkers and oh-so-worthy intellectuals, mingling with slumming trust-fund activists. All of them smug, self-important, and bored — very, very bored with each other, and the whole protest scene.

And along comes Darcy — earnest, not a jaded bone in her body.

No surprise that they figured they could play her for a little fool. But trying to fake her out by introducing her to some dude pretending to be Doefen was just a dumb fuck thing to do. And he said as much to Darcy when she told him about the whole first meeting.

Of course, she refused to be outraged. Called the whole thing a prank. "Doefen had nothing to do with it," she assured him in the ever-respectful, ever-loyal, I-live-breathe-and-die-for-Doefen tone that made Robert want to hurt her. Hurt Doefen.

The effort of tamping down the anger in his heart, combined with the spirit-sapping events of the night, exhausted Robert completely. He sank onto the cold stone floor. Darcy's rhapsodic detailing of the little huddle she got into with Doefen after the conclusion of the whole identity stunt came to him as though from a long distance. And when Darcy declined to reveal exactly what she and Doefen discussed, a strangling sadness rose to his throat like pain. He heard himself make a small, choking sound.

Darcy did not fail to notice. Squatting down alongside him, she gently kneaded his arm. "You do know that I couldn't have done this without you."

Robert had no reason to doubt that Darcy was being honest, but he knew better than to believe that it was true, and remained silent.

In response, Darcy wrapped him in a light embrace, and whispered, "I'm so glad that you're here now."

What choice did Robert have but to let her go on and on and on about Doefen like she used to go on about frogs, or Alar, or wood park? He could only hope that her passion for Doefen would soon pass and be replaced by a more worthy enthusiasm. Only a hard-hearted bastard would have considered hauling Darcy home at that point. Much wiser to hang in there, make himself useful and see that she didn't get into any major trouble.

Darcy laughed off any and all concerns Robert articulated. Good people, she called the crew in the Castle, worthy people, even if they had made some crude remarks, and indulged in some jokes at her expense. "I ignore all that stupid stuff, and people lose interest."

She was eager for Robert to meet everyone. As the day went on, a steady stream of WE big shots did stop to talk with Darcy in the courtyard. Most of what was said amounted to meet and greet bullshit, but these were grown men, experienced activists with names that he recognized and they were consulting with a teenage girl. That in itself was impressive. Never mind that the press that Robert had read about a lot of them pretty much showed them to be assholes.

Like Tre Moyle, for instance. He was the one that Darcy introduced him to first. Tre's most recent claim to fame was for a DWI with a near fatality. And then there was a story about his altercation with a girlfriend that turned violent. Charges were dropped. And going further back, a murky story about the shotgun death of his best friend in high school that ended up being called a tragic hunting accident. Somehow, this black sheep son of a rich and conservative family, whose millions came from sugar plantations located in countries too impoverished to worry about details like labor laws or exploited cane cutters, always got away with it. After each such incident,Tre took up a worthy cause. Doefen was his latest.

"Good to meet you, man," Robert said, but it wasn't. He didn't for one minute buy any of Tre's bullshit about his commitment to WE. Bankrolling people like Doefen barely made a dent in the family fortune that Tre hadn't actually earned himself. It was all about image. And maybe feeling cool. As far as Robert was concerned, Tre could very well be a mole his family had planted in WE to protect their investment in the fast-food industries that Doefen opposed.

*Paranoia, the destroyer...* Somehow meeting Tre started the old rock and roll lyric looping in Robert's head. He did his best to ignore it and focus on the skinny guy with a bushy grey ponytail and rimless glasses, who Darcy introduced to him next.

Lee Hire! Another name Robert recognized. This one from his own days in SDS. Word back then was that Lee, who styled himself as a tough talking organizer, best known for his fuck this, fuck that foul mouth, turned out to be a total wimp who shit himself at the sight of a Pig, and ratted out a bunch of people after being busted at the Columbia takeover.

What the hell was he doing hanging out with WE?

*Paranoia, the destroyer ... the destroyer.* Hard as Robert tried, the rest of the lyrics and the name of the band refused to come back to him. A bad sign. Right up there with the post-piss dribble. *I grow old, I grow old/ I shall wear the bottoms of my trousers rolled.* T. S. Eliot. *The Wasteland.* At least he remembered that much.

Robert missed the name of the goofy looking kid on a skateboard who came tearing out of nowhere, and slowed down next to Darcy only long enough to toss her a cell phone. "It's a new one from Frank," the kid called out over his shoulder as he disappeared into the crowd. "He said you can toss the other one he gave you."

Darcy got right on the thing and began to text and I.M. with someone as effortlessly as all of the other kids flitting around the courtyard. Dumbfounded, Robert just stood and watched. True, kids of her generation had never known life without cell phones, and text messages, and internet. But Darcy was not one of those kids. The mountains around Glen Eddy were just high enough to block off cell phone reception. Most of the community was too poor to own a computer. The few PCs in the library were down more often than not, and so out of date and slow that they might as well have been coal-powered.

So how and when had she so effortlessly mastered the technology that she'd never owned and that so intimidated Robert?

To this day, he can't say why he didn't ask Darcy more about the phone, or who she was texting, or why it didn't occur to him to tell her to call her mother.

He tells himself that it would not have made a difference.

Phone or no phone, Darcy was just doing what she'd been raised to do. Act on her beliefs. Speak her mind. Be a leader, not a follower.

He can't help but remember the favorite song of her child-hood.

> *Blackbird singing in the dead of night*
> *Take these broken wings and learn to fly*
> *All your life*
> *You were only waiting for this moment to arrive.*

On that day in the courtyard, Darcy had given him a whole-hearted and earnest earful about how WE was all about de-centralized action. Individual responsibility. Multiple points of view. Small affinity groups — like an ant colony – each repre-senting specific causes. No leaders. No followers. No institu-tional organization.

> *Blackbird fly*
> *Blackbird fly*
> *Into the light of the dark black night*

"Right on," he'd told her. What else could he have said? That it was all blah, blah, blah bullshit. That WE was a movement, and like any other movement, it needed a leader. A voice to speak for it.

Followers. Leaders. That was the way of the world. People need a leader. And Doefen was not the one who would lead.

Without a doubt, it was Darcy who had been in charge of the Belvedere courtyard that morning. A buzz, an electric charge crackled the air as she'd walked around the grounds saying hel-lo, introducing him to people.

The fiery girl itching for battle had clearly roused even the most veteran activists in the crowd. Against every dictate of common sense, they'd embraced her. Signed onto her cause. Lee Hire trailed after her docile as a puppy, and took orders without uttering a single expletive.

"I just asked him to stop swearing and he did," Darcy had told Robert like it wasn't in the least bit extraordinary.

They'd all become her workers. Her army.

Robert didn't think for a moment that Darcy had ever asked Doefen for the leadership of WE, or that Doefen had offered it, but it did seem like everyone at Belvedere had only been wait-ing for her to arrive.

> *Blackbird fly*

"Our numbers are small," Darcy shouted that evening from the top of a stone wall at the far end of the castle courtyard, the setting sun robing her in orange light. "So we must be careful and clever."

Darcy spelled out for the crowd what Robert had already figured out at the *West End* the night before.

Hardly any organized protest against the WTO meetings existed because applications for marching permits had been denied. Demonstrators who attempted to speak out were penned, pepper sprayed, chased, beaten and arrested, leaving the WTO free to go on creating policies that would leave the poor, poorer, the hungry, hungrier, and insure that the natural world would continue being exploited, polluted, destroyed.

"Just say No to WTO!"

Billy, sitting on the wall, legs dangling, looking like a boy gone fishing, roused himself long enough to tap his skateboard in punctuation

"WE are not for sale."

Tap, tap, tap, tap, tap.

"People before Profits."

Darcy raised her hand, silencing the calls of protest.

The one and only permit issued to WE was for a rally at an abandoned shipping pier way far, far away from the meetings, she informed the crowd.

Robert was not surprised. Out of sight, out of mind and media coverage. Pigs! Business as usual.

Robert scanned the crowd. Maybe a dozen of the protesters looked old enough to remember the Sixties. The rest hadn't even been born then. No wonder they listed with rapt attention when the nerd with the camera planted in his glasses climbed up onto the wall alongside Darcy to give them a rundown of the obvious.

The only footage from the non-violent action that had taken place outside the Waldorf, he told them was the footage he'd put up on the net.

"But will WE give up?" Darcy demanded of the crowd.

"No," a couple hundred voices shouted.

At which point, Doefen materialized and nattered on about

a current art event that involved a Plexiglas machine being fed gourmet food, and a paying public lining up to watch the food be digested. Chefs were competing for the honor of serving the machine. The city's largest newspaper gave the installation almost a full page of coverage, praising it as an important critique of consumerism. He pulled the offending page out of the bib pocket of his overalls and held it up like a kid doing show and tell. "Meanwhile, WE's efforts to stem rampant materialism didn't get so much as a mention," he bleated.

Doefen didn't exactly rock the crowd, but Darcy flashed him a smile that was like a high-five and a kiss rolled into one.

For the life of him, Robert didn't get it. What was it about the guy that allowed him to obliterate every bit of Darcy's good sense?

The disparity between himself and the usurper of Darcy's heart was hard for him to swallow. There he was, standing at her feet, cheering his heart out, supporting her now as ever. But did she look at him? No, not once.

Along came Doefen, Mr. Lackluster with his pipsqueaky voice, not to mention weak chin, squinty eyes and she glowed.

Could it be a female thing? Something hormonal?

Darcy picked up the speech where Doefen left off. "Tomorrow the WTO meetings at the hotel will continue in the same spirit of indifference to the desperately poor of the world and to those who would protest on their behalf. But WE can change that."

The WE plan was simple, elegant. A small number of demonstrators would go to the assembly sites designated in the police permit and make a show of protest. Nothing too disorderly or disruptive — just loud enough to make the police notice, and to keep them occupied without giving them any excuse to make arrests. At the end of the protest period, everyone was to break up into small groups and disperse peacefully in different directions. After dark, everyone was to assemble back at Belvedere Castle, singly and unobtrusively.

Meanwhile, a contingent of WE activists would stay away from the protest, and use prepaid cell phones to place untraceable calls to community activists and organizers of groups sympathetic to WE with details for a Free Action. These contacts would, in turn, be asked to place untraceable calls to members of their organization. While this phone tree was being activated and the cooperative action was being mobilized, WE and fellow organizations would maintain their usual web activities, put up postings condemning the erosion of the public's right to free speech and assembly, and urge their membership to contact their government representatives to object. The Free Action was not to be mentioned anywhere.

A good plan. Doable, requiring coordination, cooperation and commitment. But also dependent on complete confidentiality and loyalty.

Robert couldn't help but wonder who the traitor would be. Because there always was one — a narc, a plant, an impostor. And if there wasn't an actual traitor, then there was bound to be some self-serving ego-maniac who'd go to the media for the sake of five seconds of fame, or some pathetically scared wretch who'd spill everything to the first Pig that asked. That's how it went down in the Sixties, and Robert doubted things had changed much since.

He surveyed the courtyard. Who'd be the one to sell out the plan, betray Darcy?

Tre was an obvious candidate.

Ditto, the goofy kid on the skateboard. Did he really give Darcy an untraceable cell phone, or was it a direct line to a Pig wiretap?

*Paranoia, the destroyer.*

M3 was another possibility — constantly eying Darcy like an oversized grackle, camera always on and transmitting. His footage could be going straight to the Pigs. Too obvious? Or maybe so obvious that it was perfect.

*Paranoia, the destroyer.*

The one lesson Robert learned from the Columbia takeover was to never let your guard down and to trust your gut.

Of all the characters who glommed on to Darcy, Frank Arras buzzing around her like a huge housefly, made Robert's insides heave right from the get go.

Obnoxious. Loud. Voice like a bullfrog. Always going on about being a crip, just in case you'd missed his wheelchair — a monstrosity with huge tires, fenders customized with orange and purple lightning bolts, and a motor that roared like a goddamn Harley. Frank rode the thing at motorcycle speed, a menace to himself and others.

Any sympathy Robert might have felt for the sorry fuck turned to rage as soon as he opened his mouth, calling Darcy chickee and babydoll, even though she asked him not to. And talking to her in dirty double speak like she was too young, too stupid to get it. "Girlee, girlee, give me a hand," stretching out his grimy paws towards her. "Help me get up." Wink, wink. "Come on, chickee. I know you can do it. Come on, babydoll, you've got the power." Yuck, yuck, yuck. Laughing so hard that the rhinestone skeleton on his too-tight t shirt danced obscenely over his gut.

Very fucking funny. Robert could hardly resist pulling Arras out of the wheelchair and knocking him unconscious. Even if he was a crip. And that was a big if. As far as Robert could see, the only thing wrong with the guy was that he was too fucking heavy for his legs to carry him. Robert didn't want to distrust a man just because his language and behavior were grotesque, and he chain-smoked rank, low-tar cigarettes, and guzzled liters of soda, but suspect him he did. The whole crip this, crip that routine was just a little too over the top to be believable. Did being a crip really make Frank a secret weapon in Darcy's plan, like he said? Or was it just a snow job to get an in that he could use to fuck her over? It didn't help that Robert overheard Frank tell someone he was talking to on his cell that the situation with the skinny little twit was in control. Was it paranoid to think he meant Darcy?

*Paranoia, the destroyer.*

Paranoid. Yeah, he could be. But even if he was paranoid that didn't mean that Robert wasn't also right-on.

# CHIEF CUCHEN
Fire Starters


At 6:45 a.m. Officer Warwick and Officer English of the horse patrol unit covered their beat along 59th Street from Fifth Avenue to Amsterdam without reporting anything or anyone worth noticing.

"All clear," English radioed base headquarters.

At 7:01 Chief Cuchen received word that seven wooden barricades outside the Waldorf had just gone up in smoke. He immediately ordered the deployment of two fire units to the Waldorf sector, and placed all foot and horse patrols in the area on high alert.

A few minutes later he received reports of small, fires bursting out further up on Park and Madison, mostly in front of banks and corporate offices. Trash baskets were filled with smoke. Out of nowhere Molotov cocktails exploded into flames. There were smoke bombs. And stink bombs. But no apparent protesters.

All patrolmen, including Warwick and English, were instructed to proceed East in the direction of Park Avenue. None of them reported any unusual activities or suspicious individuals. Nonetheless, small blazes continued to break out here and there along the avenue. To Cuchen that meant that the fire-setting had to be the work of solitary, guerrilla-style perps who, in all likelihood, were disguised to blend in with the usual early morning dog walkers and commuters.

He ordered Park and Madison closed to all pedestrian and vehicular traffic.

Fifteen minutes later, the fires had been put out, and no new ones were spotted. Up to that point, nothing really bad or truly dangerous had happened. Mostly, it was like goosey night gone bad.

But then, at 8:12, a taxi blew up near the back entrance of the Waldorf.

Cuchen deployed another fire unit, a riot control troop, and all horse patrolmen in the vicinity of the hotel to the scene. The towel-head his men barely managed to rescue from the burning cab swore that it had been leaking oil and overheating for weeks. A subsequent check with the Taxi and Limo Commission confirmed that the cab's medallion had a long history of violations.

So, the burning cab was not part of the arson action. Just a dramatic and lucky coincidence for the pyromaniac miscreants.

No sooner had the force secured the Waldorf sector and doused the burning wreck, than all hell started to break loose on 59th.

Officer Warwick had returned to his post on Fifth at the 59th Street entry to Central Park, only to radio-in that wheelchairs in tight formation were blocking the entire south end of the street starting at the doors of the Plaza Hotel all the way to the St. Moritz. To make matters worse, kids – three rows deep – were lined up in front of the phalanx of wheelchairs. By kids, he meant little kids. Not the usual pierced and tattooed college crowd. He requested headquarters to send back-up.

Cuchen immediately checked the surveillance monitors, which not only confirmed Warwick's report, but showed that much the same situation was taking shape further south on Fifth. Panning the cameras from the doors of FAO Schwartz to the Plaza fountain and down the Avenue, all Cuchen could see were kids. Young children. Like a school field trip gone AWOL.

He switched back to the feed from the real-time video cams planted on all the lamp posts along 59th and beyond. The street behind the wheelchairs was now filled up with crips — rows upon rows of them with crutches, and walkers, and canes. Behind them, came women. All ages. All sizes. Women filled the streets from Central Park South up to and around Columbus Circle, and out onto Broadway. There wasn't a man to be seen until somewhere past Lincoln Center. From there, it was men way the hell up into the 70's.

"What the fuck?" Cuchen shouted at his captains.

How had the mob managed to gather so fast? And where did it come from?

He checked the monitors again. A crowd that size didn't just materialize out of thin air. Somebody, somewhere should have known about it. What was the use of deploying the *Archangel* unit out in the field if they didn't know?

"Everything is status quo" they'd reported that morning. A

couple thousand people mobilized in a matter of hours was not Cuchen's idea of status quo.

The unexpected, unregulated crowd was bad enough, but the camera feed showed that there were animals along the perimeter – what the hell was that about? Dogs, cats. All kinds of caged beasts too. Birds. Lizards. Frogs. Hamsters. Gerbils. Snakes. The animals and their owners made a more or less unbroken ring around the kids, wheelchairs, women, and men.

Cuchen panned the security cameras down to a guy with an albino python the size of fire hose slung around his shoulders. That snake had to be one of the two hundred exotic animals specifically banned from private possession within city limits by the City Health Code. And if it wasn't, it should be.

Before the day was out, he'd have that guy in custody and the snake where it belonged – in a pen at the zoo.

By 9:00 a.m. because of the illegally occupied streets, vehicular traffic was backed up to the New Jersey side of the Hudson crossings. The East River crossings weren't any better. Cuchen ordered a shut-down of all the Central Park transverses. Traffic wasn't moving through them anyway, but the closings gave the impression that the force was in control.

Control was key. Always. But especially in an unauthorized mobilization like the one unfolding before Cuchen's eyes.

From what he could see on the monitors, it wasn't a bad or scary crowd, as crowds went. Not loud. But not exactly quiet either. Mostly everyone was talking and laughing like the whole thing was some huge party. The animals were busy making the kinds of sounds they usually make. And the kids were whooping it up the way kids do.

Usually, controlling and dispersing that kind of crowd was a snap. All it took was a tight phalanx of police motorcycles nipping at the edges of the illegal assembly — like sheepdogs corralling a herd — to drive everyone into side street that would be barricaded at each end. There, they'd all be zip tied – and in this case, kids and crips included.

The problem was the cameras. Not just the usual media guys covering the protest, and video freaks with cameras doing their thing, getting in everyone's face, but the cameras in this crowd. Every goddamn man, woman, and child was carrying some kind of camera — still, video, digital — or a camera phone. Even some of the larger dogs were rigged with camera equipment. The minute one of his men approached, or tried to, each and every one of those cameras was trained on him, and the crowd took to chanting. "WE see you. WE are you."

It shouldn't have mattered, but the men were spooked. Even the seasoned guys on the force basically shit themselves and did nothing. Just stood there like a bunch of dumb fucks.

Ditto, the brass sitting on their asses at headquarters. Instead of mobilizing the troops, they decided it would be best to let the crowd do what it was going to do, and burn itself out. In principle, Cuchen could see their point. No use in giving the illegal gathering a chance to create heroes or martyrs. But it was a stretch. What was the point of standing by and allowing the rule of law to be flouted?

# ROBERT
WE Are You and You Are WE and We Are All
Together


The morning of the march, Robert opened his eyes to the sight of Darcy in the middle of the castle courtyard on a horse, cell phone in one hand, reins wrapped loosely around the other, looking like she'd been born to ride.

A goddamn horse! Never mind that it was one of those squat carriage nags that took tourists around the Park, the effect was brilliant. Robert wished that he'd listened to Chuck Lorrain. The girl deserved a stallion.

"Chuck and I had planned for you to have a horse," he told Darcy, "I was going to bring *Black Lightening* but I bagged it out of respect for your mother. She would have freaked."

Darcy smiled, patted the mare's mane. "No worries. Flo is all the horse I need," she said. "Aren't you Flo?"

*A horse is a horse of, course, of course.* The point was to have a horse. Any horse. *My kingdom for a horse.*

And how exactly had Darcy managed to rustle up this iconic steed?

"All I had to do was ask."

Ask who? And when? And why without telling him?

Hadn't he always been her go-to guy? Wasn't he the one, the only who'd always taken her seriously? It wasn't like he expected her to share every little thing with him, but he'd always believed that she'd include him on the big stuff. Like a middle-of-the night excursion from Belvedere Castle down to 59th Street where the horse and carriage trade hung out.

Without a doubt, the girl knew how to break his heart.

If he'd had any clue that Darcy was going to slink away from the Castle in the middle of the night, Robert sure as shit wouldn't have left her alone with Billy. He would not have spent the whole night hanging out with Lee Hire in the room at the top of the tower, where the FCC, Freedom Communications Center, as Lee called it, was buzzing with all kinds of back and forth on cell phones, laptops. Robert had figured that he was doing Darcy a favor by keeping an ear, an eye open to make sure she wasn't being excluded from something important. But all he'd gotten was a whole lot of Lee going on and on about his bullshit political actions, writings, and oh so important academic appointments. For all that Robert knew, Darcy had engineered the whole set up, told Lee to take him to the top of the tower and chew his ear off, and get him wasted on beer in order to keep him out of her way.

*Paranoia ...?*

"Not wise, what you did," he told Darcy, "going alone through the Park in the middle of the night. Unprotected."

"I'd rather die than do nothing," Darcy said with hardly a downward glance from the saddle.

"Not wise," he muttered. "Absolutely, not wise."

"You worry too much." Darcy smiled. A warrior on her steed. Certain. Invincible

What did it matter to her that she was armored in nothing more than innocence and a *djellabah* — wisp of fabric shot through with silver thread?

Oh, the sweet, sweet arrogance of youth. Robert had to admit that in his long night of rapping with Lee about who did what back in the day, there were moments when he'd felt *cool* again, and *groovy,* and remembered what it was like to be *with it* and *right-on;* remembered the pleasure of it.

Darcy on her horse. Totally sure and pleased with herself. It was enough to bring a tear to his eye.

Had he ever been that certain, that young? Regret rose to his throat like pain. *I have measured out my life with coffee spoons.*

"D Girl," he said, invoking her childhood nickname, his voice hoarse with emotion. "Please be careful."

"I'm fine. Really," she said in a tone that felt like she'd given him a small pat on the head.

The hell with the dismissive little brat, he remembers thinking as she snapped the reins, and turned the horse to face the crowd. The hell with her.

Her little army of 150 maybe 200 souls, max, would probably have milled around the Castle courtyard all morning if she hadn't stood in the stirrups and called out, "Listen up everyone. Walk together. Keep your heads up. Fear nothing. No harm will come to us."

At the sound of her voice, the courtyard fell silent. A charge, like electricity, crackled in the air, passing from one body to the next, pulling everyone in tight and close. Even Robert felt gripped by a sensation that reminded him of the total body rush he would get from standing under the high tension electric power towers that ran along the ridge out by the Glen Eddy dam – ears pricked to a sound that was almost out of hearing, teeth vibrating in their sockets, limbs pulsing in concert with the current that throbbed in the wires, mouth gone dry with the knowledge that if unleashed, the energy of that current could reduce everything in its path to cinder and ash.

Darcy knew the power she had. No denying that. But no matter what anyone said later, she had no intention of abusing it. Her closing words before WE hit the streets were, "Just remember, be kind to the cops. They're people like you and me. They've been deceived by their own disguise. Make it safe for them to do the right thing."

Clever girl paraphrasing Ginsberg like that. What the poet laureate of the Sixties protests had actually said was *make it safe for cops to get a hard-on*. Or maybe it was for straights to get a hard-on. Robert couldn't remember exactly.

But he definitely knew that he'd never read that particular poem to Darcy. Of the many topics Robert willingly covered with her, sex was not one of them. Not ever. Darcy didn't seem to have any desire to go there. Which was just as well as far as he was concerned. The Free Love of his era notwithstanding, he somehow found the whole topic of sex vaguely embarrassing, distasteful and dirty in a dumb, retro sort of way.

Darcy must have found that Ginsberg passage all on her own.

A smart strategy to woo people to your cause by making them comfortable, making it safe for them to get a hard-on.

Woo. An old fashioned word with an old fashioned definition — as in to court, to win the love of.

Wooing represented one hell of a change from Darcy's usual style, which until then had always been all about challenging – whether the cause was banning Alar, or saving Wood Park, or wearing a *djellabah*.

"Right on," Robert shouted. "Right on." His little girl was growing up, getting wise to the world.

By the time the Castle contingent reached the 59th Street exit

171

from the Park, WE supporters stood in the streets many thousands strong.    Thirty thousand according to media estimates. The cops claimed much lower numbers. But the footage from traffic helicopters, which played exactly once on TV and innumerable times on the internet, showed all of the streets from 59th and Fifth Avenue up to Broadway and 72nd crammed with marchers.

As Darcy turned her horse onto 59th Street, Joni Mitchell's anthem hummed in Robert's head.

> *By the time we got to Woodstock,*
> *We were half a million strong*
> *And everywhere there was song and celebration*

He watched Darcy unfurl a beautiful WE banner that he'd never laid eyes on before. Another secret she'd kept from him. As the white silk caught the breeze, a cheer rose up from the crowd. Darcy slowly made her way from the edge of the Park to the front ranks of the gathered protesters with Doefen on her right side, Lee Hire on the left. Billy, for once minus skateboard, walked alongside holding on to a leather lead attached to the bridle. For sure Darcy would have had Billy up in the saddle with her if the kid hadn't been such a wimp. Robert walked behind Billy at the horse's flank. Per usual, M3 buzzed around like a horsefly.

Frank Arras made a spot for himself right next to Robert, and remained mercifully silent up until they reached the rows of wheelchairs, at which point he raised a fist and shouted, "Yo, hommies. What it is!" sounding more surprised than pleased by the numbers of his fellow kind.

The march advanced slowly with Darcy at the head. A military parade could not have been statelier. Darcy held the banner straight up, never once letting it slope back over her shoulder.

To cover the few blocks from 59th to the Waldorf took the marchers at least an hour. Plenty of time for the Pigs to deploy. No surprise that by the time WE arrived at the barricades surrounding the hotel, cops stood in tight ranks – nine deep by Robert's count – with a mounted unit at the front.

The air smelled of burning.

Darcy raised the banner and waved it slowly right to left and back again. The crowd, as one, came to a stop. She smiled, leaned down to squeeze Billy's hand.

"No matter what I say, don't get scared, OK?" Robert heard her tell him — ever mindful of her little buddy.

After checking that Doefen was in place alongside her, Darcy nodded to M3 who positioned himself to face the wheelchair brigade now headed by Frank Arras.

Darcy stood up in the stirrups.

"Good soldiers of the National Guard, and honest officers of the law, step out of the way and let Doefen pass."

The cops pressed closer together, fingers twitching on the triggers of their guns. Those with rifles that they'd cradled across their chests now positioned the barrels to point at Darcy. The mounted cops tightened-up on the reins until their horses' teeth were bared.

"Doefen comes in peace and good will to speak to Dick Burgundy and the delegates of the WTO," she said patiently, as though the cops were her friends and she was explaining a particularly hard math problem.

The blue line of cops held perfectly still. A tiny image of Darcy burned on each of their bug-eye mirrored visors like a galaxy of pinpoint suns. The static squawk of radios and walkie talkies was their only answer.

"Go back to your homes." Darcy said making it sound like both a request and a command. "Do not squander yourselves on the corporate heads of multinational businesses that do not have your interests at heart. Doefen represents you, represents us. All of us."

Darcy hoisted the WE banner high above her head. "WE stands for all of us. WE are all of us together."

"Nobody gets in without a permit," Chief something or other with badges and stripes all over his uniform said.

"Whether you like it or not, WE will pass."

The police chief cocked his head, and the cops behind him raised their big ass plastic shields like they were knights protecting their keep. The rows behind them cocked their rifles. One of the mounted cops rode up to Darcy, reins in his left hand, gun in his right.

Darcy cradled the pole of the banner against her chest with her left hand, and slowly, deliberately raised her right as though to say "Stop." Except that she held a camera clasped against her palm. Right on cue, every other camera in the crowd was out and put into action.

The image of Darcy's stubby grey mare nose to nose with the cop's gleaming dark stallion, her camera, his gun positioned barrel to barrel was captured, recorded by countless cameras.

Over the crowd's rumble of "WE see you," Darcy addressed the Chief again. "If you order your men to take up arms against us, WE will defend ourselves. Blood will flow. And for what?" She pointed at the crowd. "WE are no different than the children, and spouses, and parents you left at home."

A dog yelped.

Darcy smiled. "And the pets WE love are just like the ones that you pamper and spoil."

She stopped, and looked off into the sliver of blue space that separated the buildings at the head of the street like she'd said all she had to say. But Robert standing near, watching closely, could see her brow furrow as if she was straining hard to listen to something, someone only she could hear.

"Yes," she murmured so softly that it seemed more a breath than a word, and looked right back into the eyes of the Chief. "WE are not faceless, nameless, numbers. WE are not "protesters," or "anarchists," or "rebels.""

She turned to the children. "Say your names."

And they did in the reedy sing-song way of little kids.

A few cops smiled. Some stared at the ground as though they were wishing a passage of escape would open at their feet.

"Very pretty," the Chief snarled, looking uneasy.

Robert could easily guess the calculus that stymied the Pig — he was not about to have some teenage girl on a horse flaunt his authority, but also not about to risk giving an order that he wasn't sure his minions would follow.

Frank Arras laughed. "Just look at those cops squirm, shift from one foot to the other. Get them to decimate a bunch of rugrats in public? Not here. Not in America. Not yet."

"I wouldn't be so sure," Robert said, a flashback to the Kent State shooting that ended the Sixties raising prickles of anxiety on his whole body.

"Nah. It's like I told Doefen and the girl back at the Castle at their planning meeting. Kids and crips, and kittens. Those are WE's best weapons."

174

"Oh for Chrissake, it's not about weapons," Robert said. "First and foremost they've got Darcy,"

"Oh yeah, they've got Darcy," Arras brayed and laughed so long and hard that tears came into his eyes. "They *do.*"

# CHIEF CUCHEN
Principles of Police Work


Cuchen stared at the Waldorf surveillance feeds. Three precincts of the city's Finest mobilized to secure what was basically a business pow wow at a swank midtown hotel, and they couldn't even stop a girl. Because, when all was said and done, that's all she was. An unarmed snot of a teenage girl.

They just let her trot up the avenue. Literally, trot. On a horse.

There had to be at least a dozen statutes she had violated. Illegal assembly. Inciting to riot. Stealing a horse — they could have charged her with those for starters.

The very same security teams that managed to chase down and arrest dozes of bicyclists for participating in a Transportation Alternative's rally – even though they had stopped at every traffic light, obeyed every traffic law – didn't seem to find it necessary to get a girl on a horse off the street.

Cuchen was hard pressed to decide who pissed him off more. The girl. Or his own men.

At the very least, his ground force should have controlled the mob that gathered around her. All it would have taken was following the few basic principles of police work that he had drilled into them time and time again.

Number one – Bladder control is crowd control. The key to breaking the back of any demonstration was to corral everyone into a smaller and smaller space and keep them there. In no time at all, the crowd would go from furious indignation to despair. Why? Because no one wants to piss or shit themselves in public. Even the most rabid protesters penned up for a few hours in a tight space without facilities, turn docile as sheep.

Number two – Photos are not facts. Like eyewitnesses, they can be challenged, refuted and dismissed because the camera's eye is not neutral, and film is not objective. What matters is where the camera is set, when the shutter is pressed, what's in the frame and what's left out. The angle of a shot can distort or hide the truth. The department's legal team excelled at proving the worthlessness of so-called eyewitness photos.

One camera. A thousand. It shouldn't have mattered. Just because the girl and her mob pulled a few cameras on them was no excuse for the force to act like a bunch of pussies. You'd think the sad fucks had never heard of a body block, or the wonders of a little judicious water cannon, or heard mention of pain induced compliance. It wasn't like they didn't all have a Taser in their gunbelts.

Letting the girl get away with promenading all over the avenue on a horse was bad enough, but the force allowing itself to get into a face-off in front of the hotel was beyond stupid. A rookie mistake. It just gave the crowd an opportunity to sound off about anything and everything from homelessness to climate change. What better way to legitimize the pleadings of obscure nobodies like One-World Vegans than to have half the police force sitting on their asses taking it all in?

And drawing guns on her – even dumber. It instantly transformed a naive and overzealous girl into a person of stature, a person to reckon with.

As a rule, Cuchen did not get personally involved with criminals. It gave them an exaggerated sense of their own importance. But this crowd had to be controlled, and the girl had to be brought down before she became a real menace.

An underground passageway, formerly used to transport elite guests from the Waldorf to private trains awaiting them at Grand Central, allowed Cuchen to pass unseen from the surveillance trailer and to materialize in the hotel lobby.

"Stand down," he commanded the uniforms who weren't actually engaged in anything he'd be willing to call an action.

Once they recovered from their surprise at the Chief of Police actually coming to the protest site, the men, with the exception of the Captain, seemed relieved, almost eager to get out of the way and let him take over. Cuchen treated the Captain to a flash of a smile as fleet as the display of tooth a dog flashes before lunging, and the Captain stepped aside too.

After a little show of negotiation at the doorway of the hotel, Cuchen allowed the girl – minus the horse — to proceed inside to the security checkpoint. She'd had some idea that she was going to ride the horse right into the lobby.

Allow a hourse to make a mess all over the marble floor? Not on his watch.

In return for dismounting, the girl insisted that he allow the

WE delegation to accompany her. After a show of reluctance, Cuchen agreed. Keeping her little posse together would facilitate surveillance and control.

A clever touch, the horse. Girl and horse. So classic. So innocent. So sexy.

Except that up close the girl was anything but sexy. And you couldn't call her delicate or pretty either. And she wasn't exactly a picture of innocence. The indistinct video images on the surveillance footage were deceiving in that regard. In them she looked like a pixie waif. Proof, yet again, that like he always said Photos are not Facts.

There was a kind of knowing, a wisdom in her eyes that he couldn't name. It gave her face the look of an ancient. And there was a stillness about her that made her seem impenetrable as a statue. She was a compelling presence for sure, but she wasn't going to grow up into the kind of woman men would be dying to fuck. Or want to fuck at all, unless they found themselves stranded on a desert island with her. And maybe not even then.

So the whole robe cover-up was an unnecessary precaution. As was the chopped off hair.

Quite possibility she was just a mixed up girl who wanted to be a boy. Gender dissatisfaction, or whatever the hell it was called, seemed to be an up and coming trend. In which case, in his humble opinion, she was probably already on her way to coming to a bad end. It wasn't in his power to prevent that. But that was no reason to allow her to go around acting like she could do whatever she damn well pleased, like she was entitled to.

"Who told you to dress like that?" he demanded in lieu of her name, which thanks to belatedly an energized *Archangel* unit he already knew.

"No one."

"Why would you deliberately choose to wear the kind of clothing worn in the home country of the extremists responsible for the atrocities of 9/11?"

"I will be judged by my words and actions, not my clothes."

"You would do well not to place yourself in unnecessary danger."

She replied to his threat with one of her own.

"Anyone who does harm to me because I prefer these clothes

will suffer in both body and soul."

A girl willing to fight, itching to fight. Possibly a full-out wannabe martyr to a cause. Cuchen regarded her with new and invigorated interest. Maybe she did have the potential to be truly dangerous.

Without a doubt, the girl's choice of dress was a source of her strength. Put her in some ordinary clothes, and she was just another puny girl no one would look at twice. And she probably knew it.

Thus far, the girl had chosen to align herself only with a group that was fairly inconsequential. WE could hardly be dignified with the appellation of an organization. But experience dictated that this could change.

The question was how strong was her allegiance to WE?

Cuchen made a show of forbidding the girl to bring the WE banner into the meeting room.

"I love my banner forty times better than you love that gun of yours," she told him.

"An original response," he laughed, acting like she'd succeeded in charming him. Truth to tell, he'd pretty much heard every variation of what any perp was ever going come up with at least twice before his first promotion. But her spunk did surprise and amuse him.

The girl waved the flag above her head.

Cuchen smiled, pleased to see her look so pleased with herself. Vanities, even small ones, were often a useful addition to his arsenal of weapons. He made a show of capitulation.

All through the security process, the girl stuck close to Doefen, and, surprisingly, to the paunchy guy with blowsy hair – Robert Baudry.

Doefen, Cuchen could understand. That was her boy, her project. But so far, the *Archangel* data on Baudry didn't add up to much. He seemed to be nothing more than just some nobody from her home town.

Cuchen called Baudry first for the check through. The guy turned pale, like he was going to shit himself. Cuchen made him walk through the metal detector twice – just for the fun of it. Not a peep out of him. A real pussy.

So he ordered a pat down — again, just because. The inspecting officer found a peanut butter sandwich in one jacket pocket and a fan-shaped leaf attached to a hard white pod in the other.

No wallet. No ID. Some loose change – for a jailhouse pay phone, no doubt. To judge by his age, Baudry must have learned those precautions in his younger days. Could it be that Cuchen had caught himself a real, live, gone-to-seed relic of the big, bad, rebellious Sixties? The *Archangel* archives weren't as thorough or complete for that decade. He'd have to order a manual search. Look deeper. If Baudry was anybody back then, somewhere, in some dusty paper file there'd be some data.

Cuchen pronounced the sandwich a health hazard and had it confiscated, allowed Baudry to keep the leaf, and waved him through the check point.

Baudry scampered inside like an obedient little hamster, and even said thank you in a way that gave Cuchen a pleasant sense of having done a good morning's work. And, Cuchen noted, the little shit never so much as gave the girl a backward glance.

Ditto the Doefen guy. Marched on through the security check, and kept on going like he was a one-man show.

If the girl felt betrayed or scared to be left behind without a word by the two men, she hid it well. And her mettle did not desert her though Cuchen deliberately left her to cool her heels at the checkpoint while he disposed of the rest of her entourage of WE activists.

First, Tre Moyle – a fleshy brute, like a linebacker gone slack. Cuchen figured him for Doefen's bodyguard, though why the ridiculous goatherd would need one was a mystery. He looked like he would be packing heat, but turned out clean.

Next the nerdy dickhead with thick glasses. He refused to let Cuchen touch his backpack, and was therefore strongly encouraged to leave voluntarily. On his way out, he spewed whole paragraphs about how *The People* were always being watched by the *Police State*, and how it was not a crime for *The People* to watch back. Cuchen gave orders to have him tailed.

That left only the scrawny boy — Billy, who clung to the girl for dear life. Billy. Little, ittle bitty baby Billy. Cuchen could have scooped him up for being an underage runaway, which he clearly was. Had him and the girl escorted to the precinct to wait for their happy Mama and Papa to pick them up. Assuming that either one of the brats actually had a parent that gave a shit about them. A big assumption in his experience. But there was little fun in that, and the girl could be put to better use by allowing her to stay with WE.

So he waved the two of them through with a flourish that almost suggested a bow. No ID check. No pat down. No nothing.

The boy gulped like he'd surfaced from a long, deep dive, but the girl stepped past him, head up so high she looked an inch taller. Cuchen's palm itched to slap the little snot senseless.

Still, all in all, Cuchen counted the intervention a success. The security cameras at the checkpoint insured that he would now have crisp, digital close-ups of the girl and each of the WE headliners. Everything they touched would be brushed for prints. With any luck, there'd be a little residue for DNA testing to enter *Archangel's Protective Security Inventory* data base.

The information contained in the *PSI* was the most extensive in all of police history. Cuchen's own special project. Rightfully, his pride and joy. Whatever *PSI* didn't collect was probably not worth knowing. Cuchen had already read all about Doefen in the *PSI* briefs. Soon enough, he'd know all there was to know about all the other players in WE.

In the meantime, Cuchen was quite content to let the WE gang relish their illusion of victory. It wasn't like he'd allowed them access to a critical asset. The Waldorf was nothing but a hotel with a Swiss cheese of vulnerabilities. *PSI* had deemed it not worth squandering resources on. Ditto their recommendation on the subject of dedicating resources to protect Doefen – a full-of-himself goat herd for chrissake. And Burgundy too for that matter — a totally dispensable target who happened to cash in on the whole organic food craze and make a pain in the ass of himself. If by some chance some lunatic managed to eliminate either one of them, there wouldn't be any major fallout. In fact, as far as Cuchen was concerned, eliminating the Doefens and Burgundys of the world was entirely to be desired.

The mayor's office said it was good business for the city to indulge Burgundy, so who was Cuchen to do otherwise. But just because his duties as head of the *Archangel* Critical Asset Protection unit included establishing and maintaining a symbiotic relationship between the public and private sectors, that didn't mean he was the mayor's puppet.

Allowing two losers like Burgundy and Doefen to have their

little pow wow was no sweat off his back. Sure there would be reporters. But no one who really mattered gave a shit about what either Doefen or Burgundy had to say. Doefen was clearly a nut job. And, in the larger scheme of things, Burgundy was just a guy looking to make a buck. Next week, next month he'd switch to selling some useless tech gizmo or alternative energy bullshit.

In the meantime, there was the matter of the girl and the horse to amuse Cuchen. Impound the animal. Slap a citation and fine on the girl, and the sorry, dumbass hack driver who let her take the grey nag out of the Park. Nothing made Cuchen happier than a nice game of cat and mouse.

# ROBERT
Showdown at the Empire Suite

Robert squeezed Darcy's shoulder. "We did it. We got in."

They'd all gotten through security. How amazing was that? Even M3 could have made it if he'd cooperated even a little.

He wished that Isabelle could have been there to see it. Jack too. They would have been proud. Amazed.

Inside the lobby, Darcy waved the banner in a slow arc above her head. "I told you that the road for WE and Doefen is wide open," she said, as if it were all a given.

Robert was old enough to know better. Darcy had fought the Man and she had won. That was totally extraordinary. Who would have believed that the Man could be brought down, could be shamed by something as simple as pointing a camera?

The security check at the hotel door was just posturing, a little chest thumping to cover up the Man's defeat. Robert was relieved and almost disappointed that he hadn't been called upon to use his alias after spending hours and hours finding the perfect one.

The lobby of the Waldorf had to be the biggest room Robert had ever seen. He could only image how it must have looked to Darcy or Billy. What did they have to compare it to? Their high school gym?

The carpet – all giant blue swirls – made it seem like the center of the room was a pool that had overflowed and sent water lapping at the marble pillars near the entrance, and the hooved legs of the couches, tables and chairs arranged at its edge, before draining down distant corridors. In the huge mirrors that enclosed the room, everyone looked like they were walking on water.

Robert sneaked a peek at Darcy's face as they walked through the lobby. She looked totally blissed out. He figured that Farmer boy Doefen would look lost and out of his element, but he had the satisfied look of a goat that had just landed in a field of unmown clover.

After crossing the lobby, they entered the Empire Suite, a huge room with a chandelier the size of an asteroid. At the front, a TV screen stared out of a recess in the silk-paneled wall like a big blue eye, reminding Robert of the story about wild things that he used to read to Darcy.

Dick Burgundy and his handlers sat under the TV screen at a long table set with spiky bouquets of microphones and glasses of water. On either side of the room, TV cameras stood at the ready for Burgundy's press conference.

For a long moment, no one said anything. The Burgundy people stared at the WE delegation staring at them from the door of the suite. And then Darcy marched down the center aisle toward Burgundy like she'd been born to do nothing else, Doefen loping alongside her. She stopped a short distance from the dais.

"Gentlemen, I bring you the best leader that anyone could ask for."

Dick Burgundy responded by calling for security. A guy the size of bulldozer commanded Darcy, commanded all of them to get the fuck away from the table. At which point, Darcy gave the signal for everyone to turn on their cell phones and point their cameras at him. Stopped him dead in his tracks. Just like she'd stopped the cops.

"WE has full authorization to be here," Darcy said once everyone got quiet. She nudged Doefen, "Take your rightful place."

And he did.

Doefen seemed to grow taller and stand straighter at the mike, to bloom under the lights of the TV cameras so dramatically that Robert couldn't help but wonder if maybe Darcy had been right all along. Maybe Doefen really was the guy to lead the people out of the calamity of apathy and complacency they'd sunk into since the Sixties.

Not that Darcy was ever able to explain why Doefen was the one. Or how she knew it. She just quoted Ginsberg when Robert tried to ask.

"Because knowing how to walk across a street is the same thing as knowing how to write a haiku."

Really? The best she could do was a bit of Ginsberg? Always Ginsberg. Admittedly, *Howl* and *Kaddish* were great poems. But the rest? Pretty much forgettable. And yet, somehow Darcy had never really taken to the really powerful, beautiful poems Robert and Isabelle had introduced her to — poems that would wring tears from your eyes, peel the thick callus of indifference from your heart.

She didn't need poems about sensations, Darcy said. "Ginsberg teaches me how to behave."

Robert got the behave part. Without a doubt, Darcy was a girl who needed to act, to set something, even one small thing right. As a toddler she went around picking up discarded cigarette butts and paper scraps in her chubby hand while railing against litter in a squeaky voice. The picketing and protesting — against Alar in apple juice, against the destruction of Wood Park, against the maize field, and now the committment to WE — were all points on a continuum.

But Robert was hard pressed to understand how a girl who hacked off her hair and hid her beautiful body under a robe, a girl who had never, ever had a lover, a drink, or a cigarette, who never swore, who demanded that everyone stand at moral attention could possibly see a mentor in a profligate poet like Ginsberg who promoted scabrous living, rampant fucking, and went around saying that the purpose of life was to make the world a safe place to get a hard-on.

Sex. As far as Robert could tell, that's what it all came down to for Ginsberg. But somehow Darcy overlooked that. Ginsberg's poems shouldn't have been anything for a girl like Darcy to live by, to stake her life on.

And yet she did.

*You're led to believe a lie when you see with not through the eye,* Darcy quoted Ginsberg quoting Blake, and said it was Ginsberg's voice which stopped her dead in her tracks when she was thirteen, and allowed her to see the whole universe in a blade of grass. His poems, their words and rhythms, played in her ear like music, and entered every cell of her body, and her entire being was forever altered.

The Voice, Darcy called Ginsberg — a singing voice, a dancing voice, a sunflower voice that said what needed to be said very clearly with honest words, and said the most necessary things in the silence, in the space between the words. "I hear the Voice and it's the color of water," Darcy once told him. "I always understand the Voice and it steers me well."

The Voice. As in voice inside her head, inside her heart, her conscience. Not some hallucination. No matter what the world said, Robert knew for sure that Darcy was not some schizo hearing voices.

Not that hearing a voice sounded really sound crazy to him. Hell, anyone who'd ever dropped acid knew what that was like. Trouble was that Darcy was going up against a world that wasn't into expansion of consciousness, thank you very much. Even those who'd taken LSD or peyote at some point, now pretended they never had. And they certainly hadn't learned anything from the experience.

Duke Burgundy was a perfect example — a rich kid who, if Chuck Lorraine was to be believed, went from being a stoner to being the biggest, fat-cat capitalist he could be without ever actually having experienced so much as a moment of true awareness. He sat in the blaze of TV lights, in the Empire Suite looking like a bottle of beer was as close as he ever got to a mind-altering substance, and like his idea of transgressive behavior was to sneak some white bread, or gulp a soda. Hair as neatly trimmed as a privet hedge had replaced the ass-length dreads of Chuck's description. No more jeans or crushed felt hat with an eagle feather. Instead he sported a bespoke suit — casually sumptuous – that probably cost more than Robert earned in a year of keeping bees. The one-time hippy freak, Merry Prankster wannabe turned CEO of Burgundy Enterprise was polished and groomed to within an inch of his buffed nails.

With a crook of his finger, Duke bid Doefen to sit at the end of the dais, waited for him to settle into his seat before allowing Darcy to take the floor.

"Let's begin, shall we?" he said flashing a smile of orthodontic perfection.

Ignoring the mike, Darcy announced in a voice that carried to the furthest reaches of the room, "WE are here to tell the elected officials and business leaders of the globe that you can't just do whatever you like without consulting us." She smiled and gave Duke a look that clearly said, "And I do mean you."

In response, he treated her to another full Cheshire tooth display of porcelain whiteness scarier than the first.

Unfazed, she continued. "WE will not accept the selling of citizens' rights to the multinationals or the WTO. WE will not let ourselves be manipulated."

"Burgundy Enterprise and WE have the same goal, really," the sell-out fucker whose multinational, multimillion company had reaped untold profits from genetically manipulated crops said, giving her a snarky look – as if she was no more than a mildly amusing puppy. "Both of us want to help people lead better, healthier lives, and to accomplish this without further harming the environment."

*BE for BEtter Living,* a slogan that had racked in millions. Fooled many. Robert despised BE's phony paeans to pasture-bred cows inscribed on cartons of milk that were full of growth hormone. Ditto the bullshit PR about free-range hens that came with eggs laid by poultry that was fed a factory-produced glop of corn and chemicals, not to mention, the totally bogus pictures of green fields that adorned Burgundy's patented seed packets of single harvest crops.

Pastoral Porn.

"WE will happily join arms with Burgundy Enterprise just as soon as it renounces agricultural biotechnology, and embraces true farming instead of producing irradiated, adulterated, genetically engineered products that are forced on the public though strong-arm consumerism tactics and Wall Street marketing," Doefen called out from the end of the table.

Duke responded with a sigh and momentarily baleful look mostly for the benefit of the cameras and the press. "Without biotechnology the world's demand for food cannot be met. BE's biological knowledge is the best tool we have to make it possible for all people to live better."

"Before BE decided to focus on biotechnology, it gave the world PCBs, dioxin, and the defoliants used to make war on Vietnam," Doefen said. Like Burgundy, he was now addressing his remarks to the TV cameras. "The damage these products have done to human life and the environment needs no review."

"BE has divested itself of all those holdings"

"And has now cornered the market with a weed killer that wipes out everything – other crops, even bees and birds."

"And don't forget frogs," Darcy called out.

Burgundy ignored Darcy. Doefen also gave her the smallest of smiles before continuing. "And because the BE weed killer wipes out everything, including the crops it's supposed to protect, BE goes ahead and breeds plants that are resistant to it. Catch is that the plants are bio-engineered to make a toxic chemical that sterilizes their own seeds. So, no more saving seeds from one season for the next season. No more sharing them, passing them around. To grow a new crop, the farmer must always buy new seeds from BE. And to insure that the farmer has no other choice, BE is in the process of buying out all the other surviving seed companies."

"BE is doing no more than farmers have done for centuries — breeding seeds to make better plants. Biotechnology allows us to insure that the product is not polluted by hybridization with inferior crops."

It wasn't exactly scintillating oratory, but Doefen was more than able to counter Burgundy's boundless hypocrisy with the power of his sincerity. No one could deny that he knew as much as there was to know about the issues of sustainable agriculture, or that he cared deeply for animals, goats in particular, or that he had a vast and abiding passion for matters concerning cheese. But when all was said and done, he failed to generate any excitement in the room. The press snoozed until Darcy spoke up.

"You are a godzillionaire," she said pointing at Burgundy. The cost of your suit would support a family of four in one of the too many poor countries of the world for a year. Your base salary last year was like ninety million dollars, far more than any farmer will ever earn in a whole lifetime. And that doesn't even begin to include all the perks and privilege that come with being super rich."

Ninety million. Robert glanced at the reporters. Every last one of them was scratching that number into a notebook pad.

"BE is nothing more than a big bully shoving unwanted products down the throat of the people, like strawberries with fish genes to make them resistant to frost, and square tomatoes that don't have any flavor, but are easier to pack," Darcy continued. WE will not stand by and allow Frankenstein foods to take over."

Frankenstein food. A sound bite if ever Robert heard one. Apparently, the reporters thought so too. Hints of animation flickered across their faces. Their pens were out and moving.

Duke spread his arms like he was Jesus. "Of course making changes in something as fundamental as food scares people," he said in a tone of gooey sincerity. "But the application of current biological knowledge to food is going to happen. It's inevitable – like the Industrial Revolution and the Information Revolution."

"No," Doefen shouted. "BE is not about progress. It's about waging war on nature, hijacking genetics, encoding genes like they're silicon chips and making the farmers pay for the information. It is ensuring profit at the people's peril."

Gradually, the reporters stopped taking notes. Some turned off their mikes and cameras. No matter how long the shouting would go on, for them the press conference was effectively over.

At which point Darcy got up to the mike again. "Wait," she called out. "I have something very important to tell you."

"You are probably asking yourselves, who is that girl and why should we listen to anything she has to say?"

And then she laid it out.

"My name is Darcy Pucelle, and I come from a village so small it's not on most maps. Until a few days ago, I did what kids my age do. I went to school. Tried out for soccer. Played trumpet in the marching band.

I'm sure a lot of you out there are thinking that I have no business being up here. That I should be back at home doing school work, getting good grades, worrying about getting into college, thinking about the prom, and wondering who I'll marry.

Trouble is, on my way to school I keep finding weird, deformed frogs with missing limbs, and toes like question marks. And sometimes I see birds fall out of the sky like stones. Some mornings dead crows with feet sticking straight up litter the playground. And a couple of days ago, a field of experimental maize planted in an empty field near my school burst into flames. Went up in smoke. Just like that.

No one can explain why the maize did that. But here's one thing everyone knows for sure. That maize was genetically engineered by BE."

Burgundy pounced with evident pleasure. "Spontaneous combustion." He rolled the syllables against his teeth. "BE has never been blamed for that before."

The exchange eventually made several kinds of headlines – *Combusting Corn -- No Way, Says Head of BE. BE Corn -- Kills Bugs and Burns. BE's Bad Seed* – were the ones the stuck with

Robert.

Darcy waited for the snickering in the press pool to subside before she continued.

"When I was in kindergarten, the cafeteria at school stopped serving apple juice because it was contaminated with ALAR. You all remember ALAR, right? It was a chemical that growers sprayed on trees to give apples a better color and keep them on the trees longer. Trouble was it caused cancer."

Doefen held up a manicured finger. "First of all, ALAR was not a BE product. And secondly, it was shown that children would have to eat a boxcar of apples daily to be at risk."

Fifty cancers per million was what Isabelle's research turned up, as Robert remembers. The industry said five per million. As if that made it alright. He and Isabelle made sure that Darcy never ate an apple unless it came from the trees on his property, even if she didn't like them very much. After ALAR, the tart, heirloom apples from his orchard that had probably been planted at the turn of the century brought a good price at his roadside stand. Even with worm holes. The ALAR thing scared people. Woke them up to the dangers that lurked in the most innocent and wholesome of foods. "Apple a day, keeps the doctor away." No one dared claim that anymore.

"OK. OK," Darcy continued. "Probably by now you're all thinking – this Darcy girl is some country hick. What do her stories about deformed frogs and dead birds and maize that goes up in flames have to do with us? So let me tell you that in the next county from where I live, a few years ago a kid died of an intestinal infection after he drank apple cider. And then a city kid died of it too. E.coli. Somehow a bacteria that used to just give people diarrhea had turned into a toxic killer. Pretty soon everybody knew not to drink cider unless it was pasteurized. Then people all over the US came down with the same infection from eating spinach. Yeah, the green healthy stuff that kids and grownups love to hate. No big deal, right? Nobody really wants to eat spinach anyway. But then the same bug showed up in hamburgers. And Taco Bell. And salsa. And other stuff."

Burgundy countered with the obvious. The culprit bacteria came from animals.

"From cowshit to be exact," Robert shouted hoping to conjure up the offensive smell. A look of displeasure passed over Burgundy's features, before he remembered himself and smiled. "BE is not in the cattle business."

"Oh, but it is." Doefen took over and patiently, lucidly explained how BE corn in need of a market ended up in the stomachs of cattle penned in feedlots where it fattened them quickly and cheaply, but wreaked havoc on their digestive system. Unable to digest a diet no ruminant was ever meant to eat, the animals developed bloat, ulcers, liver disease, diarrhea and *E. coli* intestinal infections. Multiple antibiotics in high doses were required to keep the cattle from dying. The *E. coli* fought back and evolved into more and more deadly forms.

"Given grass and space, the cattle would not carry and shed impossible-to-kill superbugs, and we would not be talking about how and where our food became contaminated with them. If BE was not burying the natural world under an avalanche of its genetically modified corn, I'd be on my farm milking my grass-grazed goats, making cheese. The only question you'd ever need to ask yourselves about that cheese was whether you liked it, not whether it will kill you."

A tear came to Robert's eye, but then he was more easily moved than the average guy. Sentimental, Isabelle called him. However, the reporters – red-blooded, meat-eaters to a man by the looks of them — had heard more than they'd ever wanted to hear about the intestinal life of a cow, and seemed indifferent, even hostile to Doefen's plea for a return to the pastoral.

It took Darcy to open their hearts.

"I start each day hoping that I don't wind up getting a bad salad, or apple, or burger. But I know that I could. That you could. That your kid could. Today could be the day.

So, if you're still thinking, 'This kid should be at home,' know this. I wish I could be. But for me to be at home, the world would have to change. Or I'd have to be a different kind of person. And maybe if I live long enough, I will be. Maybe I'll grow out of caring about the world, and I'll stop believing that there are things that need doing, and that I, you, we are the ones to do it.

But until that happens, here's what I will leave you with. Make the world a better place. WE — meaning you – have the power to make that happen. All you have to do is elect Doefen. It's not too late to nominate him as an Independent in this election. Let's make him our next President. We need him. The rest is

191

politics."

In the instant of stunned silence that followed, Robert sang out in his loudest, deepest baritone, "You go, Girl," even though proposing Doefen for the Presidency was another little something Darcy had neglected to share with him. Until that moment, he'd thought that Doefen was supposed to be Darcy's mascot for clean food, a green environment, nothing more. While the rest of the room babbled in surprise, Robert stood stock still, arms crossed against his chest, eyes locked on a stripe in the wallpaper to the left of Darcy's head. He arranged his lips in a knowing smile, resisted the urge to strop his fingers on the day old stubble on his chin.

Darcy stretched out her hand to quiet the room.

"Put Doefen in the White House. That's your goal."

"Yeah, you tell 'em, Girl," Robert said, softly this time, as though it was a private, little communication meant for her ears alone, hoping that a reporter would notice, would understand that Robert wasn't just some random guy, that he was someone with a special connection to Darcy.

"Once Doefen is nominated, his opponents' strength will steadily weaken. They will not have the power to defeat him. Act bravely. Have no fear. All will be well. WE will not meet much resistance. Many will join us. WE will fight to make your voices heard and speak for those who can no longer speak for themselves. The world is in your hands."

Those were Darcy's words. Verbatim. Thanks to the Freedom of Information Act, and the Pigs who taped the conference, Robert was able to get the transcript and read it again and again, confirming that nothing she'd said that day was in the least bit crazy, included naming Doefen as a Presidential candidate. History was full of third party and independent nominees. They didn't make it to the White House, but they made a difference. They won and lost elections for the main party candidates, got things on the agenda. Hell, Robert, for one, had voted for Ralph Nader. Just because a guy wasn't elected didn't mean he was a throw away vote.

Burgundy was the first to dismiss the idea of nominating Doefen, calling it a big, stupid joke. Laughing, he declared the conference done and marched out of the room. The reporters laughed too, though one of them did remark in his report that in the course of Darcy's speech, Doefen went from being a quiet farmer to a man with visible energy in his walk, and gestures, and voice.

The world should have paid more attention, taken Doefen's nomination more seriously.

Sadly, the few who did listen closely to the things Darcy said weren't looking to do her or Doefen any good.

## BILLY
Come On, Come On


After the speech about making Doefen President, Darcy was pale, licking her lips like it was a hundred degrees outside and she hadn't had a sip of water all day. Not that it was obvious. You had to really know her to notice. To anyone else she probably looked totally cool.

But all I could think was, she's just a kid. Just a kid. It's too much. They'll never let her get away with it.

I mean, there she was dissing Burgundy, a totally a big-time dude. She didn't come right out and call him evil, but you couldn't walk out of that press conference and not think that he was worse than evil. That he was Death.

At first, Burgundy didn't look like he gave a shit. Maybe he even kind of got off on a kid daring to call him out. It wasn't until Darcy started talking about Doefen running for President that he lost it.

"I am not going to honor this absurd proposition by my continued presence," he said making it sound like everything Darcy said was a complete joke.

A millisecond after he left, the reporters were all over Darcy.

Ms. Pucelle. Ms. Pucelle. Is that the name? Darcy?

They pushed mikes up to her mouth like they were popsicles. Look here. Smile.

The camera shutters went off like rounds of gunshot, and Darcy had to cover her eyes against all the flash.

"Ms. Pucelle, you just called upon the public to make Mr. Doefen the next President. Are you really saying that we should consider Mr. Doefen as a potential candidate?"

These weren't serious questions. She was just a kid and the pres was having a little fun.

"Not consider," Darcy said, not letting them put her down. "Count on it."

Oh, big laughs on that one.

How so? Why? What makes you so sure?

"The voice of truth demands that Doefen take his rightful place."

That got even bigger laughs. It was all they could do to keep from peeing their pants. "The voice of truth? Does this voice speak to you?"

"Of course."

At which point, everyone got busy hurling questions at her about the voice, and completely ignored anything else she tried to say about Doefen or WE.

She was just a kid, and what could a kid possibly say about the serious matter of politics that was worth hearing, let alone reporting. That was the attitude. But a kid who says she hears a voice telling her that Doefen should be President, now that was something.

In the frenzy to get a good sound bite, the press closed in so tight and hard that they all but squeezed the breath out of Darcy. And me.

"Come on. Come on." I tried to wiggle us out of there, but someone made a grab for Darcy's arm to keep her from leaving and yanked it really, really hard.

"Hey," she cried out. "Hey," looking a little shocked as she rubbed the arm and held it close to her chest.

She was hurting. I could see that. Her face got all clouded over, like she was afraid she was going to start crying or screaming and was trying really, really hard not to.

Which was when Robert stepped in. Late as usual.

"Interview is over," he announced, and putting his arm around Darcy's shoulder started to walk her out towards the back of the room like she was some kind of bride and he was the father. "Thank you."

"Yes, thank you," Darcy seconded, like she was suddenly channeling Miss Manners "Thank you everyone."

She turned and pointed with her good arm to Doefen who was still at the dais. "Doefen will be President."

The reporters made an immediate beeline back into the room to Doefen.

"Sir. Sir. Is what the girl says true?"

"WE is about individual responsibility," Doefen responded and started on his usual blah, blah, blah.

Within seconds he had everybody yawning and looking to leave.

Darcy gulped the glass of water I'd brought her, brushed away

Robert, who was making noise about taking her for an x-ray of her arm, and plunged back into the thick of things. Robert and I were right behind her.

"Truth will make a road for Doefen. *WE will make a road for Doefen,*" she shouted.

*WE will make a road for Doefen.* Who knows how many time she repeated that.

For as long as the reporters were willing to stick with Darcy, Robert – Mr. Don't Let Anyone Know Your Name – stood next to her introducing himself, smiling, butting in every two seconds to make it sound like he was in on the whole idea of running Doefen for president, and like everything that Darcy did was because of him. And first chance he got, he switched the topic away from Doefen and Darcy, and started talking bees.

His bees. His hives. His design for the bee screens along with a blow by blow on how he built them. His farm. His orchard. His organic produce. His honey. His blah, blah, blah.

Dumb fuck reporters chowed it right down.

I kept waiting for Darcy to get pissed and tell him to shut it. But the weird thing was that the longer Robert ran his mouth, the shakier she got.

"I don't think I want to do this," she whispered to me looking up at Robert like he was *all that* and she was nothing. "I'm in over my head. I should go home and just let grown-ups like Robert handle this."

I hated to hear Darcy sound so unsure, even though I liked the part about going home. I mean, her job was done. Doefen was launched. The rest was really up to him.

So I put in my vote for telling Robert to take us back to Glen Eddy, and right away Darcy turned totally schizo on me.

"I can't. I can't. Robert would be so disappointed in me if I quit on Doefen."

Robert disappointed? Without a doubt, he was getting off on shoving his way into Darcy's scene and being a part of something big. I mean, hell, it was either that or herd bees in Glen Eddy. But it wasn't like he gave a shit about Doefen.

Smart as Darcy was she had to know that. So what could I think except that, for some reason, she'd gotten scared? I patted her arm – the one that wasn't hurt — and told her not to worry, that everything would be alright.

Darcy nodded, but didn't look at all convinced, just kind of cradled her hurt arm with her good one.

Eventually, the reporters ran out of questions and the photographers had all the photos they wanted to take, and they all started to drift out of the conference room. Doefen followed them out. The rest of us closed in behind him.

Doefen came out of the hotel to a cheering crowd. Which improved Darcy's mood a lot. She started to smile again and waved with her good arm, gave a thumbs up to the blue, blue sky.

"Listen up, people," she said. "Doefen is going to Washington, as in Washington, D.C."

She waited for the cheering to stop before adding, "And WE will make the road for him. You, me WE have to stay all the way."

"Stay all the way," the crowd answered, even as the cops edged in on them.

"Look at them. Fucking, Pigs. Doing the same shit they did when I was at Columbia." Robert said, never one to miss a chance to reference his hippy protest days.

"Those cops don't scare me one bit," Darcy said. "I'm taking Doefen to Washington."

# ROBERT
The Voice


"WE is about individual responsibility, multiple points of view, small affinity groups representing specific causes, all separate and all one, like an ant colony. People already know the truth and have the power to make it heard. WE are speaking out so that this country does not end up being sold off to a web of multinational businesses and the military. I am only one of many. Really, there's no need for a leader or an organization. Truth will win out."

Darcy put Doefen in the spotlight, and that was the best he could manage. A minute after Darcy stepped away from his side, he succeeded in confusing the hell out of the press and boring them to tears at the same time.

No wonder they ended up ignoring Darcy's clear message — WE will make a road for Doefen – and seized on her bit about the voice of truth. There wasn't any juice in a story about some goat guy going on and on about the need to put leadership and power into the hands of those who weren't looking to grab it. But a kid who said she heard the voice of truth telling her what to do, that was something that would sell copy. Overnight, Darcy became the kid who heard voices.

A kid who was looney tunes. Crazy. Fucked-up. Dismissible.

All of which could have been easily avoided if Darcy had bothered to confide in Robert. Only someone as young and naive as she was could have possibly imagined that bringing up the voice of truth was anything but a big mistake. Mercifully, she hadn't actually tried to explain about Ginsberg.

Not surprising that the media totally distorted everything she said. Misunderstood. Robert tried his best to convince reporters that Darcy was just a normal kid. Normal in the way that the media meant normal. He told them about her love of animals, the Frog Rescue Hospital, her intuitive and easy way of being around bees, horses.

He told stories about her moral passion. She was a girl who needed to act, to set right even one small thing in the world. He described toddler Darcy picking up discarded cigarette butts, four year old Darcy asking her mother to hang a sign over her bed – *Remember to stop drinking baby bottles and to save the manatees,* her school petitions against Alar in apple juice, and the planting of the BE maize field.

But no matter how Robert tried, or how carefully he worded things, somehow each story he told got turned around, twisted, and, by the time it went into print, ended up making Darcy seem weirder and crazier.

Eventually he was forced to accept that no matter what he might say about Darcy, the world would continue to see only a girl with shorn hair who went around wearing a type of robe that had come to be associated with terrorists, and hallucinated some voice that instructed her to lead a goat herd from no-where USA to the presidency.

Thanks to the net and cell phones, any news about her went out and around the world in milliseconds. No investigative reporting was done. At least not till later. Way later. By which time Darcy had been turned into a crazy girl commanded by voices to overthrow the government, elect an unknown farmer as president, and, inexplicably, according to some religious faction, a delusional heretic claiming to be an incarnation of the Virgin.

# A.K.A.
Daily Report


A.K.A. Cherub, and Flaming Sword, and Eliot, and Ed, and Richard, and Phil, and John, and Blue Lips, and more names than he could remember tried to set the Chief straight right from the get go.

"Nobody gives a shit about a goat herder running for office." The whole thing was nothing more than a sound bite, he told the Chief. A video clip, a bit of comic relief to perk up a dull news day. Because who the fuck could stand to hear about the ins and outs of trade rip offs, also known as free trade agreements all day long? The reporters were bored out of their gourds, and the public, sure as shit, wasn't going to give the topic their undivided attention. The goat guy was a joke. In a day or two, everybody would forget about him.

"Exactly," Chief shouted at a.k.a.Cherub like he was deaf. Or stupid. "What they won't forget is the girl on the horse."

No doubt about it. The girl irked the Chief. Who the hell was she to think that she could do whatever she pleased? No respect for permits or procedures. A loose cannon.

Way before anyone had started calling her Angel Girl, the Chief already had his shorts in a knot over what to do about her.

"Deactivate her." That was the order. The sooner the better.

Chief didn't really want to hear that there was no point in wasting manpower to take her down. Chose to ignore the obvious – that she was just a young chick, who left to her own devices, would find a boyfriend in the next five minutes and the whole activist thing would be over. Poof. She'd be too busy fucking, and worrying about her boyfriend cheating on her to give a shit about a goat guy and government.

The part about a boyfriend caught the Chief's interest. "What's our availability to deploy a resource like that?"

Christ on a crutch. A resource to pose as a boyfriend? For a minor? Zero. Nil. None, he told him.

"Recruit one."

A.k.a. Cherub promised to give it his best shot. How exactly was he supposed to insert this resource? The girl was never alone. The scrawny kid from her home town who was ready to walk barefoot on broken glass for her, never left her side. And M3 didn't let her out of his sight. From the moment, he'd brought her to the Castle, he had his camera on her practically 24/7. And then there was Baudry, the hick bee keeper, who was always looking to horn in on her scene, always trying to keep the young dudes away from her. Called himself a friend, even though he was old enough to be her father. The perv.

Deactivate. That was the order. By whatever means necessary.

Having that kind of latitude was a good thing. Any other time a.k.a Cherub would have been happy. But for a kid? That made him nervous.

He should have bowed out. Never mind that Chief said, "Put this one to bed, and you'll get your pick of the next assignment. Narcotics. Corporate. Vice."

"And I'll get wheels."

"Absolutely."

"A Humvee."

"No problem."

"No more small time activist shit?"

"Never again."

What undercover in his right mind was going to say no to that?

# ROBERT
The Circle


Darcy and everyone from WE who'd been present at the show-down between Burgundy and Doefen came out of the hotel with hope in their hearts, and a sense of having won a round against the Man. Not that anyone except Robert would have used that term. Once again, he wished that Isabelle and Jack could have been there to see it.

Damn, if Darcy didn't do all of them proud. He rubbed at the tears that collected in the corner of his eyes.

The crowd outside the hotel greeted them with cheers. There was dancing in the street. It was a moment of almost complete happiness.

Darcy's discovery that the horse, Flo, was no longer tethered where she'd left her threatened to undo the mood, but then Frank assured her that he'd seen a guy in top hat and tails lead-ing the mare toward the Park, and just like that everything was right with the world again.

As Darcy walked away from the hotel, the cops manning the barricades stood as if bewitched, silent as stones. No pushing or shoving or threats. No hassles at all.

Getting back to the Park felt more like a triumphal procession than the continuation of a protest march. Of course, none of them knew at the time that, round ups and arrests were being carried out at the outermost reaches of their gathering.

Darcy, Doefen and Robert along with the front ranks of WE arrived at the field below Belvedere just before noon. The last of the marchers didn't arrive until hours later – that's how big the crowd was, never mind the puny police estimates. Somewhere along the way, the movement to elect Doefen was named *Spontaneous Combustion* because of the way it was going to ignite the hearts of the electorate with a passion for a leadership that spoke truth. Lived in truth. Fought for truth.

Everyone in WE loved, loved the name. And it was a good name. A fitting name.

*We are stardust. We are golden,* Frank sang in a loopy, over-the-top falsetto take on Joni Mitchell's *Woodstock* as they walked onto the field. With Frank it was always like that - too much, way more than necessary.              "We need a little song and celebration. If I wasn't a crip in a chair, I'd be twisting and shouting and kicking up some dust. Trust me, all of you really have to dance."

And they did. Without too much prompting, everyone linked hands in a circle that spiraled and spiraled and spiraled around itself and grew until it filled the entire field.

With his left hand Robert held on to Darcy. Her palm burned against his own. He marveled, not for the first time, at how small and spare her hand was — like a prototype of some elegant device whose uses were too marvelous and many to comprehend.

The hand that slipped into his right hand as the protesters linked to make a human chain was unfamiliar — deliciously cool, like the underside of a pillow in summer is cool. And petite — he could encircle it with his thumb and pinky. And soft, shapely, delicate. Probably a pampered hand. Not the sort of hand to be held in his blunt and hardened mitt. But then his thumb found a tiny calloused patch of skin – a possible indicator that this was a hand that had done some kind or work. Encouraged by the thought, he proceeded to explore further. The nails were cut short and gently rounded. Unpolished. The skin felt silky but not lotioned.

A sensible hand, he decided. A hand he could study for a long time without tiring.

Robert hardly dared to look at the woman it belonged to. But when at last he did look, he was not disappointed. She was young, but not too young. Attractive without being unduly beautiful. Her hair was loose. He liked that. Loose.

He smiled and she smiled back. Neither of them tried to speak. Robert gave her hand a squeeze, and fell in with the rhythm of the chanting. "Say No to WTO. Say No to WTO. Say No to WTO. WE are not for sale. WE are not for sale."

It was not an angry outcry. The cadence of the calling was peaceful and patient and rocking. More a meditation than a denunciation. A determined chant. Unflagging, but gentle.

The whole circle swayed to the lulling tempo while gently swinging their arms up, and then down, and slowly making a circuit around the lawn below Belvedere Castle.

All things move in circles, Robert thought. The earth and

moon and stars. Time. The seasons. All of life. His life. This circle.

Outside the circle, there was nothing. Or rather, chaos. The chaos that was every day existence. A tumult of sound. *Sound and fury, signifying nothing.* Noise.

Dimly, Robert registered the far-away blaring of stranded traffic, and the wheezing of overburdened buses, and the occasional yelping of a distraught dog, and the piercing hysteria of a police siren. Entranced as he was by the unknown hand, he did not immediately identify the staccato beat that first tapped, then thudded out of the distant din for what it was — a maelstrom of hooves, the thunder of charging police horses.

"Run," someone screamed. "Run." The protesters broke and scattered away from the horses bearing down on them.

Robert felt Darcy's hand slipping out of his own. He clenched, but too late, grasped at empty air with his left hand, even as his right held tight onto the hand that belonged to a woman whose name he didn't know.

In the next instant Darcy was swept away. Out of reach. Scooping empty air with his left arm, Robert strained after her, struggling not to fall in the crush of bodies surging past. He managed to hold fast to the hand in his right hand.

With all the strength in his body Robert fought to reach Darcy. His eyes strained to keep her from slipping from sight. And yet, all the while, his brain insisted on trying to divine the name of the woman whose hand he held fast. Linda. Lovely Linda. Maybe Angela. Or Clara. She looked like a Clara.

Yes, Clara, he thought, just as he spotted Darcy far off, well ahead of the mounted cops, her *djellabah* spread on the wind like wings. She was most of the way up a rocky ledge below the Castle, Billy clambering up after her. Other supporters closed in a tight vee behind them.

It looked to him like she was safe. And she was definitely too far away for him to reach her. No need for him to keep worrying about her, he decided. Especially, since she had spent the last two days going out of her way to make it clear, very, very clear that she didn't need him, that she had her own life now, thank you very much, a life with grand plans for Doefen, which didn't really include him, and which she'd never even bothered to share with him.

Robert clasped the unknown woman's hand tighter. Not Clara. Maybe Dawn. Or Hope. Or Lilly.

*"Her name was McGill, and she called herself Lil. But every-one knew her as Nancy."* The Beatles tune played in his head as the horses that had driven Darcy to run south and west, sud-denly turned, and left Robert no choice but to escape in the opposite direction.

He ran north, away from the Castle as fast and hard as he'd ever run, without losing or loosening his grip on Eleanor. Lucy. Sophia.

"Stay with me," he urged, though she already clung hard to him, and made no attempt to let go.

Monica. Rose. Julia. Louise.

Her name was Celeste.

"I haven't done this in a while," she told him when they finally made it to his truck and caught their breath.

"Me neither," Robert confessed and moved to sit ever so slightly closer. His head reeled from the intoxication of being in the presence of an attractive woman. A woman with nar-row hips, a pert little ass. A sexy woman — now that he had a chance to examine her more closely. Dressed in form fitting jeans and a supple, black leather vest. He couldn't remember the last time he'd been this near to a desirable woman, a women he desired. The summer yuppies he occasionally bedded didn't count.

Celeste laughed. "Not this." She waved her arm to include Robert, his proximity, and the cavern darkness of the truck bed under its rusty canopy. "I mean being at a protest march."

Robert liked the straight and honest and amused way that she looked into his eyes. Her gazed precluded nothing, and suggested that much was possible. He wished that he'd been able to bring her to a van with carpeting, and leather seats in-stead of a battered pick up. The occasion positively demanded a kick ass stereo to blast Joplin, *"Take a little piece of my heart now, baby,"* or a Hendrix riff of electric ecstasy.

"I missed out on the Sixties," she said as though she could read his thoughts. "I always wished that I'd been old enough to be a part of the sit-ins, and be-ins, and demonstrations."

"They were highly overrated," Robert assured her gladly as-suming the role of older, experienced activist.

*But are you experienced? Have you ever been experienced before?* Hendrix crooned in his head.

An anti-nuclear march, Celeste said, was the last time she had taken to the streets. Marched to the UN, weeping most of the way. Not so much over nuclear arms proliferation, or the violations of the SALT treaties, but because she was newly divorced, and heartbroken, and her best friend was walking with a newborn asleep in one of those sling things that go across the chest.

Robert wondered, but didn't ask, whether she'd remarried, or had babies. He just let her talk, encouraged her, "Tell me. Tell me about yourself."

She'd grown up in the burbs, bored senseless. An outsider and geek. "Like a lot of girls, I wanted to be a dancer. But I took longer than most to outgrown the fantasy."

"I bet you were good," he insisted over her demurrals to the contrary. He pictured her suspended in mid jeté, like the young deer he'd once seen crossing his pasture in the moonlight – improbably arched, defying gravity. "But you needed someone to encourage you."

She did not deny it and Robert's heart ached with sympathy.

She became a massage therapist, later a paralegal to pay the bills. Raised a child, a daughter. The love of her life, she said.

"What about a husband?" Robert asked, heart pounding unpleasantly fast.

"Oh," she laughed. "Husbands and lovers and a love. I've had them all."

Had them, but not now. He breathed a deep sigh.

And to his amazement, somehow between loving and divorcing and parenting and working, she'd found the time and wherewithal to travel – a trek to the remote reaches of the Himalayas, the further reaches of the Amazon.

Listening to her Robert felt like a kid left on the bench in a pick-up game of basketball. Hers was a full life; a life well-lived.

"Where were you when I was twenty?" he moaned.

"You wouldn't have liked me then," she sensibly replied, and Robert knew that it was true. He'd have called her straight. A sellout. He would have mocked her. He might have tried to fuck her while remaining blind to her beauty. He would not have understood her kind of courage.

They talked for a long time, and with each hour, Robert felt like he was slowly awakening from the long sleep that was Glen Eddy. How and why had he stayed there for so long?

Glen Eddy was supposed to be a temporary stop, he told her.

After the Columbia take-over devolved into a rampage of tearing up student files and smearing the Dean's desk with dog shit, he'd ended getting booked by the Pigs. And while that file was still open, he'd gone on to ignore his draft notice. And that created another file. Bottom line, he found himself in need of a nondescript place with no connection to anything to hide in until things chilled out and the war was over.

Glen Eddy, he told her, seemed perfect. A depressed area in the middle of nowhere. No industry. A little subsistence farming. Landscape pretty enough, but not spectacular — hills, but no large mountains, an undistinguished river without great fishing or white water rapids. Nothing to attract second-homers or suburbanization.

In the beginning, squatting in a long-abandoned bungalow colony with Jack and Isabel had felt pretty "alternative," he explained. Radical. Anti-establishment. As did the business of helping Jack hock jewelry for dope when the economy tanked. Jack did the negotiating. Robert weighed the gold, commiserated with the hard luck stories, paid out the cash, and carried the gun that Jack had insisted on "just in case."

"A gun?" Celeste exclaimed, and Robert feared that he'd lost her. "You carried a gun?"

"Just a 38." A faint nausea rose to his throat just remembering it.

The drugs Jack sold and liberally indulged in made him whacko. Paranoid. He became convinced that they needed a gun for protection. Robert volunteered to carry it, tucked into the waistband of his jeans, knowing for sure that he wouldn't use it. He feared that letting Jack hold it could turn out to be a whole other story.

"You armed yourself with a deadly weapon," Celeste said and let her eyes slip down past his chest over the small mound of his belly. And below.

He felt shy as a virgin. And thrilled.

"Only for a short time." Sucking his abs as flat as he could, he explained how the whole scene got tired really fast once Jack almost died muling dope — a condom full of coke that he'd swallowed broke and put him in the ICU, but luckily not in jail.

Jack recovered, he assured Celeste. Went straight. Took a job stringing wire for the phone company. Which, to Robert's annoyance, Isabelle pronounced groovy because it was about "getting people connected." A detail he didn't share with Celeste. Nor did he reveal that Isabelle considered Robert despicably bourgeois for buying the farmhouse and some land with his cut from the dealing.

"I'm clean, now," he told Celeste. No weapon. You can search me."

And she did – running her long fingers over his shirt.

He shivered, his nipples hardened. He liked her liking him.

"I would like to get the hell out of Glen Eddy and maybe buy a little hotel in the Caribbean. If only the local county would get around to building a casino or racetrack like they keep promising, I could sell my place and make a decent profit."

"Sweet... a life in the Caribbean," Celeste murmured, her fingers coming to rest at the top of his belt.

"I thought that all I had to do was to be patient and wait," he told her, struggling to keep his voice cool. Neutral.

He'd waited and waited and waited. Only nothing ever got built in Glen Eddy. And the world he'd left never became a better place. A place to return to.

Celeste held onto the waistband of his jeans with one hand, unzipped him with the other. "So what did you do while you were waiting?"

He let her slip his jeans and briefs down over his hip bones. Showed her what she clearly wanted to see, but just for a moment. Then pulled up the briefs again.

"I dropped out for good," he told her. "Just planted my own garden, so to speak."

Though he'd barely done that, if the truth be told. For all his talk, he'd pretty much retreated from his college days idealism the way a factory worker retired from the assembly line.

"I hear tell that a lot of people did that after the Sixties," Celeste said and drew him to her.

He allowed her to embrace him.

She may have looked as delicate as a winged creature, easily crushed, quick to alight, but Celeste's hold was sure. Robert liked that. Surrendered to it.

For a moment, he imagined the life he could have had with someone like her – a city life in rent-controlled apartment on a leafy street in the West Village, windows overlooking the sprawling limbs of an ancient sycamore. An aerie nest with a woman who loved him. And a child. His own child, for real. Not a maybe daughter like Darcy.

As he traced the long line of Celeste's neck with his calloused fingers, touched the firm nubs of her nipples through her shirt, Robert thought that maybe, just maybe, it wasn't too late. No one remembered or cared anymore about the Columbia take-over or the draft. He should sell the farm. Set the bees free. Make his life alongside, next to, with Celeste.

He could do, learn to do something other than poke around in his own little plot.

# BILLY
Chased


We scattered as soon as the cops showed up. Darcy laced her fingers in mine and we made for the Castle. Fast as we ran, we couldn't outrun the thumping hooves. Even when we reached the bluff, we still heard them behind us.

Sweating, panting we scrambled up onto the rocks. The climb was not as steep or rough as some parts of the short cut we took to school, but we needed our hands.

Darcy only had one good one, and I was afraid to let it go. She wrenched it free.

"Just stay next to me," she said. As if I was about to do anything else.

Flying, burning things whizzed all around us. Glass bottles exploded into shards against the rocks. Black smoke blotted out parts of the sky. The air reeked of gasoline.

Molotov cocktails. Neither one of us had ever seen one. But somehow we knew that the fiery things flying over our heads from the direction of the Castle and crashing at our feet were gasoline bombs.

"No," Darcy screamed. "No way." The petroleum stench that she loved at the pumps, and I'd learned to appreciate, had no place in Central Park. "Please, no. They can't be ours."

The idea that WE, pacifist, non-violent WE, might be responsible for the fire balls seemed to stress her out more than the flames that were jumping from one clump of weeds to the next.

At this point, anyone but Darcy would have been totally focused on getting away. Which got my vote. But she stood straight up and turned to scan the field and Castle to determine exactly who was responsible for the fire bombs.

"You're crazy. Outta your mind," I blubbered.

Oh yes, I was back to blubbering again, practically blind with tears. I yanked at her sleeve, tried to pull her down.

Too late.

Something hit her hard in chest, up above the heart, near the shoulder. I heard the thump, looked for flames and didn't see any.

The already hurt arm that Darcy had been holding against her chest fell to dangle alongside her body.

"I've been hit." She reeled back in shock and pain. With the fingers of her good hand she probed for an open wound. "It's not bleeding," she said, like the tears on her face had nothing to do with her. Like crying was just some reflex no different from the one your knee makes when the pediatrician hits it with that little rubber tomahawk hammer.

With Darcy clutching her hurt arm, and me using my entire body to brace her, we stumbled up toward the castle. The blizzard of bottles, and sometimes cans, and rocks continued. The threshing of horses' hooves followed us from behind.

The wind shifted. A smoky fog that burned our eyes, and made our lungs seize up closed in around us, separated me from Darcy. Between sputtering and coughing, I called for her. I felt, rather than saw, figures flit past. A horse snorted close to my ear. Its breath brushed my cheek like an invisible hand.

I ran harder. The horse did not follow. The wind shifted again, blew away the smoke. I turned to look back.

A horse with a saddle that said NY Police Department, but minus any rider stood snorting and shaking its bridle, pawing the ground with one hoof. No cop came to claim the spooked animal.

For like the nine hundred ninety ninth time, I yelled for Darcy. This time, she materialized out of the smoke and ash, her finger to her lips in a shhhhh sign. As if I was making the only noise in the world, and there wasn't screaming, and neighing, and the pop, pop, pop of things exploding all around us.

With slow, even steps she approached the riderless police horse.

"They're awful careless with you," she crooned at the horse as she hoisted herself into the saddle, one handed.

The horse whinnied and Darcy leaned to whisper in its ear, "Yeah, they're awfully careless."

Still leaning over the horse's neck, she turned to look at me and in the same whispery voice said, "Come here. Hop on and let's get out of here."

Panicked as I was, not even Darcy could convince me to climb on a beast whose rump stood higher than my head.

I preferred to take my chances on foot.

# ROBERT
Because She Wanted Him To


Robert pressed his belly into the hard bowl of Celeste's pelvis — because she wanted him to. Because her body demanded it. Commanded it.

Something smooth, round dug into his thigh.

A stone? Darcy collected small ovoid ones, and he was always on the look out for another to add to the collection that she kept lined up on the radiator in her bedroom.

He shifted his weight, remembered the gingko seed in his pocket. If it got crushed, the stink would kill the whole vibe.

He braced himself on his elbows. No graceful way to stop now to retrieve the thing. Celeste was already taking sippy little breaths, calming her excitement with longer, slower exhalations, and unbuttoning her shirt to expose naked breasts.

No bra. He swallowed down his disappointment at that, caught her hand, brushed it with his lips to stop her from slipping out of the leather vest.

The vest was good. A leather corset or a bustier with cut-outs to show the nipples would have been better. The better to suck them. Women liked that, having their nipples sucked. Biological. Came from suckling babies, no doubt.

He would do that for her. Suck her tits. And buy her leather lingerie. Dress her in it himself. All she'd have to do was stand there. Maybe hold a crop, make like she was going out riding. Just stand there and hold the crop while he knelt before her, did whatever she liked, whatever she wanted, whatever she commanded.

He pulled the leather vest closed, tightening his grip on it until her smallish breasts were squeezed into mounds with cleavage.

"The framing," he told her, leaning back to admire his handiwork, "makes it so exciting."

She murmured contentedly, cupped her breasts and thrust them upward. He brushed them quickly with closed lips. As he allowed his body to press up against hers, he began to smell the ginkgo – still faint, but unmistakable.

He shifted up off his right thigh, lay on his side ready to reach into his pocket, but she caught his hand, brought it to her lips, ran her tongue around the tip of his index finger. With her free hand she undid his shirt.

The cool air on his chest was a shock. The sticky warmth of her skin against his was equally unnerving. The whiff of ginkgo was now a growing stench. How could she not notice?

He raised himself off her into a full cobra position in an effort to shift his weight off the foul seed.

She whispered something undecipherable and pulled him back down.

Burying his face in the leather vest, he nuzzled the buttery warmth of the dressed and tanned hide, inhaled deeply. One breath, another. The leather's powerful essence extinguished every trace of the ginkgo stink, and even imbued the too floral scent of Celeste's hair with the dark smokiness of animal musk. Robert pressed his wind worn, sun parched lips against the leather, touched and teased it with his tongue. Gently, he lifted the edge of the vest with his teeth, held it softly at first then bit it harder, held on tight to the leather while Celeste tossed and writhed beneath him.

As though from a great distance, he heard her moan — softly at first, then louder. He sucked up the leather until it was a swollen wad that filled his mouth, until it became a gloved fist sinking deep down into the back of his throat to choke the breath out of him, to force him to come. Plunging his tongue into the wet leather, he emptied himself with a groan.

Celeste slept almost immediately. Robert lay next to her, his pulse hammering in his ear, the damp leather vest cooling against his cheek. Once again, the acrid stink of ginkgo rose up to fill his nostrils. It seemed to be everywhere, everywhere all at once, an unseen cloud, a vapor enveloping the van, twining around him and onto Celeste. He reached into his pocket to dispose of the foul fruit.

Inexplicably, it was whole and undamaged. Carefully, quietly Robert sat up to stow the ginkgo in the wheel well.

Celeste's eyes flew open. "Stay," she murmured, and he obeyed.

Clearly she was looking to cuddle and curl, just like most women in Robert's experience. And he would have indulged her even though he barely knew her, but now Darcy was weighing on his mind again. Knowing Darcy, she was probably alright. Better than alright, still he needed to check on her. Make sure.

He had to hand it to Celeste. She didn't need a road map to understand his predicament. Two minutes after he'd explained about Darcy, she was up and ready to roll. No attitude. No reproach. The way she fretted about finding Darcy, you'd have thought that she was her own kid. Probably, it was a woman thing; something in the DNA meant to insure the survival of the species.

As they ran together around the pond and back down to the Castle, he couldn't help but notice that she gripped his hand tighter than before, all the while urging him to go faster.

# BILLY
The Capture


From the moment Darcy got on the horse, she'd been trying to climb the ridge to get to the Castle, but it was like the ridge was made of glass and ice. The horse couldn't really get moving on it, and I kept slipping and falling.

On the field below the ridge – a godzillion cops, on horses, on foot, were grinding the dry grass to dust. Yellow fingers of light from the lamps on their helmets poked through the smoke of the Molotovs that had been thrown down from the castle.

Darcy decided that our best shot at escape was to get down from the ridge and make our way around the lake below. The demonstrators who'd already made it to the Castle would be able to see us. Could give us cover in case the cops followed us. All of a sudden, Ms. Non-Violence was OK with WE throwing a few rocks at the cops if it meant giving us the lead time we needed to get to the wooded path that would take us back up to Belvedere.

We were halfway around the lake, her on the horse, me running alongside, when Darcy screamed, clutched her thigh. She was hit again. But no giveaway thump this time. Or at least, I didn't hear one. I looked around, saw nothing. No one.

Thinking back, I realize that there must have been some kind of sound. There had to be. Law of physics of something. But at the time I was quick to imagine that she'd been hit by invisible lasers, secret weapons no one had even heard of yet because once again there was no blood, no open wound.

I crouched down low.

Darcy clicked her tongue quietly, and the horse did its best to giddy-upped. The soft mud along the bank sucked and slapped at its hooves. Each slow and clumsy step must have branded itself into Darcy's injured thigh. She scrunched up her face but didn't complain.

We were almost at the woods when, out of nowhere, a cop appeared and charged straight at Darcy. I was close enough to see his outstretched meaty hand, his yellowed thumbnail that was gnawed down to its moon. He closed his fist on Darcy's beautiful, delicate *djellabah*, and pulled her off the horse. As she fell, I saw the shapes and shadows that were the woods sprout, transform into men in uniforms. They charged the horse, wrestled Darcy face down onto the soggy ground.

"Stop," she sobbed as her arms were wrenched behind her and cuffed.

"You have the right to remain silent," a winded voice wheezed at her, just like they do on TV cop shows.

More tears than Darcy had ever cried at any one time poured out of her eyes.

"You have the right to counsel."

How brave was I? Not very. I mean I screamed "stop" and "no" and "let her go," but with the horse neighing and all the other commotion it made about as much difference as a gnat buzzing in a thunderstorm.

I did hit the cop who was putting a choke hold on Darcy. Slammed his back hard as I could with my fist. But he was all padded out in one of those body armor things, so all I did was hurt my hand.

Then I bit him, dug my teeth into the soft spot above his elbow and held on tight. That got his attention. Not that he let go of Darcy. But he did turn to look at me. And I saw right away that if that cop ever got his hands on me, I wouldn't live to tell it, so I dove into the bushes and crawled on my belly away from the path. Which was just what M3 had taught us was the thing to do in that kind of situation.

I went to ground and stayed there until things got quiet. By which time it was dark.

I was alone. Darcy gone. For the first time ever, I was all alone in the dark.

I got up, took one step. Then another. Without signs or strings, I made my way past the Castle, avoiding the cops staked out around it, and headed for the rendezvous place up by the fort that Darcy and Doefen had planned out the day before.

I crept through the gathering night like I was with Darcy, and we were taking the short cut to school through the woods. I wasn't fast, but my steps were silent. Or pretty close to silent. An insect's breathing would have sounded louder. And I was invisible, or almost. Carefully hunched down, I made myself into a small brown blot, a shadow passing over the ground, between the trees.

I smelled things I'd never smelled before. I could have totally picked out the scent of a human from the stew of all other odors – rotting leaves, worms, dirt, the high sweet gasoline funk emitted by cars far outside the Park. My ears were open to sounds I'd never heard before – blades of grass rubbing one against the other, the snuffling of small animals dug down in their underground hideouts. I could see further than I'd even seen before, as though I'd just put on a brand new pair of glasses with a stronger prescription. Each rock, each tree had its own recognizable character. My skin prickled with every shift in the air, each tiny hair on my body was a finely tuned antenna. Never had I felt more alive. Or more scared.

The shriek of a jay flew out of the trees, a quiver of silver arrows.

A shriek. Silver arrows. My whole body shook like I'd stuck my finger in a live electric socket. I had never seen sound take a shape before! This had to be what the world was like for Darcy. What it must have been like to be Darcy.

How did she manage to live with such intensity?

I don't know how long I walked, or what route I took. I only know that by the time I found myself at the fort where WE was hunkered down, the world had reverted to being just a landscape that lay outside my body.

There wasn't much of a WE crowd left after all the people who'd gotten busted, and all the one's who'd cut out at the first sign of real trouble. But Doefen was there, sitting on a big rock drawing circles in the dirt with a stick. Tre and Frank and a couple of the others were planted around him, arguing about who had the best plan for what WE should do the next day.

M3 lay propped up against a tree. The standby light on his camera blinked on and off like a psycho firefly.

And yeah, like a minute later, Robert came out of the woods, ran up and tried to hug me like everything was going to be OK.

All of which changed in a hurry once he got it through his head that Darcy wasn't with me.

Little fuck, he called me. Prick bastard. Accused me of losing Darcy. Ran around spazzing out, making a scene. He was all tears and heartbreak.

But the girl with the licorice hair who came out of the woods with him had his number. She just left him to rant, and came and put her arm around my shoulder like she was my mom.

"OK." she whispered into my hair. It was kinda, sorta a statement, but a question too. "OK?"

And so I nodded yes, because I was. I was as OK as I'd ever been in my life. I'd gotten through the night. I hadn't cried. Not once. Not a single tear. Not then. Or since.

Maybe it wasn't so much. But it was what I could do for Darcy.

## ROBERT
Not Part of the Plan


Violence wasn't part of the plan. Neither was getting arrested. Darcy must have been shocked to find herself being treated like a dangerous criminal — hands cuffed, patted down, *djellabah* yanked up around her neck, the laces from her boots confiscated. She was forced to lie face down in the police van that hauled her off to a holding pen.

The details of the arrests made that day have become common knowledge, documented in the civil lawsuits that came afterward. Violations of due process. Strip searches. People held without food, water, denied access to a lawyer. All of those were the norm of the day.

Over two thousand arrests were made, most of them before the big round up at Belvedere Castle. During the march to the Waldorf, at key locations all over midtown, side streets full of people were penned – hundreds at time. The Pigs claimed that the arrests were directed at protesters who'd refused repeated orders to disperse. The lawsuits proved that the Pigs had, in fact, sealed off the ends of cross streets with orange mesh barricades making it impossible for the protesters to comply. They opened the barricades only to herd the marchers into prison vans.

Massive numbers of vans with metal grids on the windows, along with armored vehicles, and regular patrol cars were staged within a few feet of the protesters. The idea was to unnerve anyone on the street, and to give the Pigs the means to disappear detainees quickly without attracting attention.

The sweeps that day included a bunch of innocent bystanders – a toll collector on his way to work at Port Authority. Also a dad from the burbs bringing his daughter to a college interview. And a retired biology teacher on the way to see her cardiologist. And some Japanese tourists looking for the Empire State Building.

That day, instead of the cops issuing a summons – the usual procedure for a minor offense – the detainees were fingerprinted and assigned a special code identifying them rioters.

219

After processing, which took many hours longer than usual, they were kept in custody for up to forty hours without seeing a judge, almost a day longer than the suspects arrested that day for rape, robbery, and even murder. When the detainees were finally allowed to make a phone call, it was registered in a special police log.

Two months after the march, thanks to the ACLU, charges were either dropped or dismissed against more than ninety-seven percent of those arrested. The individuals who chose to sue the city found that the Pigs had collected massive amounts of their personal information in the name of national security — not just the usual financial data and employment records, but medical information, report cards, and e mails sent to lovers, parents, children, friends.

The public was shocked to learn that such things could happen, did happen in America. Of course they were shocked for about ten minutes, and forgot about it. That was the American way. And so was leaving it to the ACLU and other organization like it, to fight for justice from an unjust system, to press for the dismissal of all trumped up charges, and for cash settlements for physical injuries. Of which there were many, thanks to the Pigs' zealous enforcement of "peace and order."

As it turned out, WE members were singled out for "proactive arrests" because of utterly untrue, probably fabricated "received intelligence" indicating that WE attracted anarchist sympathizers who were "very prone to violent and disruptive tactics." No one blinked an eye at the revelation that the Pigs had WE, and other private citizens with no criminal record under active ongoing surveillance.

In the end, the inquiries initiated by ACLU just proved that Jack's rants against the Man were right-on. The Man was the Man. Nothing had changed. Documents, draft reports from the Pigs' own Department of Disorder Control outlined a program of covert tactics that included using undercover cops to distribute misinformation within WE so as to spread lies that would instigate distrust within their ranks.

It was like the Man's whole Independent Service for Information program from the Sixties had come to life all over again. History had proven that ISI was, in fact, an operation designed to engage activists in "front organizations," which were meant to diffuse, discredit, or subvert them. Or worse, make them play into the system. In its heyday, ISI had even succeeded in co-opting the likes of Gloria Steinem – Isabelle's personal saint of just and politically correct causes.

The Handschu Agreement of the Sixties, designed to regulate police behavior, was supposed to have taken care of that kind of subversion of the Constitution. But the way the Man treated the WE protest, it was like the courts had never ruled that collecting information on political groups with the express intent of destabilizing them was a violation of the First Amendment right to free speech and assembly. It was as if the military vets who'd secured the right to oppose the Vietnam War had never gone head to head with the police state.

From day one, Chief Cuchen had an answer for every charge of police violence, every violation of due process.

"The force did its best under a sudden flood of arrests."

He attributed any delays in processing the arrests to the extraordinary numbers of detainees, and the time needed to check fingerprints and records for outstanding warrants.

"Nearly 1200 arrested in a one hour period. It was the largest number of arrest in the history of the city."

He cited that stat as if it was the norm to arrest any citizen who wanted to improve the status quo, as if suppressing democratic dissent was a thing to preen over.

He called the forty-hour holds without charges "extended detentions," an unfortunate byproduct of the city's diligence in maintaining public order. With a straight face, he declared that the city had done an excellent job of keeping the streets safe while still protecting civil rights.

For Robert what it all came down to was really simple. WE had fought the Man and the Man had won. Because that's what the Man does — by whatever means it takes.

For things to have gone down the way they did, as fast as they did the day of the Waldorf showdown, the Man's whole machinery had to have been in place and ready to roll ages before WE came along. WE just happened to set it in motion, and Darcy was the coin that dropped into the slot. Cha-ching.

Sometimes when Robert couldn't sleep and was wrung out with crying, he consoled himself with the thought that there was really nothing he could have done to change what happened. It had all been inevitable.

Because really, what reason was there for Cuchen to make an example of Darcy? What had she done? Her nomination of Doefen couldn't have meant squat to him. Or the bigger powers either.

They could have taken care of Doefen in the usual fashion. Let him win a few primaries, then seen to it that he petered out, went back to his goats. No one would have been the wiser.

Robert knew all about handling that kind of defeat at the hands of the Man. He would have been right there standing by, ready to console Darcy when the whole Doefen thing crashed and burned. She would have been hurt for a while, then found another cause. That was the way these things worked. Basic as gravity.

How was he supposed to know that Cuchen would make it personal?

# CHIEF CUCHEN
Key Concepts

It was like he always taught the recruits. Pre-emptive defense. Pre-emptive detention. Those were key, the best shot at defusing a situation.

Questions about errors? Of course there would be questions. They were, mostly, a nuisance, an unavoidable and time-consuming distraction for those in the front lines of response, who already had their hands full defending liberty, peace, and all the things that make the nation great.

Which was where pre-emptive justification came into play.

Terrorism.

One simple word was all it took to explain why WE was handled the way it was. Terrorism.

Since 9/11 it was the biggest, baddest bogey man going. Everyone from the bum on the street to the big boys of government was preoccupied with it, wanted it stopped.

If you see something, say something. Do something.

And that was exactly what the police force was doing. Responding. The answer was as straightforward as that. It was their business to watch for was going on and to do something about it. Lest anyone forget, the police were the first line of defense, the best protection against terrorism.

Forget about all the legislation that slathered on another layer of bureaucracy over already existing agencies of the intelligence community without giving any one of them the power and authority to take action against potential terrorists. What was the use of electronic surveillance programs like Total Information Awareness collecting stats about possible terrorists and then not using them? All that data about suspicious patterns of communications, medical usage, travel, education and financial transactions going to waste in Washington.

Terrorism existed in a borderless world as a network, not a state. It was not an army. Its recruits had no uniform to identify them. A terrorist could be anyone, look like anyone – even a girl in a *djellabah*, or a boy with punk hair and nose piercings. Terrorists co-opted and exploited the freedoms of a democracy by posing in the guise of peaceful demonstrators. Farmers. Beekeepers.

The sad and scary truth was that terrorists could and did wage their war anywhere and everywhere. Let Washington haggle with the American Civil Liberties Union over the government's supposedly unjustified intrusion into the personal lives of Americans. Cuchen and his men would do what had to be done to protect the streets and the citizens of the city. If routing terrorism required vigilance, surveillance, a close attention to nuances of behavior, and yes, responding to suspicious actions with pre-emptive detention – then so be it.

The trick was to understand potentiation, and to use it to boost the effectiveness of all the agencies already on the lookout for the signals that could spell trouble, and to cut out all noise from the bleeding hearts who were sapping the strength of the country. Of course everyone got 9/11 after it was a done deal. The trick was to catch on before it happened. Too bad that it took a shock to the psyche like 9/11 to get some action. It wasn't a lesson Cuchen was about to forget. Once a group like WE succeeded in undermining the best nation on earth, it would be too late.

No matter what anyone said, the US was still the best country on the planet. What other nation paid its workers better, had a better standard of living, more cars, TVs, phones, you name it? What government allowed more freedom – to travel, get naked on TV, or whatever. Nobody in the US of A had to go to bed without a meal if they were willing to work.

Cuchen wasn't about to let a two-bit outfit like WE and a pipsqueak girl to bring down the mighty land that bred them. Not on his watch.

The Darcy girl only got what she had coming to her.

## BILLY
Fact. Truth. Authenticity.


Fact. Truth. Authenticity.

All of them different. All of them almost the same. Related.

Fact. Darcy was arrested. I was there for that part.

Fact. I wasn't with her in the jail. But others were. Lots of others. Everyone noticed her. Remembered her. I mean duh, how could they not? She was the only one there dressed in a robe with sparkly threads. Her face was already all over the net. And the word was out on how she'd launched the whole Doefen for President nomination thing. So, of course, there were tons of people who wrote about her, and blogged about her, and talked about her for 30 seconds at a time on TV.

Truth. I read every eyewitness account, every document, every police report, and newspaper article I could get my hands on. Not when it all happened. But later.

And I knew Darcy. So I could tell which stuff was real and which was just shit that somebody made up. I mean for about a minute, all kinds of people were looking to claim a connection to Darcy so they could grab a minute of fame. Which meant there was a lot of totally bogus stuff out there. But since I knew her — really, really knew her — I could sort it out, put together the real and true and authentic story of what happened.

A lot of the facts were the same no matter who they came from.

Fact. People all over the city — in the Park, out on the street — were scooped up in big orange nets. Some were protesters. A lot were innocent bystanders — like these two really old, old tourists from Japan. They kept showing a clip of them on TV after it was all over —- heads bobbing a mile a minute, repeating, *"Mistaku. Mistaku."* And then there was the wino geezer guy who got all bugged out by the orange netting and wound up keeling over from a heart attack. And the bike messenger girl with red hair who spent the night in the same pen as Darcy. She was one of twenty bike people the cops arrested that day— just because.

Truth, none of these people were violent or doing anything

but minding their own business.

Fact. Everyone got cuffed, hands behind the back. The cuffs looked like no big deal – thin, plastic tie things like the ones they use to bundle vegetables at the supermarket. Except that the sharky teeth on one side made the ties go tighter and tighter when people tried to wriggle out of them.

Truth. People came out with cuts all over their wrists, their fingers blue from the cuffs cutting off circulation.

Fact. Everybody was shoved into prison vans that took off for a hellhole part of the city over by the river. Picture a dark and dangerous spot — deep black water with concrete piers sticking out like teeth. Nothing for miles but warehouses with blacked out windows, empty lots of heaved-up asphalt, all of it choked off by coils of razor wire.

Fact. The area used to be Navy shipping yards. Abandoned since like forever. I had to go back a couple of decades to find a map old enough to show them. I saw pictures and they gave me nightmares.

Fact. The vans – some done up to look like yellow school buses, some stenciled front and back with EMERGENCY VEHICLE in big blue letters – screeched to a stop behind the Navy yard warehouses where lines of cops stood guarding metal double doors. It took seven cops to move each door, and once the doors were wide open there was room for two Mac trucks to drive in side by side

Fact. The whole transport trip from arrest to the place of detention took maybe half an hour.

Truth. People stumbled out of the dark vans feeling dazed, disoriented, dizzy, off-balance like they'd traveled for a thousand miles.

Fact. The vans arrived while it was still day. Darcy sneezed as she always did in bright sunlight. A lot of people remembered that because of how some cop yelled at her to cover her mouth and slammed her across the back of the head. Never mind that her arms were in cuffs.

Truth. People said that the whole place felt like night, even though the sun was still out. They swore that the dark waters of the river were like those black holes in outer space that swallow up everything — sound, light, even gravity.

There are documents about all the usual stuff that goes with

arrests and detentions. Cops with batons, dogs. Lots of pushing, prodding, herding. Lots of shouting through megaphones
– "Listen up people, for your own safety..." Demands. Instruc-
tions. Confiscations. Inventorying, tagging of dangerous items
like back packs, cell phones, clothing and food.

After those, came the walk through metal detectors, which
according to an eyewitness, Darcy said reminded her of rose
trellises.

Truth. Darcy had an eye for beauty, saw it even when everyone else missed it. Called it out in a metal detector.

A cop or two or three or ten dissed Darcy for wearing a *djellabah*. Called it a terrorist get-up. Threatened to strip it off her. But
didn't. Not then. Not right there.

Fact. Nobody at the WE march wore anything like it, or would
dare to. Not after 9/11.

Mug shots were next. A number was taped onto each person's chest and back. The background was a sooty black wall
that had made it through some long ago fire, but just barely.

Fingerprinting followed – which should have been a non-
event, except that the cops made a point of pressing people's
pinky finger really hard onto the plate like they were testing to
see if they could manage to break the bone and still be able to
call it an accident.

Fact. The ACLU was hip to this kind of shit, and sued.

Truth. The fingerprint thing kind of made you understand how
stuff like waterboarding and Abu Ghrab and Guantanemo could
happen.

Fact. After "processing," it was into the holding cells deep inside the warehouse, which smelled of vomit and piss, and a little of rotting apples. A lot of people mentioned the apple smell.
Nobody explained it.

Not a fact. I'm betting it was from some toxic chemical left
over from the Navy warehouse era.

Fact. People were jammed together so close that the shoulder blades of one person were totally stuck into the belly or
chest of the person behind. It was impossible for the detainees
to look anywhere but down.

Fact. The floor crawled with huge brown bugs – nobody had
ever seen anything quite like them before. They swarmed over
rotted pieces of food that were so gross and ground into the

floor nobody could tell what they were. Sometimes, the bugs climbed up on people's shoes or up their legs. There was lots of screaming.

Truth. Darcy got freaked out by bugs, but believed she was supposed to love them even if they looked like space-alien, boggle-eyed, dragon-faced, robot-jointed, I-can't-believe-we-live-on-the-same-planet weird. Six legs, eight, a hundred? Darcy did her best to love them all, even went around looking for them under rocks, in dead wood, and leaf piles. Called them beautiful.

Fact. Between the bugs and the claustrophobia, people were actually glad to be taken out of the cell for questioning.

Fact. The process started out the same for Darcy as everyone else, but quickly got way different.

"Name?" Three times a cop asked. Three times Darcy didn't answer.

Fact. Truth. Robert taught her not to give her name to the cops, and she didn't. Even though by then her name and picture were all over the net, and she knew it.

Authentic detail. The cop's voice was the color of lilies, but without any softness to it. That's what Guy Laval, Darcy's cell-mate and big time blogger, reported that she'd told him. In his blog, he called her poetic.

Fact. The Guy Laval dude spent a lot of time with her in that cell, and most of the time he was good on the specifics.

Truth. White was Darcy's least favorite color. A non-color. White was the absence of spirit. The color of death.

Fact. The cop smiled. I'm betting his teeth were white and smooth as squares of tile.

Fact. He tapped his pen against his clipboard.

Truth. I had the same nervous habit of tapping my pen on things until Darcy explained that the sound clattered against her body like hailstones that were covered all over with tiny clear spikes.

Darcy asked the cop to please stop and tried to cover her ears.

Still smiling, the cop pressed his stick into her shoulder — the already hurt shoulder and used it to pry her hand away from her ear. She screamed. Two other guards closed in on her.

One forced her to squat, the other pulled the *djellabah* over her head. Or tried to.

Fact. The accounts disagree. Some have Darcy naked and probed. Other say she whispered to the cop, "You can't like working here like this. It's got to feel like you're a prisoner too." Which did not make him suddenly act like a very nice human fooled by his own disguise. Thank you very much, Allen Ginsberg.

According to Guy Laval, Darcy fixed the cop with a look of such force and fire that his face burned red and caused him to turn away in shame.

Which I believe. Want to believe. Because it follows the you-can't-make-this-shit-up rule of truth and authenticity. And especially because it comes out better for Darcy.

Fact. During the arrest and booking, strip and body searches were done mostly on young women by male guards, right out in the open for everyone to see. Private parts were exposed, probed with cop sticks.

Fact. Cuchen called it a psychological tactic used to set a tone of compliance.

Truth. It was rape.

Fact. The ACLU sued the cops and won. Which was a good thing, but not good enough. Could never be good enough. Not for anyone, but especially not for Darcy.

Fact. Truth. Authenticity. Darcy was totally private about her private parts. For sure, she had never, ever been touched down there before. No way, no how. In health class she once asked why tongues weren't considered private parts too. Or fingers for that matter.

So what fucking good did winning a lawsuit against the NYPD do for a girl like Darcy? Or for any of the other girls, for that matter.

Fact. Truth. Authenticity. Whatever the cops did, all of it was too much.

# GUY LAVAL
Blog: WE Protest, Day #2
Are You Experienced?
Have You Ever Been Arrested Before?


Seven hours go by. Singing, chanting.

"Protest is not a crime. Why are we doing time?"

The usual stuff that goes down while you wait for the lawyers to come and spring you. But this time — nothing. No legal aid. No ACLU. No food or water. Not even a trip to a porta potty.

Eight hours after the bust, they bring food. At least eight hours, hard to tell for sure. Nobody has a watch or a cell phone. First things they took away from us. For safekeeping.

Yay food! I make a grab for it, even though it's the same standard shit they always give you. Three kinds of sandwiches. Bologna, cheese, peanut butter. Meat, vegetarian, vegan. Fucking cops are getting PC as all hell.

Anyway, the Girl — the WE See You Girl, the Girl on the Horse, the Elect Doefen Girl, the whatever her name is Girl – takes a PB sandwich, unwraps it, peels off the rectangle of white spongy stuff also known as bread and says, "Crap."

She's not wrong. The bread is mostly high fructose corn syrup held together with a little bleached flour. There isn't a freshly ground peanut in sight. Just oozy brown glop. Hydrogenated to death. Also full of fructose.

"Dude," I tell her. "Better eat it." No chance we're going to see anything else in here anytime soon. Forget about organic, local, cruelty-free. The PB is the safest bet.

She'd rather wait and get something when she gets out she tells me.

Alright then. A newbie. A first timer.

I get her talking. Head to head. Heart to heart. Five, ten minutes later we're close. Like brother and sister. Somehow, that's how it goes, even though she's a hottie. I mean robe thing or not, you can see she's a babe. But something about the way her eyes burn through you if you even so much as think of hitting on her, makes you stop before you get started.

Turns out she actually has had the tinniest bit of experience.

I mean, organizing a boycott of her school cafeteria when she was eleven and passing out petitions against BE Frankenstein corn, that's something. But it's not the same as getting arrested. It's like first base compared to going all the way.

So I clue her to the way things operate. The police, as in P-O-L-I-C-E, as in mother-fuckers with guns and live ammo, have a lot of time on their hands and a really big urge to show you how badly they can fuck with you. The law is whatever they want it be. Which means you eat when there's something to eat, and drink when there's something to drink, because you're going to get out when they say you're going to get out, and you need to keep yourself together so you can get out and do it all over again.

No. No, she says. She's doing it just this once for Doefen and then it's back to Glen Eddy for her.

As if. The whole WE thing is about to break into the big time. And once you get started, this protest stuff gets into your blood.

Me, I've been into the whole WE thing for a while. Three marches with them so far. The first two, the cops hardly bothered with us. WE hadn't really made it onto their radar.

But this time, the busts started on day one. All because of the Doefen for President thing. Holding cells full of WE people. All kinds of ages. Even the Who's Who of really established activist movements are here.

Like Margaret Goodright for starters. The queen mother of all activists. Civil rights, voter registration, anti-war, anti-nuke, pro-choice, pro-environment, you name it. She's been marching since before most of the people in this cell, including me, were born. I'll bet this protest is like her ten thousandth one at least. And here she is, over in the corner, nodding off on the bench, WE banner wrapped around her shoulders like a shawl.

So any minute now, the WE protests are going to become like Davos or WTO. Way major and totally out of control. I mean, get anywhere near a WTO meeting and they arrest you for breathing. It'll be like that with WE too.

I spend a good part of the day, telling the Girl all about the time I got busted at the Seattle WTO. First day out. Bam, I'm locked up. In Cancun I lasted until the second day. But in Italy, they got me coming off the plane.

I'm talking to her about experience. The need for strategy. And what does she tell me? That I'm sort of a groupie, not so different from her friend, Robert, some dude who trailed after the Dead — as in Grateful Dead — for a good long while.

I have to laugh. Even when the Dead were hot, they weren't. I mean, the Girl so doesn't get it.

But after awhile I get to thinking that maybe she has a point. That maybe the whole activist thing is just like a groupie thing that gets really tired after a while. And old.

I mean how different is Doefen from your average rock star? Gets up on a platform. Gives a little performance. And then, it's off to the next gig with press, a VIP lounge, good food, nice hotel, room service. You don't see him in a fucking holding cell.

So all the while that the Girl is going on and on about how Doefen really needs and deserves everyone's support, needs my support, and I'm saying yeah, and right on, my brain is really going, "Been there, done that."

I clear a little space around me on the floor, and lie down for some shut eye. And I tell her to do the same.

Maybe later, she says.

"Whatever, Dude," I tell her. "Suit yourself."

I know that it's only a matter of time. Sooner or later, she'll conk out. Just like me, just like everyone else.

# MARGARET GOODRIGHT
Memoir Excerpt
Innocents

I look at them all, asleep on the filthy floor, gently breathing, and my heart is full. They are so young. So beautiful. So very, very beautiful. As beautiful as they're ever going to be. And they don't even know it. They're busy sweating the small stuff. Zits. The size of their breasts.

I want to hug them all, hold them to me, tell them to love. To pay attention. Which would be advice. And that's not what I do.

The important thing is to just to pay attention. Stay interested. Be in the moment, as my Buddhist friends put it. The doing comes on its own from that. I've learned a lot from doing. All my life, I've been doing. Doing wonderful things.

Loving, hollering, lusting, drinking wine, fucking, raising children, planting gardens.

All of them necessary. Things that needed doing.

Like getting arrested. Such a happy feeling to be hauled off to jail for a good cause. I probably won't see the inside of a cell again. Forty years since the first time – an anti-nuke protest. A lot of close calls with the law since then. Bookings. Releases. Dismissals. They'll dismiss this bust too. They'll have to. So many illegalities.

My days of jumping up onto the barricades are over. Never mind jumping. Even with all my friends pushing, I couldn't climb a sawhorse now. Not anymore.

Too stiff in the joints. Wobbly feet. Bunions big as a robin's egg, the bone pecking its way out through the skin. Not enough breath. A cinch for the cops to catch me now. No more outracing them – even the fat ones, never mind playing dodge ball with tear gas canisters. Circulation not what it used to be. Rogue cancer cells – chemo survivors — gnawing at my bones.

The spirit is willing, but the flesh is weak. It is ever thus. From the first breath to the last, it'll be the body that betrays you. A fact of life. A fundamental flaw in the great design.

I look at them all, snugly sheathed in their youth, and I too am young. Young as they are. Young as I ever was. Hungry and thirsty and eager. Afraid of nothing. Knowing everything.

Because they do know. The young. Newly emerged from the cosmic soup. They still know in their limbs and bones all that is essential. They know what's right. What needs doing. They know. It is clear and simple. And necessary as water.

I look at them all, and I know that they will wake, most of them, into tremulous maturity. Rub the bright sunshine from their eyes, and buzz off to the honeycomb office buildings set out along all the humming financial thoroughfares where the sweat and labor gathered from all the fields of the world are transformed into gold. Loyal drones, they will not taste the royal jelly, but console themselves with houses and cars and barbecue grills.

They will make babies. Beautiful babies. Babies who will one day take their place on some other concrete floor in need of sweeping, who will give harbor to hope, and dream of making and remaking the world. And that is all as it should be. The creation of the world is a job that's never finished.

They'll do alright, most of them. Those sleeping here now, and those who will come after. The worst that will happen to them is that instead of doing, they'll choose to live for thirty, forty, fifty years like they're dead from the dandruff down. Sad. But not tragic.

They're not revolutionaries, this crowd. Which is just as well. The world has enough deluded, self-indulgent narcissists already. The high drama, the posturing of the revolutionary, the dull and tired agitprop – how radical are they, really?

The calls for armed struggle. Old as the world. I understand the frustration, but violence is just laziness.

A combative pacifist. Now, there's something new. Or newer.

Love. Compassion. Tiny, everyday acts of decency, fellowship. Those are what I call subversive. They make a movement. A revolution. The rest is thunder. Smoke.

That's what I told the girl. The one they're calling D Girl and Angel D. She is that. An angel. Not one of those pastel creatures fluttering around like oversized swallowtail butterflies. No. She's the real deal. A force of heaven for truth and good. A warrior spirit. Even when she sits with her chin on her knees, her hands over her ears, it seems more a meditation, a consultation with her conscience than a withdrawal. No doubt about it, she is someone to be reckoned with.

And so, I fear for her.

She is severe as a nun. All covered up. No tight jeans or cleavage shirts or thongs for her, thank you very much. For all that, she's hot. The kid with the purple hair, Guy Laval — he knows it. Feels it. We all do. The fire in her. The radiance.

Guy Laval – all the makings of a CEO and a name to match. Protest is a phase the kid will grow out of like comic books. Just a matter of time till he loses the purple porcupine look, and goes back to natural brown hair, exchanges the thick lace-up boots for buttery leather loafers. But his heart is in the right place. He's spent the day trying to protect the girl. Sit here. Eat this. Do that. As if that will save her. He's not looking to make her, and I like him for that.

"Cute boy you've been talking to," I told the girl when Guy nodded out, chin on his knees. For all his bravado, the kid was exhausted. Sitting in a cell will do that. Wipe you out. Going on forty hours for him. Twenty-eight for me. Just twelve for the girl. None of us has seen a lawyer yet.

"I'm not here to pick up boys," she said as if this was news.

We talked a while about being serious. About Doefen. And WE. And Causes. Her Cause.

All of it so elating and so *deja vu* all over again for me. Old world dying, the new just waiting to be born. Now and forever.

Making change takes a long time, I told her. You have to be patient. You have to do the work it takes to make change. You don't do it to win, but because it's a good way to spend your life.

So, all the more reason for her to check out the boys.

"I met my favorite husband at the '69 march on Washington," I told her.

"Your favorite?" Her pretty brow puckered with disapproval, incomprehension.

Second of four. Died young of cancer. Kind of movie of the week. But life is like that. No tragedy that it cannot render trite.

"Maybe if he'd lived, you would have ended up not liking him so much."

I laughed, tears in my eyes. Oh the heartless logic of youth. This girl is a truth teller. An idealist. Intolerant of compromise. Unforgiving of the world's imperfections. She's the kind who will still be charging around on a horse when she is my age. If she lives that long.

Pace yourself, I tell her. Burn with a slow, steady fire. Do other things. Raise children, bury parents, write books, build a playground where there isn't one, plant a garden in an abandoned lot, and love – friends, food, wine, music. That's important. The part about love.

"It's why I'm still here today."

Without a doubt, the girl is in danger. And dangerous. The innocents always are.

She's not looking to die. Her intentions are pure. She longs only to spark a fire that will banish the dark vast with a bright and beautiful light. There's not a thought in her head that fire consumes. Immolates.

I look at her sleeping. She moans gently. The kid with the purple hair snuggles her. Her eyes snap open, she look past him to something only she can see. The boy croons into her ear, a few words, a song that I'm too far away to hear.

# CHIEF CUCHEN
Damage Control


The Mayor demanded that Cuchen give him a briefing on the arrests — as if he gave a shit about civil procedure and all that. The short, little fuck was on his way to buying his re-election. The flap over the arrests was all about PR. The Mayor knew it. Cuchen knew it. The Mayor knew that Cuchen knew it, and Cuchen knew that the Mayor knew that he knew it.

But Cuchen also knew that the Mayor had more than enough millions to buy a new Chief of Police, and so he explained.

If he'd said it once, he'd said it a thousand times. Arrest was not the goal. The critical thing was to deactivate. Isolate. Discredit.

Deactivate. The Mayor got that.

Close a street. Tell the crowd to keep moving, which of course it can't. Then round up the bastards like the dumb cattle they are and drive them into a holding pen.

The point was to take a chunk out of the hindquarter of the beast before the head knew what was happening.

Most of the disorderly conduct busts were made at the barricades while the girl was still holding forth inside the hotel. And once she came out, the procedural pick-ups were done quickly, quietly by separating the stragglers from the main pack. Bottom line, the number of arrests didn't have to be huge, just big enough to be noticed. Significant enough to bleed the crowd of morale and purpose, but not rouse it to fury.

Hitting the WE contingent when it was back at the Park feeling safe, celebrating victory was all part of the plan. The orders Cuchen gave were clear. Shake them up, don't injure them too much.

Doefen needed to be taught his place right from the start. Before things went too far, got out of hand. And so did the girl. Especially the girl.

She thought she was creating a leader for WE. But it was WE that had created Darcy Purcell. That was how things worked in real life. Movements created leaders, not the other way around.

Luckily, whatever momentum WE had created, would be unmade.

The arrests were targeted, precise. Nothing random. Especially where the girl was concerned.

So were the releases. It was no accident that the ACLU was able to spring most of detainees on a technicality. The Pucelle girl was supposed to be part of the package — eventually. First she needed a few extra jail hours to impress on her that she didn't want to end up there again.

Hundreds of the WE crowd released. Records expunged. And were they grateful, did they crawl back under the same rocks they came from? No, they milled around shouting for the girl, mugged for the cameras. Everybody was looking to get five minutes of TV time. Five minutes of glory and fame.

Dar - cy. Dar -cy. Dar- cy. Hours and hours of shouting. A media frenzy of rolling cameras. A field day. And why? All because some incompetent asshole at the detention center failed to act on Cuchen's rescind of the special hold order he'd originally put on the girl. One little slip up and what was supposed to be her nice, quiet, well-planned, routine, middle-of-the night non-event release went straight to hell.

Heads were going to roll Cuchen promised the Mayor.

A show of accountability. Hissoner liked that.

Back in the day, Cuchen could have salvaged the situation in a second, no sweat. He would have presented it at a news conference as the minor, bureaucratic snafu that it was. The media would have given the arrest 30 seconds play on the evening news and moved on. But thanks to M3, the media agitator with the cheap camcorder strapped to his head, who'd glommed onto WE and made Darcy Pucelle his pet project, the news of her continued confinement was all over the net in a heartbeat. It brought the ragtag WE remnants running down from the Castle, and recruited a fresh, new batch of demonstrators.

Which got the Feds attention and brought the Mayor breathing down Cuchen's neck. Suddenly, the Washington boys wanted in on the action, demanded a trial of the girl, which was no more than business as usual. But it pissed off the Mayor and turned the whole situation into a major pain in the ass.

As for the noise on the street. It came from the usual dickhead, two-bit activists with too much time on their hands. That was business as usual too.

The only surprise was Doefen. The scruffy cheese maker had to know that the girl didn't get out of detention with the rest of his WE gang. But did he care? No. Not a word out of him on the girl's behalf. Off he went to hold forth at a meeting of Concerned Scientists, and a Business Council luncheon, ready, willing and able to put all his effort into sucking up to power and money — a useful little tidbit that sank right into the Mayor's synapses.

No worries, Cuchen assured the Mayor. Doefen and his measly outsider contacts were no match for the power of the force. Neither Doefen nor WE was going to be hard to take down.

Let them make noise. Cuchen was an intelligence and security expert long before Doefen and the rest of his pipsqueak supporters were born. The attention they might get could make Cuchen's job a little harder. But not undoable. It could delay, not stop the inevitable.

Operation Flaming Sword would proceed to completion.

Whatever it takes, the Mayor agreed, and Cuchen shook his hand, took his leave.

Holding the girl for an extended period of time and sending her to trial had not been Cuchen's goal. But now that he had her, he had to make sure that she was good for something.

The girl was arrested in the city – his city, his jurisdiction – and if she was going to be tried, she'd be tried in the city. No way was Cuchen going to hand her over to the Feds. Let the Feds buff their record on Homeland Security somewhere else, on someone else's watch.

It was Cuchen's intelligence work, his connections, his commitment to police work of the highest order that made her capture possible. He wasn't about to entrust her final disposition to some other agency.

He'd see to it that her trial was impeccable. By the book, letter of the law. No plea bargaining. No wiggle room.

Conviction. Sentence. Time. Any other outcome would be a farce, a miscarriage of justice.

Oh yes, she was going to end up doing the maximum inside. He'd see to that. Make an example of her to all the other pampered brats who thought they could trample the law, take over the city. Make trouble.

He'd show her trouble. Give her a lesson she'd never forget. By the time he was done with her, she wouldn't be able to pass a background check for a job stocking shelves in Wal-Mart.

She wasn't just some little teeny bopper shouting a few slogans. No, she was a real menace. Worse than an enemy. With an enemy, things are clear. You are at war with them. You fight. You win or lose or come to a cease-fire. But she was a traitor who disrespected all the things that made life, made America great. She deserved what was coming to her.

There were rules. Procedures. She'd violated them all. No permit. No fucking permission to march on foot, never mind prance around on a horse. And lining up crips and kids. That was low.

The horse bothered Cuchen the most. How did she manage to pull off a stunt like that? Even Cherub said he didn't know, and he was as good an undercover as Cuchen ever had. Any other agent would have given him some song and dance explanation to cover his ass. Lying came easy as breathing to the lot of them.

But Cherub was different. Like a son to him. A good son. Not the ungrateful piece-of-shit sons he read about in the paper who repaid all the sweat their fathers put into them by getting into partying, and drugs, and whores. Or worse, alternative life styles.

If Cherub didn't know about the horse, it meant it wasn't a scheme that the best and brightest gathered at the Castle had dreamed up. It had to have been the girl's idea. Maybe Raymond Duke, the carriage driver was telling the truth — he just up and gave the girl the horse, because she asked. Something about her hit a sweet spot in him that made him want to help her.

No surprised that the likes of him – a sentimental, clown-faced little wino — could be suckered in by the girl. But Cherub's report more or less confirmed that she had the same effect on other people. Sober people. People with a lot more smarts than the carriage driver just went ahead and lined up to do her bidding.

When she first appeared at the Castle, Cherub and the WE operatives thought she was a pushy little brat. Full of herself. A few of the men thought she was hot. And Cherub reported that he'd heard a dyke or two say the same.

The plan was to play her a little, maybe even have one of the guys in the undercover detail at the Castle hook up with her, then give her the boot. But when push came to shove, all of a sudden everybody got cold feet about the hooking up. Acted embarrassed and guilty. Cherub razzed them, but they told him to lay off. Said the girl was just a kid. Probably a virgin.

Just a kid? That sure didn't keep the crowd at the Castle from taking her seriously. One day after she arrived on the scene, grown men were willing to do whatever she wanted. It was like they didn't have the will to resist.

Terrorist networks. Opportunists. Those, Cuchen knew how to deal with. But if the girl really was able to make people think that by following her they were signing onto something grand, and true, and just. That was trouble.

Nothing worse than a true innocent. Taking down one of them wasn't as easy as undoing a clever agitator. An innocent had the potential to recruit the vilest kind of element – zealots. So, assuming the girl really was the innocent she made herself out to be, the world needed to be protected from her. Or she had to be protected from herself. One way or the other, she needed to be stopped.

The more Cuchen thought about it, the less a public trial of the girl seemed to be the way to go. A trial would only give her a forum. Draw more followers. More support.

She needed to be disarmed. Discredited. The little fires she'd set in peoples psyches needed to be snuffed out before they blazed out of control.

Cuchen would start with a word or two or fifty. In the beginning was the word — it said so, right there in the Bible. Sticks and stones would come later, if necessary. Words had plenty power to hurt her.

# ROBERT
Say What?


It's not like you can keep people from talking. And no one tried. Doefen certainly didn't do much to manage the media after the big bust at Belvedere. Which he somehow conveniently missed. Delayed by a spur of the moment press conference, he said, and by a spontaneous gathering of supporters who insisted on discussing a platform, planning a coalition, launching a campaign.

As far as Robert was concerned, the explanations never quite added up. Doefen had an obligation to be at Belvedere, alongside Darcy, as a show of respect, if nothing else. Until she came along, he was just some dude squatting in a make-believe castle accomplishing nothing. But did a single expression of gratitude cross his lips? No. Not ever. That was the part that really burned Robert. The guy never even copped to what Darcy had done for him. You'd never have guessed that she was the one to name him as a candidate for President. As in President of the US of fucking A, not some 4H Club.

Illegal assembly, the Belvedere arrest warrants said. Disorderly conduct. Inciting to riot. As if. The scene at the castle consisted of a thousand plus living, breathing individuals chanting, humming, singing, spiraling slowly, letting the sun shine into their lives. A convocation of monks couldn't have been more orderly. Or more peaceful.

The mass round up by the Pigs was completely unwarranted. Arbitrary. Pre-planned.

And there was Doefen — right smack in the middle of his ten minutes of fame, the press ready to repeat his every word – and not a peep out of him about the arrests in a single interview he gave the day after. No mention of the brutality — Pigs beating up on unarmed people, running them down with horses, driving motorcycles right into women, and even children. Two hundred thirty-seven reported wounded – sprains, fractures, seven concussions, one life-threatening punctured lung, and who knows how many unreported injuries, and what did Doefen talk about? Cheese. His goat cheese. To hear him tell it, his creamy little smelly bars of goat's milk processed in the ancient French style held the promise of a cure for America's epidemic obesity.

Which was both hilarious and more than a little sad considering that Doefen's mother was grotesquely fat. Not so fat that she had to be fork lifted out of bed. But almost.

How was it that the press never mentioned that? Was Robert the only one who had ever seen the picture of Doefen's family in the local paper back in the day of the fast-food restaurant sit-down? Doefen's mother stood at half her son's height and three times his width. Fence post legs. Sandbag breasts.

There were men who liked that – a woman to drown in. Chuck Lorraine, who knew Doefen's mother since they were kids, said she got around in high school, and continued to get it on with all kinds of guys even after she was married and grew big and bigger.

With a mother like that, no wonder Doefen was ready to lie down in front of bulldozers to keep a fast-food joint from being built. Better that, than dealing with her. Or his father, who was known to wander around Glen Eddy wrapped in plastic saying he was made of atomic particles that would blow up if anyone touched him, or screaming that he was being pulled apart by a thousand magnets.

And yet, the press chose to go after Darcy, an innocent kid with nothing to hide.

Right from the get go, she was made out to be a fanatic vegetarian organic food commando, praised or ridiculed depending on which interest group was writing about her. She was, simultaneously, a poster child for the Left and the Right. It would have been funny, if it weren't so sad.

The Left thing was pretty much what Robert would have expected. Darcy was their mascot for free speech, empowerment of the People.

The Right's smear campaign was also utterly predictable. Darcy was their example of a radical extremist looking to overthrow the government.

Some woman looking for her 10-minutes-of-fame got on national TV and claimed that Darcy had attacked her down in the subway and beat her without provocation.

A kid from her school said in an interview that Darcy had a violent streak and no sense of humor. Told a story about now she tried to break his arm just because he made a joke about her Halloween costume.

Then there was the whole evangelical and Christian zealot thing that went down — a new one on Robert. A sect of nut-job nuns with a thing about the Virgin — as in mother of Jesus – decided that Darcy was an incarnation of the Virgin.

How? Why? It didn't matter because it took TV anchors all of about a day to start saying that it was Darcy who was going around calling herself an incarnation. Which pissed off mainstream religious factions who accused her of sacrilege and slandering their faith. And that was before the story became that Darcy truly believed that she was, in fact, the Virgin. Amidst calls from a far right religious extremist group for a good old-fashioned inquisition, an interfaith council pleaded for rational discourse. Of which there was none.

Muslims, cowed by the aftermath of 9/11, said nothing. Or, if pressed, disavowed any association with Darcy. A Moroccan newspaper pointed out that her *djellabah* was typical of a robe worn by a groom on his wedding day. Which didn't matter one iota to the red-blooded patriots of the US of A, who were determined to call Darcy a terrorist. The *djellabah* told them all they wanted or needed to know. Darcy could easily be wearing the garb of a Muslim groom to disguise her terrorist intent, they said.

It was *America, love it or leave it* all over again. And clearly loving America still meant embracing big industry, and making nice with *uptight short sighted, narrow-minded, hypocrite* CEOs like Dick Burgundy, and allowing giant advertising companies to *Mother Hubbard, soft soap you with just a pocketful of hope.* As far as Robert could see, the current state of the body politic was just as bad as when the Beatles first sang *Gimme Some Truth.* Or worse. This time around there didn't seem to be a shred of evolved consciousness to be found.

*Consciousness.* What ever happened to that word? And *Consciousness-raising.* It was certainly time for that practice to make a comeback.

The way things went down for Darcy – it was enough to make a grown man cry. And Robert cried plenty. No shame in admitting that. After all, how many years could he go on singing *where have all the flowers gone* and not fall into despair?

He was grateful that he'd spent his youth in the *Age of Aquarius* — that brief, giddy moment when a whole generation of the young could allow itself to believe that it was witnessing the dawning of a new era in which *peace would guide the planets and love would steer the stars.*

> *Harmony and understanding*
> *Sympathy and trust abounding*
> *No more falsehoods or derisions*
> *Golden living dreams of visions*
> *Mystic crystal revelation*
> *And the mind's true liberation*
> *Aquarius! Aquarius!*

Robert finds it hard to believe that he'd ever been that naive. That hopeful.

Of course, the difference that allowed the Aquarius illusion to thrive was that back in his day, being part of a movement meant something. Only those in the know, those with a raised consciousness, really knew what was going on. Word of political action took time, you had to wait for it to spread through the underground, and get handed out in leaflets, and written about in the alternative papers before it made its way into the mainstream media.

Now everything was instant fodder for a sound bite on the evening news, and every clueless Mr. Jones could suck his teeth on it.

> *You raise up your head and you ask, "Is this where it is?"*
> *And somebody points to you and says, "It's his"*
> *And you say, "What's mine?" and somebody else says,*
> *"Well, what is?"*
> *And you say, "Oh my God, am I here all alone?"*
> *But something is happening and you don't know what it is*
> *Do you, Mr. Jones?*

*Ballad of the Thin Man.* Robert still knew all the words. Or at least the ones that counted.

> *Ah, you've been with the professors and they've all liked your looks*
> *With great lawyers you have discussed lepers and crooks*
> *You've been through all of F. Scott Fitzgerald's books*

*You're very well read, it's well known*
*But something is happening here and you don't know*
*what it is*
*Do you, Mr. Jones?*

*Something is happening here and you don't know what it is,*
*do you Mr. Jones?* A question as relevant for Darcy's time and
place as it was when Bob Dylan first posed it in the Sixties.

*Relevant.* There was a word that the Sixties had bled dry,
and which needed a revival.

Thanks to the net and cell phones, news was out and around
the world in milliseconds, and Truth was whatever was playing
on screens – the big ass screens in homes and bars, and the
laptops and cell phones that everyone but Robert and Darcy
seemed to carry around. All the instantaneous media didn't
give anyone time to figure out what was *relevant.*

In Darcy's case, no effort was made to do investigative reporting. At least not till later. Way later. By which time it was
too late.

# CHIEF CUCHEN
A Choice

To ensure that the Feds didn't have a first go at the girl, Cuchen went to the lock up to question her himself. "Do you play an instrument, Ms. Pucelle?" he asked the girl after the guard closed the gate of the interrogation room.

"I took a semester of trumpet in seventh grade."

"Just one?"

"My school doesn't have enough music stuff to go around, so I had to give another kid a chance."

"Pity," he said without a bit of sincerity. Her slacker generation had an excuse for everything. He grew up without any musical in his home, but that didn't keep him from educating himself.

"I wasn't very good on the trumpet."

Cuchen hummed the lento from the prelude to *Lalo's Concerto in d*. Why that piece and not some other favorite he couldn't say exactly.

"Pretty," the girl said. "Mr. Mortimer never tried to teach us anything that nice. We just did scales."

Cuchen smiled. "Lalo's concerto is for a cello and requires years of practice. Dedication. "

He surveyed the hold outside the bars of the gate. Chaotic. Smelly. A colossal waste – all of it — the kids, the protests, the arrests. If only he'd been able to make a life in music...

Out of the corner of his eye, he saw the girl grimace at something on the floor.

"American cockroach," he said, easily identifying the source of her distress. "Often mistakenly called a waterbug, which it isn't." He smiled.

The girl suppressed a gasp as the cockroach skittered past her feet in search of a dark crevice,

"They're harmless," he assured her. "But I take it that you dislike bugs." Knowing people's dislikes often proved quite useful.

"I try very hard not to," the girl said, her lips pale, her voice constricted.

"Love all creatures, large and small, including the hideous

247

and horrifying, is that it?" He clapped his hands twice. "Very admirable. What a good girl you are."

She gave him a hard look and shrugged.

Could be that she was a good girl – in her own way. Or maybe she could have been, if she'd had a proper upbringing, decent parents to guide her. A few years of musical education would have helped. What better way to learn discipline, patience, and to sharpen the ability to understand the nuances of creating harmony between the solo performance and orchestra?

It wasn't Cuchen's fault that the girl was the prickly and difficult creature she was, but it was his obligation to bring her into line. If helping her to find her place in the order of things required making her spend a night sharing quarters with a few American cockroaches, it was a small price to save her from a life of further, graver error.

That, more or less, was Cuchen's line of thinking later that night as he sat in front of his stereo relishing the repeating phrases of the Lalo concerto's first movement, waiting for the entry of the dark and masterful cello. The deep and fearless tone, the commanding pitch of the cello often played in his head as he delivered his morning briefs.

Without a doubt, after the annoyance of the WE protest and the debacle of the Pucelle arrest, listening to the cello solo of the *lento* was the best part of Cuchen's day. Unfortunately, just as the cellist was drawing the last majestic notes from the throat of the instrument, Cherub called — rudely intruding on the opening bars of the clean, hard brilliance of the *allegro maestoso* — with news of an unhappy turn of events in the already troubled detention of Darcy Pucelle. Despite all of Cuchen's express directives to his men on how to handle the girl, and the whole issue of the *djellabah*, so that the correct and necessary outcome was achieved, she was still in the holding cell.

"I'll take care of it myself," he said evenly, resisting the urge to hurl the cell phone across the room.

All he'd expected of the men was to follow up on the choice that he'd offered the girl – wear normal clothes, and get an immediate free pass out of jail. Or keep the terrorist gear, and pay the consequences. He'd even given the men more or less free rein to take whatever steps were needed to ensure that she made the right choice.

Put it in writing, the little snot had told Cuchen when he'd made her the offer. As if she had leverage. As if she was somebody to make demands. As if he had to offer her a deal. But in the interest of getting her out of detention — as long as it was minus the *djellabah* — he'd been willing to go along. Gave her his word that she wouldn't be paraded in front of the press when she was released, and gave her time to think about the offer.

And despite all that, she'd told his men that giving up the *djellabah* was not a choice she could make. She'd given her word, sworn an oath to wear it, and no other kinds of clothes. Made an oath, not to anyone in particular. Not to any group or organization. No. It was Truth that held a claim on her, she said.

So now it came down to a question of wills. The girl was tough, but he had the better arsenal. Experience. It always trumped moral certainty.

Right and Wrong. Black and White. The was the girl's only weapon.

But that kind of either/or thinking was really nothing more than a sign of her immaturity. With any luck, like most sane people she'd outgrow it around the time she started to cut her wisdom teeth.

In his youth, Cuchen had been a little like her – self-righteous, sentimental, ready to boo hoo over Anne Frank hiding in the attic – that innocent, blameless girl full of hope, that poor minnow, caught in the vast nets of power as they trawled the dark waters of history. But then, he grew up and realized that life was all about nuance, and that the likes of Anne Frank didn't mean jack shit in the larger scheme of things. The Ann Franks of the world never do. All the blah blah blah about their heroism and moral courage was just that – blah, blah, blah lip service.

So whatever high and mighty thoughts the young Miss Darcy Pucelle might have about herself, she was just another minnow. A little, itty bitty minnow. And if she'd only been smart enough to behave like one, Cuchen could have let her swim away. But a minnow carrying on like she was a shark — that upset the order of things.

A great country remains great because men like himself are willing to defend it from those who, knowingly, or not, would destroy it.

249

Cuchen's sworn duty was to uphold the law, maintain order, and keep the city, the nation safe from harm. And whatever his personal sentiments about Darcy might be, he would do no less.

# BILLY
Breaking Out


Well, duh. Of course, Darcy tried to break out. She wasn't the kind of girl to put up with being caged. And she was desperate. Who wouldn't be? Especially after Cuchen released everybody except her.

In the holding pen all alone. Cops coming and going. Day and night. Checking her out like she was some exotic animal at the zoo. Poking their sticks between the bars. Mocking her – "Who is the big terrorist now?"

As if she ever was. Or wanted to be. All she ever did was to try to bring a little truth into the world.

She was definitely not somebody who was looking to kill herself. The drop from that cell window was just about as high, maybe a little higher than the river bank we jumped down every time we took the shortcut to school. OK, so she had to land on asphalt instead of mud, but she took that into account. I mean, she came out of the jump with just a sprained ankle. If she'd been trying for suicide, she would have dived head first. Went for a broken neck. Gotten a concussion, at least.

Just because she said she'd rather die than be in prison didn't mean she was suicidal. I mean, what prisoner doesn't dream of escape? It's what you do if you're locked up. Everybody wants freedom. Has a right to it. I mean it's there in the Constitution and everything.

Plus, Darcy admitted that it was stupid. She wouldn't have jumped if hadn't been for how much she wanted to get back to WE so that she could keep the whole Presidential nomination thing going for Doefen. It's not like she knew, or any one of us knew then that the fucker never even tried to get her out of jail.

# CHIEF CUCHEN
Catch and Release

Stupid, stupid, stupid girl. Making a break for it. Lucky she wasn't killed.

Not that Cuchen would have shed a tear. But what a mess it would have made for him and the department if she'd ended up dead. Thirty seconds after her body hit the morgue, every human rights and legal this and that organization would have been crawling up his ass.

Bad enough that he had to bring in the medical people. They confirmed just what his men told him. A sprained ankle. She came away from the incident with nothing more than an ace bandage. Not a shred of evidence that she was suicidal.

Cuchen conducted the interrogated on the subject of her intent himself.

"Did you jump on the advice of that voice of yours?"

"The voice of truth doesn't command. It speaks of freedom."

"It never crossed your mind to kill yourself?"

"I only thought about escape."

Spoken like a true teenager. Not a thought in her head of mortality.

Not suicidal, but a little paranoid, for sure. Didn't trust the pain medicine the paramedics offered her. Requested some herbal remedy her mother always used.

Still, Cuchen instructed his people to make a case for a mandatory psych evaluation. A danger to herself – check, and others – check. It wasn't too much of a stretch to ask for a 2 PC. He knew docs who would sign a physician certificate and agree to put her under observation.

Too bad the judge refused to see things Cuchen's way.

"This girl has already been the victim of your department's violations of due process," he bleated. "I am not able to accept your statement that you are making a good faith effort to comply with my prior orders to release all the detainees who haven't already been arraigned."

As per usual, getting any decent work done with a judiciary system infested with liberal bias was an impossibility. Clearly, any plan Cuchen might have had for going to trial in order to demonstrate the legal process at work was out the window at that point. The girl was going to be nothing but a headache, and the sooner she was out of his immediate jurisdiction the better. Whatever happened to her after that, could not and would not be his responsibility.

He had the girl released on a technicality. Just like most of her pals in WE. Even the ones who had been booked. By the time it was all over, ninety percent of them had all charges dropped by the judges.

An outrage. But still, that meant that Cuchen had gotten ten percent of them. Ten percent were inactivated. Would stay inactivated. He'd see to that.

And all of them would stay in the data base. Let the court expunge or seal their records. Operation *Archangel's* archive was in no way tied to the disposition of court records.

Anyway, next time it would be different. The arrest and detention stats would be better. It's like he told the Mayor. He couldn't just stand by and watch a lawless bunch of extremists like WE violate the rights respectable citizens, and visitors, and business people like Burgundy.

Hizzoner – a chicken shit politico if ever there was one – nattered on about how in America, cradle of liberty and free speech, WE had to be allowed to have its say. He could not, or would not grasp that WE was basically a terrorist band intent on keeping a decent business man like Dick Burgundy from expressing himself. No surprise that he caved to the judiciary and supported the order to let the arrested protesters go.

No matter. Cuchen was prepared to play the long game. By the time the next big trade and banking meetings came to the city, the Mayor would be gone — term limits were a beautiful thing! Age, decrepitude, and death would take care of the other left-over bleeding-heart liberals from the Sixties who were still on court bench and had issued the writs foisted on Cuchen — *Release all protesters held for 38 plus hours (a mere 120 people) by 1:00 p.m.* or have them arraigned by 1:30. Those held between 36 and 38 hours (no more than 350 people) had to be released by 3:00 or arraigned. The tiny fraction held from 24 to 36 hours (just 90 people out of 1983 detainees) had to be released or arraigned by 5:00. That was the ultimatum.

"We're doing our best to move people through the system," Cuchen told the court. "The force is overwhelmed by the number of arrests within a four hour period. Over 1900 were taken into custody at several different locations for offenses that ranged from disorderly conduct to resisting arrest to various degrees of assault."

Processing the detainees as the speed that the judge demanded just wasn't doable. Charge sheets had to be written. Evidence logged — a lot of it in video form. Even the supremely efficient *Archangel* team using the better than state-of-the-art video processing equipment needed more than the allotted few hours to log all the confiscated video footage.

"Get it done now," the judge replied, and ordered a fine of one thousand dollars for every person not released per the court decree.

Not really a huge sum to pay to uphold the rule of law, but the City Council and Hizzoner shit their pants and refused to provide funds for fines. Cuchen had no choice but to comply.

If he learned anything from the detention debacle, it was that amateur videos posed a huge problem. Ultimately, four hundred cases were dismissed because of videotapes donated by "concerned citizens," and "casual passers-by," and "impartial observers" that savvy defense lawyers presented in court. Four hundred videos selected and edited to make extremists look innocent — five hundred sixty perfectly legit arrests went out the window

Next time it would be different. Never again was *Archangel* going to be hamstrung by every Tom, Dick and Harry with a cheap camera.

And were the detainees grateful to be released? Not one bit. They did nothing but snivel to the press about conditions in the holding pen – nowhere to sit or sleep, boo hoo. People lying on concrete floors covered in "toxic residue." As if a little motor oil ever killed anyone. What were they expecting? Down pillows? A vacation resort?

The list of complaints went on and on. The food was bad. Nothing but warm water to drink. The toilets didn't have stalls.

Anyone with a cut, or a rash, or a simple cold blamed it on the "grossly unsanitary conditions" at the holding site.

Admittedly, some of the photos of the detainees coming out of jail with their skin and clothes covered in black motor oil sludge made for bad PR.

Were the photos real? Fake? Staged? Photoshopped. Cuchen didn't care. In the future, there wouldn't be any such photos or videos.

Whiney, wimpy bunch of brats. Some of them went so far as to call themselves political prisoners, victims of the war on terrorism. As if.

Next time, he was going to give them something to whine about. Unlike most Americans, he'd read the Homeland Security Act very carefully and more than once. He knew just how much he could do.

# BILLY
The Ride Out


A horse. Darcy should ride away from the jail on a horse. That was Robert's big idea.

"No way," Frank said. It was so yesterday's news. Cops would be expecting it. They'd snatch it at the first clip clop of its hooves. And it wasn't like WE had one ready and waiting, anyway.

Instead, he was all for celebrating Darcy's release with a float — as in parade float with music and lights. "Picture it. Her riding to the WE rally in the Park like she was the Queen of the Rose Bowl."

Which was so not Darcy.

But neither Robert or Frank gave a shit about that. They were too busy getting into each other's face about whose version of Darcy's exit from jail would make more of an impression on the crowd, get more media play. I wished that a peace monitor, like the one we had for recess at school, would come settle them down. Scared as I was to get in the middle of them, somebody had to stick up for Darcy.

"She wouldn't want to make the whole thing be about her," I told them.

"Right," Robert said, obviously glad to have somebody, any-body even me, go up against Frank with him. "We should forget the float. The focus needs to be Doefen."

"That's where the kid is wrong," Frank insisted.

Spinning his chair around to zero in on me, he hit me with a bunch of buddy buddy punches to the shoulder that were just hard enough to hurt. "You know those crowds that have been standing outside the jail, did you once hear anybody shouting out for Doefen?"

He had a point. For three days and three nights there had been a steady chant outside the jail of Darcee, Darcee, Darcee.

And that was the problem. People were so totally into the whole girl-on-a-horse thing, and the to-do over the *djellabah* that they just blanked on what Darcy stood for in the first place. No one was talking about clean air, and clean water, and clean food, and representation in government to fight for them. No one was talking about Doefen's mission to keep the Dick Burgundys of the world from getting away with their shit.

"Let's face it. Take away Darcy and you got nothin," Frank said, sticking he face in mine. "You're a bright kid. You can see that, right?"

I knew that Frank was really talking to Robert. But I nodded, because that's what you do when grown-ups use you to talk to each other.

What I wanted to see was all of us doing something to get people back to thinking about WE and Doefen, and the things that Darcy cared about.

Somehow, Frank was able to make it sound like the float was just the thing to do that. It was like he was channeling one of those Home Depot dudes who help you find the aisle with the light bulbs, and end up selling you a whole lighting system.

Years afterward, Robert swore that the float was all Frank's idea and no one else wanted anything to do with it, that the bastard pushed and pushed until everybody went along. Truth is, I signed on for it, and so did Robert, and Celeste, and a bunch of other people. By the time we were hammering that float together, we were all way into it, and acting like we owned the idea, like it popped up into our heads, all at the same time.

The weird part is that I signed onto Frank's whole plan, even though way down in my heart I didn't trust him. I tried, but could never get over the creepy feeling that I had from day one that he was a fake. And the whole gross "miracle" stunt he pulled with Darcy the day she made the Doefen for President speech pretty much convinced me that I was right.

After the showdown with Burgundy, everybody was on the field below the castle gathering for the *Circle of Combustion*.

Frank joysticked his chair up to Darcy. "Angel, angel, people are talking, saying that the way you made Doefen stand up all tall and proud is nothing short of a miracle."

Of course Darcy denied having any special powers, and tried to walk away.

Frank zipped around her, reached out and grabbed her wrists.

Darcy tried to shake him off, but he held tight, and slowly, very slowly he got to where he was half-standing out of his chair.

"Hallelujah, Girlee. You really can work miracles – I'm a crip

257

and you have me rising up and standing."

Wink, wink. Smirk.

Darcy's eyes went dark in a way that scared me. "Touch me again, and you will be a dead man."

Frank had himself a long wheezy, sleazy laugh, like he'd never heard anything funnier.

As soon as he wheeled off, I ranted to Darcy about what a big, horrible fuck ass he was. And how much I hated him, and hated the way that he talked to her, and treated her, and looked at her.

But Darcy being Darcy, put her hands on my shoulders and said, "Don't hate him."

"Like you don't?" I said, breaking away from her. Confused. Angry. Flailing my arms to keep her from getting near me.

"But I fight against it," she called as I ran away.

Well it wasn't like I didn't struggle to follow Darcy's example, but I ended up yo-yoing between hating myself for being a heartless shit where Frank was concerned, and hating him for making me feel like a heartless shit.

And yet somehow, when it came to the float, I let all that go, and wound up giving Frank a pass. Go figure.

## ROBERT/BILLY
The Float


Robert hated to admit it, but Frank had a point. WE needed a change. Marching in quiet circles with some sputtering little lighters did feel tired – so been there, done that, old-style protest. It wasn't like his idea for a truck float was something new in the history of man either, but at least it was a way to honor Darcy, and everything she'd done, everything she'd tried to do. Even if Doefen was a big bust, a media whore who was having the time of his life hanging out at fancy parties given by fancy people who were having five minutes of fun slumming with a hick farmer from Nowhere USA, Darcy still went to jail for him, took heat from the Man because of him. She deserved some kind of recognition.

Frank swore that he could make it so the whole float thing would be on the up and up with the Man, went on about how "as a crip and a vet" he knew how to handle bureaucracy, knew who to talk to, and what to say to cops so they couldn't, wouldn't turn down his application for a permit.

Sure as shit, a few hours after heading down into the city for the necessary permissions, Frank came zipping back up to Belvedere at full speed in his souped-up chair waving a bundle of official looking papers, which no one actually took the time to examine too closely, and things just took off from there.

People got way excited. Energized. Everybody actually started to think that persistence could win out, that WE could have its say and be taken seriously.

Suddenly, Frank, or maybe it was someone else, knew someone who was in the trucking business and could make a flatbed available for free. Someone else was an audio guy who had friends who had huge speakers, and he knew just how to rig them. Someone else had a trucker's license, for real, and knew how to handle a thirty-five foot flatbed. In all of two hours, WE rounded up enough musicians not only to play on the flatbed for the whole ride, but to do a three day festival if that's what WE wanted.

Robert and a bunch of other people volunteered to work on

decorating the flatbed in the Chinatown warehouse where it was parked. Once again, Frank was in the middle of all the action. He knew the cheapest place to buy everything — the foam and spray paint to make a model of the signature globe that represented WE, and the cable for the sound system.

But it was Robert's hive-building skills that made the enormous globe possible. Without them, WE's symbolic planet would have been the size of a watermelon. And it was Robert who found the honeycomb foam to sculpt convincing continents and oceans to cover the bent wood frame.

A guy with theatrical lighting experience set up a strobe system around the border of the flatbed to go off like flashes of fire — as in *Spontaneous Combustion, Circle of Combustion.*

"Great visual." Frank enthused at the test run, making a camera frame of his fingers. "Perfect photo-op. Except, for one thing. If you're talking excitement, energy, you want the real deal. Not some bullshit lights."

He proposed pyrotechnics.

Which didn't strike Robert as all that cool. He remembered all too well the stories of Sixties activists accidentally blowing themselves to kingdom come with incendiary devices.

But Frank explained that what he had in mind were gerbs — canisters that shot off cold sparks. Spectacular, but harmless. Like the stuff at rock concerts.

By the time he was done, everyone including Robert was convinced that the gerbs were safe and got busy setting them up.

\*\*\*

The float turned out way cool. The WE banner was stretched across the whole length of the flatbed. Yeah, my banner, the banner I designed was up there, five by fifteen feet. For sure, that gave me a thrill.

And so did seeing the huge foam globe in the middle of the platform with the WE logo on it. Musicians from all over the world would stand next to it to play their hearts out. Six foot speakers mounted at the four corners of the truck would blast the music for miles and miles. And flashing lights at the edge of the platform would make it look like Darcy and everyone on the float was riding inside WE's circle of *Spontaneous Combustion.*

I have to say, I didn't love the name *Spontaneous Combustion*. Every time I heard the words, the whole Christmas tree catching fire episode played in my head. But there was no point in talking about that, especially since the push to elect Doefen was being called *Spontaneous Combustion*, as in fire up people to vote for him, and Darcy was one hundred percent behind the name.

The one other thing besides the name that I really I didn't like was the whole gerbs thing Frank came up with – long metal tubes packed full of some kind of powder, sealed off with a little metal cap. It made me nervous that they were so big — at least four feet tall. Just about my height. They were supposed to light up the air above the float with showers of sparkles. Pretty. Non-flammable. Totally safe, according to Frank. But no matter what he or anyone said, they looked like giant firecrackers to me.

Every talk the fire department gave at school about fire safety had a part in it about the dangers of fireworks — stories about kids blowing off their fingers and noses and ending up blind. So I was worried about the gerbs being part of the float. And it didn't help that at some point while Robert and Frank hammered alongside each other like blood brothers, they started screeching out some old song both of them knew.

> *The time to hesitate is through*
> *No time to wallow in the mire*
> *Come on baby, light my fire*
> *Come on baby light my fire*
> *Try to set the night on fire*

Set the night on fire?

Yeah, that did not make me happy.

The lighting guys had already done a great job of wiring up the float with strands of colored bulbs and strobes. I didn't see why WE needed some kind of goddamn gerbs.

Gerbs. Even the name grossed me out. Sounded short for gerbils, as in rodents. Which reminded me of the way bored gangs of kids in Glen Eddy went around catching mice and exploding them with firecrackers. Especially around the Fourth of July. Grossed me out and made Darcy cry.

So, I asked about fire extinguishers. And Frank blew me off.

"Dude," he said — not kid – which made me hate him for trying to sound like he was only about ten minutes older than me and we were friends. "We're talking little fountains of cold sparks. Rock bands use them all the time." He claimed you could stick your bare arm in them, and they would bounce off your skin like confetti. "These gerb babies can only shoot the sparks about four feet into the air, where they will burn for only about four seconds."

Which was four feet, four seconds too much for me, considering that the float was going to be full of musicians, not to mention Darcy. And, maybe even me. And then there would be all the people marching right alongside.

And I said, "Shouldn't we have some fire extinguishers anyway," but it wasn't a question. Not in my mind, anyway. Because the truth is that fire, in any form, scares me. Yeah, the kids in school used to call me Pyroman and I let them. But only because it made me sound a little dangerous. And that was a good thing when you were the kid who other kids picked on and beat up. But really, my main interest in fire had to do with how to put it out. I mean, I collected fire trucks and wore a fireman's hat to bed. So what does that tell you?

No matter what anyone said or thought, I didn't set my Christmas tree on fire. I didn't make the maize field burn. My dreams were about saving tiny, scared and screaming children from fires that resulted from their parents' careless smoking, or the crappy construction materials used by cheap contractors. It wasn't like I had some secret wish to burn shit down.

More than anything, I wanted a fire extinguisher on that float. I kinda, sorta nagged and begged, but no one listened. For once in my life I wished there was a Home Depot somewhere nearby. I think I probably could have dragged Robert or Celeste into the store to buy at least a small extinguisher like the one my dad put up on the wall next to the stove in the kitchen.

But eventually, I let myself get sucked into Frank's vision of the float – gerbs and all.

How and why?

I keep thinking that it probably was all because of that five by fifteen WE banner.

Darcy called the sketch of it that I first showed her back in Glen Eddy, my all-time best-of-the-best design. Of course, I immediately fell in love with the banner too, mainly because Darcy loved it. And because I loved that she loved it.

So, the float was a way to show off a five by fifteen foot display of Darcy's message, and of my love for Darcy. Or at least, that's what I told myself. But the complete, cross my heart and hope to die truth is that I also loved the idea of flying that banner on the flatbed because I designed it. I was proud of my work. The float was a chance to show it off. *Everyone*, and Darcy especially, would get to see it. Admire it. And I loved that.

Truth is, I should have loved Darcy more. Loved her more and better.

# BILLY
Release


The day of Darcy's release from jail, Frank plowed in and out of the crowd like he was some kind of drag racer, terrorizing people — because he could. Because he figured that people wouldn't come down on a crip in a wheelchair.

M3 was zig zagging around the margins like an oversized dragonfly.

Robert was clawing his way up to the landing at the top of the courthouse stairs where cameras were rolling and photo flash was going off like fireworks. Moth to flame, that dude.

Celeste started out with her arm around Robert's waist, her thumb hooked in the belt loop of his jeans. But then Robert shook her loose. Or maybe she just let go. Anyway, he got to the top of the stairs alone.

And me, I was standing at the back of the flatbed trying not to panic. People were pressing up alongside the truck in a way that made me nervous. Everywhere I looked, there were people, and more people. Frank had figured on a crowd of a couple hundred. A thousand, max. But the turnout was big, bigger that the first day of the WE march. Only not as quiet or peaceful. The vibe, as Robert would call it, was not good. It was like watching the school bullies walk down a hallway look-ing all cool and calm, and knowing that any minute they could exchange a look and decide that today was going to be a day when they beat you up again after all.

Cops – in uniform and out — were all over the place, but just standing around, doing nothing. I heard one of them report into his squawker, "We've got a situation down here," and give a crowd estimate of 10,000. I couldn't make out the response he got. All I remember is that he laughed and said, "I read you, loud and clear."

Ten thousand, or thirty like the media said later, what did it matter? It was enough of a crowd to leave me standing there shaking, thinking stampede, body crush. It didn't help that peo-ple kept coming up to the float to hi-five the bands. Some of them were acting like groupies gone wild, and trying to climb up to touch a guitar player's hand or shirt or whatever.

The cops didn't lift a finger to keep them off. Not then and not later.

There was supposed to be a clear lane in front of the truck so we could drive away. But the cops just stood there and watched as people trampled the orange traffic cones around the flatbed as they pressed close and closer filling up every square inch around the float.

I wanted to get out of there in the worst way. But I held on and waited for Darcy.

# ROBERT
The Way Things Are


They led Darcy out of custody between two hulking cops. She was in cuffs – the old-fashioned metal kind connected by a heavy chain – like she was some kind of criminal. The Pigs.

You could see that they weren't happy about the crowd at the foot of the courthouse stairs, or all the press people. If the Pigs could have had their way, they wouldn't have let her anywhere near the mikes. But with all the eyes and TV cameras on them, they had no choice but to let her speak.

Darcy had tears in her eyes as she addressed the crowd.

"Thank you, thank you everyone for being here. Thank you for believing that the world can be changed. You have come together to be counted, to join others who are willing to be responsible for their own actions. They tell me there are thousands of you here, thousands of individuals ready to continue their own struggle, thousands mobilized to collective action. Thousands to gather, and disperse, and gather again as many times as necessary. We are the new way of conducting politics. We are the body, the voice of the world."

To cheers and chants of *WE are the world,* she started down the stairs to the float.

The press quoted her brief greeting for weeks to come, but only to point out that she hadn't mentioned Doefen. And why the hell should she? It wasn't like the guy had worn himself out trying to get her out of jail. Or even bothered to show up for her release.

Never, not for a moment did Doefen bother to give the girl who put him in the spotlight her due. And the worst part was that he wasn't even sorry. To hear Doefen tell it, he was out there doing exactly what Darcy would have wanted him to do — meeting with concerned scientists, slow food advocates and political movers and shakers in order to mobilize the forces necessary to protect a society at risk. He was working hard to make Darcy's dream of a world with wholesome food, unpolluted air, clean water a reality.

"By my every action, I honored Darcy's intention," he said.

A load of self-serving bullshit if ever Robert heard any.

Not that the crowd that came out to greet Darcy's release from jail was any better. For all the difference her call to responsible action made, she might as well have shouted —"Listen up people. You've all seen the movie. You know what to do. Take your places. Moderates in the middle. Fringe at the fringe. Bad guys — you know who you are — disperse yourselves to inflict maximal harm and betrayal."

Because that was more or less the way things went down. Every group played its expected part to the hilt.

All the fucked-up mother-fuckers who wanted to bash a few heads, and get their own bashed managed to commandeer the fringe for the five minutes it took to get the pent-up adrenalin out of their system.

The traitors, undercover cops, spies – Robert knew that they had to be there, they always were – got right out in front where they would be most conspicuous and therefore best camouflaged.

For the few true-blue, die-hards idealists, any place in the crowd was a good place because there would always be the next action and the next one after that.

For all the chanting and cheering, the bulk of the crowd that day was there to check out the scene and each other – mostly each other. After it was all over, they would go right back to doing what they'd been doing before — hanging out in bars, going to college, taking dance class and acting class. They were gonna grow up and get fat, and barbecue on big grills in the burbs, and harangue their kids to do well on tests and get into a good college just like their own parents did

The people who were really going to change the world, probably weren't even there. They were in some garage putting together a band, or holed up in a room writing the next big novel, or doing something that really, truly couldn't even be imagined, but would turn out to be the equivalent of making the first computer or sending the first rocket to the moon.

They sure as hell weren't hanging out in a narrow street outside a courthouse looking to jump up onto a float called *Spontaneous Combustion*.

Because that's how things work – as it was in the beginning, and in the Sixties, so it was then, and ever shall be. World without end. Amen.

# BILLY
A Ball of Fire


Once Darcy stepped up to the mike and all the cameras were on her, the cops more or less cut her loose. They unlocked the cuffs, and she raised the attached chains above her head, waving them like they weighed nothing, like they were a ribbon of silk or something. The crowd went wild.

The legal aid dude – Celeste's friend – who had been to court about eight hundred times to get Darcy out of jail came over to her and gave her a big hug. Robert didn't even wait for the dude to step aside before he stuck his face next to Darcy's and kept it there.

*Darcy, Darcy, Darcy, Darcy* – the sound rose and crashed, rose and crashed like ocean waves. You couldn't blame people for being excited. I mean, they got it — totally got what Darcy had done. If a young girl like her could launch some random goat guy to run for president, and face down a bunch of bully cops, and deal with being locked up in jail, then anything was possible. For them. For anyone.

Darcy reached out her arms to the crowd and *abracadabra* everybody went quiet.

Hello... WE... .Thank you. A few words, and a minute later, she was done. Typical Darcy. No making a big deal of herself.

Without a doubt, Robert had to be disappointed. I mean, the dude loved hanging out in the spotlight next to Darcy acting like he was supposed to be there. So, even though she headed right down the stairs, he just couldn't rip himself away from the cameras and mikes.

Everybody else broke out into more cheering as Darcy ran down to the float, smiling a smile you probably could have seen from outer space. The crowd surged up behind her, hands out to touch her, grab her. Everybody was looking to connect to her, or her *djellabah*, at least.

Darcy began to run faster, paddling the air with her hands like she was swimming in heavy water. She didn't look panicky, but she didn't look happy either. As soon as she was near enough, I leaned way out over the back of the float to pull her up onto the platform.

She was breathing too hard to saying anything, just squeezed my hand, her palm warm against mine. I shook like I'd been kissed. A moment later, we were both down on our bellies pulling Celeste out of the throng around the truck. Robert was still up on the steps near the mikes, talking into a TV camera.

The driver had the engine running and started pulling away the moment Darcy got on board. The crowd moved out of the way, but just barely. Instead of blowing his horn and continuing to move slow and steady, the driver revved the motor and pressed down on the accelerator. People at the front of the truck scattered. Behind us the crowd surged to follow the truck.

Right then, the feeling I got was like being at the beach in the water, and seeing that a huge wave was coming, and knowing you weren't going to catch it. You could stand there and let it smack you down. Or you could dive into it and hope for the best.

"We need to get off this thing," I shouted at Darcy.

For the first and only time that I know of, she looked pale, shaky. "It's all because of this." She rattled the handcuff. "If it weren't for my arrest, none of this would be happening."

"It is so not your fault, dude," I said, and pulled her away from the crowd that was heaving itself at and onto the truck. I tried to work the two of us away from the edge toward the middle of the platform. I had this idea that if Darcy and I could somehow duck inside the WE globe and wait for things to settle down, we'd be safe.

Right about then, as the lead guitar guy from one of the bands was on the mike to begging everyone to chill the fuck out, the first of the gerbs went off.

Everyone ooohed at the pretty spray of sparks that flew up and up over their heads and showered down onto the banner, the globe, and all over the flatbed. Even when the first flames started to lick across the banner – which took all of about two seconds – people kept watching like it was part of some show. It took a choking, black smoke blowing across the flatbed for them to figure out that maybe things were not going as planned.

The band stopped playing. "This is not cool, definitely not

cool," the bass player shouted as the rest of the gerbs started to explode. Big chunks of burning embers went shooting all over the place. The bass player dropped his bass. "Fucking, hell," he yelled as his shirt lit up with flames.

Everybody started jumping off the flatbed into the chaos below. Swept up in the surge of bodies, I was ripped away from Darcy. Next thing I knew, I was down on the ground, in a forest of legs, limbs, falling bodies, and I was crawling, choking on smoke, struggling to get up — all in that slow mo kind of way of a bad dream that you can't wake up from.

There was a roaring in my ears, which must have been the sound of my own blood rushing out of my heart, and sometimes a crackling noise — like the air had turned to ice and was falling to pieces. And far, far away there were screams – sharp and pointy and silver as scissor tips.

I wanted to roll myself up tight and small as a fist, but knees, legs, arms – not my own – kept me stumbling, falling, scraping, stumbling, falling again and again. I kept telling myself it was just like being beat up in the playground, and that sooner or later it would have to stop. All I had to do is wait. But really, I didn't believe I'd ever see Glen Eddy or my Mom or Dad again.

Maybe that's why in my head I saw myself standing with my Dad in the bright aisles of Home Depot, staring up at sheetrock stacked in neat piles that went all the way up to the ceiling, and we were squinting because the lights were glaring into our eyes... when all of a sudden, there was a swooshing sound like someone had turned on a giant vacuum cleaner, and I was sucked up into the air where a bright red ball of fire burst into a million spidery arms.

The force of the WE globe exploding into a fireball sent me, sent everyone near the flatbed flying, knocked us all flat. Somehow, I managed to pull my head up off the ground just high enough to see flames swallow up the entire flatbed.

Blue and green sparks kept showering down from the burning globe. Iridescent, delicate, very pretty... People were twisting, and turning, and opening their mouths wide and wider, but the whole scene was completely and totally silent.

Turns out the blast left me deaf for about a week. Others stayed deaf forever.

Scattered around the truck, I saw small dark mounds covered all over with yellow tongues of flame. It took me a while to understand that these were humans whose clothes had caught fire. A long, slow minute went by before I finally located Darcy.

# LEFT, RIGHT AND CENTER
Initial Reports

Originally estimated to draw no more than ten thousand supporters, the court-ordered release of Darcy Pucelle, the WE activist last seen riding a horse down Fifth Avenue, brought out a crowd three times that large. The mostly orderly crowd allowed her to proceed peacefully down the Court House stairs. But minutes later the float that was carrying her away erupted in flames, and the crowd turned into a stampede. Many hundreds suffered crush injuries.

Although the intense blaze burned for less than 10 minutes, it left 37 with serious burn injuries. Tragically, Darcy Pucell did not survive the fire.

Police halted the march immediately and moved in to quickly extinguish the flames.

Onlookers said the float was set on fire by an anarchist group, although those statements have not been confirmed.

***

Just minutes after the court-ordered release of Darcy Pucelle, the last detainee from the recent WE protest melee, a group of self-proclaimed anarchists set fire to the float meant to carry her away. An alleged spokesperson for the group shouted at the press photographers to stop taking photos, then took his fist to a camera to enforce respect for the principles of anarchy.

***

Chaos erupted outside the Court House earlier today when a WE float was set on fire, scattering demonstrators. Police quickly extinguished the flames, and seized 15 people said to be carrying smoke bombs.

As the suspects were being arrested, members of Black Death, an anarchist group, threw traffic cones and metal barriers at the police. Three officers sustained minor injuries, another required hospitalization for facial trauma. Black Death members were charged with felony assault.

The Police Chief Cuchen dismissed questions about his department's handling of the crowd. "My men showed that we're prepared, flexible, mobile, and fully capable of keeping our city safe," he said.

Preliminary reports indicate that WE activist Darcy Pucelle succumbed to the fire, and upward of 30 demonstrator sustained burns requiring hospitalization. Chief Cuchen cited WE's blatant disregard of fire and safety regulations for the otherwise avoidable fatality and injuries.

***

A WE float carrying at least thirty musicians, who volunteered to play world music in celebration of Darcy Pucelle's release from police detention, was set on fire earlier today. Ten arrests were made in connection with the incident. Police claim that WE supporters, who had come to witness the release, pelted them with bottles and sticks. Chief Cuchen called it an unprovoked attack, despite numerous videos showing it to be a response to mounted police running down the crowd with horses and motorcycles. No footage was found to confirm police claims that the melee was begun by people lining the sidewalks chanting "Two, four, six, eight, f*** the police state!"

Two of the ten people arrested were charged with felonies, and one with arson. Bail for the alleged arsonist was set at $200,000.

Within 30 minutes of the fire, some WE supporters attempted to convene at Belvedere Castle in Central Park, despite having been denied a permit earlier in the week due to concerns about trampling the newly re-seeded Great Lawn.

Tragically, Darcy Pucelle lost her life in the fire and over thirty individuals sustained potentially life-threatening burns.

***

Martin Laven, an alleged anti-WE activist, was arrested and charged with allegedly setting fire to the WE victory float during yesterday's release of Darcy Pucelle. However, our reporter has learned that the DA's Office plans to dismiss all charges against him next week in light of photos provided by a number of different press photographers, which show that Mr. Laven was standing some distance away from the incident, and could not have been involved with the fire at all.

## CHIEF CUCHEN
Police Press Briefing

*Spontaneous Combustion.* Not exactly original. But fitting.

The whole float — a tick-tacky project if ever Cuchen saw one — was practically guaranteed to go up in smoke. The center-piece globe — molded from highly flammable foam and paper, the electric cables – non-code, poorly insulated, snaking from one end of the flatbed to the other, the generator — sparking like a Roman candle on the 4th of July, and the crowning touch — strobes to synchronize with pulsating music. Not only were the flashing lights a sure hazard to visual acuity, and the nervous system, but also a well-known cause of disorientation, vertigo, nausea – all very useful and much to be desired in maintaining crowd control.

Kudos and congratulations to Cherub. Cuchen couldn't have come up with a more ridiculous representation of WE if he'd tried. For it to self-destruct, all he had to do was instruct his men to overlook the flatbed's total disregard for fire safety rules, and it's traffic violations – illegal parking, truck length exceeding street access limits, blocking a crosswalk.

"A tragic, tragic event," Cuchen intoned at the press conference. "And sadly, an entirely avoidable one. If WE had simply abided by the laws and regulations created to safeguard the public against the kind of tragedy that was witnessed today, we would not be here mourning the loss of a young woman's life, or anxiously awaiting news about the many, many of our injured friends, relatives and loved ones.

The dedicated doctors and nurses in our best burn units are at this moment struggling to save the lives of 37 victims of the fireball explosion on the WE float. These victims – some inno-cent bystanders, some police officers felled in the line of duty — will face years of surgery, treatment and painful rehabilitation. Several hundred of those less gravely injured are being treated in our emergency rooms, or have already been processed and discharged to the care of their own physicians. Were it not for the quick and selfless response of our fine police force, there might well have been more fatalities, more injuries.

The WE organizers and members, which just last week spread chaos through our street and disrupted an important economic meeting, today once again launched an illegal action with reckless disregard for human life.

Their float – ironically named *Spontaneous Combustion* – was illegally parked at the Court House stairs where it blocked vehicular traffic. Before our police force could remove it, the flatbed was boarded by Ms. Pucelle and a large number of her overly-enthusiastic supporters, and proceeded to drive onto our streets without a permit.

Unfortunately, all the decorative elements of the float were made of extremely flammable materials rather than the more costly fire-retardant materials that would have been required had WE obtained the proper permit from the fire department. In addition, the sound system was being run off a defective generator that was seen by many to spark repeatedly. And finally, in further violation of common sense and fire codes, WE chose to set off pyrotechnic devices without sufficient clearance for safety, and not a single fire extinguisher. These illegal pyrotechnic devices ignited an enormous fireball on the truck with tragic consequences."

After a few more paragraphs of praise for all the fine men and women — uniformed, medical and merely civilian – who responded to the situation, Cuchen offered condolences to all the victims of the tragedy on behalf of himself and the City.

# ROBERT
Déjà Vu All Over Again

At first, the media aired Cuchen's statement in its entirety. Later they cut it to a clip, a sound bite. No matter how abbreviated the format, the sight of Cuchen's sanctimonious mug and the sound of his slithery voice were too much for Robert.

The occasions to see replays of Cuchen's self-serving pronouncements were unfortunately many, first in the immediate aftermath of the event, then for the entire duration of Cuchen's run for mayor one year later.

His abuse of power, suppression of civil liberties, and murder of Darcy didn't seem to hurt his candidacy in the least.

Robert was not surprised. The Man was the Man was the Man. And it would never be otherwise. People like himself, Darcy, Isabelle and Jack didn't stand a chance.

Sometimes Robert screamed at the image of Cuchen on TV. Sometimes he slammed the TV screen hard with the palm of his hand. Sometimes he opened a beer and drank it in one thirsty gulp. Sometimes, he sat stony silent and still staring past the flickering screen onto the fields outside his window. Sometimes he heaved a tired sigh. It was all just so fucking *déjà vu* all over again.

## EXPERT TESTIMONY
Gerbs, Plumes and Sparks


A gerb is a type of firework which produces a jet of sparks lasting from 15 to 60 seconds. It consists of a thick walled tube filled with a pyrotechnic composition, and a choke, which is a narrowing in the tube. Gerbs are often referred to as fountains. Those intended for use indoors or near a proximate audience, such as at a rock concert, typically have short durations of action lasting about 1/8th to 30 seconds and reach a display height of 4 to 50 feet.

These types of gerbs are packed with titanium, which produces so-called cold sparks. Think 4th of July sparklers. The sparks burn at several thousand degrees, but bounce off skin harmlessly.

Unfortunately, the gerbs from the WE float were packed with zirconium, iron, ferro titanium and glitter spritzels. Unlike titanium, the sparks from these metals go molten before the final reaction and embed themselves in flesh causing a severe burn. Hence, the unfortunate incidence of injury at the event in question.

Gerbs are usually measured in terms of time and height. For example a 4x4 burns for 4 seconds at a height of 4 feet. Industry standards require that all spark plumes, even the titanium ones, be treated with the same safety precautions as would be used with any pyrotechnic material. In the case of gerbs, spectators must be kept at a clearance distance that is one and a half times the height of the device. When angled fallout is expected, the clearance requirement increases. For example, a 10 foot gerb must have a 15 foot vertical clearance and a minimum spectator distance of 20 feet. The concussive effect extends to 25 feet.

In the case of the WE float, there were a total of 7 gerbs: one at each corner of the flatbed and three around the globe. The ones at the corners measured 8 feet, those are around the globe 4 feet. Meaning that the closest spectators should have been at least sixteen feet away from the edge of the flatbed. We know from video footage that there was, in fact, zero clearance between the crowd and the devices.

Presumably, all of the gerbs had been set to point straight up. However, either through error or due to being trampled by the crowd that rushed the truck platform, two of the corner gerbs diagonally across from each other were found to be at a 45 degree angle pointing toward the center of the stage. The remaining two were at 50 degrees aimed out toward the spectators. The gerbs flanking the globe were variously tilted 15 to 25 degrees away from the vertical, 2 in the direction of the globe, one away.

The flanking gerbs were probably the principal source of the sparks that hit the flammable foam construction of the globe and ignited the fireball explosion. The resultant heat and flames set fire to the electrical equipment. The gas-fueled generator exploded scattering metal shrapnel for as much as thirty feet.

Spectators on the flatbed were either overcome by smoke or burned by the fallout from the fireball. Sparks from the remaining gerbs landed mainly on the streetside spectators, with those closest to the flatbed being the most severely affected.

It would appear that the sparks and flames were initially perceived to be part of the event, but within 30 seconds thick smoke began to billow down from the flatbed and the crowd stampeded. In less than a minute the entire flatbed was engulfed in flames.

By the time firefighters were able to approach the flatbed 15 minutes later, all that was left besides the metal components of the truck and flatbed was the steel armature and support rod of the globe.

The charred but still recognizable body of the single fatality was found near the base of the globe.

## BILLY
Holy! Holy! Holy!


Darcy burned and died.

There are those who said that Darcy escaped the fire, that the whole thing was a set up.

If only.

Others said that when the ashes were raked, her heart lay untouched.

There are those who said that when the flames burned out, a bird – a white dove – fluttered up out of the ashes.

Skeptics said it was a pigeon flying overhead.

I'm here to tell you that no such things happened.

I was there. I saw it all.

One minute there was a ring of fireworks with Darcy in the center. The next, a ball of white light burned where she'd been standing.

The flash came first. Then the sound. The force of the explosion threw some people to the ground, sent others flying like they were stardust from the original Big Bang.

I picked myself up off the sidewalk, saw Darcy's *djellabah* go squiggly like a mirage inside the burning, saw her arms wither above her head. She must have been screaming.

Where she had been standing, a piece of white paper floated on an updraft, drifted on a thermal, fell. Rose again. In the wind it fluttered open, and closed, and open along a fold that ran down the middle of it like a spine. A blank sheet of white paper. Nothing on it. A leaflet bleached of all text by the fire.

*Holy! Holy! Holy!*

According to some, that's what Darcy cried out like six times.

Stop. Drop. And Roll. Darcy never had the chance to follow the fire safety rules we'd been taught in school.

*Holy! Holy! Holy!*

According to Robert it was a line from some Ginsberg poem he claimed Darcy knew by heart. Wiping away a tear, he'd quote it for anyone willing to listen.

*Holy! Holy! Holy! Holy! Holy! Holy!*
*The world is holy! The soul is holy! The skin is holy! The*

*nose is holy!*

Fucking Robert. And fucking Ginsberg. I used to wish that neither one of them had ever existed, or at least that Robert had never read Ginsberg to Darcy.

One time I sat down and read the *Holy! Holy! Holy!* poem over and over again to see if I could figure out what the hell Darcy thought was so great about the Ginsberg dude.

*Holy! Holy! Holy! Holy! Holy! Holy!*
*The world is holy! The soul is holy! The skin is holy! The nose is holy!*
*Everything is holy! everybody's holy! everywhere is holy!*
*Everyday is in eternity! Everyman's an angel!*

Okay, that part sounded like something that Darcy would be into. But The tongue and cock and hand and asshole holy! That was so not Darcy.

Could it really be that as Darcy was burning, she was shouting, *Holy! Holy! Holy!* as in Ginsberg's *Howl*?

*Holy! Holy! Holy!*

I wanted to believe that maybe Darcy was trying to shout, Holy shit! Or Holy hell. Or Holy fuck, get me out of here. Because the Darcy I know wasn't some poetry spewing little saint. She was just a girl; a plain, ordinary girl, who more than anything else, wanted to live.

The fire burned away her *djellabah* completely, leaving behind a few strands of silver thread on her skin. Her charred, but still recognizable body lay on the flatbed — stripped, exposed by the flames. All the girl parts of her girl body were out there for anyone and everyone to gawk at.

The cops strung up yellow crime scene tape right away, and told people to get a move on, but there was no keeping the crowd from staring. Besides, the cops themselves were staring too. After all the press about Darcy refusing to give up her *djellabah*, and all the stupid wondering if she was really a boy, or a girl trying to pass as a boy, everybody was checking out that body to see if was female, and then taking a hard long look to see just how female it was.

I know I had to be screaming, "Cover her! Cover her!" I mean, whatever else Darcy said about why she started wearing the *djellabah*, the whole point of it was to keep herself – all of herself – private.

Holy! Holy! Holy!

So while the cops alongside the truck were busy waving their hands at people like they were directing traffic at a busy intersection, I did what I had to do. I crashed right through the yellow tape, climbed onto the flatbed, tore off my jacket and shirt, covered Darcy, and protected her with my arms and body.

The cops slammed me. I didn't care. I kept on kicking, and hitting, and biting and screaming, "Cover her!"

The media got all over that. And so did the shrinks and the courts.

I tried to explain at first, but nobody ever really got it. So I stopped talking. That didn't help clear anything up. But I felt better.

For about five years, I went around not saying a word. Not to anyone about anything. Not once. Not ever.

The shrinks labeled me PTSD at first, then some other kind of acute mental condition, and tried to pump me full of drugs. I just laughed and kept my mouth shut.

# ROBERT
There's a Photo

There is a photo.

Sometimes it's titled, *The Girl Who Went Up in Flames* – as though Darcy was no more than an illustration of a rare phenomenon of physics.

Sometimes, it's titled, *The Girl Who Burned.*

Darcy was that – a flame. A fire. A blaze.

The photo has made the career of the guy who shot it. His name will always be remembered. Darcy will always be *The Girl.*

Because the girl who burns is an icon. She has no name and doesn't need any for the chicken shit people of the world, who go on without a shred of courage, to hold her image holy. They raise their voices in praise. Words of admiration fall from their lips like kisses. Oh yeah, they honor the girl who burns, esteem her, stand in awe of her. How could they not? The girl who burns, burns for all that they hold dear and dearest. She is their ideal.

She is also their nightmare. A horror. They avert their faces from the girl who burns, shield their eyes from the glare of her. By her very existence, she asks too much, demands too much of them.

For Robert, there is no looking away. The image of her is seared in his brain.

But what if Darcy had survived like the other thirty-seven?

Would she have ended up like the women and men that Robert saw day after day at the inquest into the "accident." Some had faces that were wrinkled masks with skin like bleached leather and red slits for eyes and lips. Some actually no longer had ears, eyes, a nose, or lips. One young woman testified that five years after the fireball she still saw the world like she was wearing sunglasses smeared with Vaseline. And because of all the smoke she'd inhaled on that anguishing day, she could no longer walk across a room without getting winded. She never said that she wished she were dead, but Robert wondered if that would have been more merciful.

Then there was the young guy whose hand had hardened into

a claw that could not tie a shoe or button a jacket.

Would Darcy have lost her hair? Of all the survivors, the one who came to court wearing a cheap black wig that hung crooked, and didn't quite cover her scarred scalp broke Robert's heart the most. The very least that the Man owed her was a settlement that would allow her to buy a wig that didn't look like it came out of a Halloween kit from Wal Mart.

And then there was Celeste. Robert could only manage to look at her in short glimpses from across the courtroom. To talk to her was out of the question. Mercifully, she did not try to speak to him.

Celeste told the court that she'd needed dozens of surgeries to salvage her face, arms, and hands. Thick burn scars kept her from sweating normally, and left her unable to distinguish hot from cold. "A burn injury is a life injury," she said, without a hint of self-pity.

Robert both admired and was vaguely sickened by the way she decorated her despoiled flesh with delicate necklaces and bangle bracelets. He could not begin to imagine how she got from one day to the next.

What if Darcy too had ended up with skin like the bark of an oak, every lick of flame engraved in swirls and grooves of petrified flesh?

Robert couldn't bear to think about it, couldn't bear to imagine Darcy, his precious Darcy maimed like that.

The worst of it, the fucking absolute worst of it was that the Man won. Got away with it. The whole float and gerbs thing had to be a set-up from start to finish. But that was not the final finding of the inquest.

All the technical testimony and blah, blah, blah about the gerbs came down to one thing. They were not packed with titanium powder, like Frank said they were, but with iron and zirconium. Unlike the titanium that burned at several thousand degrees, and by some mystery of science that was beyond Robert produced harmless cold sparks that bounced off things, the gerbs on the float were full of metals that went molten before the final reaction, and ended up embedded and burning whatever they landed on. The explosion from the instant and huge fireball they created could be heard miles away.

Somehow, Frank managed to produce a receipt from some

supplier in Chinatown that specified titanium gerbs. Mysteriously, no one at the warehouse could or would cop to having written it. He could not say how or when the gerbs came to be packed with other metals. Instead, he suggested that many others, including Robert, had opportunity and motive to tamper with the packing.

"For all I know, WE may have been looking to create a martyr to raise its profile and figured me for the patsy," Frank whined.

At which point, Robert wanted to throw himself on the fucker and choke the life out of him.

Frank also claimed ignorance about the foam being highly flammable. "I went for cheap," he said. "An honest mistake."

As for failing to obtain a permit from the fire department for the pyrotechnics, Frank insisted that it was simply an unwitting oversight. His understanding was that the parade permit covered everything, and that an amateur set-up involving only half a dozen gerbs was exempt from an additional fireworks permit.

He professed remorse at the harm done and even shed a tear on cue. "I didn't mean to kill nobody," he told the court. "I just wanted to give the girl a spectacular welcome."

In return for a no contest plea of involuntary manslaughter, Frank received a sentence of a year's probation and three hundred hours of community service. He offered to write a letter of apology to each of the victims.

Robert could have sworn that he smiled when he said victims. Frank reeked of cop. Pig. The Man. Sabotage. Even if Robert didn't have a way to prove it.

The Man was the Man was the Man. Jack had been right to drop out totally and completely. Robert should have done the same. Should have raised Darcy to stay away from the corrupt and despoiled world of the Man.

Bees. Poetry. It could have been, should have been enough. He would have loved Darcy her whole life through. Loved her better than any father ever loved his daughter.

Not a day went by that Robert didn't mourn Darcy. He wept first thing when he opened his eyes, and went on weeping until the sound of his own sobs and the salt sting of his tears narcotized the pain. A few tokes of weed helped the process.

He would then lose himself in mournful contemplation of the crystalline perfection of his image of Darcy. In his memory, she was forever the young girl bounding across the pasture, full of promise and exuberance. She was the girl sitting on the split rail fence shouting out lines from Whitman and Ginsberg and all of his favorite poets, giving life to the poetry he'd taught her.

Forgotten was her propensity to be cruel in her honesty, punishing in her inflexibility — which could have been unbearable, if it weren't that it was always on behalf of the small, the halt, the lame, the injured, the defenseless, the pure. He forgot how he used to gird himself to be with her, because in her presence he would feel like someone thawing out from a numbing frost, and the pain of blood returning to body and limbs, the warmth that swelled his skin taut often seemed unbearable.

With Darcy gone, he felt shrunken, his hands and feet had become dull implements, and his heart nothing more than a pump.

After weeping a while longer, Robert would conclude that in some way Darcy was better off for having died in the midst of her passionate mission. She could not have lived a compromised life. Her desire was for the clarity, purity and the absoluteness of fire.

He'd been right to let her do what she needed to do. It was the only thing to do if you really loved her. And no one loved her more than he did.

It was not the fire on the float that consumed her. Rather, it was the flame that was always there in the center of her being, smoldering in the crucible that was her heart, which had flared into flames. Her very own vigil flame had exploded into a fire, and burned down the bodily edifice meant to contain it.

There was nothing Robert could have done.

Consoled, he'd get out of bed, wash his face, and go tend to the bees. At the end of the day, he'd return, draw the shades in his bedroom, and turn for distraction to the blue light of his secret videos ...

...A long thong of braided leather binds his manacled wrists to the center post of the barn. He is down on all fours, sucking on the sharp toe of a red stiletto... no a black stiletto. Black is sexier. Angelica, no Veronica, Veronique towers over him wearing a black beekeeper's veil and a few bands of studded leather with strategically placed buckles.

She snaps her whip across his bare ass. "Down, slave!"

He presses his chest, his nipples harder into the straw, savors the coolness of the barn damp on his flesh, raises his ass high.

"Down!" The whip burns the command into his skin. His cock, already sprung and hard, swells still more between his thighs as he licks the stiletto.

Veronique shoves the handle of her crop hard against his forehead, forces him up onto his knees.

"Cover that puny prick of yours."

Quick to obey, Robert arches, thrusts his pelvis towards his hands. The leather thong holds tight causing his hard-on to stand even more exposed.

The manacle cuts deep into his wrist as he attempts to heave his cock into his bound hands.

His bound left hand. Because it will feel less familiar. More like someone else's hand. Not his own.

"Cover it." The whip crackles alongside his ear.

"Please, mistress," he whimpers. There is no hiding his enormity.

"Silence, slave."

The whip bites hard into his fist, flicks, just flicks the head of his cock.

Veronique strides over to one of the hives, unlatches it, dips the handle of her crop inside, paints his cock gold with honey. Within seconds, bees are crawling along his shaft, his tight and aching balls, up onto his butt, down into the soft pink rose of his asshole, down into the tenderest, darkest whorl of the rose. Prickles of heat, electric sparks shoot along his limbs and spine...

Eventually, he'd fall asleep, and in the morning wake to a dream of Darcy. The tears would begin again as he contemplated the triptych arrangement of his memories of Darcy.

Most days, he got it together to take care of the bees. Some days not. Occasionally, he'd go into town, grab a bite at the diner, then take a drive out to the dam for a taste of real leather.

It wasn't much of a life, but with Darcy gone, Robert couldn't manage more. Didn't want more. Nothing, no one was worth living for except Darcy.

Darcy – first, last, and forever.

# BILLY
## So What Changed?


The world is full of good stories, stories to rip your heart out, but they don't really change dick. I'd like to think that Darcy's story is different. But is it?

I've asked myself a godzillion times, "So what changed because of her?"

Not Robert. Not him.

Maybe if Darcy hadn't made him out to be her best friend, and said that she loved him, and chose him as her go-to-guy for all the big stuff, maybe, just maybe I wouldn't give a shit. Maybe I would be OK with seeing him around Glen Eddy blah blahing to everybody about what a special place Darcy had, has in his life and boohooing about everything that went down.

Mr. Amazingly Sad. He has that act down. And the look to go with it – we're talking droop-eared little dog that's been drop-kicked.

Nice guy. Poor guy. He's taking it really hard. That's what people in town say about him.

Can it really be that I'm the only one who sees him for the fake, liar, skank that he is? Or is it one of those things nobody talks about. Like his nose-picking.

Every time you see the dude, he's rubbing the boney part of his nose like he's just lost in thought, pinching the wing of his nostril between his thumb and pointer finger. Who can miss that when he takes his hand away from his nose, he's busy rolling, boogers till they crumble off his fingers? Back at Belvedere, when he thought no one was watching, I actually saw him smear the booger on a rock he was sitting on.

I mean, who hasn't stuck a finger up their nostril and dug out a nice, thick yellow one? Except then you learn about Kleenex and you stop. You outgrow it. Not Robert

So yeah, forget him and change. I would settle for just seeing him outed.

I want the bogus cool of his whole beekeeping thing to stop. No more letting him get away with the bullshit about the special design of the frames he builds to make the bees more comfortable, and to keep them safe from bears – there hasn't been a fucking bear anywhere near Glen Eddy in like twenty years. No more letting him carry on about all his hard work. It's not like he has to get up in the middle of the night or to spend all day delivering a foal the way Darcy and I once watched Chuck Lorrain do. He doesn't have to spend all morning milking goats like Doefen does. The bees make the honey. All Robert does is to collect the credit.

And no more using the Darcy story as his con and cover for every damn question. Like why he lives alone? Why he's never had anybody "special" in his life? Why he never socializes with anyone?

I'd like to know why no one is talking about Robert's late night drives up to the reservoir dam. It's no secret what goes on at that old guard house with the rusted chains on the wall. I mean, it's not like the cops raiding it a few years ago put an end to anything.

And I can't be the only one who knows about the skank porn shit he's into. I was just a kid when I found his stash in the wheel well of the truck back in the city, and I remember what I saw – nasty, nasty shit you don't pick up in the magazine rack at the check-out lane of the supermarket. I figure him for a regular at the adults-only section at the back of the candy store where the local Glen Eddy druggies deal weed and crystal meth.

So yeah, I don't think it's asking too much for Robert's tongue to fall out of his mouth the next time he gives his teary-eyed, little speech about how much he admires Darcy for wearing the *djellabah*, and for her commitment to the dignity and sacred-ness of the female body.

I'm betting that Celeste got his number. She was way too bright to have bought his line of shit. Generous, kind, dignified Celeste.

There's someone whose life has changed. I cried when I saw her in court — her beautiful face scarred, the rest of her body twisted and deformed by the fire into crippled parts. Robert never so much as said a word to her. She must know that fire or no fire, Robert would have dumped her. So why isn't she talking, telling everyone what a self-serving piece of shit he is?

I want to see Robert ravaged, hollowed out, for real. I want to hear him screaming because life is chewing a hole in his gut and slowly eating him alive. I want him to never, ever be able to smile again. Not ever. I want him to wake up in the morning and wish that a SUV would jump a curb and smash him dead, that some random thing, or someone would finally put an end to him. Because sure as shit, he doesn't have the balls to do it himself, or the decency to just heave off and stop stinking up Glen Eddy, and the rest of the planet for that matter.

He should go, and take Frank with him. Another piece of shit. He didn't change either. Before, during and after the inquest, he went right on claiming credit for WE's successes – like the peaceful march to the hotel, and never, ever took responsibility for the total fuck-up of the float.

He and Robert are like twins separated at birth when it comes to having an excuse for everything. By the time of the whole court thing, they were even starting to look like each other. Robert had already started to get fat – and is still getting fatter – and Frank was looking thinner.

Fucking Frank. Who could say if he actually lost weight? Maybe it was the jacket and tie he wore to court instead of the sweats he dressed in at Belvedere that made him look like he'd lost a ton of weight. Or maybe, he was thin all along and wore a fat suit under the sweats. That's the thing about Frank. There's just no knowing. Nothing you can say for sure. Not then. Not now.

So what changed?

I wish I could say that the world changed, that people here, there and everywhere, in places near and far were touched by Darcy. And maybe they were. For five minutes. Or at least they talked like they were.

"A good and innocent girl has died," the mayor's press secretary and lots of others said.

Talk. Talk. Talk. Just like after 9/11. I was a little kid, but old enough to remember the way everybody went around saying they were going to be their better selves forever and ever. It didn't last back then. So why would it for Darcy? Her story was so much smaller. Just one girl.

Once she was gone, no one really stepped up to work on the things she cared about. Even the small things, like frogs. I see articles all the time about how frog populations are going down the tubes, and pretty soon will be gone. There's lots of talk, talk, talk about what's to blame — global warming, pollution, loss of habitat, pesticides. But nobody does anything. Or tries to figure out what to do. Because, it's just frogs.

And bees are dying off too. There's a name for it now — Colony Collapse. The name doesn't explain why it's happening or how to fix it. But sure as shit, it hasn't scared Burgundy out of selling genetically engineered seeds that grow into plants that kill insects. Kill bees.

The right thing to do is the profitable thing to do, the beneficial thing to do. That's the Burgundy's operational model. Now as ever.

Which explains how Doefen comes to be the head of a new division in the Food and Drug Administration with special oversight of organic agriculture. Sounds good, until you find out that it was Burgundy and his industrial-style agricultural posse who lobbied to have him appointed to oversee the patchwork of food growing regulations. We're talking bullshit PR — Doefen as lap dog, not watch dog. Doefen in a position that has hardly any bark and even less bite. Yeah, that's Doefen — Mr. Food Czar.

He never did try to run for president. And he stopped raising goats. So I guess that's a change.

OK, so what else?

If Darcy could come back, she'd see that the hill behind the school got a buzz cut. No more trees. The school district sold off the woods for lumber after the deal with Burgundy Enterprise for the monster corn went up in smoke. Now you can stand in the playground and see all the way up to the Interstate at the top of the hill with its snake of yellow headlights sliding along the rim at all hours of the day and night. Commuter traffic. Yuppies have started to invade and take over Glen Eddy, just like Darcy's Dad always said they would.

And then there's the cell phone tower. I guess that counts as a change. Glen Eddy was like the last place on earth without cell phone or internet service, which was why Darcy's Mom and Dad never got any real-time information on what went down in the city with the WE protest. Once word of that got out, the town was finally connected to the grid. Too bad that some bright light in industrial design decided to try to disguise Glen Eddy's one and only cell phone tower as a pine tree. So, there it stands twenty times taller than the tallest tree, sticking up out of the top of High Point Mountain. You can see it for miles. Twice a day, every day, Glen Eddy is famous for 15 seconds during rush hour radio… "Traffic on the Interstate moving well up to the Glen Eddy Tree Tower."

The net result of the good people of Glen Eddy finally receiving cell phone service is that they can act just like the people I saw in the city. Instead of paying attention to their driving, or having a conversation with their kids while they're taking them to school, they can ignore them and yammer on about nothing on their cell phones.

So, yay, cell phones. They're a wonderful thing!

Darcy's Mom still doesn't have one, and I doubt she ever will. She hardly talks at all anymore. To anyone. Not that she was ever one of those chit chat kind of ladies to begin with. But now, she hardly even comes out of her house except at night to go to her job at the hospital.

And she has stopped cutting her hair. An ancient mourning thing, some people call it. Breaks your heart they say — that cloud of white hair floating around her like a veil, puts you in mind of a bride who got lost on her way to the wedding.

So not that. I saw her one night in the hospital parking lot, and it was like she was a delicate moth-creature fluttering out of the dark towards the lights burning in the windows.

Yeah, me — out in the dark, alone. Now there's a change! It's not that I'm not scared of the dark anymore, but I've gotten to where I can deal with it better. I have Darcy to thank for that.

For the longest time after Darcy was gone, I wanted to do for some kid what she had done for me. Trouble is, I'm not brave like her. I can't just take some lost kid by the hand, and lead him to where he needs to go.

So I make signs, instead. Signs for highways and airports, and schools, and baseball fields, and stores — even for Home Depot. I make signs that are better and clearer, signs that can be read in bright light and dim light and even no light. I try to make the kind of signs that will keep some kid with a whole lot of heart and an idea from having to spend a whole day lost on the subway.

Signs are important, because even with GPS and Google Maps, you still need to know if the street corner you're at is Main Street or Yearance Avenue, and you still need to know which way is east and which way is west.

And that's where my signs come in.

They provide a point. Identify a locus. Tell you where you are, mark your position so that you can see how to get from point A to point B. And really, when you come down to it, wasn't that what Darcy did? Or tried to do?

I design each of my signs with a tiny D hidden in it. A tiny D and a flaming heart — just like the one I've been re-inking on my chest with a laundry pen since I was eleven. Whenever anyone reads one of my signs, it's like Darcy is there pointing the way.

So even though I don't have it in me to be bold like Darcy, I try to remember that she believed that each and every person could and did change the world – even the one whose name we don't know, and the one who was attacked by police dogs, or water cannons, or was sent to jail so that some other person whose name we don't know would be able to vote, or to earn a living, or would not end up being sent to die in some stupid war.

Make the world a better place – that's what Darcy lived for. Either she didn't know or was too brave to care about how much the world could hate her for it.

Me – I just try to do my part, and not think too much about that.

## ISABELLE
Epilogue/Elegy/Eulogy


I know the sound. It's the cry an animal in a trap makes just before it falls silent and begins to gnaw on its own flesh in order to get free. The sound used to come with tears. Those stopped.

The sound comes from me. It wakes me from sleep. Eventually it subsides, and I am able to walk from the bedroom, stop at the stove, put on the kettle, walk from room to room, open the shades. In the winter dark I see my own face reflected in the window glass.

*Uba* stares back at me from the window pane. An old woman in a deranged state – according to the conventions of Noh masks that I once learned about in my college art class. I wore the face of a *Ko-omote* then. The face of youth. I will never display the expression of a *Deigan,* the enlightened middle-aged woman with gold-flecked cat's eyes, and an open smile illuminated by tiny gold teeth.

The shades – opened or closed — it doesn't matter. I no longer see outside. Neither, I think, does Jack.

I brew coffee. Dress. Sit down in the dark at the kitchen table and wait for the sound to subside. To stop completely. When it does, I walk to the car, drive to the hospital, open the door, greet the sleepy guard, receive sign-outs from the evening nurse, and for eight hours attend to my duties. Diligently, wordlessly I spend the night ventilating people.

Back when Jack and Robert and I first came to Glen Eddy — back when we were young enough to believe that squatting in an abandoned motel was a political act, that we were living Underground and that it mattered, back when we were naive enough to think that our stay would be temporary, that we'd resume our lives, our real lives, once the world came to its senses and the war ended – the one in Nam, that is – there have been so many wars since — back then, I once came upon a fox in the woods. For a long time, we stared at each other in silence. The fox and I. Stared long enough for me to wonder why it didn't run away. Hide. Flee. Like a wild animal would. Should. Stared, until I saw the trap.

I rushed off to get gloves and a tool, ran back to set the fox free.

I found the trap empty except for a bloodied hank of fur and flesh, a chewed off foot.

I sometimes see, or think I see, that fox hobbling through the brush. I know it's crazy. The fox couldn't have survived all these years. No doubt it met a swift and merciful end in the predatory teeth of Nature. Better that, than the cruelty of sickness, starvation.

Whenever I remember that fox, the sound that comes from me — the sound that is me— turns pointy and sharp in my mouth. I spew blades and arrows at the indifferent dark, in memory of the feral splendor of that fox that flicked through the wood like a flame. And always, in memory of Darcy. My fiery, fervid girl. Heart of my heart. For my Darcy.

The sound that comes out of me used to come with words — complex words at first that eventually gave way to simpler ones —

I can't justcan'tIcan'tIjustcan'tIcan'tIcan'tIcan't... Then even those words faded away.

Tonight, I sit with my hands wrapped around the coffee cup, same as I usually do. But the sound is more fierce and shakes my body. Coffee sloshes up against the cup's chipped rim, seeps down onto the table. I hold the cup tighter. I know that when the warmth is gone, it will be time to stand up. Get dressed. By then, the sound should have subsided.

But this night, along with the usual baying sound that issues from my mouth, torrents of words tear through my brain.

Darcy is gone. My beloved child. Gone. There will never be another like her.

One and only one. Irreplaceable. Gone.

Of the millions upon millions of swirling, burning stars in the night sky, it's the falling stars that catch the eye. Some of them have collided with the earth, and the cataclysm of their fall changed the planet forever – extinguished dinosaurs, caused flowers to flourish in place of jungle vines, moved brutes to awe and the dumb to speak. Even those that merely streaked by the earth in long ellipses left it transformed. What if not a blazing star lit a path to the Messiah's crib? And yet for all the wonder that each fiery, burning, falling celestial body trails in its wake, it emblazons across the cosmos a reminder that to be extinguished is inevitable.

Fire is the life and the silent language of stars.

There was an inevitability to Darcy's trajectory. A bright and fiery girl. A girl on fire.

Read to her, the learning specialist said. Poetry in particular. The testing he'd done when Darcy was seven identified strengths in creative thinking, empathic reasoning, auditory memory, a facility for the rhythm of language, not rote skills like spelling. A learning difference he called it.

"She's very musical. Use that."

From the first, Darcy sang the world to herself. She sang the song of "Windy the bird, bird" lighting on the power line at the curb, and the song of the road passing by the car window. She sang the "siskrimpilindo" of oil sizzling in a frying pan, and of Jack's joy in sucking down his morning brew, "Yippee, yippee Daddy has coffee."

She sang the pictures in her readers instead of the words that she just couldn't sound out.

I, we, read poetry together. We read and reread every book of poems on the shelf of the school library. *Rhymes for the Very Young, Poetry Classics for Children.* By the time she was six she could easily recite long stretches of *The Song of Hiawatha* and knew all of the *Cat in the Hat* by heart.

Before long, we graduated to more grown-up poems, the poems I studied in my freshman English class in college.

> *"Beauty is truth, truth beauty" that is all*
> *Ye know on earth, and all ye need to know.*

At night, I sit on the darkened ward reading by the blue band of fluorescent lighting at the lip of the nurse's station. I read the same poems I once read to Darcy.

Behind me lie rows of inert patients tethered to life by thin plastic lines. A line for Oxygen. Another for fluids and medications. Pinch the lines, and the patients would float free.

It is my duty to make sure that they are held fast. All of them — the wife beaters, and abusers of children, the torturers of small animals. The gun dealers. The dopers who extinguish cigarettes on the flesh of their nearest and dearest. Even suspected murderers.

In a town the size of Glen Eddy, you can't help but know things about people. The patients I tend to, some of them are not good people. Not by anyone's standards.

How much do I contribute to the misery of the world by keeping them alive?

One small pinch... that's all it would take... a pinch...

But it's not for me to sort the worthy and unworthy. To judge. Darcy had no such compunction. Full of passionate intensity. She *would* live a good and decent life, become a vet and share a farm with an Arabian stallion, a Rhodesian Ridgeback, two Chihuahuas, and an Abyssian cat.

And she *would* change the things that needed changing. No one should go hungry. No one should eat tainted food. She *would* do her part. Everyone else had to do theirs.

She chose Doefen to change the world. Who is to say that she chose unwisely?

The media portrayed her as a reckless girl who became involved in things that were over her head. They call her naive. Inexperienced.

In my heart, I know that she knew more than anyone understood, or gave her credit for.

Working nights, sleeping days, it wasn't unusual for us to miss each other's comings and goings. But the day she left for the WE protest, when I came home, there was an emptiness in the house I'd never felt before. I called Robert. Somehow, the way that his phone rang and rang and rang with a hollow sound told me that she wasn't at his house or in his pasture, or in the barn, or in the orchard tending to the bees with him.

I found her note in her bedroom. A single page in her bold hand lay at the foot of her bed. As I came into the room, a sudden autumn gust from her open window sent it flying to lodge under the dresser. Darcy insisted on fresh air while she slept, kept the window cracked even in the dead of winter, often went without covers, deliberately cultivated heartiness as though somehow she knew that the life she intended to lead would require more than the mere natural strength and resilience of youth.

Dear, dear Mom:
It's important that I drop everything and devote my-

self to this cause. I would really like to just stay at home and be a good daughter, spend my time listening to music, and dancing around, and having boyfriends, but I have to do this.

Please understand.

I love you very much.

Darcy

"I have to do this." So Darcy. And so much like Jack — my long ago, passionate street fighting man Jack. And like me. The long ago me.

I too once had to leave. Had to flee the itchy, boiled wool sweaters of winters in New England, flee the dour woods and the dun light. I ran off to a place where the sun was hot and high in the sky.

Morocco!

Nineteen — only a little older than Darcy — away from home, on my own for the first time. I rounded yet another turn in the labyrinth medina of Marrakesh — hungry, tired, lost, and scared. Scared enough to cry, but not crying. I stood looking this way and that, searching for a way out.

Hovering above my head in the pale and sifting light of the passageway I saw an angel with outstretched arms. I watched it float on the faintest breath of a breeze.

"For you a special price," the stall owner crooned, and I understood that the angel was a *djellabah*. A garment strung on a line that he offered to take down just for me.

The fabric in my hand felt shockingly sumptuous after a lifetime of nylon and polyester. I bargained, for the first time, for an object of my heart's desire.

How naive I'd been prancing around in that *djellabah* for months afterwards, certain that I was dressed for a life that was not going to be this life. Not the life I am living now.

I was mistaken. So sadly mistaken. But I was not wrong.

When Darcy took the *djellabah* for her own, I could not deny her the pleasure of wearing it. Especially after Principal Toul called her choice of dress "alarmingly provocative."

"All of her private parts and then some are totally covered," I pointed out knowing full well that the fat-ass, ignoramus meant to call it a "provocation." I let that bigoted, uptight, short-sighted, narrow-minded, illiterate hypocrite sputter and sweat in his too tight suit made of something synthetic and shiny before I quoted chapter and verse from the school rule book to prove that there was nothing in the dress code that prohibited the *djellabah.*

The likes of Toul were not going to break and fetter the spirit of my daughter.

Darcy — delightful, willful, exasperating, idiosyncratic heart of my heart would live — had to live — a life that was better and freer than my own.

> *All I want is the truth*
> *Just gimme some truth*

Truth. I'll never have another life, only this one. Truth. There will be no other kind of tomorrow. Just this one endlessly repeating. No other kind of yesterday.

The march Darcy led was a mere blip on the TV news. Or so I've been told. I don't watch TV and Jack keeps it tuned to reruns of cop shows. I didn't see what happened to Darcy. I wasn't there. But I saw the photos and they were enough for me to know everything there is to know. I wasn't there, but I know what went down.

A flash of light so intense it sucked up all air and sound.

A flash of light so bright that all the light in my life went out.

Darcy is gone. There will never be another like her.

I will never have another child. Not with Jack. Or Robert. Or anyone else. My body has spent is cache of fertile moons.

Darcy. Flesh of my flesh. Born squalling out of my body.

Naked. Both of us. Naked. Made flesh.

My flesh, hers.

Bone of my bones. Flesh of my flesh. Taken out of me. Naked. Life of my life.

Blood of my blood.

Once. Just that once. With Robert. He stood looking at me with such yearning. Looking like in me he could see possibilities. Futures. A window. A door. A net.

So like, and unlike Jack. No wildness in Robert. No daring. Only nostalgia. Not for the past, exactly, but for the idea of a life he, I had meant to live.

I never shared his wistfulness, just an inclination towards the melancholy that overcame him, us in November. "Sad attacks" we called them long before anyone came up with the concept of Seasonal Affective Disorder. Oh, how very, very restlessly sensitive we were. A jagged patch of spring's neon green sprouting in an expanse of yellowed grass could and did move us to tears. So too, did the sight of the Central Park Meer morphing into vapor. Scarlet leaved autumn trees burned for us like sanctuary lights in a damp church. We shuddered to see the elongated shadows our bodies cast in the low sun — so like the Giacomettis we were studying in Art History. Like those sculptures, we felt hacked and hewn, starved and starving, scraped down to our essence by unnameable hungers.

Sometimes, on our walks in Central Park, we'd sink to the ground, hug our knees to our chest, and cry.

"All this beauty, such beauty." Robert once said, including in the sweep of his arm the pond, and autumn trees, and sky and cosmos. "So vivid. So painful."

He meant the dying away that was fall. We could accept the stark solemnity of winter. By then our hearts were as benumbed as the frozen ground. But November...November was an unmerciful reminder that we are born astride a grave.

For consolation we read the *Ode to Autumn*, and committed *Howl* to memory.

Once. Just that once. In November. Standing together with Robert at the door of his barn. The hills graying to smoke. The sky turning to smoke too. A single shaft of light fell across his face. Faded away.

Such beauty. His. Mine. Fading...

He turned and looked at me with such yearning.

I slipped my arms under his jacket, around his waist, under his shirt.

There was no fire. I knew that as soon as I let him touch me. Felt his chapped hands on my face and neck.

No fire. Just the yearning. Not lust. Or real desire.

A much more private thing, that yearning. In him. All about him.

His green eyes. Like a cat's. Sly slits for pupils. Secret.

Still very lean like a dancer back then. A prowler from the black heart of a desert. Lean and yearning.

Beauty faded. Fading.

Just that once.

No wildness in him. I wanted to burrow down into the straw. It was still soft, redolent of new mown grasses and wildflowers. I wanted to heap it on him, on me. On us.

I wanted to dance naked. Throw handfuls of the pale straw—summer's fading bounty into the air, and let it rain down on us like a blessing.

Jack would have done that. Jack, my wild, wild boy. My black-eyed lover. In his hands the straw would have turned to clover.

Wild Jack. Back in the day. Back when he would stay in bed with me to see if we could fuck 27 times continuously, because 27 was a good number. Back when he'd jump a washed out bridge in our beat up old Dodge Dart sooner than detour 2 miles. Back when he'd take my hand, and we'd run from the house butt naked to roll in newly fallen snow. Back in the day when each day was a Nantucket sleigh ride. Back before he twelve-stepped right out of life to string phone wire by day and drum paradiddles on the kitchen table at night...

Jack would have danced round and round with me until the horizon tilted up to kiss the sky, then fallen down with me onto the heaving earth, and picked the straw out of my hair with his teeth...

Not Robert. Leave your clothes on, he whispered. Leave your clothes on... clothes on...

Like with clothes on it was supposed to be sexier

His hands on my arms. Pulling at me. Pleading for me to hold him, mount him, take him with our clothes on...

It was too much and not enough. For both of us. Like a glass of wine, when a whole bottle was necessary. A momentary haze instead of the mercy of an obliterating dark.

A mistake.

Just that once.

A cruel fact of nature – men not knowing. Never knowing for sure who their children are. Even with blood tests, there is room for doubt.

Jack never thought to ask. Robert never stopped asking. Not in words. Always the question, the uncertainty. In his eyes. Afterwards. And forever after.

Flesh of my flesh. My daughter.

The public calls her hero, saint, pawn. And a fool – holy or not. What are such names to me? Gnats that draw the last drops of blood from the flesh of her tender life.

Some weep for her. Pronounce her name with pity, with reverence. Awe even. Tears fall from their eyes like kisses.

Tears. Laments. An old word that — lament — from an old world. Not this world. Not the one I inhabit.

They lament her fate.

Fate. Is there a word more ancient, more out of date? But fate is what they call the thing that was done to her.

Fate. They are innocent. The word absolves them. They lament and emerge clean. Cleansed.

Lamentation.

> What would they do if they had the motive and the cue for passion/ That I have? They would drown the world with tears and cleave the general ear with horrid speech/Make mad the guilty and appall the free/ confound the ignorant, and amaze indeed/The very faculties of eyes and ears. Yet I, can say nothing.

Borrowed words. Words I read to Darcy once. True words. I know none that are truer.

I poisoned her with poetry. Fed her hard, harsh, beautiful, true words. Taught her to speak in a language foreign to the one required for everyday life.

I sit silent. Dry-eyed and silent. Not a word crosses my lips.

I sit in the dark saying nothing. Remembering.

Let others raise monuments in Darcy's name. Memorials. Let them tell their stories. She is all stories. And none of them.

> What we call the beginning is often the end
> And to make an end is to make a beginning.

Darcy was born an old soul. There will be other girls, passionate girls who will burn and shoot across the indifferent sky like comets. Girls whose lives will make it possible for those who are left behind to light a candle and not curse the darkness.

But once I'm gone, there will be no one to remember Darcy. My Darcy. No one to know the way she tapped against the tight drum of my pregnant belly with her still-forming fists, and the way Jack tapped back gentle paradiddles and crooned, *Baby you are a rock star, oh yeah, you are.* No one to remember that way she pointed at the moon and called it a silver button on the velvet dress of the night. No one to know that she wished she could see a thousand ladybugs at once and know that there were exactly a thousand, not one more or one less. No one to remember...

To keep Darcy from being extinguished, I must stem the torrent that that each day bursts out of my ravaged heart. I must stifle the sound that breaks out from behind my clenched teeth. I must silence the sound that comes from me, that is me.

Darcy, dear beloved daughter. Flesh of my flesh. One and inseparable. I am you as you are you as you are me and we are one together. Such is a mother's curse. And enormous blessing.

www.ingramcontent.com/pod-product-compliance
Lightning Source LLC
Chambersburg PA
CBHW071111250626
47159CB00002B/696